2/14

Ahmet Hamdi Tanpınar

A Mind at Peace

Translated from the Turkish by Erdağ Göknar

archipelago books

Second Archipelago Books Edition

Library of Congress Cataloging-in-Publication Data
Tanpınar, Ahmet Hamdi.
[Huzur. English]
A mind at peace / Ahmet Hamdi Tanpınar ;
translated from the Turkish by Erdağ Göknar.
p.   cm.
Novel.
ISBN 978-0-9826246-3-0
I. Göknar, Erdağ M. II. Title.
PL248.T234H8913 2008
894'.3533–dc22   2008028157

Archipelago Books
232 Third St. #A111
Brooklyn, NY 11215
www.archipelagobooks.org

Distributed by Consortium Book Sales and Distribution
www.cbsd.com
Printed in the United States

Cover photo: anonymous, 19th century, Adoc-photos/Art Resource, New York

This publication was made possible with support from Lannan Foundation, the National
Endowment for the Arts, the National Humanities Center, the New York State Council
on the Arts, a state agency, Republic of Turkey Ministry of Culture and Tourism TEDA
Project, the Turkish Cultural Foundation, the Moon and Stars Project, the American
Turkish Society, the Duke University Center for International Studies, and the
Mary Duke Biddle Foundation.

A Mind at Peace

Part I

İhsan

I

(City of Two Continents, August 1939)

Mümtaz had not set out on a long walk since his paternal cousin İhsan, a brother to him, had succumbed to illness. Aside from tasks like summoning the physician, taking prescriptions to the pharmacist, and making calls from the neighbor's telephone, he'd whiled away the measure of the week at his cousin's sickbed or in his own room perusing books, reflecting, or attempting to console his niece and nephew. İhsan had complained of backaches, fever, and fatigue for about two days before pneumonia heralded its onset, sudden and sublime, establishing a sultanate over the household, a psychology of devastation through fear, dread, rue, and endless goodwill scarcely absent from lips or glances.

The entire household slept and woke with the remorse of İhsan's affliction.

Mümtaz again rose to sorrow from sleep that train whistles had bloodied with altogether different anxieties. The hour approached nine. He sat at the edge of his bedstead, preoccupied. A host of errands awaited him. The physician had said he'd arrive at ten o'clock, but Mümtaz wasn't obliged to wait. His first order of business was to hire a nurse. Given that neither İhsan's wife, Macide, nor his mother, Sabire, ever stepped away from the sickbed, the children languished in ruin.

The elderly servant could easily handle Ahmet, but someone had to occupy his little sister, Sabiha. More than anything, she needed conversation. As Mümtaz mused, he smiled inwardly at the various postures of his young niece. His affections for her had taken on new proportions since he'd returned to the house: *Is it a matter of habit alone?* he mulled. *Do we always happen to love those in our midst?*

To rid himself of such thoughts, he returned to the quandary of the nurse. Macide's health wasn't too stable. What's more, he was astonished she could withstand such stress. Excessive worry or exhaustion would again reduce her to a shadow. He had to get hold of a nurse, yes. And in the afternoon he had to face that headache of a tenant.

While he dressed, he repeated to himself, "This reed stalk known as man." Mümtaz, who'd been quite isolated during a formative period of his childhood, liked to talk to himself: *And that entirely separate thing called life.* Then his mind turned back to little Sabiha. The thought that he loved his little niece solely because he'd moved back into the house troubled him. In truth he'd been bound to her from the very first. Considering the circumstances of her birth, he was grateful even. Few children could so quickly fill a house with such ease and elation.

Mümtaz, having tried to engage a nurse for three days now, had collected a handful of addresses and made countless calls. But in this land, one's aims simply receded into the distance. Doubtless, the East was the place to sit and wait. With a modicum of patience everything arrived at one's feet. Six months after İhsan regained his health, for instance, a couple of nurses were certain to call seeking work. When one was genuinely needed, however . . . This, then, was how the ordeal of the nurse went. As for that tenant . . .

The tenant boded trouble of another sort. Since he'd let the small shop from İhsan's mother, he'd been dissatisfied and complained, but for a spell of, say, a dozen years, he hadn't once considered moving, and for a fortnight running, he'd been making inquiry upon inquiry requesting that one of the gentlemen of the house – or the good lady herself – honor him with a visit posthaste.

The entire household met this turn of events with disbelief. Even İhsan, squirming with fever and cramps, expressed amusement. They knew that the principal trait of the picaro was to keep out of sight, go into hiding, and if not being sought – or even while being sought – to respond as belatedly as possible and only after the greatest of griefs.

Mümtaz, having taken the responsibility of late for renewing the lease and collecting rent, knew how difficult it was to see the man even while standing right before him in his shop.

As soon as Mümtaz would step into the store, the shopkeeper would shade his eyes with a pair of black glasses as if they were a potent talisman and, for all intents and purposes, vanish behind a glass shield, from where he'd drone on about the stagnation of the market, the difficulty of eking out a living, and the blithe fortune of men who worked on fixed incomes, such as civil servants; consequently he'd grow livid, berating himself for having quit his job as a state employee and submitting to the *elkâsibü habibullah* hadith – Muhammad, beloved "merchant of Allah." Indeed, it was solely for this reason, to avoid consciously violating the example of the Prophet, that he'd started out in trade. At last, he'd cut to Hecuba:

"My good sir, you are *aware* of what's happening, it's out of the question at present – all due respect to dearest Sabire. She'd do well by granting me a few days' grace. She's no landlord in our eyes, not at all, on the contrary, she's been a benefactor, a fountainhead. If she'd be so good as to stop by in a fortnight, I'd be both deeply honored by her visit and, inshallah, able to offer her a little something." And by so stating, he'd leave the matter hanging in the balance; nevertheless, as Mümtaz stepped back through the door, the shopkeeper, his voice quavering, would continue where he'd left off as if startled by the enormity of the promise he'd made: "But I'm not certain it'll be possible in a fortnight, either." Because he couldn't possibly say, "She'd do well by not coming at all, really, the lot of you would do well by keeping your distance! For what purpose would you come anyway? As if it isn't enough that I live in this decrepit building, am I also to pay you for it?" Instead, he'd request a delay of deliberations to another, distant time: "It'd be best if the good lady honored me with a visit toward the first of the month, or better still, midmonth."

Now then, this pismire, annoyed at being sought and sounded out, had sent repeated messages asking after them and requesting that the fine lady, or in her absence, one of the fine gentlemen, appear at their earliest convenience to negotiate the status of the abandoned outbuilding of the old estate, including its two second-floor rooms, and to attend to the fact that his lease had expired. They had every cause for bewilderment.

Come afternoon Mümtaz would trudge, as he did each month, to the shop he was loath to visit because he knew by heart the responses awaiting him. Yet this occasion was different. Last night when his aunt goaded him with, "Mümtaz, go pay a visit to that tenant," from behind her back, İhsan wasn't able to gesture and mime, "No use tiring yourself out for nothing, you know what he'll say, just go out for a stroll, take in the air, and come back!" İhsan lay as if spiked to his bed; his chest rose and fell with labor.

İhsan's philosophy toward this bête noire rested in the wisdom that it was senseless to make futile attempts when the outcome was apparent. Mümtaz, all the same, wanted to avoid disappointing his aunt, who was quite incapable of forgetting about the rent that amounted to an inheritance from her beloved pater. Furthermore, in the lives of this family living cheek by jowl, as Mümtaz would have it, on the "Island of İhsan," the saga of rent provided fodder for a multitude of puns and witticisms.

Most amusing, mirabile dictu, was how after Mümtaz returned and shared with his elderly aunt the range of responses he'd received, her initial anger, "I hope the bum dies, the geezer," would gradually and by shades turn toward compassion, "Poor soul, he's helpless, the dear man's afflicted anyway," or how she would then grow heavyhearted and say, "Maybe he really doesn't earn a profit," and subsequently attempt to resolve the situation over and again; or how she declared, "That's all that's left of that great manor, or else I'd have sold it and been done with it long ago," indicating that the rent, which she never received in a timely fashion, was a source of genuine remorse. One day, however, Aunt Sabire would resolve to make her customary visit to the tenant, and since this daughter of the lamented Selim Pasha wouldn't deign to go out onto the streets unaccompanied, word would be sent to Arife, the maid in Üsküdar, who would arrive on the appointed day, after which the following three or four days would be spent in deliberation, "Let's go pay a visit to that man tomorrow," and frustrated attempts to do so would be made while visiting the neighbors or at the Grand Bazaar; but finally, one fine day, she'd return triumphantly in a taxi heaped with presents.

Doubtless, her visit to the tenant was never made in vain; she'd at least get a portion of the rent, regardless. Her temerity astonished both Mümtaz and İhsan, though, all things considered, it wasn't that surprising.

Though İhsan's mother cherished Arife, she couldn't stand her chatter. As Arife the gossip's visit to the house dragged on, Sabire's rage, which Arife had known since childhood, mounted. When it finally peaked, a taxi was summoned, and they would set out together, Arife not in the least bit wise to where she was being taken; first the elderly, faithful maidservant would be dropped off at the Üsküdar-bound ferry landing with a "Farewell, my dear Arife, I'll have them call for you again, won't that do?" before İhsan's mother would head straightaway to the shop.

As might be expected, snubbing the landlady when she appeared in such a state of mind constituted something of a challenge. The pitiful man had attempted to do so a few times by complaining of stomach pains and what-not. On the instance of the first occasion, Sabire suggested he brew mint leaves, and on the second, she advised him to try a more complex remedy, but on the third visit, when she again was met with complaints of ill health, she asked, "Have you taken my cures?" In response to his negative reply, she snapped, "In that case, don't ever mention such ailments to me again, is that clear?" During this third visit the shopkeeper realized he couldn't evade the old matron whose temperament fluctuated between fury and guilt. On her arrival he ordered her a customary coffee, feigned one or two calculations at his desk, and as soon as she'd finished her demitasse, he shuffled her off while stuffing an envelope into her obliging hands. Afterward she roamed from shop to shop, a taxi to sport her about, hunting for gifts appropriate for all, only to return home after spending every last penny. İhsan and Mümtaz considered this store, its rent, and the tenant, along with Arife, who might even be considered part of the old manse herself, the lady's sole amusement and diversion, the single greatest entertainment with which she filled her spare time; and because she was heartened by it all, they did nothing but indulge her.

On the Island of İhsan, whatever one did was tolerated; each phantasy, each curiosity was met, if not with a chuckle then with a smirk. The lord of the island wanted it so; he believed if things were this way, everyone would be content. Brick by brick, he'd built this happiness over long years. Now, however, fate was testing him a second time. İhsan was infirm. *Today's the eighth day*, thought Mümtaz. They'd come to believe that even-numbered days would pass quietly.

Shrugging off the daze brought on by poor sleep, Mümtaz plodded downstairs. Little Sabiha had put on his slippers and was sitting resentfully in the open hall.

Mümtaz couldn't bear the way the wild sylph sat silently so. Granted, Ahmet was reserved too. But he was this way by nature. He felt forever blameworthy. Especially since he'd learned the heartrending circumstances of his birth – from whom? How? A mystery. Perhaps one of the neighbors had told him – he was always in a corner and always felt awkward at home. Were he indulged overly much, he'd assume they were patronizing him

14

and tears would well in his eyes. Misfortune of this sort was rife. Some were condemned from birth – the reed stalk snapped off on its own. Not Sabiha, who was their enchanted fairy tale. She wandered about, spun yarns, and sang songs. Her jubilation, the riot and ruckus she made, often reverberated over the Island of İhsan.

She'd hardly slept at all for three days. Feigning sleep on the broad divan in the oriel window, she'd watched over her father with the others.

With delight, Mümtaz regarded the nymph's wan countenance and sunken eyes as much as he possibly could. Her hair had been missing its bow now for days.

"I won't wear the red ribbon now. When father gets better, I'll dress up!" she'd said three days ago with her usual coquetry and through the grin and charm that appeared when she wanted to be friendly. When Mümtaz showed her some affection, however, she began to weep. Sabiha wept in two ways. The first was a childish cry, the forced cry of one playing the brat: Her face contorted, her voice hit an odd pitch, and she kicked and stomped; all told, like every child swathed in selfishness, she became a petite afreet.

Then there was the way she cried when confronted by genuine sorrow, to the extent that her young mind was able to grasp, a suppressed and halting cry. At least she'd withhold her tears for a while. Her expression changed, her lips trembled, and she averted her wet eyes. She wouldn't square her shoulders as with the other, but virtually let them droop. These were tears she shed when she felt ignored, belittled, or treated unfairly. When she did shut off the rest of the family from her child's *âlem*, a world she so wanted to make decent and cordial, an eternally vibrant realm embellished with coral branches and mother-of-pearl flowers, Mümtaz sensed that even her red velvet ribbon had lost its luster.

Sabiha had chanced upon the bow herself a few months after her second birthday. She'd simply handed her mother a dark red ribbon that she'd found on the ground and demanded, "Tie it in my hair." Thereafter she wouldn't stand to have it removed. Over the years, the ribbon had grown from a fashion accessory into a signature item. A red ribbon marked everything of Sabiha's, and she handed them out like a queen bestowing knighthood. Kittens, dolls, objects of which she was fond – particularly her new bedstead – everyone and everything that was the object of her affections received one. Not to mention that the honor might even be revoked by special proclamation. On one occasion, the cook had scolded her for acting spoiled and, not satisfied with that, complained to her mother, sending Sabiha into a tantrum; later the girl politely requested that the cook remove the bow she'd given her. The truth of the matter was that Sabiha's dainty girlhood warranted such rewards and punishments. At any rate, she was the one who had established the sole sultanate of the house before the onset of the disease. Even Ahmet found his little sister's dominion, which had begun to take root in everyone's heart, natural. For Sabiha had arrived after a tragedy that had shaken the house to its foundations. Certainly, Macide was still unstable when she'd given birth to her. And Macide's return to life and sanity coincided with Sabiha's birth. Macide's affliction hadn't passed completely. She suffered small episodes: concocting stories as before, giving her voice the cadence of a sweet little girl's, or for hours on end waiting at the window – or wherever she happened to be – for the return of Zeynep, the oldest daughter about whom she never spoke.

The accident was a misfortune of epic proportions. İhsan and the doctors had done everything within their power to keep news of the tragedy from Macide, but no one could conceal the distress and anguish from this woman yet writhing through her first contractions. In the end Macide learned of what had befallen her daughter from the nurses. From where she lay, she dragged herself with difficulty to the body, saw the corpse laid out, and stood petrified before it. After that she wasn't herself again.

She lay in bed with a high fever for days, giving birth to Ahmet in that state.

One June morning eight years ago Zeynep had come with her grandmother Sabire to the hospital, only later to remember that she'd forgotten to bring her gift; without telling anyone, she went out to the front of the hospital to await her father, and in a moment of distraction, the girl, pondering God knows what, was spirited away by Death.

İhsan, who'd persuaded his wife to give birth in a hospital, under the sway of doctors claiming that she displayed truly severe symptoms, never forgave himself. He witnessed the devastation minutes after the fact, the body yet warm, still bloody, and he carried his daughter into the hospital only to witness the quiet passing of last hopes.

Fate had orchestrated the tragedy so that nobody bore responsibility. Not once had Macide wanted her daughter to visit the hospital. Sabire withstood the girl's insistence and tears for two full days. İhsan hadn't been able to find a single taxi to take him to the hospital in time and was forced to come by streetcar. Hoping against hope to locate an empty cab on the way, he'd even ridden on the trolley's steps. Many held him responsible. But Ahmet lived with the burden of death more than the others did.

Mümtaz found Ahmet at the foot of his father's bed, ready to scurry at the slightest gesture. Macide stood, fiddling absently with a loose strand of yarn from her wool cardigan.

On seeing Mümtaz, İhsan ws heartened, his face sanguine again. His chest rose and fell slowly. In the morning sunlight, to Mümtaz, he appeared much thinner than he actually was. His stubbled chin lent his face a strange mien. His condition seemed to imply, "I'm nearly done with being İhsan. Soon I'll be something else or I'll be nothing at all. I'm preparing for that eventuality!"

He made a vague sign with his infirm hand.

Mümtaz leaned toward the bed. "I haven't read the papers yet. I don't think there's anything to worry about," he said.

In truth, he was convinced of the approach of war. "When the world is about to slough its skin, mayhem is inevitable." İhsan, with whom he always discussed current events, would often repeat this quote by Albert Sorel. To this warning, Mümtaz now added the bitter prediction of a poet he quite admired: "This is the end of Europe." But he couldn't discuss such things at present. İhsan lay ailing.

From where İhsan lay, he contemplated the situation. His hand fell to the quilt in a gesture of pleading and despair.

"How did he pass the night?"

"There's been no change, Mümtaz," Macide answered in her gentle voice like a dream of spring grass. "He's always and forever the same."

"Were you able to sleep at all?"

"I lay down here together with Sabiha. But I couldn't sleep."

She gestured to the divan with her hand, grinning. She might have indicated this spot where she'd slept for five days, as if pointing to a gallows with horror and a shudder. But for Macide, this astounding and exceedingly precious creature, her smile made up half her character. So much so, she was unrecognizable without it. *Thank God those days are behind us!* The days when Macide had lost her smile were over.

"Why don't you sleep for a spell?"

"After you return . . . I couldn't sleep all night for the train whistles. I wonder if troops are being mobilized or some such thing?"

Mümtaz recalled: *I learned of the tragedy by telegram while I was in Kastamonu. I came immediately. Macide and baby Ahmet were in two separate rooms. Everyone was preoccupied with Macide. My aunt Sabire was frantic. İhsan was a mere shadow of himself. I'll never forget that summer. If İhsan hadn't maintained faith in life, what condition would Macide be in today?*

İhsan pointed to Macide. "This one–" He stopped as if powerless to finish his words. Then he mustered his strength and continued, "Give this one a word of advice."

Good God, his labored speech. This man, who was the most articulate of anyone Mümtaz knew, whose classroom lectures, conversations, and repartees would stay with him for days, could barely string together these few words. But he was content nevertheless. Despite everything, the "old codger" – this was his expression – had come through. He'd been able to express himself. Mümtaz would, of course, find a way to keep Macide from exhausting herself; İhsan's eyes, fixed as they were on the young gentleman's face, lost all focus.

Stepping outside, Mümtaz stared at the street as if he were observing it in the wake of a long absence. At the entrance to the mosque opposite the house, an urchin toying with a length of twine gazed at fig branches lolling over the low wall. Perhaps he was contemplating the assault he'd soon make on the fig tree and the pleasures it promised. *Just the way I sat and thought twenty years ago . . . but back then the mosque wasn't in this condition.* He completed his thought remorsefully, *Neither was the neighborhood.*

A street suffused in radiance. Mümtaz ever so absentmindedly studied the sunlight. Then he looked back at the urchin and at the fig branch and, above it, the dome of the mosque, whose lead sheathing had been commandeered for military supplies – slipped off like a glove from a hand or effortlessly peeled away like the skin of a fig from this very tree. *The historic Mosque of Hazel-Eyed Mehmet Efendi*, he thought. *I'll find out who that man is yet!* The man had once endowed another mosque in Eyüp, where his tomb was located. But would Mümtaz ever be able to unearth the charter of this charitable trust to verify the fact?

II

Most of the addresses given to Mümtaz were false leads. A nurse named Fatma had never lived at the first house of his inquiry. The daughter of the family had simply begun a nursing course. The girl greeted him with a smile. "I signed up for the course so I could be of some use in case of war. But I haven't learned anything yet." She was solemn of voice. "My brother's in the army . . . Thinking of him." An actual nurse had lived in the second house he visited. But three months ago she'd left for a job she'd found in an Anatolian hospital. Her mother, greeting Mümtaz, said, "Let me look into it. When I see one of my daughter's friends, I'll pass the word."

With the patience of one who didn't want to spoil a charade, Mümtaz scribbled his address on a scrap of paper. The house was old and ramshackle. *What do they do in winter? How do they keep warm?* he thought as he walked away. Anyway, these questions were moot. On this late August morning, each street seized him in its ovenlike maw, then gobbled and swallowed him whole, before passing him on to the next one. An intermittent shady patch or a pocket of cool air at an intersection seemed to ease life's toil. "İhsan, this summer I can't avoid the libraries. I have to finish the first volume no matter what!" he'd said. The first volume . . . before his eyes Mümtaz saw pages crisscrossed with threads of writing: annotations in crimson ink, extensive marginalia, and scratched-out lines that resembled an argument with himself. Who knew, maybe the history would never be completed. Under the torment of this thought, he went from street to street, speaking to corner grocers and proprietors of coffeehouses. The only nurse he was able to locate at home said, "I've taken leave from work because my husband's sick. It's not that I'm unemployed. After admitting him to the hospital, I'll return to my job." The woman's face was a veritable building on the verge of collapse.

Mümtaz, reluctantly: "What's he have?"

"Paralysis from stroke. I wasn't with him. They brought him home, half his body limp. If they'd had any sense, they'd have taken him to the hospital then and there. Now the doctors say we should wait ten days before moving him again. How many times I begged of that wench, 'Let him out of your clutches, he doesn't have a penny or a thing, he isn't young or handsome, find someone better for yourself.' No, it had to be him above all, and now I'm stuck with three kids."

At the threshold of this family tragedy, Mümtaz bid farewell to the woman facing him. Three children, a paralyzed husband . . . on a nurse's wages. They lived in two rooms of a large house. Even their water vats were stored in the entryway, meaning they might not have use of a kitchen or toilet. The wooden house had been built by some wealthy Ottoman bureaucrat, finance minister, or provincial governor when marrying off his daughter. Despite its faded paint, the elegance of its construction was still evident through meticulously carved window casings, oriel windows, and eaves. Twin five-stepped staircases curved up to the entrance. On the right side stood the door to the coal cellar. But the owner had rented it to a coal merchant. Perhaps the kitchen was rented separately as well.

Loping and rumbling, the massive body of a coal-laden truck clogged the street.

Mümtaz veered into an alleyway . . .

He mused about the previous summer, how perhaps on one such day, he'd wandered these very streets with his beloved Nuran, strolling through the Koca Mustafa Pasha and Hekim Ali Pasha neighborhoods. Side by side in the heat, their bodies nearly entwined, wiping sweat from their foreheads, conversing all the while, they'd entered the courtyard of this very *medrese* or deciphered the Ottoman inscription on the fountain he'd now passed. One year ago. Mümtaz cast glances about as if seeking the shortest possible route to the previous year. He'd come as far as the Seven Martyrs beyond the city's ancient land walls. The martyrs of Sultan Mehmed's conquest slept side by side in small stone tombs. The street was dusty and narrow. Where the martyrs rested, however, it opened into a diminutive square. From the window of a two-story house, so run-down that it almost appeared – like those tiny sports cars – made of pasteboard, came the sounds of a tango, and in the middle of the street, dusty girls played a game. Mümtaz heard their song:

Raise the gate, toll keeper, toll keeper.
What will you pay me to pass on through?

The girls were hale and hearty, but their clothes were in tatters. In a neighborhood where Hekimoğlu Ali Pasha's manor had stood at one time, these houses like remnants of life, these poor clothes, and this song brought strange thoughts to his mind. Nuran had certainly played this game in her childhood. And before that, her mother and her grandmother sang the same ditty while playing this game.

What should persist is this very song, our children's growing up while singing this song and playing this game, not Hekimoğlu Pasha himself or his manor or his neighborhood. Everything is subject to transformation; we can even foster such change through our own determination. What shouldn't change are the things that structure social life, and mark it with our own stamp.

İhsan understood such things well. He'd once said, "Every lullaby holds the thoughts and dreams of a million children!" İhsan, however, lay bedridden. Furthermore, Nuran wanted nothing to do with him, and the headlines announced a tense state of foreign affairs. Since morning he'd been under the assault of forces he didn't want to acknowledge, relegating them to a corner of his mind.

The poor girls played over a tinderbox. Still, the song was the same old song; life forged ahead even atop a powder keg.

He sauntered along, passing gradually from one thought to the next.

He realized that he wouldn't be able to find a nurse in these outskirts of the city. He'd forgotten about the last address in his hand. After following the lead, he'd phone a relative near the American Hospital before trying to look around there.

He plodded through decrepit, grim neighborhoods, passing before aged houses whose bleakness gave them the semblance of human faces. Throngs surrounded him, wearing expressions forlorn and sickly.

They were all downcast, anticipating what the impending apocalypse of tomorrow held in store for them.

If not for the disease . . . and what if he were drafted? What if he had to go and leave İhsan infirm like this?

Returning to the house, he found Macide asleep. İhsan's breathing had steadied. The doctor had left good news in his wake. Ahmet was at his father's bedside together with his grandmother Sabire. Curled up near her mother's feet, Sabiha was truly asleep now.

Overwhelmed by an eerie quiet, he climbed the stairs to his room. He'd seen the characters that made up his entire circle, almost, for he'd had no news of Nuran. *What was she doing?* he wondered.

III

İhsan and his wife held vital places in Mümtaz's upbringing. Following the deaths of both his father and mother within a span of just a few weeks, his cousin had raised him. Macide and İhsan; İhsan and Macide. Until he'd made Nuran's acquaintance, his life had passed almost entirely between them. İhsan had been both a father and a mentor to him.

In France, where Mümtaz had been sent for two years about the time Macide had regained her health, his cousin's influence persisted; in those new surroundings with so many temptations, he'd been spared initial experiences of decadence in part due to İhsan's guidance, and thus hadn't squandered his time.

Macide, meanwhile, had entered his life when he most needed a woman's compassion and beauty's counsel. When she came to mind, he'd muse, *I've spent part of my youth beneath a spring bough.* Thus, İhsan's affliction had shaken this already troubled youth to his core. From the moment he'd heard the word "pneumonia" leave the doctor's lips, he'd been living in a perplexing state of distress.

It wasn't the first time Mümtaz had known such anguish. Anxiety in part constituted his inner self, that entity resting beneath the surface yet controlling everything. İhsan had strived to banish the serpent coiled within Mümtaz, and to extract its tree, whose roots extended into the boy's heart. But it was essentially with Macide's arrival that Mümtaz improved and turned to face the sun. Until he'd passed into her hands, Mümtaz was a creature of resentments, closed to the world, expecting nothing but calamity to fall from the skies – and rightly so.

After the Great War, during the armistice-era invasion of S. by Greece, a local Anatolian Greek, an adversary of the owner of the house where Mümtaz's family lived, mistakenly shot his father instead of the landlord. The town verged on capture. Many Turkish families had already fled. Mümtaz's ill-fated father had found conveyance for wife and son that same night. Their bags and belongings had been prepared. He'd spent the entire day in town arranging for the trip. A little after nightfall he'd returned home to say, "*Haydi!* It's all set! Let's eat something, and we'll be on the road within the hour. The routes are still open." They ate on a cloth spread on the ground. There came a thump at the door. The servant informed them of someone waiting to see the man of the house. His father rushed to the door, assuming he'd receive details about the wagon he'd spent dawn till dusk procuring. Then they heard the report of a gun, a single, hollow shot without so much as an echo. The large man, one hand pressed over his abdomen, almost slithered back upstairs, collapsing in the hallway. It all lasted no more than five minutes. Neither mother nor child knew what words had been exchanged below or even who'd come. The shot was followed by the downhill patter of men running. While still numb with shock, they heard the sound of approaching artillery. Shortly, the neighbors arrived and an elder tried to pull them off the body, saying, "He'd always treated us with reverence. Let's not leave him out in the open but bury him. He's a martyr and can be buried without rites in his clothes."

Hastily, a grave was dug under a sprawling chinar tree in a corner of the yard within the light of a sooty lantern and an as-yet-unpacked oil lamp held aloft by a half-mad gardener.

Mümtaz never forgot this scene. Upstairs, his mother continued to weep over the corpse. As if spellbound, he was glued to one wing of the garden gate, staring at the men by the tree trunk. The three men worked under the lantern they'd hung from a branch. The flame of the lantern verged on blowing out in the breeze; meanwhile, the old gardener raised the edge of his jacket to keep the other oil lamp lit. Beneath two sources of light, shadows expanded and contracted and amid artillery thuds, his mother's wails mingled with the rasp of shoveling. When they were nearly finished, the air turned crimson. The glow came from the direction of the house; the town was burning. The fire had broken out an hour beforehand. The men continued to work under reddened skies. Shrapnel began to fall here and there. A roar louder than the sound of water bursting a levee rose from town, followed by an apocalypse of sounds. A man, hopping over the fence into the yard, shouted, "They're entering town." Everybody froze. Only his mother came downstairs, pleading. Mümtaz could withstand no more, and his hand, which clung to the gate wing, loosened and he collapsed to the ground. From where he lay, certain sounds reached his ears, but what he saw differed from what actually surrounded him. His father, as he did every night, had taken out the base of the large crystal lantern and tried to light it. When Mümtaz came to consciousness, he found himself outside the fence. "Can you walk?" his mother asked. He gazed about absently and said, "I can walk." He did walk.

Mümtaz couldn't fully recollect the journey. From which hilltop did they watch the town burn? On which main road did they join the ghastly, miserable procession of suffering hundreds? Who'd put them on the sprung carriage toward daybreak, seating him next to the driver? These questions remained a mystery.

He had fragmented memories, one of which was the way his mother was transfigured on the exodus. No longer was she a wife who wept and moaned over her husband's corpse. She was a mother who'd set out and was trying to deliver her son and herself. Silently she did what those who led the refugee column said. She walked, holding her son's hand tightly. Mümtaz could still feel the clench of her hand, a grip that would outlast her death.

Or else the memory was more vivid. He'd see his mother standing stiffly beside him with her torn headcovering and her gaunt, rigid face. Later, in the carriage, each time she cast her head back, she seemed a shade paler, a little more withdrawn, a veritable wound of withered face and withheld tears.

The second night of their exile they spent in a spacious inn lime-washed white, seemingly waiting alone for the Anatolian steppe. The stairs of the inn ran along the exterior and the windows of the rooms opened onto a terrace, where fruits were dried beneath the autumn sun. Mümtaz slept in one room with four or five other children and as many women. Before the entrance of the inn lolled a group of camels and mules free of wagons and stables. When one of the intermingled gathering of dormant animals stirred, the whole lot began to move; the clink-clank of their small bells and the cries of the watchmen disrupted the silence of the steppe night and the sense of exile gathered by slight gale and solitude from who knows which remote foothills, deserted valleys, or emptied villages and piled around the sooty lantern illuminating their quarters. At whiles, in the blackness, whatever the cigarette-smoking men before the entryway uttered reached his ears. The words filled Mümtaz with despair and resentment though he didn't fully understand their significance; the sentences made the petty, spoiled, and privileged life he'd lived till then at once very harsh, cruel, and absurd. Then winds blew through open windows, bedsheet curtains billowed, and sounds from distant locales mingled with voices of the closest proximity.

A commotion woke them in the dead of night. The surrounding muteness had so hermetically sealed off their lives, like an incredibly dense yet thin substance, that the faintest sound or slightest noise became a resounding racket, like an object shattering glass, and conveyed feelings of devastation and collapse. Everybody rushed to the window, some even began flocking outside. Only Mümtaz's mother remained still. Four men on horseback appeared, one of whom lowered a figure from the croup of his horse. Mümtaz, sidling up to the horses' muzzles, heard a young village woman mumble, "God be pleased with ye." The lamp held aloft by the innkeeper illuminated her large black irises. A waistcloth covered the lower part of her body, the kind worn by women who worked the opium fields. On her upper body, she wore the traditional embroidered coat of the Zeybek fighters of the Aegean mountains. These horsemen drank water from the terra-cotta jug passed around by the innkeeper's apprentice, who'd earlier brought tea up to the rooms; they shared bread offered by the innkeeper and filled their haircloth sacks with barley; as if rehearsed beforehand, everything happened swiftly. Men congregating before the inn asked repeatedly of news.

"There's a battle raging over S. You've got till tomorrow. But don't stay too late, there's a flood of refugees on the way."

Then they quickly spurred their horses with nothing so much as a fare-well. Where were they going? What were they doing?

Mümtaz went back upstairs where he discovered the newcomer, a girl of eighteen or twenty, stretched out beside his mother, sobbing open-eyed and stone-faced. Moving aside, his mother had made a space for her. Mümtaz lay next to the young woman for only a few hours, but in his sleep on subsequent nights, he relived bodily the sensations roused by her nighttime proximi-ty. Even long after the fact, he'd awaken as if he were in her arms, her hair veiling his face, her breasts pressed against his chest, and her sultry breath on his forehead – as he'd actually experienced a few times that night. She wrenched awake sporadically. During such intervals, she moaned with halt-ing, nearly inhuman sobs perhaps as heartrending as his mother's silence, but the moment she nodded back to sleep, she'd clasp Mümtaz with her arms and legs as if forcefully prying him from his mother's bosom, and her face would graze his in a full tumult of tresses and panting, or she'd draw him toward her, pressing him against her torso. As Mümtaz arose to these frequent embraces and groans, it surprised him to find her body, teeming with bewildering and mystical desires, entwined with his own; and this body, willing, with every iota of its being, to die a separate death from the one he'd experienced the night before, alarmed him, as did her sweet breath, which seemed to melt everything it contacted into soft ore, as did her eerie and tense face, and Mümtaz tightly shut his eyes to avoid the incognizant glint of hers in the light of the still-burning lantern.

Carnal desires churning by themselves, burning embraces, and moans that filled their barrenness in opposite proportion contained a sorcery unknown to him. He couldn't manage to free himself from her embrace and simply abandoned himself to that peculiar twinned state of one weary of body who'd fallen asleep in warm, aromatic water, afraid of drowning on one hand, yet unable to resist the numbness of sleep on the other. Never before had he experienced this. His body, which had previously felt nothing beyond simple arousal, opened as if to an entirely new realm; within a state of intoxication, moments of pure delight continually settled in utterly mysterious and unfamiliar vertices of his body. Internally, he felt a delicious feeling of being expended that recalled certain final stages of sleep, and what's more, these hot embraces and caresses themselves bore desire for depletion. The moment it reached its pinnacle, one of consciousness lost, when he practically merged with his surroundings, his body, ravished by fatigue and anguish, suddenly slipped into unconsciousness. Oddly, as soon as sleep overtook him, he always had the dream of the previous night, when he'd passed out, and he saw his father with the large crystal lantern; but since the dream occurred within the torment of an initial experience, it roused him frequently and violently. Thus his inner suffering united with the ecstasy emanating from the woman's figure and overwhelmed his whole being, and he became a grotesque creature doubled in body and meaning.

Toward daybreak he awoke fully to find himself in the arms of the woman, his jaw resting against her diminutive chin, in complete command of his senses with every ounce of his being, when her eyes suddenly opened with unnerving insistence. To avoid her gaze, he shut his eyes again, and rolled anxiously toward his mother.

His second memory wasn't as convoluted. Around midafternoon, the carriage they rode left the rest of the column far behind. He was with his mother, three women, and two younger children. *She* was also there, crouched just behind the sprung seats.

The carriage driver announced that they'd approached B., constantly glancing inside the wagon. Mümtaz realized quite well that the driver's need to chat and provide details had to do with her. But she didn't say a single word either to him or to the mounted gendarme, who wouldn't alter his horse's gait beside them, or to anyone for that matter. Her moans of the previous night had ceased. Mümtaz was delirious with the desire to look at her, but because he didn't dare turn his head, he couldn't even see his mother. As night fell, he was intimidated by the woman's presence, and from time to time, as she let her shoulder press against his, the sensation became rather merciless.

The contact was startling, devoid of the warm intensity of the night before, yet laden with memory; involuntarily, Mümtaz wanted the heat to approach, and within such anticipation, his shoulder nearly went stiff. During one spell of anticipation, his eyes fixed on the driver's turquoise-beaded leather whip, waiting emptied of thought, he remembered his father with a distinct agony that far exceeded anything he'd ever felt, agony ready to hurdle every separation, diminishing every distance between them. He'd never see him again. He'd withdrawn from life forever. Mümtaz would never forget the moment of this epiphany. Everything lay spread before his eyes, in plain sight: The turquoise beads on the tip of the rawhide whip glimmered gloriously as they caught the autumn sunlight, some of them midair, some of them on the haunches of the horse before him. The horses sauntered, tossing their manes. From the top of a telegraph pole ahead, a broad-winged bird took to the air. Everything was mute in the washed-out landscape except for the sound of the wagons and the cries of a three-year-old girl; he sat next to the driver; the woman from the night before, who'd held him until morning and ignited mysterious desires in his naïve body, sat behind him; and just opposite her was his mother, who had no idea what was transpiring or, what's more, what would transpire.

Unexpectedly, he saw his father, an imago before him, and this vision reminded him that he would never lay eyes on him again, that he'd be separated from his presence in perpetuity, with the sharp and insurmountable pain of departure, of never again hearing his voice, of never again being a part of his existence.

The village woman, perhaps realizing that Mümtaz verged on fainting, supported him from behind so he wouldn't fall. The amazing sensuality of the night before united anew and inextricably with his father's death. He felt deep inside that he'd sinned irrevocably; he felt guilty of unnamed transgressions. Had they interrogated him at that moment, he might have said, "I'm the one responsible for my father's death." It was a horrendous sensation that made him feel utterly deplorable. This paradox of mind would plague Mümtaz for years and trip him up at every step and turn. Even after he'd reached adolescence, Mümtaz wouldn't be able to escape these feelings. The images that filled his dream-chambers, the confounding hesitations, anxieties, and the array of psychological states that comprised the agony and the ecstasy of his existence were all bound to this chance convergence.

The woman parted company with them at B. The carriage stopped within a vast stain of sunlight on one of the city's half-ruined streets. Without uttering a word or looking at anyone, she leaped from the carriage. She dashed swiftly in front of the horses to the other side of the street, from where she glanced at Mümtaz one last time. Then, running again, she turned down an alleyway. For the first and last time, Mümtaz saw her luminous face. A freshly healed knife wound ran from her right temple to her chin. The scar lent her face a queer harshness; yet, while gazing at Mümtaz, her expression softened and her eyes smiled.

Two days later at twilight, Mümtaz and his mother arrived in A., at the house of a distant relative.

IV

The Mediterranean: Mümtaz later learned through books how the White Sea embraced humanity with a life of leisure; how the sunlight, the crystalline weather, and the clarity – extending to the horizon and emblazoning each wave and crest into one's vision – refined the self and filled the soul; in sum, how the quality of nature here permitted grapes and olives, mystical inspiration and rational thought, or the staunchest desire and the anxiety over individual satisfaction to coexist. Not having cognizance of these things at that age didn't mean that Mümtaz failed to savor his experience of them. His sojourn here, despite life's continuing misfortune, constituted a season of exception.

The feverish state that had scorched a stretch of their lives in S. persisted here as well. Each day the city was shaken with news; today there would be fearful word of a great rebellion to the north; tomorrow news of a victory would fill the streets with a celebration to be forgotten by nightfall. On almost every street corner raged heated debates, and at night the clandestine transport of troops and matériel continued. Daily, the hotel opposite their house filled up and emptied out anew.

Yet this all occurred beneath a sun as luminous as a diamond, within the intoxicating perfume of orange blossom, honeysuckle, and Arabian jasmine, and before a lapis lazuli sea that accepted him with his thousand frailties, transforming with him, a sea whose wrath, serenity, long bouts of listlessness, and delight always accompanied him.

No matter how angst-ridden he might be, before long the luminance would find a crack in the misery, through which it slithered like a golden serpent. Sunlight released him from his inner confines and described an array of possibilites as if recounting a fable, as if to say, "Have faith in me, I am the source of all miracles, I can do anything, I can turn earth to gold. I grab the dead by the forelock to rouse them from sleep. I can easily soften thoughts and make them resemble my essence. I am the efendi of life. Where I am there can be neither despair nor depression. I am the elation of wine and the sweetness of honey."

Any life-form heeding this advice chirped and twittered merrily above every sorrow. Each day the cargo and passengers carried by one or two steamships, a horde of camels or beasts of burden were deposited in front of the hotel opposite their house, bundles were opened and repacked and reloaded, crates nailed shut, and metal straps cinched around wooden chests; travelers sat in chairs before the entryway, conversing; as in a Futurist painting, simply an eye or a sole ear and its curiosity, or an eager female head, protruded through windows; out of idleness, brazen Italian soldiers of the Allied occupation played with children in door fronts for hours, calling out to them with repeated *cara mio*s, carried trays of raw pastries and baklava prepared by housewives to hot bakery ovens, and when they got a little fresh and met with a scolding, they bowed their heads as if quite ashamed and walked away jeering openly before wandering down a backstreet to reemerge. In front of the depot, enormous dromedaries, the world's most pacific animals, were made to wrestle; everybody was gratified to see nature's disproportioned and tranquil creatures succumb to the mind of mankind. At night boys and girls went to the Palisades district, or to other places beneath the moonlight or in pitch-blackness to route water to the gardens of their houses. Life was restricted, but nature was vast and inviting.

On only the second day of his arrival, Mümtaz had made numerous friends. He'd wander together with the boys of the house to the citrus groves and to the Karaoğlan district. They'd even go as far as the walnut groves on the outskirts of the city. Much later he'd come to like the Kozyatağı neighborhood in Istanbul because it reminded him of this walnut orchard. But for the most part they'd spend their days at Mermerli or at the seaside on the wharf, and toward evening they'd go up to the bluffs of Hastaneüstü.

Mümtaz liked to spend the twilight hours perched on boulders between the road and the sea. The sun above the Bey Mountains girded the hilly undulations in golden and silver armor as if arranging the rites of its own death by preparing a sarcophagus of gilding and indigo shadows; then the arc that had descended and toppled backward spread open like a golden fan, and large swaths of light, bats of fire, fluttered here and there, hanging from the rocks. The ineluctable modality of the visible was as bountiful and lush as a season. The boulders, during the daytime, were only seaweed-covered blocks of stone that wind and rain had eroded with holes like sponges, but because they abruptly came to life in twilight, Mümtaz was besieged by a horde of fabulous beings whose numinous powers and physical forms were superior to man's, who were mute like fate itself, only communicating through echoes of their existence within mankind. And his small body in their midst – an understanding of life expanding inside him – Mümtaz tried not to be scattered by that astounding gust of apprehension whose origins extended deeply into the past and whorled about his entire being. It was the sea mated with the sun . . . the hour when all things were reborn in a new form, when voices augmented, when humanity receded as it moved toward the infinite under a firmament that deepened and lost its warmth and friendly countenance, when from everywhere nature declared, "For whatever reason did you go and become the plaything of dreary suffering? Come, return to me, dissolve in whole synthesis, you'll forget everything, and sleep the comfortable and blithe sleep of dumb matter." Mümtaz sensed this calling until it reached his vertebrae, and to avoid lunging at the invitation, whose meaning he didn't fully understand, his tiny being stiffened and recoiled.

At times he did go farther, to the rocky outcroppings that overlooked the sea from the heights; there, at the edge of the precipice facing seaweed patches, he observed how the placid water exposed itself to the last bounty of the evening like a viridian and porphyry mirror, gathering shards of light and harboring them like a maternal womb before occluding them gradually. After the muffled rasping of waves, moving to and fro far below, after the fleeting pianissimo, the whispers of love, the fluttering of wings, the splashing; in sum, after the enunciations of mysterious beings living only for the twilight hour filled quiet interstices between dusk and nightfall, he was summoned by vast invitations with scalloped edges and colorful spectra, by the articulations of thousands of life forms dormant in who knows which mother-of-pearl shell, fish scale, rock hollow, moonbeam, or starlight. Where were they inviting him? Had Mümtaz known, maybe he would have rushed to the occasion. For the sound of the sea is mightier than the sough of love and desire. In darkness, the roar of water spoke in tongues of Thanatos.

With a telltale tremor that showed he was ready to accept the roaring invitation, Mümtaz sought out friendly visions of his as-of-yet incipient life in this black mirror; he sought out the chinar under which his father made his eternal repose, as well as the blithe childhood hours that he'd abandoned abruptly and the black-eyed village girl at the inn, a deep inoculation into his innocent skin; and when he realized this was only a blank mirror, he stood and tried to escape the gigantic shadows of the boulders as if from a nightmare – staggering and stumbling at each stride.

The boulders might very well come alive as he passed them, it seemed, or a hand might verge on reaching out to grab hold of him, or somebody might toss his mantle over his head.

The crowded rockscape made him shudder even in broad daylight. Rather than being a living part of nature, the stones resembled life-forms that had frozen still in the midst of some unspecified cataclysm. But truly horrifying was their appearance during the arrest of his imagination. At such moments they would be ousted from life, eternally alien to him and rejecting him. They seemed to declare, "We are removed from life. Outside of life . . . That all-nourishing, life-giving sap has withdrawn from us. Even death is not as barren as we." Verily, next to these rocky outcroppings how vibrant was a lump of clay, clay that he so loved to play with as a boy and would always love. Its soft, malleable existence might take any form or surrender to any will, or any idea. Yet these solid fragments of stone were forever removed from life; the wind might blow, the rain might fall; atom by atom they'd erode, deep lines and furrows would appear on their colossal bodies, but none of it could rid them of the state in which they were formed by the hands of some primordial apocalypse. Inasmuch as they had no apparent inquiry to make on life's trajectory, they were crude and coarse symbols issuing from infinite time, posing all questions at once.

Occasionally a bat would dart from where he'd stepped, and in the distance another winged beast would call to its fledglings. Once free of the rockscape, he felt relieved. On the flat macadam road he slowed his pace and affirmed his resolve: *I won't be coming back here again!* But tastes of the unfathomable are seductive, and the next evening he was back again, or at the seaside, or simply crouched on a boulder beside the road. For the sake of experiencing this titillation alone, he even made excuses to take leave of his friends before nightfall.

The day came when his companions took him to Güvercinlik, to a grotto between Hastaneüstü and Konyaaltı quite some distance from the city. They rambled along the coast for a while, then turned in to the boulders, and finally went underground through a tunnel. Shuffling and crawling on hands and knees in pitch-darkness didn't appeal to Mümtaz. But at the end of this passage everything was suddenly illuminated, as if the sun were shining through lush, verdant leaves, and within this luminescence they entered a sea cave. Despite their hands and knees being covered with cuts and sores, the light, shifting between deep turquoise and naptha green, excited Mümtaz. When the waves ebbed inside the mass of rock that the sea had hollowed out, there remained a calm, somewhat deep body of water, like an artificial rocaille pool similar a natural pond, with a small island of stone, whose waters were clear enough to reveal fish swimming in its depths and crabs and crustaceans along its rocky edges. This part of the grotto was accessible by sea. Behind it, the part through which they had entered was wider and constituted a slightly elevated, largish cavern filled with rock fragments. When a wave struck and sealed the mouth of the grotto, all was suffused in verdigris light. Then, in a series of odd, seemingly subterranean sounds, the water emptied out, and everything was illuminated again through refractions cast by the sunlit sea. Hands on his chin, Mümtaz watched the chiaroscuro play of light and shadow silently for hours from the perch of a boulder.

What did he contemplate? What did he expect? Had he assumed that the waves would convey something, or had he just surrendered himself to the curious drone made by the water filling and draining the grotto? The sounds bore an invitation, but where, to which arcanum?

By chance, toward nightfall, a caïque that had meandered out along the coast transported them back effortlessly to the pier. Hastily, Mümtaz abandoned his friends and ran home. He wanted to describe what he'd seen to his mother. But she was in such a state that he didn't dare utter a word and was mindful not to leave her alone again.

He passed his days there, beside his mother's sickbed, at times attending to her, at times lost in thought or reading. Each day toward noon he went to the telegraph office to learn whether any response to his mother's telegram had come. Then he sequestered himself in her room, and within the sounds reaching him from the ever-animated, ever-lively street, he consoled her.

As evening fell he sat before the window. Over recent days a girl had been walking down the street. Each night she passed before the houses singing *türkü*s as she carried an empty bottle or some other vessel. Mümtaz recognized her voice when she was still at the far end of the street:

> 'Tis nightfall and I haven't lit this lantern o' mine
> The Almighty has written this fate o' mine
> I haven't caressed my lamb to my heart's content
> Should I die, darling, your fate will be torment

Mümtaz's heart ached, assuming the gaze his mother trained on him every time she lifted her head bore a meaning close to that of these lyrics. Nevertheless, he couldn't keep from listening. The girl's voice was beautiful and strong. But she was still quite small, and in the middle of the rendition her voice cracked oddly, like a whimper.

A little beyond the houses, at the end of the street that led below, the song changed. Her voice suddenly grew bolder and more radiant, to such a degree that it seemed to resonate in intensely luminous echoes against the walls of the houses, the road, even the air itself:

> *Mother-of-pearl, dear Mama, adorns İzmir's minaret*
> *Pour and I'll quaff, dear Mama, from a drinking goblet*

By means of the second *türkü*, Mümtaz was liberated from the woes of his short existence, whose meanings he couldn't yet fathom, to be transported without warning to some other luminous realm, yet laden with longing and suffering. This realm began at İzmir's Kordonboyu esplanade and ended with the death of his father, which also escaped his full comprehension. Here, too, dwelled a residue of torments that didn't fit into his childhood imagination; here, too, gathered death, exile, blood, seclusion, and *hüzün*, the Hydra-headed dragon of melancholy coiling within him. For Mümtaz, that entity called "day" ended when the girl passed by; an anonymous girl, yet one whose arrival he anticipated, however fearful he was that it might disturb his mother's peace. Until the next evening, there passed an undisturbed monolith of time.

That week, one night toward daybreak, his mother migrated to other worlds. Before she died, she requested water, then tried repeatedly, yet unsuccessfully, to impart something to him; her face went pale, her eyes rolled upward, a tremor moved across her lips, and her body stiffened. Mümtaz's mind recorded her final moments in immaculate detail.

Following her death, a cavernous void opened that he couldn't manage to fill. Perhaps by trying continuously to forget troubled days, Mümtaz himself had created this temporal abyss in his mind. However, he did precisely remember the day he was placed on a ship to Istanbul. His kith and kin gathered and took him to a little grave in the courtyard of an old mosque; indicating a mound of recently smoothed-over earth, they said, "Here lies your mother." But Mümtaz never accepted this final resting place. In his mind he'd buried his mother next to his father. The time span between their deaths was negligible. Having her rest beneath the large tree of death with his father was easier and more appropriate. Maybe because Mümtaz had grown accustomed to seeing them together, he could hardly think of them separately in eternal repose.

He remembered the day vividly. The landscape was suffused in white radiance. Sunlight conducted crystal lutes at every turn, on the wooden exteriors of houses, on terra-cotta shingles, on the pure white macadam, on swaths of sea appearing at intersections, on the lemon-yellow wall of the old mosque, on the small and dusty trees of the cemetery, on their sharp stones, on the ruined fortress ramparts where he saw his erstwhile friends at play; indeed, light was crooning its peculiar, contagious, and omnipotent song of radiance. The bees, the flies, the scrawny alley cats, the dog who'd commandeered the area in front of their house, the pigeons flocking on all sides, everyone and everything was besotted with the musical harmony and invitation of *lux*.

Only one figure, it seemed to him, only he alone, had been excluded from this banquet. Fate, through one of its decrees, had culled him from others.

What would happen to him? He didn't know. He'd go to Istanbul, but to stay with whom? How would they regard him there? Never again would he see his mother and father. Into this agony now mingled the despair of an orphan. He felt an overwhelming urge to weep, though he restrained himself. Sobbing in the midst of this sunlight, on this road where each passerby practically hummed a tune, crying before this crystal sea seemed something of an impossibility. Weeping would do nothing but elicit pity from those around him. By now they must certainly be tired of him. For days on end, he'd sensed the shaking of heads and sidelong glances that pursued him like a veritable fiery hand on his back. He assumed he'd been a burden and cursed fate. No, he wouldn't cry. He certainly seemed to possess a peculiar fate, distinct from others.

Toward midafternoon, the ship was to embark. The entire family accompanied him to the pier. There they entrusted him to a civil servant of long standing and his wife who would escort him to Istanbul; and Mümtaz, disgruntled by destiny, gladly bid farewell to the gathering then and there. He'd scarcely noticed the absence of the oldest son of the household, who'd shown him such camaraderie. A bizarre sense of revulsion overcame him. The sunlight gouged his eyes, and the merriment, in which he could not partake, annoyed him. He longed for an extraordinarily gloomy, somber, and muted place. A place like his mother's grave. A place at the edge of a secluded mosque wall, shielded from the sunlight, where the crystal lutes of illumination didn't mock his fate, where the bees, drunk with lifeblood and sun, didn't buzz, where children didn't laugh and shout shrilly in the light, like a shattered mirror whose shards pierced his flesh.

The blackened hulk looming in the offing heartened him. He spoke of nothing, didn't even offer his thanks, only hastily took his leave by kissing hands and cheeks – and hurriedly at that.

In Istanbul he was greeted by his aunt and İhsan. İhsan had recently returned from a military imprisonment in Egypt. Reasons of health prevented him from going to Anatolia to fight in the resistance. As a consequence, he was working for the underground in Allied-occupied Istanbul. Mümtaz's father, at home, had mentioned his nephew İhsan frequently. Statements like, "I'm quite impressed with İhsan. Hopefully, Mümtaz will grow up to be like him," or, "The brightest one in our family is surely İhsan," or, "I only wish for that boy's safe and sound return," could be heard almost daily. Hearing his father's comments at once conjured a number of visions of this cousin, who was twenty-three years his elder. When greeted at the ship by İhsan, Mümtaz realized that he was actually more agreeable than the personae of his preconceptions. A man with a wounded leg, a pockmarked face, and smiling eyes grabbed him and proclaimed, "That's no way to greet your old cousin!" lifted him into the air and advised, "Don't be so long in the face, son, forget it all," and declared his friendship without expecting a thing in return.

Mümtaz adjusted to the Şehzadebaşı household of old Istanbul with difficulty. His elderly aunt had seen much suffering. İhsan was very busy. In addition to his teaching, he had a great deal of writing and reading to attend to. Outside of school, Mümtaz passed his days in near isolation. They'd given him the top-floor room above İhsan's. The large adjacent library would later provide him with a place to study and write. This first encounter with so many books, stacks of pictures, and curios astounded him. Once he grew accustomed to life in the household, the library beckoned. His first books came from its shelves. Novels, stories, and poetry – whose meanings he couldn't quite decipher – were his truest friends that year. The following year they enrolled him in the French lyceum Galatasaray. One week afterward İhsan and Macide married.

Mümtaz approved of his cousin's bride at first sight. "I'm very pleased," was his response to İhsan's inquiring, however joking, *so-what-do-you-think* gesture. His naïve response bore a truth. Macide always infused her surroundings with a sense of contentment. This was part of her essence, secondary to her beauty, moral decency, and composure. With her arrival, life in the family changed dramatically. İhsan's long silences eased and Aunt Sabire's longing for bygone days waned. As for Mümtaz, he struck up a friendship with a woman twelve years his senior. Within a few weeks' time, when he was accepted as a boarder at school, he felt the stirrings of remorse. The household in which he'd felt himself a guest had somehow become his own.

By belonging to a family that he loved, Mümtaz had staked a claim on life. The youth, who'd assumed on his last night in S. that everything would end and, due to his particular fate, that he'd remain ostracized from social life, suddenly found a new existence. Life besieged him and he was part of that life.

At the center of this life rested that exceptional creature, Macide, a petite woman who drew in her wake everything and everyone, magically transfiguring them. On weekends she'd pick Mümtaz up from school and, on empty stomachs, now stopping before shop fronts, now watching passersby come and go, they'd roam through the European quarter of Beyoğlu for hours; then, like two truants who'd cut class, they'd return home in fear and dread of getting caught. When he was ready to go back to school again, Macide was at his side. She prepared his schoolbag and checked his clothes. She wasn't a mother or a sister but rather a guardian angel of sorts; her presence was like that of an alchemist who understood many mysteries, transforming everything, reconciling matter and man, and infusing the hours of the day with an air of sweetness and light.

Mümtaz came to know İhsan later, upon entering into an intellectual life. Without letting on, İhsan had kept an eye on the youth, observing and nourishing his aptitudes and inclinations. When he'd reached the age of seventeen, Mümtaz felt ready to cross a threshold. He'd read the classical Ottoman divan collections and had savored the delicacies of history. İhsan himself taught the history course. On first seeing his older cousin in the classroom, Mümtaz thought, *How am I to learn anything from a relative?* But as class began, he understood that İhsan's persona as teacher was distinct from that of the brother he knew so well. The entire class was awed from the first day. To them, İhsan was something like the eagle that had abducted Ganymede. He'd seized and capitivated them, and though he hadn't taken them up to any Mount Olympus, he'd transported them to the heights of a path they'd subsequently descend by themselves.

Years later he and his classmates recalled lines still fresh in their minds from this first lecture. And lessons continued at home for Mümtaz. He was astounded to realize that he'd become something of a young colleague to İhsan, who shared many of his ideas, argued with, and mentored him. One after another, he'd make requests like, "Search for this matter in Joseph von Hammer," or, "Go see what that charlatan chronicler Şânizâde Mehmed Ataullah has to say," or, "Find out about this business from Hoca Sadeddin Efendi's *Tâcüttevarih*." Mümtaz would take up a large tome, sit at the table reserved for him in a corner of the room, and for hours, depending on the task at hand, note for İhsan details about the life of Hâlet Efendi, about the gifts sent with some embassy to Istanbul by the Hapsburg dynasty, or about the rationale for the Ottoman campaign to Egypt. İhsan aspired to write a comprehensive history of the Turks. It was to be a vehicle for organizing the social doctrine he espoused. Gradually he'd imparted his ideas to Mümtaz.

Listening to İhsan, Mümtaz felt that he was rushing from one epiphany to another. They debated the format of the project together. İhsan wanted a chronological history: Beginning with the economic conditions the Ottoman Empire had inherited from the Byzantines, and proceeding year by year to the present. Conversely one might write up a series of great events; however, this wouldn't constitute a collection of comprehensive surveys as İhsan desired, although institutions and events would be better addressed. Mümtaz favored this second format. Following a heated debate, İhsan agreed. Mümtaz would help with the project; specifically, he was to prepare the art and intellectual history sections. While continuing down the path that İhsan had blazed, Mümtaz's inclinations drew him toward poetry and aesthetics. An aspiring poet's greatest hope is to find his own voice through tools that developed an inner realm. By and by he'd discovered the French poets Régnier and master of the sonnet Heredia, then the symbolists Verlaine and Baudelaire, and each of them gave him a new horizon.

Whatever he read or heard about later played in the peculiar stages erected in Mümtaz's mind: the rocky outcroppings in Antalya and their house in N. All of the scenes in the novels he read took place in these two settings, from where they'd seep into his private life.

Mümtaz found himself in Baudelaire. He was more or less indebted to İhsan for this discovery. İhsan wasn't an artist. His creative side had been subsumed by history and economics. Even so, he understood poetry and painting well. In his youth he'd read French writers methodically. For seven years, he'd lived in the Latin Quarter together with other international cohorts. He'd lived through many trends, witnessed the birth of various theories, and participated in the roaring harvest fires of aesthetic debates. Later, after he'd returned to Istanbul, he'd abruptly forsaken it all, even the poets he loved the most. In an unanticipated way, he occupied himself with topics pertaining to Turks, cultivating this interest to the exclusion of others. Since he'd developed the measure of his aesthetic sense in Europe, he didn't particularly distinguish local choices in art from others. He introduced Mümtaz to the works of Ottoman poets like Bâkî, Nef'î, Nâilî, Nedim, and Shaykh Galip, along with musicians like Dede and Itrî. And it was İhsan who handed him a copy of Baudelaire. "Since you're reading poetry, you might as well read an alchemist of genius," he said, before reciting a few poems from memory. That week Mümtaz hadn't gone to school. A mild grippe kept him in bed. It had been a bitter winter besides. All of Istanbul lay swathed in snow. İhsan, at the edge of his aunt's bed, holding the leather-bound *Flowers of Evil* he'd just bought Mümtaz – perhaps with his eyes trained on his own youth, when a group of them were enamored of the red-haired Mademoiselle Romantique, when they pined for her, spending entire nights till dawn roaming from café to café – İhsan read in his gruff voice, "Invitation to the Voyage," "Autumn Sonnet," and "The Irremediable."

Mümtaz couldn't put Baudelaire down. Much later the Symbolist Mallarmé and the Romantic Nerval joined the poets he admired. But by the time the young gentleman became acquainted with them, he was of an age to determine his own course and savor the literature that appealed to his own sensibilities.

———————

Mümtaz had witnessed an ordeal during this period. Like a figure in a novel, he'd confronted tragedy at a young age, ensuring that it would always afflict him. His mind had blossomed to love and thought during the span between his father's death and his return to Istanbul. These two months had nourished his soul in a strange way. He still relived those days in his dreams; agony frequently roused him from sleep, covered in sweat. Like a leitmotif, a vision of his first instance of consciousness lost colored these dreams: his father trying to light the crystal lantern amid the thud of artillery fire, the rasp of a pickax and shovel, murmurings, and his mother's wailing. And the convoluted memory of his first carnal passion never faded. As he lay beside his afflicted mother, the coiling of the young peasant woman's tired body about him, the gaze of her incognizant eyes, the pleasure wrapped in anguish, disturbed his thoughts and being. Yet, everyday events, that is, time, made him forget about this level of affliction and unendurable suffering. But when melancholy found him, it stirred within him like a Hydra-headed serpent, slithering around and constricting him. Classmates told him that he howled in his sleep. For this reason he'd stopped boarding in his last years at Galatasaray.

V

Come afternoon, he paid a visit to the tenant, and on his return he stopped at the Beyazıt coffeehouse. This two- or three-hour journey, like poking one's nose out into the dark night of a snowstorm, had quickly informed him of a number of circumstances. When he'd just about arrived in Beyazıt, the trolley stopped for the crossing of a military detachment. Taking advantage of the opportunity, Mümtaz stepped off the streetcar to walk the remainder of the way. He'd long enjoyed this route. He was fond of watching the pigeons beneath the huge walnut tree beside Beyazıt Mosque, browsing through books in the Sahaflar book market, chatting with booksellers of his acquaintance, entering into the half-light of the Grand Bazaar, whose coolness overwhelmed him after the sweltering day and bright radiance, and rambling as he sensed the abrupt chill in his flesh. Not to mention that if he'd been in no rush and felt the impulse, he'd enter through the flea market and meander through labyrinthine streets to the Old Bedesten, the heart of the bazaar. The market contained cheap imitations and makeshift goods today; he came across only knockoffs, shoddy imports, and knickknacks, or inexpensive wholesale products. Normally, were he paying careful attention, he'd always find something astonishing in the flea market or Bedesten.

Here two opposing and difficult-to-imitate polarities of life, which didn't appear without latching on to one's skin or settling deep within, actually merged: genuine poverty *and* grandeur, or rather, their castoffs . . . At each step, remnants of out-of-fashion entertainments and the traces of old and grand traditions, whose origins and means had been forgotten, could be found heaped together. In one of these narrow, contiguous shops, old Istanbul, veiled Anatolia, and even the last remnants of the Ottoman Empire's heritage would glimmer in the most unanticipated way. Vintage outfits that varied from town to town, tribe to tribe, and period to period; old carpets and kilims whose locale of weaving he'd be sure to forget even once reminded, yet whose motifs and colors he'd remember for days; a store of artwork from Byzantine icons to old Ottoman calligraphy panels; embroidery, decorations, all in all, caches of objets d'art; jewelry that had adorned the neck and arms of some forgotten beauty from a lost generation or two; all of it, in this humid and crepuscular world, could keep him in its thrall for hours with the allure of a by gone age and the appeal of the mysterious added in for good measure. This represented neither the traditional nor the modern East. Perhaps it was a state of timelessness whose very clime had been exchanged for another. When Mümtaz left this setting for the hubbub of the Mahmutpaşa street bazaar, he felt the inebriation of a man who'd gotten drunk on laced wine in a cellar before stepping into direct sunlight. And the satisfaction imparted seemed to be quite a middle-aged pleasure for a man his age – like an addiction.

On this occasion, he relented again. First he watched the pigeons. Then he gave in and fed them. While he did so, he was prodded by an urge to make an appeal to Allah, as he used to do in his childhood. Mümtaz, however, no longer wanted to mix everyday matters with his personal conception of the divine. The divine should be like a fountainhead, unencumbered by humanity, robust, removed from all types of experience, and should simply provide the resilience to endure life. He didn't think this way solely to resist the pagan superstition that often reared its head during times of trouble and had recently established a vast shadowy realm within him. Perhaps he wanted to remain faithful to the notions that preoccupied him. About a month ago, a friend of his whom life had staggered rather profoundly had told him how society filled him with revulsion, how little by little the ties that bound him to the community had loosened. He was in full-scale revolt: "The social contract won't continue, it cannot continue," he raved.

At that time, Mümtaz tried to explain to his friend the absurdity of the connection he'd arbitrarily made between his experience and his ephemeral mental states. He said, "Just because things have taken a bad turn, let's not blame the gods. Our affairs are always susceptible to the betrayal of circumstance and to trivial mishaps. Things might even go wrong for a few generations. The breakdown and disorganization shouldn't alter our relationship to our inner beliefs. If we conflate these two distinct things, we'll be left naked and exposed. Furthermore, we shouldn't assume that success is granted by the gods, either. Matrices of probability contain failure. What's the relationship between the postponement of your uncle's trial and our historic rights over this nation? Between your sister's marriage and the morning prayer called at the Süleymaniye Mosque or to your birth to a Muslim father? Or between the real estate broker who swindles you of your money and the values that constitute our inner character or the colossal realities that make us who we are? Even if these realities ultimately rest in society, they shouldn't incite us to *inkâr*, denial of ourselves, but to change the conditions in which we find ourselves. Of course there are countries and citizens more content than us; of course we feel in our lives – rather, in our flesh and blood – the vast fallout of two centuries of disintegration and collapse, of being the remnants of an empire and still unable to establish our own norms and idioms. Allowing this suffering to drive us to nihilistic *inkâr*, in effect, would be to accept even greater catastrophe, would it not? Motherland and nation are cherished because they are the motherland and the nation; religion is disputed, rejected, or accepted as religion, and not based on the ease it purports to bring to our lives . . ."

As Mümtaz spoke, he realized that his expectations of others were high. He knew that when the social idiom changed, people changed and the faces of the gods paled. Yet he also realized it shouldn't always be this way. While he fed the pigeons, he contemplated such thoughts; at the same time he noticed that the fine grain coating his palm irritated him like an aperture shutting somewhere in his person.

No, he wouldn't ask anything of Allah anymore. Mümtaz wasn't going to confront Him with his fate or the missteps of his life, because were his plea ignored, his loss would be twofold.

The pigeons, indifferent toward the grain in the midafternoon heat, approached reluctantly, hovering close to the ground and gliding in one at a time. Like the hand of a magician producing a bright blue handkerchief out of thin air, they still made surprising and illusive movements as they flew, but they didn't flock and crest all at once with the swiftness of a wave under a southerly breeze as they did when in full feather and hungry; they didn't pivot in the airy void as if there were a whirlwind above them; and they didn't lose all speed in the aether and plummet as if they'd come to an unseen pier or the wall of a manor by the sea.

They made a rather tranquil arrival, sluggish and languid. Some of them looked dubiously – almost with pity – at the grain on the ground from the wall of the opposite building where they'd perched in a line. Yet, beneath them a small, oneiric flock gathered and pecked, each detail of its movements depicted separately and as an isolated form, like seas issuing from the brushwork of the Fauvist Raoul Dufy.

Despite their avarice and exploitation of one's affection, they were beautiful creatures. Especially in the way they trusted, they were beautiful. Humans were this way, they delighted in being trusted. This sensation deeply satisfied man as master and singular, eminent creator of life. Despite man's brief and tormented life, his absurdity and selfishness, this hobbled and deficient deity recognized such trust as the sole expression of worship toward him. But he took pleasure in betraying those who trusted in him. Because he liked to change, and he enjoyed the cognizance of himself during different moments and situations. Because he was narcissistic, yet the conversation within him wasn't merely one-sided.

He sprinkled the grain from above, raising his hand over his head in a circle so that the pigeons might rise and he might sense the winged flutter about him. But none of them moved the way he desired; a few feeble and sporadic attempts resulted in a fluttering ascension of a half yard above ground before the momentum died.

For Mümtaz, the pigeons were a vice of sorts in Istanbul, like lures that attracted men to women of ardor. They might also be compared to the fables children spun to magnify themselves, to fill their inner worlds, whose mysteries we couldn't fathom; and like a fable of this nature, this large tree and this Ottoman architecture – whose gilded door was visible within a purple shadow each time he turned his head back – might even have conjured this covey. A coffeehouse apprentice swung a pendant tea tray to the fullest extent as he purposefully passed through the pigeons so they'd flutter about. The apprentice was a handsome youth of about seventeen. The slow and plodding walk that he affected didn't strip his body of its agility. He wore a navy blue and white striped flannel shirt, and behind one ear he kept a pencil stub, certain to be replaced, maybe tomorrow, by a cigarette. Despite this catalyst, the fairy-tale ship and the wave cast by a *lodos* southerly that Mümtaz so desired still didn't manifest. Instead, the interconnected, circular lines of the compact cerulean waves suddenly separated, and the primitive depiction of the sea, gradually, with an offhand, virtually dampened sound of applause, moved farther onward, flying low and landing at the feet of another man sprinkling seed. One of the pigeons nearly grazed his forehead as it flew, perhaps alarmed by such a close encounter with a human being.

The woman selling the seed said, "The hawker there has sick relatives at the hospice. Help her out by buying grain from her too; it'd be a pious deed." Her voice, rather than imploring, verged on sarcasm. Then Mümtaz noticed her face. Her eyes stared intently from a face unable to conceal its bloom beneath a black head scarf – eyes foreign to all notions of piety. With a hostility toward men seen only in common folk-women, her eyes momentarily bared themselves, exposing her entire body naked in the sunlight. Before this gaze, Mümtaz, heart in tatters, handed her his money and entered the Sahaflar book market.

The small alley was a narrow passageway where in summer all the smells of the bazaar floated by the square and its environs. The season subdued this alley with aromas. Yet before the door, Mümtaz's previous desire faded. What would he see after all? A bunch of peculiar though familiar oddities.

Not to mention that he was anxious, his mind was divided into two, even three, parts. The first Mümtaz, maybe the most vital, dreading fate and trying to suppress his thoughts, stood beside İhsan's sickbed, staring at his unfocused eyes, chapped lips, and rising and falling chest. The second Mümtaz tore himself apart trying to reunite with Nuran on each and every Istanbul street corner where she might appear; he tossed a scrap of himself to every gale that arose. A third Mümtaz marched into the wilderness of the unknown and the harsh whims of fate behind the military detachment that had caused the streetcar to stop suddenly. For days now he hadn't contemplated politics. For him, the train whistles that had increased over recent nights were enough of a portent.

Such a conundrum proved to be comforting in one respect: Thinking of three things meant thinking of none. Terrifying was the abrupt union of all three, the potential formation of an absurd and distressing synthesis, a dim, and malformed *terkip*.

The heart of the book market was quiet; at the entrance, a small shop that had landed here like a splash from the old Egyptian spice market displayed a petite, pitiful vestige of the old, opulent Orient and of vast traditions whose roots extended deep into oblivion leading to long-dead civilizations; herbs and roots whose benefits were certified over centuries, regarded as the sole panacea for fading harmony of life and health along with spices that had been pursued vehemently over the seven seas, sat in dusty jars, in long wooden boxes, and in open cardboard containers.

As Mümtaz looked at this shop, Mallarmé's line came to mind: "It's ended up here through some nameless catastrophe." *Here* in this dusty shop from whose walls hung handmade tricot stockings . . . In neighboring shops with wooden shutters, simple benches, and old prayer rugs rested the same luxurious and, when seen from afar, arcane insights of tradition, in an arrangement eternally alien to the various accepted ideas of classification, on shelves, over book rests or chairs, and on the floor, piled one atop another as if preparing to be interred, or rather, as if being observed from where they lay entombed. The Orient, however, couldn't be authentic anywhere, even in its grave. Beside these books, in open hawker's cases, were lapfuls of testimonials to our inner transformation, our desire to adapt, and our search for ourselves in new contexts and climes: pulp novels with illustrated covers, textbooks, French yearbooks with faded green bindings, and pharmaceutical formulas. As if the detritus of the mind of mankind had been hastily exposed in this market, books mixed and intermingled, texts on reading fortunes in coffee grounds alongside classicist Mommsen's vision of Rome, remnants of Payot editions, Karakin Deveciyan Efendi's treatise on fish and ichthyology, as well as subjects like veterinary medicine, modern chemistry, and the techniques of geomancy.

Taken as a whole, it constituted a bizarre accretion that appeared simply to be the result of intellectual indigestion. Mümtaz realized that this omnium gatherum had been engaged in a hundred-year struggle and a continuous sloughing of skin.

An entire society grew despondent, strove, and suffered through anomie and birth pangs for a century so that digests of detective novels and these Jules Vernes might replace copies of *A Thousand and One Nights, Tûtinâme: Tales of the Parrot, Hâyatülhayvan: Animal Fables*, and *Kenzülhavas: The Treasury of Pleasantries.*

A book merchant of his acquaintance made a welcoming sign. Mümtaz approached with an expression indicating "How are things?"

The merchant gestured with his hand toward a series of old leather-bound books, stacked and tied with twine, on one end of a wooden bench. "A collection of old magazines, if you'd like to take a look."

He untied the twine and handed Mümtaz the volumes, dusting them as he did so. Most of the leather covers were warped, and some of the bindings had cracked. Mümtaz sat on one edge of the bench with his feet dangling. He knew that the bookseller would no longer bother him; in fact, the man had put on his glasses and turned back to the handwritten manuscript on a bookrest.

Mümtaz examined the volumes that looked as if they had been slowly and gradually roasted by fire, and he remembered the last time he'd come to this shop, last May – bliss was in that spring to be alive. An hour had remained before he was to meet Nuran; he'd stopped here to pass the time and chat with the old bookseller, purchasing a handsome and nicely bound *Şakâyık-ı Numaniye*, a sixteenth-century Ottoman biographical encyclopedia by Taşköprüzade with its addendum. That day he'd gone with Nuran to the two Çekmece lakes. Though he'd explored all of Istanbul with her, they hadn't yet visited the lakes. He thought of the supper they'd shared at the smaller lake, at the restaurant nearly atop the water that invariably recalled Chinese floating houses, of the time they spent together in the stream-side garden of the hunter's coffeehouse at the foot of the bridge reached by a wooden stairway. In the vicinity, fishermen caught striped mullet as they shouted from rowboat to rowboat in piercing voices. A chorus of cries rose abruptly and men naked from the waist up made several direct and determined movements before the net strung between two boats gradually emerged from the water, glistening like a shield of abundance, with little quicksilver sparkles flailing along its perimeter, and the great haul shone like a mirror held to the sun. On the ground, at their feet, a street dog that had just befriended them wagged its tail and flattened its ears as it begged. From time to time, it strayed from its spot and roamed about, making the rounds, before turning back.

Recently arrived swallows frantically prepared nests at a distance. Rapid, twittering exchanges, whose meanings escaped them, passed at the edges of the bridge and in the eaves of the coffeehouse. Now and then, a swallow, hovering with rapid wing flaps, not unlike a swimmer treading water to keep afloat, let itself drop into the void of the boundless cerulean sky, before soaring up to great heights in a vertical maneuver; then, from a point that the naked eye could no longer discern, glided downward; and just when this trajectory aroused the anxiety of its deadly follow-through, the swoop abruptly straightened along the horizon, tracing curves and spirals upon itself, and as if proving an unsolved geometric theorem, a series of abrupt and interrelated maneuvers followed one after the other, and at last, after escaping this web of its own weaving with a final flap, the swallow arrived at its frenetic and merry nest. Mümtaz brazenly observed the broad shoulders of his dulcinea, her neck, which gave her head the poise of a delicate blossom, and her narrowed eyes, which had become a line of radiance. Last May . . . when his world was more or less intact.

One of the assembled texts was a divan poetry collection by the thirteenth-century mystic Yunus Emre that had been copied in an amateurish hand; the annotations, however, contained *gazels* by Ottoman poets from Bâkî, Nef'î, and Nabî to Shaykh Galip. Toward the end, on a few leaves, in various hands, appeared a number of remedies calling for black pepper, cardamom, rhubarb, and the like. One of them written in kermes crimson ink was entitled "Lokman Hekim's Medicinal Taffy." Another involved filling an onion with cloves and heating it over an open flame to make an "Elixir of Life." The other text was a songbook: Melodic *makam* progressions and composers' names were penned above the songs; all of them contained the intervals without omitting a single note or syllable; they'd been transcribed onto pink, blue, white, and yellow leaves, with the chalk lines still visible, in an orderly pointed script like tongues of fire. Near the end, some amusing couplets had been recorded. Next came a series of recorded births and deaths beginning in the year of the Hegira 1197, or A.D. 1783. What naïve attention to detail and ceremony. In A.H. 1197, Abdülcelâl, a son of the owner of the volume, after being indisposed for two days, passed away on the seventeenth night of Rebiülâhir toward dawn; thank heavens a few months later his daughter Emine was born. These personal events made for an extensive year; the same man opened a saddle-and-harness shop for

Emin Efendi, his "milk brother" breastfed by the same wet nurse; as for him, he was appointed to the Kapanıdakik directorship after being passed over for years. The most significant event in the next year was the initiation of his son Hafız Numan Efendi into the field of musical arts. Their neighbor Mehmet Emin Efendi would oversee his practice. Who were these characters? Where did they live? Before lives he saw no need to pursue further, Mümtaz closed the volume.

More peculiar was the third volume, most of whose pages were blank, giving the impression that it might have belonged to a child. Toward the middle beneath a title written in an odd and amateurish hand, indicating an illustration of an ostrich or "camel bird" in a tree, was a picture that resembled neither camel nor bird; and beneath it, a convoluted design smudged out by wetted ink. Many dates were listed here as well. But none of the writing made any sense together. Perhaps it was a workbook for practicing penmanship in script; and in all probability it'd belonged to an older man who'd learned to read and write late in life. Almost every line was repeated a few times in an unskilled cursive: "To our guide in pilgrimage to Holy Mecca, the Water Bearer Esseyd Muhammet Elkasimi Efendi." Later on, the address became more detailed: "To His Excellency Esseyd Muhammet Elkasimi Efendi, one of the caretakers of the Sacred Kaaba, son of Jeweler Mesut Efendi of Bâbünnebi in Holy Mecca."

And a few pages farther, beneath a rather extensive register of expenses, appeared the following: "Being the date of His Excellency the Benefactor Naşit Beyefendi's appointment as fifth secretary of the private royal chambers . . ." And farther on: "On this morning, His Excellency the Benefactor Naşit Beyefendi, whose appointment to fifth secretary of the private royal chambers has been announced by imperial writ, bedecked in the uniform of the office, embarked toward the imperial palace for the sake of initiating his obligations. May Allah, Exalted and Almighty, forthwith bestow His glorious divine guidance and assistance." A full musical ensemble from the mid-nineteenth-century reign of Sultan Abdülmecit blared within Mümtaz's mind. Farther down the page, in a very thick pen and in a hand that couldn't quite keep control of itself, appeared a couplet:

Where is the rose, where is the nightingale?
The petals of the rose do scatter and pale.

Next came a magick potion prepared by boiling in the middle of the night the shell of a baby turtle, the water of seven springs collected in a glass bottle on the fifteenth of the month, forty pomegranate arils, saffron, and black pepper; the concoction was to be stirred with a freshly cut cherry twig while reciting an incantation, before letting it sit under the sun for forty days. And after that, he read an incantation meant to be recited forty times for forty days to enable one to wander about unseen.

On the facing page appeared six words in crimson ink that didn't belong to any recognizable language: "Temâgisin," "Begedânin," "Yesevâdin," "Vegdasin," "Nevfena," and "Gadisin." An explanation below stated that repeating these words seven times before bed would cause one to dream of an object of desire. And further down the page was a long description of the pronunciation of Keldanî script. Mümtaz muttered: "Temâgisin, Begedânin, Yesevâdin, Vegdasin, Nevfena, Gadisin."

It saddened him that he wouldn't be explaining these absurdities to Nuran. Mümtaz was Nuran's purveyor of esoterica. He loved to bring her resolute skepticism and steadfast rationalism face to face with odd anecdotes he'd culled from here and there. Had it been last year, Mümtaz would have told her how he'd opened his mind to forces from beyond regarding some or another issue, then he'd have gone on to describe the dream that came to him after having repeated this incantation seven times. In conveying such nonsense, Mümtaz was forced to maintain complete sincerity without a smirk or guffaw. The charade would continue in all seriousness to the end amid Nuran's demure smiles and expressions of astonishment, and eventually, annoyed, she'd either put a swift end to the joke – opening up a delicious horizon of remorse sometimes lasting for hours – or else she, too, would simply join in the game.

Thinking this now verged on the pathetic.

He suddenly stopped at a juncture in his thoughts. *Why am I mocking these people? Is my anguish preferable to their lives, filled with countless opportunities for escape?* But did such means of escape actually exist as he'd assumed? Were they living the wealth of possibilities described in these books and others like them? Even if this were the case, wasn't he himself escaping? Wasn't merely sitting in this shop at this hour an escape? Amid a widening web of troubles, he did indeed want to steal this hour, and he'd stolen it in plain sight from İhsan and his family. Granted, Mümtaz hadn't been living a regular life since the beginning of summer. Particularly in recent days, his sleep had been disrupted. The few hours that he could sleep with difficulty passed in eerie, nightmarish dreams, and he woke from his slumber even more tired. Worst of all was the difficulty he had maintaining his train of thought. As each idea inched forward, it became a vision of agony. Today even, as he walked down the street, he realized he was spontaneously making hand gestures. During such times Mümtaz's companions suggested that he was trying to purge himself of certain paradoxical thoughts through actions and terse mutterings.

He examined the volumes, recalling again the May morning of a year ago. Summer flourished within him like an apocalypse. Next came the days he believed had poisoned his entire life, including Nuran's exasperation, his own fears and anxieties, and his feeble and exhausting insistence, each with its particular memories and moods. He knew he couldn't stay here any longer. But he couldn't stand, either. All he could do was gaze about as if asking whether a more excruciating form of this torment was to come.

The bookseller raised his eyes from the manuscript: "The outlook is pretty bleak, isn't it?"

Mümtaz didn't have the wherewithal for a long conversation: "We're tending to a sick relative at home . . . It's been a week now that I haven't been able to read a newspaper properly." He was lying. It wasn't that he hadn't read the paper. He'd just lost the strength to contemplate the news. Without even forming any opinions, he simply memorized chronologies of events as if learning a lesson by rote. Interpreting, not to mention discussing, incidents that occurred in such rapid succession was an exercise in futility.

They'd talked for years already anyway. Everybody, everywhere, at every opportunity, for years, had discussed this possibility. All variety of opinion had been expressed and all eventualities explored. Now all of humanity faced a reality of horrendous proportions.

"I don't know if you've seen the banks? They've been packed full for days now." As if it had just occurred to him, he asked, "Who's sick?"

"İhsan."

The shopkeeper shook his head: "He hasn't stopped in for quite some time. It isn't just coincidental then. I hope he regains his health soon." He was visibly upset, but he didn't ask about the illness. Mümtaz mused, *I guess he considers this a family secret.* As if to explain that a person without troubles didn't exist, the shopkeeper said: "Both our children were called up." He sighed. "Honestly, I don't know what to do. I'm at a loss. My brother-in-law fell from a horse back home and cracked his ribs . . . My wife's in such a state."

Mümtaz knew from firsthand experience about the endless sympathy of men who wanted to console others through tales of woe.

"Don't worry, things will improve, it'll all get better," Mümtaz said as he left.

These were among the stock expressions that he'd learned from a past generation. Maybe for this reason, with a curious stubbornness, he'd been reluctant to use them for years. But now, in the presence of this man's misery, they came to the tip of his tongue. *One civilization's philosophy of everyday life*, he thought. *Each experience invites one of another variety. That means our heritage not only contains miseries and sorrows but also consolations and methods of perseverance . . .*

Çadırcılar Street was bewildering as always. On the ground before a shop whose grate usually remained shuttered, waiting for who knows what, were a Russian-made samovar spigot, a doorknob, the remnants of a lady's mother-of-pearl fan so much the fashion thirty years ago, a few random parts belonging perhaps to a largish clock or gramophone, together with some oddities that had ended up here without breaking or crumbling to pieces somehow. A traditional coffee grinder of yellow brass and a cane handle made of deer antler were prominently displayed. Leaning against the shop's rolling shutter rested two sizable photographs in thick, gilt wooden frames: pictures of Ottoman-era Greek Orthodox patriarchs from the reign of Sultan Abdülhamit II or a little afterward. Their medals, garments, and emblems were identical to those that appeared in the newspapers. From behind well-polished glass, through the vantage of time past, they gazed at the objects spread out before them and at the street crowds temporarily obscuring them at each surge. Perchance they were most pleased by the roar of life sounding so many years later – by the therapy of sun and sound.

Mümtaz wondered, *Did the photographer nudge and prod them the way the man who takes my photos does?*

He sought traces of such primping in the folds of their loose-fitting robes and in their expressions, which had striven for years to merge grace with representational grandeur.

Above them hung a handsome Arabic calligraphy panel in a kitschy plaster frame: *Hüvessemiulalîm*, "the One who discerns and knows all." The rigid plaster hadn't destroyed the vitality of the script. Each curve and curl articulated its message.

The peculiar quirks of this little street, however, weren't limited to just a few. A Nevâkâr song from a Darülelhan conservatory record being played in a shop a bit farther down revealed and concealed its own numinous world like a rose garden under a deluge, while a fox-trot blared from a gramophone across the way. Mümtaz stared down the full length of the street, which seemed to rise vertically, searing his eyes under the midafternoon sun. Heaps of castoff items, bed frames, broken and worn-out furniture, folding screens with torn panels, and braziers were aligned and stacked atop each other in phalanxes along either side of the street.

Most regrettable were the mattresses and pillows, which constituted a tragedy simply by having ended up here. Mattresses and pillows . . . the array of dreams and the countless slumbers they contained. The fox-trot dissolved in the snarl of an unwound spring and was immediately followed by an old *türkü* one would only chance to hear under such circumstances. "The gardens of Çamlıca . . ." Mümtaz recognized the singer as Memo. The full sorrow of the last days of the reign of Sultan Abdülhamit II persisted in the memory of this singer, a cadet in the military academy, who'd drowned in the waters of the Golden Horn. His voice overspread these remnants of life like a grand and luminous marquee. What a dense and intricate life the alley possessed. How all of Istanbul, including every variety and assortment of its fashions and its greatest intimacies and surprises, flowed through here, composing a novel of material objects and discarded life fragments. Or, rather, everyone's quotidian life had gathered here entwined arm in arm as if proving that within our separate workaday lives, nothing new under the sun existed.

Every accident, every illness, every demolition, every tragedy that occurred in the city each day and each hour had cast these objects here, eliminating their individuality, making them public property, and forging an aggregate arranged through the hand-to-hand cooperation between chance and misery.

What a fine custom it was in some ancient civilizations to burn or bury one's possessions together with the deceased. But one didn't relinquish things only when dying . . . Two months ago Mümtaz had made a gift of his favorite pair of cuff links to a friend. A fortnight ago he'd forgotten in a taxi a book he'd had newly bound. Was this all? A few months earlier the woman he loved decided she wanted to live apart and left him. İhsan lay bedridden. For nine days now pneumonia had taken him captive and had slowly dragged him to that quiet interstice where he rested today. Something catastrophic could happen at any moment. No, one didn't just vanish and leave things behind at death. Perhaps over his entire existence, moment by moment, many things had been leaving him. They would just crust over and through a very subtle, unseen process, separate from whatever surrounded them. *Do we leave them or do they leave us?* That was the question.

The gathering of so many antique objects on this street that played the full range of the sun's lutes was powerful enough to make him forget about actual life and experience.

A soldier approached and grabbed a trinket that caught his eye from the hodgepodge. A shaving mirror. Next came an elderly man, short, thin, well-kempt, yet wearing outdated clothes. He took up the mother-of-pearl fan; like an inexperienced adolescent, he spread and shut the fan a few times tentatively, inspecting the item that his ladylove had entrusted to him during a dance, turning it over and over in his hands furtively, with a feeling of adoration surfacing as if he were stunned that it actually belonged to *her*; then he returned it with an evident feeling of relief, and asked about the cost of the carved antler handle. Because Mümtaz didn't enjoy speaking casually to Behçet Beyefendi, a one-time member of the old Ottoman Council of State, he stepped to the side and, filled with utter desolation, watched the old man's rather puppetlike movements. *You would not know by looking at him, but this unfortunate soul was in love with and jealously coveted a woman for nearly twenty years . . . and in the very end . . .*

Behçet had loved, and was jealous of, Atiye, his own wife of twenty years. First he grew jealous of her, then of Dr. Refik, one of the first members of the Committee of Union and Progress, and as a result, he made an illicit denunciation of Dr. Refik through a secret police report to the Ottoman palace; but even after the doctor's death in exile, Behçet couldn't save himself from fits of jealousy. As he'd told İhsan himself, when he heard the lady softly singing the "Song in Mahur" on her deathbed, he struck her in the mouth several times, and thereby had maybe hastened her death. This particular "Song in Mahur" was a ballad by Nuran's great-grandfather Talât. The ordeal and many like it had given Behçet the reputation of being bad luck by several factions in their old Tanzimat-era family, which had flourished through a series of well-arranged marriages. Yet, the haunting ballad remained in people's memories.

The "Song in Mahur," in its simplest and shortest version, resembled a visceral cry of anguish. The story of the song was strange in itself. When Talât's wife, Nurhayat, eloped with an Egyptian major, Talât, a devotee of the Mevlevî order, had written the lyrics. He'd actually wanted to compose a complete cycle of pieces in the same Mahur mode. But just at that time, a friend returning from Egypt informed him of Nurhayat's death. Later he learned that her death coincided with the night he'd finished composing the piece. In Mümtaz's opinion, "Song in Mahur," like some of Dede Efendi's compositions and traditional *semâi* songs or like Tab'î Efendi's "Beyâtî Yürük Semâi," was a piece with a distinctive rhythm that confronted the listener with fate in its profundity. He distinctly remembered when he'd heard Nuran sing the song and tell the story of her grandmother. They were on the hills above Çengelköy, a little beyond the observatory. Massive cumuli filled the sky and the evening descended like a golden marsh over the city. For a long time Mümtaz couldn't determine whether the *hüzün* of inexplicable melancholy falling about them and the memory-hued twilight had emanated from the evening or from the song itself.

Behçet replaced the cane handle. Yet he couldn't pull himself away from the folding fan. Obviously the small feminine accessory cast him – a man whose entire intellectual life had frozen like clockwork stuck at his wife's death, and who resembled a living memento from 1909 in his outfit, necktie, and suede shoes – far back into time, to the years when he was the fine gentleman Behçet, when he was enamored and grew jealous of his beloved, and, not least of all, when he'd been the catalyst of her and her lover's deaths. Presently, reminiscences long forgotten were being resurrected in the head of this living, breathing remnant of things past. *I wonder which of life's fragments he sees in these paving stones he stares at so intently?*

An old shrew struggled to follow behind the used mattresses she'd purchased, perhaps up the street. The street porter she'd hired was overwhelmed by the top-heaviness of the burden on his back more than the weight itself. Mümtaz didn't want to spend another second here; today neither the book market nor the Çadırcılar street market was of any consequence. He turned into the flea market.

The market was cold, crowded, and cacophonous. Almost everywhere in the small shops hung an array of clothing, prepared life-molds, like self-contained fates. Buy one, put it on, and exit as a new person! Crammed on both sides were dresses, yellow and navy blue worker's overalls, old outfits, light-colored summer wear whose tacking was visible above the sewing-machine seams, cheap women's overcoats that sheared dreams of life to zero with unseen scissors from where they hung. They were displayed by the dozens on tables, small chairs, couches, and shelves. A cornucopia! No shortage of thrift and misery as one might have thought; just disrobe from life but once and be certain to find desperation in every imaginable size!

He stopped short before a display window: A small, broken mannequin had been dressed in a wedding gown that had somehow slipped down too far; on the bareness of her neck, above the décolleté, the shopkeeper had pasted the image of a betrothed couple cut from a fashion magazine. The prim and stylish couple, located under hair tinsel and veil and above the white gown, before a landscape fit for silver-screen lovers, made this watershed moment bursting with bliss an advertisement for life and love that subdued one like a season – as would happen in the mind of the woman who might wear this gown. A small electric bulb burned over this contentment-on-sale, as if to clearly emphasize the difference between thought and experience. With no need to look any longer, Mümtaz began to walk briskly. He made a series of turns and crossed a number of intersections. He wasn't looking anymore; he knew what to expect. *After having seen what rests inside me.* For months now, everywhere, he'd seen only what existed inside him. And he realized, as well, that there was nothing so surprising or fearful in whatever he saw or stood before.

The market was a fragment of this city's life; forever and a day it would confide in him somehow. All the same, what affected Mümtaz was not what he saw but rather his own life experiences.

Had he found himself before a good canvas by Pierre Bonnard, one of *Les Nabis*, or had he gazed at the Bosphorus from atop the Beylerbeyi Palace; had he listened to a piece of music by Tab'î Mustafa Efendi or to *The Magic Flute*, which he so admired, he'd still have these same feelings. His mind resembled a small dynamo stamping everything that passed beneath its cylinder with his own shape and essence, thereby obscuring and disposing of its actual meaning and form. Mümtaz had termed this phenomenon "cold print."

Mümtaz's relations with the external world had been this way for months. He perceived everything only after it had passed through the animosity between him and Nuran, spoiling its mood, coloring, and character. His person had been secretly contaminated, and he related to his surroundings only in accordance with the changing effects of the poison.

It might be a crisis eliding everything at a single stroke, like Istanbul's rainy and misty mornings that deadened all color. No matter how much Mümtaz struggled to draw open the multilayered shroud, he'd fail to see anything familiar. Beginning with the consciousness of his existence, ashen muck, like a river whose flow was barely detectable, would carry everything away; a kind of Pompeii buried beneath lava and moving at the rate of a life span.

At such times nothing "good," "bad," "pretty," or "ugly" existed for Mümtaz. Through an effectively isolated eye whose connection with the nervous system that sustained it had been lost and whose potential for analysis had been interrupted, an objective eye experiencing final moments of hermetic perception, Mümtaz would stare dumbly at the living visions in this garden of death, and at everything that broke free from the ashen muck and accosted him, as if he were staring at reflections of a realm of nothing but echo and aftershock.

At times, seized by an anxiety that shook the entire framework, rattling everything from the windows to the foundation, Mümtaz would be agitated by all things in a frenzy that pushed the limits of his mental faculties. No accident at sea could damage a ship on the verge of sinking down to the last stave, dislodging its every nail.

He turned toward the old Bedesten of the Grand Bazaar. The auction hall was empty. But the double-sided display cases and the rooms had been prepared for tomorrow's great auction. In one of the cases, a single antique piece of jewelry, rumors of which had spread through Istanbul for the past two months, glimmered like a cluster of stars, rawly and savagely, yet not without beauty.

Within the jewel, a truth ignited and blazed in its own vast and deep essence. Only sublimity of sorts, a consciousness that had attained the utmost lucidity, or beauty that had killed off the human within it and freed itself of all weakness, could emit such light.

He tried fleetingly to imagine it adorning Nuran's neck. But he failed; he'd forgotten how to conjure visions of happiness. Mümtaz had no chance of owning this piece. Besides, it seemed to him an impossibility to meet her again in that old mind-set and for them to be drawn to each other. This impossibility unified the inhuman sparkle of the ornament before him with the beauty of the woman in his thoughts.

By distancing herself from his life, Nuran had been cleansed of all her faults and all they'd shared, assuming the radiant hardness of this diamond in an inaccessible stratum of existence. Separation had thus transformed her into a mythical presence beyond Mümtaz's realm of being.

Had I only ever experienced her at a distance like this, so alone, inherently beautiful, and removed from everything . . . Thus he'd be spared from stings of conscience and memories that bore into him like an auger. Perhaps this was one of the personas the woman who'd abandoned him assumed sporadically in his mind's eye. Yet alongside it, there was the woman with whom he'd broken and shared his daily bread for months, his beloved Nuran, a being who'd suffered so much for him, who'd shared all his hopes, who'd lived, temporarily withdrawn from all else, only with Mümtaz and for Mümtaz. But there was more. An array of Nurans wallowing in trivial episodes – whose contexts and colors were taken from inadequacies in Mümtaz's soul – which she'd all but shattered to shards and stuck into his flesh; Nurans who sought an opportunity to escape from submerged depths where they'd been trapped, surfacing to control Mümtaz's life. Each of them individually, like the characters in a Wagnerian opera, appeared with its own special mood and manner of possessing him. Each of them subdued him, agitating his person and his nerves to different degrees. Some of them left him in the same distressed psychological state for days, dragging him back and forth between anger and vengeance or the blackest death, then with the slightest cue or under the simplest pretext, she'd relinquish her place to another persona; and Mümtaz's face, tense with jealousy, his pulse racing with fury, would be transfigured, and an irresistible compassion would tear him asunder, his shoulders would droop under the weight of the sins he assumed he'd committed, and he'd believe he was cruel, insensitive, and selfish – increasingly ashamed of himself and his life.

These personas seemed to prolong jealousy, affection, regret, desire, and desperate devotion; they churned and multiplied within him and his flesh like a great tempest from the netherworld, leaving him without the smallest site to anchor or even breathe, and they incarcerated and depleted him in the very realm where they'd given birth to him; in sum, they comprised his successively changing lifeworlds.

Every outside entity depended on the order Nuran established. They adopted her color, fawned over her, grew and shrank in her radiance to such a degree that Mümtaz, especially in recent days, didn't have an independent life. He existed in a state of paradox, his conflicting natures pursuing each other; he thought, looked, and felt through their mediation. Meanwhile, time itself had quieted many aspects of this inner tempest and, according to its own rationale, had cast off numerous unnecessary contingencies. In certain respects, within the context of their separation, Mümtaz now related to his beloved through quite different personas more closely resembling his own. He no longer grew jealous of her as in the past. The cruelest and most dishonest of her semblances, the blameworthy, cruel, and mercilessly indifferent presence that obeyed only its instincts, had withdrawn. Now his thoughts and feelings reintroduced another aspect of her with a relatively more calm and remorseful countenance, a Nuran who accepted blame, whom he could envision without her listing his faults.

Above these follies and foibles of every hue hovered the image of a woman who'd absolved him – malcontent martyr to a miscellany of misunderstandings – of his every act of idiocy and inanity; a woman who'd shrouded all of the torments of his life with her beatific grin. Because this smile veiled such enormous, catastrophic, and bleak shortcomings of his, concealing a heart that had been lanced repeatedly by her malevolence, a soul that had lost its trust in people and had forsaken everything in desperation, because this grin revealed nothing, masking and eclipsing all, it became the most horrendous of weapons.

The grin resembled a mirror held aloft so he might observe aspects of his inner self, his faux pas, his guilt-ridden transgressions, and even facets of himself he didn't yet understand. Mümtaz was no stranger to the way Nuran, in moments of despair and finality, resorted to this smile that sublimated to an unrecognizable degree the woman he knew and loved, making her a foreign beacon on his horizon for the duration she wore it; he was no stranger to how she made use of muteness, which gave her the bearing of an idol whose every line and curve had been culled and created through the visions of centuries; he was aware of the way she took refuge, by degrees, behind this forced smile and quiescent poise, and how from that coign of vantage, distressed and distraught, she peered out over the landscape and over their lives, overcome by the desolation of a poignant epiphany.

During such times, were Nuran to even recognize her surroundings, she wouldn't have recognized her self.

This final vision summoned by separation and his suffering usurped the places of several Nurans. Many awe-inspiring characteristics of this lady of his intimacy had simply vanished, so the sharp dagger that played directly upon his liver, or the draught that caused him to writhe in agony without killing him outright, might be poised or properly balanced to its utmost effect. None of the childish glee that made him ecstatic remained, none of that lush springtide known only to joyous women, none of that heightened consciousness of being in the thrall of love, of existing within a realm created by being enamored, none of that sense of security, of those always creative leaps of intelligence and élan, none of it whatsoever remained. Bliss was a glass goblet lying in shards. Confronted by the hardness of the diamond before him, the nearly overwhelming flourish of a lush spring had withered. Most pitiful was how Mümtaz hoarded these memories so none of the paths he'd once traversed would vanish. In the mirror of her serene smile his imagination perpetually revealed aspects of paradises lost.

Indeed, a song, a dapple of light that played on the sidewalk, a single sentence uttered midconversation, a florist's shop along his path, another's reveries of the future, the resolve to begin work, everything, through a vision of the past, transported him back to the previous year, wherein he was roused to consciousness.

Truth be told, Mümtaz lived a twinned life, like the cobbler in the story from *A Thousand and One Nights*. On one hand, remembrances of halcyon days never left him, but as soon as the sun rose, the nighttime of separation spread within him in all its torment. The young gentleman, who effectively lived in his imagination, bore heaven and hell together. Between these two boundaries, he lived the life of a sleepwalker, punctuated with violent awakenings along the edges of an abyss. Between these two opposing psychological states, he conversed with those around him, taught his courses, listened to his students, explained their assignments, helped his friends, and argued when he was backed into a corner; that is, he forged through his everyday life.

At each step, Mümtaz suffered the tribulations of trying to live fully amid the distracting crowd.

Intermittently, his life consisted only of avoidances. Forlorn, he wandered the streets of Istanbul like a ghost ship. Shortly after arriving at some destination where he'd longed to be, a gale rising from within drove him onward; involuntarily, anchors were weighed, sails billowed, and he sailed ahead.

If not for an inclination toward the cerebral that accompanied his sentimentality, Mümtaz would have long been obliterated. But this twinned nature that had been so destructive to his relationship while in love was his saving grace now. Despite his devastation, from the outside, if only at whiles, he appeared to be more or less powerful and productive. Since he peered out over his context from a state of yearning, from a rite of passage that had deeply affected him, he better understood what he saw and knew how to adjust his perspective. That is, it was only in his personal life that he was condemned till death to remain naïve, clumsy, afflicted, or immature.

Mümtaz walked apace with the disposition of one who'd resolved not to think. From the bazaar, he exited out onto Nuruosmaniye Street. From there he descended below. He wanted to visit the tenant as soon as possible. He had to complete his errands posthaste. *If only İhsan returned to health. If only İhsan just got well.* A vagabond begged for alms. The man shuttled around on a wheeled board fastened to his underside, propelling himself with wooden bath clogs on his hands. His legs, thin and cocked like a spider's, hung over his shoulders and he pulled long drags from a cigarette placed between the toes of one foot. If not for the pallor of his face, his disheveled appearance, and the impact of disease that first overcame him, rather than a disabled beggar Mümtaz might have resembled a contortionist making involved and astounding maneuvers, a master ballet dancer who, within the ferocity of the dance and the rhythm, now became a spider, now a comet, mimicking first a swan and later a seafaring boat.

Pale and gaunt, he evidently drew great satisfaction from inhaling the cigarette smoke. His age was apparent mostly from the down of his whiskers. He took the money extended by Mümtaz, who waited as if convinced the man would transfigure himself, assuming a more astounding pose in gratitude or demonstrating another of his talents. Instead, he bowed his head, concealing his face, and pulled another breath through his cigarette before propelling himself by pushing off with his clogs, as he kept his legs wound about his shoulders and torso like spindly branches, swiftly passing to the opposite sidewalk to lean against the base of a sunlit wall with newly applied stucco. In this pose, he was nightmarish, a half-formed idea. Under sunlight, he waited like a permanent fixture of the street.

Mümtaz focused on the surroundings. Beneath the sun, the ruined, blazing white road, with its dilapidated houses, gaping doors, projecting oriel windows, and laundry-strung balconies, was long enough to instill the anxiety of infinitude, stretching onward in the brightness as if it were sloughing its skin. Here and there, weeds sprouted at the edges of the sidewalk. A cat sprang from a low garden wall, and as if awaiting this signal, a circular saw whirred in a lumberyard.

An afflicted road, he thought; a meaningless thought. But, like that, it'd been planted in his mind. *An afflicted road,* a road that had succumbed to leprosy of sorts, which had putrefied it in places up to the walls of the houses aligned on either side.

Whenever he raised his head, he noticed that a few passersby had stopped and were staring, and he understood that he must be experiencing a bout or episode. His distress forced him to lean against one of the leprous walls of the houses. The road continued onward, its skin being flayed by the sun.

A boy approached: "Would you like water?" he said. Mümtaz was only able to utter, "Nah!" If only he could get off this road. But the road had to stop sliding beneath his feet and stay put so he might walk. Was this the end? The termination . . . deliverance . . . the conclusion of everything and the lowering of the curtains? That great and mitigating release? To shout, "It's quitting time!" to all the dissonance that cluttered his mind, to open the gates and set it free, to chase away each iota of each memory, vision, and concept, to become nothing but an ordinary object, a lifeless and unconscious presence, like a shiny snake skin, to join the street, whose one end rose up, or the walls and houses, which the sunlight had gnawed away in spots like leprosy; to leave the circle of existence; to be delivered of every last paradox.

VI

With the aching distress of a cat giving birth, the tenant roamed about his diminutive shop wringing his hands as if hoping for salvation from something: the walls, the sacks and bags of hardware, the nails in bins, and the clusters of junk suspended from the rafters.

The shopkeeper narrowed his eyes as soon as he saw Mümtaz, his way of preparing to greet a visitor. Over the long years that he'd spent at his desk, he'd gotten into the habit of squinting at others this way from the hovel in which he found himself.

"Come, welcome, my fine young man. I was just expecting you." This was so in keeping with the usual routine that if not for this last sentence, Mümtaz would have thought the man's repeated messages to them had amounted to someone's practical joke. In the midst of this thought, he responded to the tenant's questions:

"He's doing just fine, it's kind of you to ask. He sends his regards. He's feeling a bit under the weather . . . thank you." As they spoke, Mümtaz understood that this wasn't the same old tenant, that at the very least mechanisms of anticipation and hope were now churning within him, nailing him up onto long, high scaffolds with little taps of the man's own heart.

"Of course you'll have a coffee or perhaps something cold to drink?"

Mümtaz declined. The shop, the sacks and bags of junk, distressed him. The man had no intention of insisting anyway. Due to the stomach cramps he'd suffered over the past two decades, the shopkeeper knew quite well how eating or drinking anything between meals could disturb the healthy balance of one's digestion. After this polite offer, like a freight wagon rolling in the wake of a luxury passenger train, he turned to the business at hand with astounding alacrity: "The contracts have been drawn up, both for the retail store and the storeroom."

Without allowing himself to be alarmed at the metamorphosis of this out-of-the-way shop into a "retail store" and at the dank cellar, which stunk up the neighborhood, into a "storeroom," the man spread two contracts before Mümtaz. "Of course, you have your aunt's seal in your possession?"

Indeed, he did. The contracts were in good order. Mümtaz endorsed them in his aunt's name. The man pulled out his wallet, said, "I've prepared a full year's rent," and removed an envelope.

Has he gone mad? thought Mümtaz.

Mümtaz took the blue envelope with a glance revealing that he expected it to contain anything but banknotes. At that moment the telephone rang. The man was seized by frenzy, which infected those around him. The onlookers, who knew both parties in the conversation, stiffened. Mümtaz, too, stood abruptly in the fear that something had happened to İhsan; they'd be able to reach him here.

"Get tin, I told you, tin and rawhide . . . that's all. As much as you can find. Just forget about the rest. Tin and rawhide."

His voice did away with everything on the face of the earth besides these two materials with a resolve that Mümtaz had never witnessed before. Then a hint of doubt mingled into his tone.

"What do we know about motors? Do what I said."

He hung up the phone. He sat back down. He was somewhat bothered that his conversation had been overheard. For the sake of doing something, anything, he put on his black glasses. From a great distance, he asked Mümtaz:

"Everything's in order, is it not?"

Mümtaz slid the blue envelope into his pocket. His eyes stared at the telephone as if to ask, "Anything else you'd like to tell us?" and he bid farewell to the shopkeeper. Swept by a peculiar feeling of embarrassment, he wasn't able to look at the man's face.

No political discussion or dossier could have informed him about current affairs as did this conversation, only half of which he'd heard. War was imminent. He ambled, staggered and distraught, wiping his brow frequently.

"There will be a war," he said. This was different from any ordinary mobilization; it was more certain, more decisive. Determination of one hundred, one thousand percent. Within all these shops, such silent preparation continued; telephones were answered and instantly tin, rawhide, paint, and machine parts were sucked out of the market; numbers changed, zeroes multiplied, and opportunities decreased. The imminence of war. *We'll be going, all of us will go.* Was he afraid? He assessed himself. He believed he wasn't.

At least what he felt at the moment couldn't be called fear. He was only disturbed. Some colorless and formless entity, a creature whose nature he didn't yet know, had coiled within him. He'd have to wait to determine what it was exactly. *I'm not afraid of death. I've lived so close to death my whole life . . . There's no reason to fear it.* War, however, even for those sent to the front, wasn't just death. Death was simple. At times one could even see it as a last resort. Mümtaz had repeatedly seen it as a land of salvation, a far shore that had to be reached, just like a swimmer who thinks his fatigue will end after the remaining five or ten strokes and his feet touch ground. In all likelihood, most people thought this way. No, death itself wasn't terrible, relative to the way it grew difficult along with everything else; to the way this fundamental event, this prearranged agreement, became a knotted ball of yarn incapable of being undone so that five or ten strokes of water filled with a thousand obstacles. *Away, alone, alas, a love, all my suffering will end there, at that threshold . . . Do we all think so? Are we the children of death or of life? Which of these two forces winds our clockwork: the hands of the seasons or the fingers of eternal darkness? Death is an absolute. But considering that my own mote of humanity hit the lottery of life, seeing that all Creation down to the tiniest element has come to life for me, in that case, in this* terra lucida, *this paradise of feelings and senses, this preposterous Walt Disney production, let me live my lot to the utmost!* No, he couldn't conceive of it like this, either. This was too simplistic as well. It amounted to remaining external, to living on surfaces. *We don't just remain at the door, we enter the abode, and take ownership of it, adopt it, declare that it's ours, we desire it, and we take pleasure in doing so. We weep after those who have left us, falling at their feet to say, "Do not leave!" We don't simply let things separate from us.*

We aren't just passive guests at a table; perhaps we're always creating and producing the things in our midst. None of us accepts life as an arbitrary condition of material circumstances. Even thinkers devoted to analyzing this have stayed in the game until the very end. Everything comes from us, comes with us, happens through us.

Neither death nor life exists. We exist. Both are inherent in us. All other things are just immense or tiny accidents passing in the mirror of time. A mountain on Mars erupts and disintegrates. Streams of molten rock harden on the lunar surface. New solar systems appear like the massive droplets of milk shimmering in the light of the sun amid the Milky Way. Coral reefs form at the bottom of the seas, and stars implode in colorful and fiery pyrotechnics in the shadow of the moon, like April flowers scattering in the wind. The bird eats the worm; in the bark of a tree, a hundred thousand larvae mature and a hundred thousand insects mingle into the earth. These are all phenomena that occur involuntarily. They're refractions illuminating, and occasionally darkening, that vast, rare, matchless pearl we call Creation, that solitary blossom of time, that lotus of the ages.

Only for mankind does time, monolithic and absolute, divide in two; and because time, this dim lantern, this sooty radiance, struggles to burn within us, because it introduces a complex calculus into the simplest things, because we measure its passing by our shadows on the ground, it divides life from death, and like a clock's pendulum, our consciousness swings between the two polarities of our own creation. Humanity, this prisoner of time, is but desperate, trying to escape to the outside. Instead of losing itself in time, instead of flowing along with all else in a broad and continual riverrun, humanity tries to perceive time externally. Thus, time becomes a mechanism

75

of torment. One lunge and we're at the pole of death, everything's over. Since we've split the unity of whole numbers, since we've consented to being fractions, we should resign ourselves to fragmentation. Momentum, however, sweeps us to the other pole; we're in the midst of life, we're full of vitality, we're once again the plaything of our hurtling inertia; but yet again, by its very nature, the balance tips irrefutably toward death, and torments increase exponentially.

Fate took shape intrinsically because humanity fled beyond the limits of time through the intellect, resisted the order of love, and sought stability in the midst of profound change. Humanity's actual fate was being slave to the light cast by a small night-lamp used only for seeing in shadows; being slave to an apparatus that tended to turn the shadows and darkness into a dungeon; in other words, being slave and sycophant to a small disembodied homunculus of light. However, the essential homunculus was born of reaction and synthesis between fire and water. It had more insight. The experiences that formed it also made it cognizant of its regrets and of the impossibilities surrounding it. Thus, as Goethe wrote, it knew to crash into sea nymph Galatea's carriage, to shatter its little glass-flask container, and to vanish into the vast and formless aether. But the small night-lamp had no such courage. It simply concocted a fable for itself; it believed in that fable and wanted to be the master of life. In turn, it was consumed by death, just like a stream that filled the first hole it chanced upon after diverging from the main source, where it would become the victim of all types of delusions, principal among them the desire to be itself. Nothing was as natural as humanity's torment! It paid for existence, its genuine existence, through consciousness. But humanity didn't leave it at that; next to this great, unchanging imperative, it created brand-new fates over and over again. Because it lived, it created various and sundry deaths. These deaths were always only the products of the anxiety of existence. For true death wasn't torment but deliverance: I'm letting go of it all, leaving it all behind to unite with eternity. I've become that enormous pearl itself, glimmering where consciousness ceases; not just a single mote; rather, I'm the entire entity. At the frontiers of consciousness, where no illumination casts a shadow, I'm an enormous white lotus shining from within, burning brightly.

But no, not at all, instead Mümtaz thought: *I think therefore I am*, cogito ergo sum. *I perceive therefore I am. I struggle therefore I am. I suffer, therefore I am! I'm wretched, I am. I'm a fool, I am, I am, I am!*

VII

Jumping frantically and involuntarily from one disordered thought to the next, he arrived in Eminönü. Now, if he could just board one of these ferries and set out on the Bosphorus. He hadn't slept at his own house for a month. His house appeared in his mind's eye; it was located in the interior of Emirgân, with an enclosed garden recalling the courtyards of old *medrese*s, and a balcony from where the entire Bosphorus seascape, from Kandilli to Beykoz on the Asian shore, could be seen. The garden, filling with the sounds of bees and insects in the sunlight, contained a few fruit trees, a walnut tree, a chestnut tree before the door, and along the borders, a variety of flowers whose names escaped him; the door opened onto a glassed corridor that had once been a larder. This area led to a stone-paved anteroom that stayed cool in the summers and contained a large low table, a small liquor cabinet, and a large divan. The stairs were broad. Sometimes he and Nuran would recline there on two cushions. But she much preferred the upstairs, the large balcony, and the hall from where the view extended clear to Beykoz. He tried to distance himself from those days, days to which it was impossible to return. This wasn't the time to think about it. İhsan lay bedridden; the disease within him, that nondescript bolus, had now assumed its full-fledged form.

İhsan spoke through the language and torment of his affliction. It extended its countless tentacles like an octopus, latching on to everything. The illness was inside and outside him. Until Mümtaz was again at his side, this situation would persist. Until he took İhsan's hands into his palms, asked "How are you feeling, brother?" until their eyes met, only then would the situation change, allowing him to pass back into Nuran's time. There the world of separation began; the world of one who found everything estranging, who felt himself to be in eternal exile and whose spine shuddered from loneliness, the world of a man without a woman. A world made up of a host of heartrending absences. For a long time now, he had lived in interconnected rooms, passing from one to the next.

The one to whom it was impossible to return had no intention of leaving him alone: She now appeared before him in the figure of two young ladies. They stood before him, one all tulle and folds in a printed silk dress whose reds were dominant, and the other flustered and panting in a low-cut yellow dress whose single ornamental button at the shoulder clashed with the simplicity of the design, giving the impression that it had just then been wrapped hastily around her body in as best a fashion as circumstances allowed.

"Oh, Mümtaz, you're happily met, how fortunate to run into you."

"Where have you been, for heaven's sake? You've been out of sight and out of touch."

Both were pleased by this chance encounter.

"Have I got some news for you," said Muazzez.

Nuran's cousin İclâl wanted to change the subject, but no pressure could prevent Muazzez from confessing everything she knew to Mümtaz.

Muazzez, however, didn't know where to begin. Mümtaz still found the sweet thing likable despite her inability to keep anything to herself; she'd be injecting venom of this sort for the first time in her short life, both describing what she knew and also taking years of revenge on him. She wanted to savor the moment, but there was yet a third matter; she had to convey the news such that Mümtaz, despite all of his buffoonery – Allah, how dense he was, how had she fallen for such an idiot? – understood that she still cherished him and was immediately available to console him. But no ideas, nothing came to her mind. All she could do was stare at Mümtaz and grin, revealing the tips of her incisors.

"Go on and say it already, what's happened?" Mümtaz laughed as he asked.

She actually had an attractive aspect. She was curt, spoiled, selfish, and senseless, yet beautiful. As sweet and appealing as a piece of fruit. He needed no convincing to like her, desire her, or love her. All it would take was to draw her face toward him from the ever-changing, ever-wavy framework of sandy brown hair and to extinguish the glint of her teeth by kissing her and biting her lips. A bright and delicious moment deep as a well. To expect anything else, to seek a further horizon was meaningless. Muazzez began and ended with herself. To the degree that one could forgo the possibilities that she openly and impulsively conjured, and continue on one's way. *At least, that's how it is for me . . .*

She would soon strike. She would tell him that Nuran was to be married.

İclâl could stand it no longer; the charade had gone on too long; evidently the young lady didn't want a matter having to do with her relative and their family to be exposed in this way. Nuran had reconciled with her ex-husband; what need was there for hesitation and evocative glances due to such a commonplace, everyday occurrence? As if surrendering herself to a void, she explained: "Maybe you've already gotten word, sweetheart. It isn't breaking news or anything that Fâhir and Nuran have made up. They're traveling to İzmir tomorrow. The marriage ceremony will take place there." She stopped as if to gaze at the route she'd just taken and blushed immediately.

Was there any need to speak to Mümtaz in such a clipped way? What else could she have done to defend Nuran against Muazzez? She softened her voice and added: "If you could only see how happy Fatma is . . . She's running around wildly shouting, 'Papa's coming back! Papa's coming and he won't be going away again!'"

No vengeance remained to be had. She took a deep breath as if she'd been relieved of a huge burden. She waited for Mümtaz to respond so that she could relax fully.

With difficulty, Mümtaz said, "May God bless them." How had he groped for these four words and strung them together? How had he uttered the syllables from his dry throat? He didn't know. But he was heartened by the fact that his voice wasn't too hoarse. When he saw İclâl looking at him as if to say, "Say more, something more . . . Save me from this snake," he commented that Fatma had a great love for her father. Then he passed on to another topic. He was gradually gaining momentum. If he exerted a little more effort, he'd be able to act naturally. As he spoke, İclâl's usual smile came to her lips. Her eyes laughed. With this expression, her eyebrows virtually merged with her listless eyes, making a languid and alluring shadow below her forehead. This much was certain, İclâl was one who lived the season of her womanhood naturally. She lived a life as modest and satisfied as a cat. It was enough that those around her were cordial toward each other; of course, this served her as well. Mümtaz knew what she'd been thinking for the past few minutes. She was content now. They were all satisfied; after so many destructive episodes, Fâhir was content with his wife, Nuran with her daughter, İclâl with her sense of family, Muazzez because she'd informed Mümtaz more or less on her own that his horizon of joy had been obliterated; indeed, they were all satisfied and now free to go their separate ways.

"I'd walk with you to the ferry, but I have so much to do."

"Oh, thanks, and we missed the 5:05 on your account . . ."

Mümtaz didn't want to mention that İhsan was at home, sick. It'd only rouse their pity for naught.

"I really do have business to attend to," he said, and departed.

Farther ahead, he turned around. The yellow outfit and the red silk print were still side by side; with small grazes, Muazzez's skirts still caressed İclâl's dress, but the pair was no longer arm in arm, their steps no longer knitting in the rhythm of mutual thought.

Part II

Nuran

I

Here follows the simplest love story ever told, so simple as to recall an
algebraic equation.

Mümtaz and Nuran had made each other's acquaintance on the ferry to
the Princes Islands one morning last May. That week an outbreak of illness
had afflicted the neighborhood children. Nuran, accepting that she couldn't
ensure that her daughter, Fatma, stayed indoors, resolved to take her to her
aunt's house on the main island, Büyükada. Since divorcing her husband
at the onset of winter, Nuran had led an existence solitary and withdrawn.
The entire winter she'd returned to Istanbul just three or four times, and
then only for necessities. Despite the divorce being the mutual wish of both
parties – Nuran had made one last gesture of goodwill, agreeing to Fâhir's
request to initiate proceedings jointly based on incompatibility – the length
of the legal process had left her all but exhausted.

The whole affair had been a matter of disgrace besides: seven years after
they'd wed, the father of her child, the man whom she'd loved and trusted,
abandoning his home and family for two years in pursuit of a Romanian
woman of questionable repute whom he'd met while traveling, had gallivanted about before one day informing Nuran that they could no longer
be together and must divorce.

Truthfully, this had been no union of contentment from the start. The
couple had been extremely fond of one another but shared no physical
chemistry; an ornery and jaded Fâhir and a simply resigned Nuran lived like
two fluke inmates of fate, side by side yet shut off from each other, though

cooperative when it came to matters of everyday concern. Fatma's birth, at first, seemed to somewhat temper this sequestered and nearly joyless lifestyle. Though Fâhir loved his daughter immensely, domestic life had always annoyed him, and he found his wife's introversion, silent and docile, forever confounding. In his opinion, Nuran was lazy of spirit. Meanwhile, she'd actually waited seven years for him to rouse her from her stupor.

A feminine life, luxuriant enough to be precarious, pregnant to all possibilities, and fecund in every sense, simply persisted like an overgrown acre within feelings of inferiority in which Nuran blamed herself for the causes of a half-dreamy, half-fallow existence caused by nothing more than the absence of a cultivating force. Fâhir, a man overcome by his sense of possession, stifled all wants and desires. Thus, without having discovered this mine of wealth, he lived beside Nuran almost in sterility, nonetheless awaiting her passionate awakenings that would excite his instincts. And his intermittent returns to his wife, because they weren't deeply nurturing and because he'd always been superficial with women, passed over Nuran like a wave cresting over a boulder without eliciting the slightest response. This nature of his might be aroused by a love affair focused on matters of the flesh, or rather by an escapade that fell into his lap. Emma, who'd encountered Fâhir on the beaches of Constantsa, entered his life through such a route. This handsome man was incapable of connecting carnally with a woman. However, Emma's fifteen-year stint as something of a trollop was enough to overcome this lack.

In the throes of jealousy, garrulous scenes, a guilty conscience, and frenzy – in short, improprieties of all stripes – Fâhir began to see himself in a new light. For two years he pursued his mistress, gasping and panting as if in a race, and when he realized that he couldn't catch or surpass her, he just surrendered the reins.

As a result Mümtaz met Nuran – the woman who would transfigure his life from alpha to omega – at a time when isolation had overcome her. Rather than be interred in the gloom of the lower deck, he preferred to sit on the upper deck, knowing full well that he'd be somewhat less comfortable. But what Istanbulite could keep from wondering who else had boarded the same ferry – especially with no risk of being left without a seat? He couldn't bring himself to go upstairs without first peeping below, where he happened to see Sabih, a long-lost friend sitting with his wife, Adile; complaining inwardly, *Couldn't you have shown yourselves on any other day?* Mümtaz went and sat beside them, and before long Nuran entered, clutching a few packages and a handbag in one hand and a flaxen-haired girl of about seven in the other. This husband-and-wife pair welcomed the new arrival with jubilation, exactly as they'd greeted Mümtaz.

From the very first, Mümtaz admired the young lady's handsome and well-formed profile, both her figure and face, which conjured a phantasy in white. As soon as she spoke, he thought, *She's most certainly from Istanbul,* and when she declared, "One doesn't easily forgo familiar places, but the Bosphorus does become tedious at times," he understood what she represented. For Mümtaz, there were two fundamental and requisite criteria for female beauty: principally, to hail from Istanbul; and secondly, to be raised along the Bosphorus. If not on that same day, Mümtaz learned in the coming weeks that the third, though perhaps superseding, factor was to resemble Nuran herself: to speak Turkish liltingly as she did; to face her interlocutor with the insistence she carried in her eyes; to lean toward one, when addressed, by cocking her sandy brown head; to make similar gestures of hand; to simply blush, moments after making a retort, astonished at her own pluck; to ply through the midst of life in a calm and nourishing manner, forever her own woman, like a river without pretension or anxiety, vast and wide – whose waters were clear enough to see all the way to the bottom.

When she'd been introduced to him, Nuran laughed and said, "I know you, we took the same ferry here this morning. You're İclâl's friend Mümtaz."

She'd stressed "İclâl's friend." Mümtaz was pleased by the recognition; yet, he was apprehensive about the light İclâl might have cast upon him. İclâl wasn't a bad person; the friendship between them would persist throughout life. Nevertheless, she was chatty.

"I wonder what that charismatic relation of mine imparted to you?" Nuran said.

"In that case, let me tell you," he replied. "You're the illustrious Nuran." Gesturing to Fatma: "The young lady was, you might say, raised in our very classroom, though she never entered it. Each morning we heard the general bulletin of the current state of affairs from İclâl." He smiled at the girl from a distance; but Fatma paid no heed to such coyness. She had no intention of countenancing any strange male; all men were a threat to her happiness. Only her mother smiled. Mümtaz now recalled how he'd at first been tempted to sit across from Nuran on the morning ferry, but upon his hesitation, as a vagary of chance he'd let himself be chewed up by Muazzez's chit-chattering teeth – he regretted that Nuran might have registered his reticence.

Muazzez and İclâl boasted of quite a delicious friendship, in which their diverse constitutions complemented and completed one another. Muazzez was a daily gazette of insignificant events and a gazetteer of unknown lands. She resembled her grandmother, who had a relative – or friend at least – residing in every district of Istanbul, whom she loved like a sibling and could always call upon.

The grandmother in question, having attained an age of social respect, roamed from dawn to dusk repeating at each visit the tidbits she'd witnessed or heard on the street or at the previous call, only to return in the evening with an assortment of gossip that had been thoroughly committed to memory. In this enormous city, there remained little to which she wasn't privy. Acquainted with all of Istanbul, that is to say those who were "above the sieve," she could discuss how people were during any particular year, month, or even day. She'd been this way for some time. "We all come home with a saddlebag of news and information," she'd say. "In the evenings at the dinner table we tell each other what's happened, and in the morning at breakfast we'll separate the wheat from the chaff, culling what's of value." Once, due to this hearsay being doled out, Muazzez's uncle had been unable to jockey for position to make a vital announcement; after three days he was barely able to interject: "Everybody, excuse the interruption, I've been meaning to tell you for days now, but I couldn't find an opening. I've received a telegraph from İkbal; we've been blessed with the birth of a baby girl!" They named the girl Nisyan, or "slip of the mind."

İclâl spoke quite sparingly in comparison with Muazzez. She was drawn to minutia, cataloging the information gathered by Muazzez, dramatizing aspects and turning them into human interest stories.

All manner of interpretation, light, and coloring sprang from her. This was why Muazzez, even if among a hundred people, would gaze at her and conclude any statement by saying, "I don't know, what would you say, İclâl?"

Mümtaz's greatest pleasure was to watch the pair leave the university each evening, head to head, arm in arm. He'd nicknamed them "the two shrews of Zeynep's boardinghouse," and he'd rib them by saying, "The president of the university doesn't know what these two know," or, "Ask Muazzez. If she's had no news of such and such, it never happened. If İclâl has no recollection of so-and-so, it's of no importance, don't worry about it." But there was a distinction between İclâl and Muazzez: The former learned only by happenstance while the latter actively investigated an event with great curiosity. Since İclâl was well aware of her friend's disposition, she'd restrained herself from introducing Muazzez – whom she'd known since high school, loved dearly, and considered a close confidante – into her own family circle.

İclâl's relatives, from Muazzez's point of view, were simply companions, frequently mentioned yet forever absent.

That morning as well Muazzez revealed a cache of information to Mümtaz. She reported on the Bosphorus residence in Yeniköy that belonged to an old Ottoman Greek family and was sold off for next to nothing; on the neighboring house that had been painted crimson, causing the bride-groom scarcely wed into the family to bolt upon seeing it, exclaiming that he couldn't live in such a tasteless home – obviously a pretense for separa-tion; on the tiff between two women of ill repute four days prior in one of the drinking holes of Arnavutköy; on Çakır, the fisherman in Bebek, who'd made purchase of a new rowboat; and on the announcements of three engagements and two weddings. Since İclâl wasn't present, however, none of the accounts could be analyzed or interpreted to its fullest dramatic potential. That is to say, İclâl's observations truly contained an important element of synthesis.

"So, have you finished your dissertation?"

"Last night," Mümtaz said, complementing his puerile embarrassment with childish glee: "Last night I drew a long line across the bottom of the last page. Beneath that, I drew another, thicker than the first, then another, and at the very bottom I wrote May 4, 11:05 P.M. I signed my name. Next I rose and went out on the balcony. I took three or four restorative breaths in the Swedish fashion. And now I'm heading to Büyükada." If it hadn't embar-rassed him, he would have continued by saying, "I'm twenty-six, I live in a comfortable house on a hilltop in Emirgân, I'm not much for dancing, I have no luck with fishing because I'm impatient, but I'm an avid sailor – at least I have a flair for surviving seaborne accidents – for your sake, I could eat two plates of yogurt-and-watercress salad a day, and even limit the cigarettes I smoke to just a single pack."

This delirium resulted somewhat from the completion of his dissertation. His pleasure mounted as he mused, because from now on he was free, he could wander and roam about at will, and he could read whatever struck his fancy. Finishing on May 4 meant earning the summer. For the first time in four years, that spectacular winged gryphon known as summer was his. For four months, Istanbul, the abode of felicity, was his. Of course, there were exams to minister, but what of it? He could always find a way out.

Wearing her mute smile, Nuran continued to listen, maintaining a peculiar attention to detail, as if she effectively existed in her eyes. The sheen of these eyes ruled her person the way the movements of the sun dictated what we knew as the day. As Mümtaz regarded her, he had to give İclâl credence: Nuran was beautiful indeed. She had a certain je ne sais quoi.

"İclâl spoke of you frequently this past winter. She'd mentioned that you lived by yourself in a house on the Bosphorus . . ."

"Yes, through an unforeseen turn of events. A few summers ago, my cousin İhsan found a wonderful house. That winter he and his family moved out and I stayed behind."

"Didn't you suffer from boredom there?"

"Not really. I'd come down to the city frequently besides. Not to mention it's a place that I've known since my childhood. Not that it wasn't difficult at first. But when spring erupted . . ."

Both of them together by separate routes meandered back to a month ago, recollecting the ruby blossoms of the Judas trees and the way they extended their poised branches over every yard. Nuran wanted to think that Mümtaz, like herself, didn't conjure these beauties through a matrix of pain and agony. But she knew that within a span of a few weeks, not to mention when he was just eleven – as İclâl had related – Mümtaz had lost his mother and father. Life could poison one at any age. Waiting in line on the way onto the ferry, she'd overheard two boys talking about the difficulties of making ends meet. Were these topics to be discussing at such an age?

". . . the old man, he has no money . . . If he did, it'd be a different story. If it were within his power, he'd sacrifice his life for us. I realized there was no end in sight, so I insisted I didn't want to go to school. Teachers aren't aware of such things anyway; they just complain, 'This one will never amount to anything!' So I put in as an apprentice. A pittance of a lira fifty a week, spend it as you like . . . In any case, I was spared paying for fees and the ferryboat. They give me lunch as well. But I can't take the smell of grease. My stomach turns. I'm like my mother was with her morning sickness . . ."

"Wasn't there any other work?"

"Yeah, but the pay wasn't enough. Because it was a craft trade, they didn't pay anything to start. Never mind, at the kitchen with tips and all we make up to ten lira. Once my father gets well, I'm going to work as a cobbler's apprentice . . . That is, if he does get well."

Nuran turned around to discover that he was an adolescent of twelve or thirteen, skinny and olive-eyed. As he walked, he leaned on a freshly cut branch that he used as a crutch. In his bearing mingled remorse, sarcasm, and inborn grace.

Sabih asked Mümtaz, "Did you find the seventy-eights?"

"I did. They're a bit scuffed. But they contain songs and pieces we've never heard before! İhsan, who's a savant in these matters, says in that case we don't know one percent of what's really out there. If only somebody would come around and promote these songs, have sheet music published, make recordings; that is, if we could just save ourselves a little from today's popular music! Just think for a minute, you're a country that's given rise to a musician like İsmail Dede Efendi; composers like Seyid Nuh, Ebubekir Ağa, and Hafız Post have come along and composed extraordinary works. Part of our identity has been formed by their artistry. We're not even aware that we're living in a state of spiritual hunger . . . This is the catastrophe: Assume that today's generation vanished. These works, many of which are only known by heart, will simply vanish. Just think about what Münir Nurettin Selçuk alone knows."

Sabih turned to Nuran. "Did you know that Mümtaz cultivated such interest in our traditional music?"

Nuran cast him a cordial glance. With a grin that made her face resemble ripened fruit, she said, "No, İclâl must have kept that detail to herself . . ."

Adile's voice twitched with the trepidation of having been abandoned, and like a cat arching its back and padding out of the cupboard where it had been napping, she said, "Honestly, I get annoyed at such types. As if they can see into others. . . ."

Adile hadn't made İclâl's acquaintance. And as for matters of music, she had no opinion whatsoever. She nourished a taste for the *a la turca*, for navigating familiar waters, and also for the pandemonium it sometimes sparked in a crowd. In her opinion, music and all else was meant to fill the void we called time. A parade, the account of a boxing match, exquisitely appointed gossip presented with the greatest of ease might evince in her the same warmth as that of an extraordinary work of art. She'd missed the ten o'clock ferry due to the details related by the doorman's wife about the second-floor tenants. In fact, Huriye the maid hadn't informed her of anything new. Adile was able to confirm only what she'd already surmised. *Yes, the man in question had coyly found a way out of the mess without his wife being any the wiser by receiving court permission for a second marriage under the pretense of her infertility. In this way, the swarthy lass he'd met three years ago on the Kadıköy ferry, and who'd also provided him with a child, had now become his second wife. The twist was that at the same time, his first wife announced that she was also in the family way. Suddenly, the poor scoundrel had become the father of two infants. Now, then, this is the way God bestows His justice!*

One couldn't say anything against Adile's deep insight into this affair. Six months before the scandal erupted, she suspected something and thoroughly interrogated her Kadıköy contacts. The man's first wife believed that she was actually barren. When this proved false – Adile believed only doctors in such matters – there remained the possibility that the man wasn't the father of either baby. Adile resembled a judge poring over the complicated report of an expert in the field. If the woman weren't in any way culpable, could she have actually stood for this disgrace? Adile imagined her neighbor – like most unmannered women and working girls, who unduly suspected that they had the power of ancient fertility gods, and thus roamed about with the pride of an Asurian bull, forever sunk within the infinite possibilities resting in this delusion, considering their bellies a vessel that must be filled at all costs – head bowed and pitiful, all of her haughty conviction gone like a flaccid balloon, and she thought, *Will I be able to look her in the eyes without laughing? That would be something like letting them off the hook . . . A slight grin and a glance that said "May it bode well!" wouldn't be a bad response either. This wasn't cruelty, simply vengeance.*

For Adile, these very thoughts abruptly tainted Nuran's gleeful laughter, Mümtaz's blind admiration, and the way they gazed at each other. These two fools had gotten to this point by having known about each other beforehand. They'd fall in love. What was it to her whether this or that was public knowledge? She'd known from the scandal on the second floor and from the anguish of Sabih's repeatedly squandering his money how ignorant they all were of the scuttlebutt.

Nuran's beatific smile turned toward Adile. But it no longer carried the same sparkle. She only wanted to convince her of the sincerity of what she'd said. "İclâl's different. She studied piano for fourteen years. She continued at the conservatory. She truly understands and loves music."

Nuran wasn't exaggerating for her relative's sake. İclâl could even at this young age be considered a *musique savant*. She'd forgotten about everything down to her college education; all that remained was music. Her world was made of melody.

"Truth be told, I know little about either. I never studied it. But I do like it. Everything I listen to overwhelms me. I have my favorites, some I find are trivial, some I don't like at all."

Mümtaz eyed Nuran as if to say, *Can one like a piece of music without understanding it? Somebody say something.*

"Were you able to find a lot?"

"More so at the Bedesten and mostly older works . . . But I do find them. Just three days ago I bought two Hafiz Osman records." *Why is it that she laughs when I speak? I'm not just an innocent boy . . . But your laughter's so sublime that instead of being annoyed, I'm simply pleased.* Something within him pivoted toward the golden fruit suspended in the offing by Nuran's astounding laughter. Involuntarily, one responded to it; the laughter grew within him like a tree that verged on bursting into bloom.

From then on, at home, without being able to help himself, he'd hear Ferahfezâ, Acemaşiran, and Nühüft *makam*s amid, and accompanied by, laughter that gilded his records and everything he happened upon, subsuming them in the redolence of springtime and transferring the heat of his own arousal to them.

Amid such thoughts, he raised his head and came eye to eye with Nuran, looking at her serenely, with a glance that emanated from depths and withheld nothing.

It was a glance, as a poet he admired had written, that dressed one in garments shorn of sunlight and yearning. Like those fortress keys of yore that were given to a conqueror on a gold platter or velvet pillow, Nuran presented her entirety through grin and gaze.

Adile fell silent. She quite fully knew the meaning of such smiles and furtive glances that fluttered about only to alight upon lover and beloved again. She was no longer contemplating the dolt from the second floor with two wives and two children who weren't his own. That affair suddenly lost all its meaning. *I won't even make a greeting. Why should I greet such a fool? In the end, he's a man who gads about with the neighborhood help . . . He's the type that would involve himself in all manner of disgrace.* And he was now the spouse of the laundress in the basement of the neighboring apartment building. Why should she concern herself with them? And through this decree, Adile shut her personal file on her neighbor, Sabit. In fact, Mümtaz and Nuran's impropriety bothered her. Mümtaz had been a frequent guest to the apartment for years. Granted, she hadn't been able to entice him to spend the night on the divan in the parlor, but he was still a family friend. She would have wanted a better future for him, rather than one with this veritable "widow." But Adile had just such luck. Because of her admiration for others, she also suffered their betrayals. Her entire life had passed this way. Her own relatives had a penchant for marrying away members of her inner circle. Now it was Mümtaz's turn. She wanted to shrug it off as if to say, "Let them do as they please." But she couldn't bring herself to do so.

One tends, more often than not, to bear one's thoughts on one's shoulders. Thus, the difficulty of moving our shoulders grows in proportion to the burden of these thoughts. Adile's shoulders were laden with Mümtaz and the full weight of his future. But this was her own foolishness; what was Mümtaz to her? Who was she to enter another's affairs, anyway? Her face recoiled before this last betrayal of fate. *Stupid fool of a man. Besides, which of them wasn't a fool? All men were buffoons. A little flattery, an aloof smile, a few words of inscrutable intent, and then the gaze of an egg-laying hen . . . time to harness the yoke.* Adile wasn't one to meddle in the lives of others. Anyway, she had no plans for anyone. She was afraid of loneliness, and because she feared being abandoned, she grew frantic when her acquaintances were no longer bound to her.

Meanwhile, Mümtaz and Nuran apparently got along swimmingly without having to rely on her at all. Unforgivable. For quite some time now, she'd accepted being a catalyst of sorts between the sexes. This natural inclination ruled her home life and her days. Men and women were welcome to come, give each other the once-over, and even fall madly in love, but only under the rays of her golden orb, only if they depended on her mediation. After such an introduction, she might make mention of Nuran to Mümtaz, exciting his curiosity with subtle strokes, almost as if needling him, and on the next day, during another visit, she might do the same to Nuran, thus bestirring thoughts in both, before one night inviting them for an evening meal; thereby, she'd make the couple something like fixtures of the house, of dinnertime, and of the evening hours that she could not fill by herself! How she loved when a couple of her design sparked and caught fire. But she was not amused in the least by relationships so intense that they established an insular, independent life – under which circumstances she'd be forgotten whether she liked it or not. She took all necessary precautions to avoid such an outcome. She did, however, love to watch an incipient friendship develop step-by-step toward full-fledged love, to hear all the petite intimacies as confidant to each party, and to resolve any potential misunderstandings. Though if the matter grew and the relationship became truly serious, she would exert all of the efforts within her means to distance the lovers from one another, and because these efforts rested on well nigh ten or twelve years' experience, more often than not, she succeeded. This much was certain: Adile could douse the flames of love as well as ignite them. Regardless, she held the institution of marriage in high esteem. She'd be much more content, however, if the women she knew married outside of her own milieu. She wanted to keep her friends to herself. They were available for limited dalliances only. Adile wasn't so unrefined as to speak openly about this. Even if in the end the couple were to marry, Adile's assistance should be sought in establishing the conjugal nest. Were the hardships of this life something worth enduring without such moments of satisfaction? Meanwhile, Mümtaz and Nuran had begun this flirtation through their own acquaintance. Adile, coincidently, had long felt the urge to initiate something between them. However, when she now saw the way Mümtaz gazed at the young lady, she quickly changed her mind about inviting them to her dinner table three days hence.

Adile made as many mistakes as the next person, but she was possessed of a virtue: When she understood her error, she didn't hesitate to take appropriate action.

No, she wouldn't be extending any invitations. Now she only desired one thing: to inform Sabih at the earliest convenience that she'd had a change of heart. It was nothing short of annoyance for a thought to remain in the good lady's head without being expressed to Sabih, especially such a vital decision, without being conveyed in the most direct and concise manner. Not to mention that the gravity of this decision was on par with a death sentence. Mümtaz would later think that this verdict really had more to do with Nuran; Adile had a soft spot for men. They weren't as devious as women; even the ugliest among them possessed such sweetness and tameness that . . .

He was convinced that Adile wouldn't make a sacrifice of him, that she'd even invite him over this very week; yet, he was also certain that Nuran would only be allowed to pay a visit alone.

Next to Adile's fixations, Sabih's were much more elementary. He was overcome with great hopes upon seeing the attraction between Mümtaz and Nuran. Since the last fiasco, having to do with bath fixtures – a Polish friend of his had circumvented that – Adile had taken out all her sorrows on her husband's treatment for uritis. For months now he'd been eating boiled carrots and buttered vegetables. Especially after Nuri's wedding, his diet had become exceptionally strict. For weeks he hadn't seen a drop of *rakı*. Would that an unexpected guest stop in for a visit! As fortune would have it, not a soul stepped foot into their neighborhood. If these two fools managed this matter well enough, tomorrow evening even . . . No, tomorrow night Sabih saw himself with a plate of boiled carrots and fresh zucchini before him again, as on the previous night and the night before. He sighed. People were cruel indeed. Life was unbearable; what difference was there between eating carrots and eating one of your own legs like a hungry spider? Eating one of its own legs . . . He'd read about it in the French newspaper spread before him that morning.

From where she sat, Adile resembled one such spider, and her thoughts – with an appetite of that voracity – were consuming her. Directly, she noticed Fatma growing increasingly more impatient at the other end of the table. The girl was rather pretty, but this beauty was undercut by an astounding brattiness. Apparently she was jealous of her mother's attentions. A glint of hope sparkled within Adile, her heart opened up like a Japanese paper flower unfolding in water, and she was overcome by eternal compassion and affection. An entire horizon opened before her. As she looked at the girl, she realized that this budding dalliance would never come to pass. *The poor little thing* . . . Adile immediately began to fawn over her. With affection that would make daemons of torment weep, she asked the girl how she was. Fatma, realizing she was being pitied, furrowed her brows, and Nuran, stunned in the anticipation of the imminent downpour, glanced at her as if to say, "Please don't." Without returning the glance, Adile pranced down a path of compassion and consideration: "Tell me then, do you still dance as well as you used to? Like on the night you came and played at our house, you remember . . . Whatever happened to your train set?" How her voice glided like velvet. How it knew to slip deep into one's inner recesses. The train set and dancing had been a part of the previous New Year's Eve celebration that they'd all spent together, her papa included. Adile's sympathy had selected this memory carefully . . . as if picking a dagger from an attic full of forgotten objects.

This alone provoked the most poignant reaction from Fatma, catapulting her out of the introversion she'd sunken into, out of the anguish of having been forgotten. That day Mümtaz learned the precise degree to which the mind of a jealous child could be an intrument of mischief. During the entire ferry crossing, Fatma didn't allow Nuran a free moment. The young mother had been all but subdued by an afreet. Only with her smile was

Nuran present among them. By the beacon of this remote smile, Mümtaz listened to Sabih's insights into the present state of world affairs. Due to the deprivations he was forced to suffer, the Great Carrotivore was exacting his revenge from mankind. As though indicating, "Here's my evidence," the palm of one hand pressed down on the French newspapers before him, he denounced one and all.

Had Mümtaz not been able to see Nuran's countenance in the arcane depths where it had withdrawn in faraway conversation with Adile, had he not been able to see her graceful smile illuminating her face, he'd have been forced to conclude that the end of the world was upon them – presently a rather welcome eventuality – and that this procession of fools known as mankind deserved such a fate as Armageddon. Nuran's smile, however, her sandy hair gathered atop her head like a season complete, convinced him that life had its horizons, aside from and surpassing politics and causes, more beautiful and more apt to transport one to realms of tranquility; her presence convinced him that contentment came within an arm's length at times, and that mortal existence was configured more soundly than he'd assumed. As the ferry approached the island, this optimism within Mümtaz met with strains of agony. Once there, he'd have to separate from Nuran and her daughter.

II

Mümtaz regretted hurrying away as soon as he'd left them. He shouldn't have abandoned Nuran like that. *Perhaps I can catch sight of her*, he thought, and waited at some remove from the ferry landing. The crowd flowed ceaselessly. As the passengers and those who'd come to greet them thinned, he first noticed Sabih and Adile – Adile could walk only a short distance on the street without leaning on her husband. For her, in all probability, one of the sound ways of fully exploiting the resource known as a husband was to have him carry her, if only partially, while they were out and about; presently they were locked arm in arm. Sabih, as if wanting to create a ballast of world affairs to counter Adile's heft, which dragged down his starboard side, carried a roll of newspapers in the opposite arm, his forehead furrowed in aggravation; doubtless, he forged ahead with a litany of ideas and comparisons about the ordered regulations of ferry docking and departure in the countries of the West.

Mümtaz shielded himself behind another group to avoid being drawn into further conversation with the couple. Soon Nuran and her daughter appeared. Evidently, so she could walk with greater ease, Nuran had chosen to remain onboard until the very last. With her face lowered toward her daughter, wearing a sweet and simple grin, she walked on, explaining something or another.

But neither the smile nor talk lasted long. As soon as they exited the station building, Fatma shouted, "Papa! Mother, Papa's coming," and bolted forward. What Mümtaz witnessed then, he'd scarcely ever forget. Nuran's face turned ashen white. Mümtaz looked about; twenty or twenty-five paces before him approached a blond woman, thick-boned and full-breasted, if not stunningly beautiful – when he thought of this scene later, he decided, *At least beautiful for some men* – accompanied by a swarthy man of about thirty-five with black hair, whose arms and face were bronzed by the sun and whose bearing gave the impression that he enjoyed water sports. Nuran's entire body trembled. As the thick-boned woman passed, Mümtaz heard her whisper softly, half in Turkish, half in French: "But *c'est scandaleux!* Fâhir, for God's sake, shut her up!" Fâhir and his mistress finally neared Nuran. In a flurry of "God bless" and "Oh, what a pretty child," Emma took Fatma into her arms. Fâhir, meanwhile, stood as if he were made of ice. He'd only managed to bring himself to caress the girl's cheek. A strange, awkward exchange ensued. From where she stood, Nuran continued to tremble; Emma, stressing each syllable she uttered to the breaking point, fawned, "Oh, what a beautiful girl!" and Fatma, distraught by this stranger's affections, and especially by her father's cool distance, clung to her mother's skirts and wept. An onlooker might have concluded that the episode had been orchestrated by Nuran, or that Fâhir hadn't missed his chance at a snub of indifference toward his ex-wife in front of Emma. Nuran put an end to the bitter episode, which could have lasted hours, with a gesture that revealed much of her character: Taking her daughter into her arms, she walked between the two of them and a short distance ahead boarded a phaeton-for-hire. As they passed, Mümtaz noticed that Fatma was convulsing in tears. He felt a twinge of distress. At the head of the road, his friends were awaiting him. He approached them:

"Where have you been? We've been waiting for you . . ."

"Has İhsan come?"

"Yes, and he's with a relative of yours!"

"Who?"

"Somebody named Suad. A peculiar fellow. He's staying at the sanatorium here!"

"He resembles a horse . . ."

Mümtaz said only, "I know him," then turning to Nuri, "It's true, he does look like a horse." Though in his mind's eye he conjured the way Nuran's hair slipped frequently from her temples toward her eyes.

Orhan completed the analysis, "He's something of a cannibal!"

"No, he's only an assassin, or a frantic assassin, that is to say, suicidal!"

These terms referred to an in-joke that had begun at the university. One day at the Küllük coffeehouse, they learned how a renowned historian, Mükrimin Halil, had separated people into three main categories – "Lackeys of the Orient," "Regulators of the World," and "Thugs." Then they'd furthered the categorization. "Cannibals" were fanatics of any ideology, whether on the right or the left. "Assassins" had certain hang-ups and discussed them with whomever they saw. "Frantic Assassins" subjectified these hang-ups to an extreme and were filled with feelings of revolt. And as for "Suicidals," they turned these hang-ups into torturous double binds.

Arm in arm, as they had been years before, they occupied half the road and walked along laughing and talking. None of them noticed Mümtaz's state of distraction.

At this afternoon hour, the restaurant filled with the presence of the sea. Suad and İhsan sat at a corner table. Light reflecting off the sea appeared to gather on Suad's face. Since the last time he'd seen Suad, Mümtaz found him to be thinner and paler. His bones seemed to protrude.

İhsan said impatiently, "Don't waste any time, come sit down." İhsan drank quite infrequently. Rather than from any concern about health, he abstained in order to give alcohol its proper due in life. He'd say, "We shouldn't let the secrets of alcohol lose their effect within us." As for the times he did partake, he'd grow as impatient as a child. He'd picked this restaurant because it was near the ferry landing, and he'd eagerly awaited Mümtaz's arrival. He abruptly turned to Mümtaz: "Your eyes are alight . . . What's going on?"

Surprised, Mümtaz said, "Seeing Suad is quite a pleasure . . ." In fact, he hadn't been pleased to see Suad, although he admired his intelligence and conversation. But there was something he couldn't put his finger on that disturbed him about Suad.

"What a joy . . . There are people in this world who are pleased to see me."

In response to his laughter, Mümtaz thought, *You see, this is precisely why I like you!* Actually, Suad's laughter had a force that came from the heart yet negated everything. He laughed and his face abruptly appeared to be alien and antagonistic. *Is he fed up with his own life or is he mocking me?*

Fahri grinned at İhsan and said, "I told you he'd come. You didn't believe me."

"But he's two ferries late."

"No, I only missed one."

"When did you get up?"

Mümtaz again recalled the great triumph of his evening, and said, "I finished the book last night. I went to bed late and couldn't sleep. No matter what I tell her, I haven't managed to get Sümbül to wake me at the right time!"

Sümbül was the maid who saw to Mümtaz's domestic affairs in Emirgân.

Suad asked, "What have you been reading these days, Mümtaz?"

Gravely, Mümtaz examined the plates of appetizers being placed before him. He'd seated himself opposite the door despite knowing full well that the young lady whose acquaintance he'd just made wouldn't appear. "Practically everything Turkish . . . Ahmet Cevdet's *History*, *Sicill-i Osmanî* biographical entries, Taşköprüzade's *Şakâyık* . . ."

Suad responded dismissively, "Disaster! Now how are we supposed to converse? Mümtaz and I used to discuss things easily enough in the past. First I'd ask him which writer he was reading, then I'd begin talking from that author's perspective or through those concerns." His inscrutable face cracked open with an abrupt, puerile laugh. Completing his earlier thought, Mümtaz mused, *You see, this is also why I like him.*

"Isn't everyone more or less reading this way?" Nuri interjected. The four of them, inseparable friends from Galatasaray, were immensely fond of Mümtaz and couldn't tolerate any innuendos made against him.

Suad gestured with his hand, "I meant to make a joke. I always needle Mümtaz this way. Of course, I know what he's all about. We're relatives. But to tell the truth, I often wonder whether everyone reads as much as we do."

Fahri's opinion took a different tack: "Europe reads much more than we do. And a number of languages at once. That's not the point, but . . ."

"There's another problem still. We're not comfortable with what we read."

İhsan was examining the transfiguration of ice in his glass, how the clear liquid slowly became clouded as if being enhanced by veins of marble. Now the glass was full of a less benign liquid.

"Bottoms up!" he said. Then he answered Suad. "The issue is this: The things we read don't lead us anywhere. When we read what's written about Turks, we realize that we're wandering on the peripheries of life. A Westerner only satisfies us when he happens to remind us that we're citizens of the world. In short, most of us read as if embarking on a voyage, as if escaping our own identities. Herein rests the problem. Meanwhile, we're in the process of creating a new social expression particular to us. I believe this is what Suad is saying."

"Indeed, with one leap to shake and cast out the old, the new, and everything else. Leaving neither Ronsard nor his contemporary in the East Fuzûli . . ."

"Is this even in the realm of possibility?" And Mümtaz succumbed to Nuran's locks again. *Does her hair always fall that way, slightly . . . Does she always brush it back with her hand while lifting her head?*

Suad listened, none the wiser about Nuran's tresses. "Why shouldn't it be a possibility?"

"It's impossible because . . ." But what was impossible was his discussing such matters at present. *I'm on this island and she's here too . . . How distant we are from each other. It's as if we are in the same house but in separate rooms.* "Because, to begin with, we'd be creating a tabula rasa in vain. What do you think we'll gain through such refutation besides the loss of our very selves?"

With a beatific look, Suad said, "The new . . . We'll establish the myth of a new world, as in America and Soviet Russia."

"And do you think they actually cast aside everything, all of it? If you ask me, neither our denial of the past nor our resolve to create can establish this new myth. If anything, it rests in the momentum of the New Life itself."

"Then what d'you expect us to do?"

But Mümtaz didn't answer. His mind was preoccupied with the episode between Nuran and her not-husband – it had to be Fâhir. *How her face fell. She was upset enough to burst into tears herself.* And suddenly, through a compassion that rose up within him, he promised to bring her happiness, for as long as he lived, to bring her happiness. And immediately at that instant he was ashamed of his childishness. *So infantile!* He acknowledged for the first time how sentimental he could let himself be.

"Don't lose sight of the fact that both the United States and Russia are extensions of Europe."

"Okay, then, what is it that should be done?"

İhsan raised his glass, "First we drink," he said. "Then we partake of these fish that this sea of splendor has bequeathed to us. And we give thanks that we are before this sea, at this spring hour, in this restaurant. Later we'll try to establish a new life particular to us and befitting our own idiom. Life is ours; we'll give it the form that we desire. And as it assumes its form, it'll sing its song. But we won't meddle with art or ideas at all! We'll set them free. For they demand freedom, absolute freedom. A myth, solely because we long for it, doesn't just materialize out of thin air. No, it erupts from social life. But to cut our ties with the past and to close ourselves off from the West! Never! What do you think we are? We're the essence of Easterners of taste and pleasure. Everything yearns for our persistence and continuity."

"Once you've let the past persist like that, why even bother with a New Life?"

"Because our existence still hasn't found its form, that's why! In any case, life's always in need of organization. Especially in our era."

"In that case we're purging the past?"

"Of course . . . but only where needed. We'll cast out dead roots; we'll engage in a new enterprise and foster new people and society . . ."

"Where will we find the initiative to do this?"

"From our own necessities and our own will to live; at any rate, we don't need initiative, we need instruction. And reality itself will provide this, not vague notions of utopia!"

Suad wiped his brow with his hand. "I'm not talking about utopia . . . but I want to hear the sounds of unadulterated folk songs. I want to look out upon the world through new eyes. Not just for Turkey, I want this for the entire world. I want to hear songs of tribute sung for the newly born."

"You want justice, you want rights."

"No, not like that! Those are meaningless words. The New Man won't acknowledge a single remnant of the past . . ."

Mümtaz, with an eye on the customers entering through the door, said, "Do let us invite Suad to provide a description of this New Man!"

"I can't! He has yet to be born. But he will be born, of that I'm certain. The entire world is moaning from the labor of his birth. Take Spain for example!"

İhsan: "If all you aspire to is that, rest assured, soon all of Europe, even the planet, will resemble Spain. But do you really think that some type of New Man has been born in Spain or Russia? To me, it seems rather that the ground is being prepared for human catastrophe."

"Are you making a prophecy?"

"No, just an observation . . . an observation that could be made by any reader of your average daily paper."

Suad fiddled for a while with his empty glass, then extending it to İbrahim, he said, "If you would, please." Topping the *rakı*-filled glass with water, he took a first sip. "If this happened, what of it, anyway? It's not that I oppose its occurrence. Humanity can only rid itself of obsolete life-molds through such a conflagration . . ."

"So it can be reduced to even more inferior molds. We all know the outcome of the last world war."

But Suad wasn't listening: "Not to mention that war has become unavoidable now. Such convoluted accounts could only be settled through war." Then he suddenly glanced toward İhsan. "You don't actually hope for anything new from humanity, do you?"

"Could one ever lose hope in humanity? I just don't anticipate anything good from war. It'll spell the end of civilization. I don't expect anything worthwhile to emerge from war, revolution, or populist dictators. War means an absolute catastrophe for Europe, and maybe the world." And as if speaking to himself, he continued: "I haven't lost faith in humanity, but I don't trust individuals. To begin with, once their ties are broken, they change completely; they become like programmed machines . . . and suddenly it seems as if they resemble deaf and senseless forces of nature. The terrifying aspect of war and revolution is that it amounts to the sudden unleashing of a rudimentary force, one that we'd assumed we'd tamed through centuries of discipline, socialization, and culture."

"That is exactly what I want, revolution."

İhsan sighed, exasperated.

"Meanwhile, we could hope for better. But what good is hope when humanity is this frail? Yes, it's hard to trust humanity, but if we consider its fate, there isn't a creature as pitiable as man."

"I admire mankind. I admire its power to fight constraints. Fully aware of its fate yet engaging in life nevertheless, I admire that courage. Which of us on a starlit night doesn't carry the weight of all Creation on our backs? Nothing could be as beautiful as the courage of humanity. Had I been a poet, I would have penned a single work, a grand epic describing the venture of humanity stretching from our first ancestors who stood on two legs to the present. Initial thoughts, initial fears, initial love, initial stirrings of intelligence gradually becoming cognizant of Creation, the integration of everything that had once existed independently, the myriad innovations with which we've augmented Nature . . . our act of creating Allah around us and within us. Indeed, I'd write only one piece. I'd describe how I longed to sing the praises of humanity awakening matter from its sleep and subduing Creation with its own spirit. Oh language that embraces all exalted things! Oh words, come to my aid!"

İhsan eyed his food skeptically: "That's quite a display of exuberance there, isn't it, Mümtaz? You sound just like one of those nineteenth-century disciples of civilization."

"No, on the contrary. Because I don't believe that these problems can ever be resolved. We'll always kill and be killed. We'll always live under some type of threat. I admire tragedy itself. True greatness resides in the courage we display despite our consciousness of death."

"Mümtaz yearns to write a poem on evolution from gorilla to homo sapien."

"Yes, the evolution from gorilla to human. Thank you for reminding me. Meanwhile, the war you crave is the obliteration of this notion. Now, are we to revert from human being back to ape? Dostoyevsky best understood the predicament in which we find ourselves." İhsan returned his glass to the table without drinking from it. "The war that you desire will take us there. After two more world wars, nothing will remain of culture or civilization. We'll lose the ideal of freedom for all eternity."

"I know that much as well. But the bankruptcy of spirit within us and the misery surrounding us, our penchant for expending men like so much fodder and the environment of fear this gives rise to . . . then just think about the calamity of people's realization that this is an obligatory part of life! All of it foretells the approach of the end of an era. We expect it, even if it proves to be an apocalypse."

———

"Keep the change . . ."

Adile glared scornfully at her husband, and in a soft voice that nonetheless glinted sharply and blindingly with a desire for bloodletting, hissed, "It just grows on trees, doesn't it?"

Sabih cocked an eyebrow, casting a customary look of sweetness at his wife. He knew the reason she'd be annoyed by everything for the remainder of the day. *I'll just sit in a corner and stay out of the conversation. Let our hosts put up with her!* Over the years, he'd grown accustomed to his wife the way one might get used to the quirks of an old jalopy. She stalled randomly, occasionally her brakes wouldn't catch, her gears slipped unexpectedly, and without warning she sped off full throttle. Sabih's task was to prevent the old rattletrap from causing an accident. In essence she was a fine woman; he'd grown used to her. And their life together was comfortable. Granted, Sabih had achieved this comfort through rather extreme sacrifices. In order to win her for himself, he'd virtually relinquished half his personality. *And I'm not quite sure one can get on in the world with just half a self.*

The phaeton driver, pleased by the tip, traced a wide arc, making the wheat-colored wicker seats and pied canopy of his carriage sparkle beneath the sunlight as he brushed past Adile. She fleetingly contemplated whether to take as a personal affront this dynamic turn made by the well-groomed horses in their spring-morning ease, and walked briskly, stepping resolutely with her heels as if she intended to pierce the asphalt that had begun to soften in the sunlight. Before her appeared a very rocky, windy, downward slope that she'd have to descend. She paused and waited for Sabih to take her arm. *In these high heels even!* She'd only yesterday purchased this pair and wasn't willing to have them torn apart on this stony path: *At least he's good for something in such circumstances!* Sabih didn't squander the opportunity presented by fate to make amends. Even though his thoughts remained on the hips of the sumptuous girl – exposed to the bikini line – lying out on a chaise lounge on the veranda of the roadside house, he didn't neglect to gently squeeze his wife's arm with provocative pressure and mastery gained from thirteen years of experience. *In any case, we're paying a social visit . . .* And he slowly whispered into her ear: "Mümtaz's life's in peril . . .

What d'you think?" He had no doubt about the effect this single statement would make on Adile. He knew quite well that presently his wife's face was convulsing in a multitude of small tremors like an oyster squirted with lemon. And simply to compensate for the torment that he'd intentionally inflicted, he continued squeezing Adile's arm, however much his affection for his wife was limited to such gestures. "In peril! Because it was certain that Nuran had a soft spot for Mümtaz as well." With hard-hearted determination to take the torment to its extreme limit, he abruptly added, "Or had they met each other long beforehand and were just playing us for fools?"

"In all honesty, I don't know, but I doubt it . . . Is there any trace of such cunning in those two? Not to mention, why should they even attempt such a charade?"

"But were you paying attention? The little girl also noticed."

"Naturally, the unfortunate dear!" And Adile, her heart in shreds out of compassion for Nuran's daughter, hung on to Sabih with the weight of her entire corpus. What's interesting is that at will Sabih can step into the cozy cadence of our engagement . . . *strange creatures these women, my word . . . I swear that poor fool Mümtaz is senselessly snaring trouble for himself.*

Sabih felt a peculiar affection toward Mümtaz. Meanwhile, running over the strategies for calculating distances that his driving instructor had imparted to him, he gauged the remaining distance between their present location and the entryway of their destination as he gently stroked Adile's forearm: "Whoa! Go easy now, dear!"

———————

Emma, with the measured coquetry of a woman who'd assumed familiarity with the male soul, expressed her delight: "Oh, they have lobster." She was on the verge of clapping with joy. "You are aware, Fâhir, that yesterday's lobster was exceptional!" Her voice was peculiar, like a cucumber marinated in mustard, and her tongue transformed Turkish words with jarring crispness. Despite this, she had almost no trace of an accent.

Fâhir stared at her vigorous chin and stark white teeth with alarm: "And the next course?"

She answered wearing one of her most endearing smiles: "Let's think about that after the lobster." But remembering how bored – naturally, like all Turks – the man with whom she lived grew waiting at the table for food, she added: "Maybe a schnitzel or a steak."

"Fine, a schnitzel or a steak for you." He turned toward the waiter: "Which do you recommend?"

The Greek waiter momentarily turned into Buridan's ass, immobilized between the superiority of schnitzel and the nobility of steak.

"But it won't do if you don't have any." Emma's voice verged on shattering out of compassion like a piece of glass in fire.

In response to this affection and its cold assault, Fâhir tensed with a shiver emanating from his coccyx.

"You absolutely must have some!" Emma insisted, displaying maternal tenderness and canny concern – for every man was partly a child in need of guidance: "And this morning you forgot to do your calisthenics!"

On the beach in Constantsa, around the time they first began these calisthenics, neither her voice nor her insistence bothered Fâhir overly much. Back then the interest that she showed in him excited him, and he found unimaginable pleasures in this measured and controlled friendship.

"Fine, I'll have some too!" In this way, at least, he'd prevent her from talking. And with an odd determination, which she, too, noticed, he buried his head in the menu and tried to avoid seeing Emma's teeth, her sturdy body, her broad chest that defied masculine strength, and all the features of this top-notch machine of gratification that had at one time driven him mad with pleasure, and now did so with impatience and even anger.

Since returning to Istanbul, Fâhir had grown alarmed by Emma's teeth.

These pearly whites, unblemished and stark, resembling a mechanism that churned incessantly inside its rather exaggerated facial housing, left him with the impression of some sort of grinder that could reduce whatever it encountered to a pulp. This grinder would pulverize the lobster and afterward chew up the Viennese schnitzel. Ever so slowly . . .

"Wine or water?"

"*Rakı.*"

Fâhir, truly caught off guard, gazed briefly in astonishment at the woman sitting opposite him. Emma, however, had lost herself in distant seas that stretched out in tropical azure between the first mimosa blooms.

"You've never had a taste for *rakı.*"

"I've gotten used to its taste now!" Then she faced Fâhir with a gaze of affection: "You are aware, I'm an Istanbulite now!"

Emma hadn't grown accustomed to *rakı* at all. And she didn't want Fâhir to drink anything, perhaps simply as an exercise of her own authority. But the encounter at the ferry landing with Nuran and, particularly, with her daughter, forced her to forgo some of her principles for a few days. In case of any eventualities, she thought it best to appear more ingratiating and docile for a spell. Till she came to better know the wealthy Swedish yachtsman whom they'd recently met, she needed Fâhir's attentions. She repeated to herself: *One month at the least* . . . Yes, she needed to remain close with Fâhir for a month at least. And then a Mediterranean voyage on a private yacht with such distinguished guests . . . Not to mention that it was just the season. *Athens, Sicily, Marseille* . . . She didn't think about anything more. Because whether summer or winter, whatever the season, above all, she longed for Paris. She ought to go there, certainly. The previous trip to Paris, which she took before meeting Fâhir, was a waste. A miserable room, a humble restaurant that resembled something of a neighborhood kitchen, the tinkling of a piano coming from the next room till the evening, a few pieces of furniture bought on a limited budget . . . Doubtless, she'd enjoyed herself immensely in carnal terms; but even for that, she could no longer stand certain deprivations. Not to mention that the time had come for her to settle down and start a family. She didn't want to miss this opportunity. But fate always played odd tricks on Emma. This time around it happened as well. The elderly and wealthy Swede hadn't just arrived on the scene alone. In tow was a young, dark youth who happened to be the yacht's captain. Worst of all, this young man behaved as if he knew all of Emma's proclivities by heart, arranging trysts for them, which she couldn't bring herself to resist, and after giving her a languorous, lingering glance with his black, olive-shaped eyes, seeing no need to stand on formality . . . This was how it had been last night at sea. How quickly he'd taken advantage of the general state of drunkenness, the moonlit night, and the silence. Along with being angry at her own shortfalls, she was happy to recall that intimacy again, and closed her eyes.

But she didn't waste time with this vision of contentment. These were all passing fancies. She mustn't lose sight of essentials. Right now, that was Fâhir. She was quite curious about the effects of the morning encounter on him. She'd only been able to see Nuran for a minute at most, and she was jealous from her vantage in life as a paramour. Nuran exuded more beauty than her in a different, deeper way. Despite this, she wasn't curious about her; their presences were foreign to each other. What frightened Emma was the daughter herself.

"You are aware, Fâhir, you behaved atrociously with Fatma!"

Fâhir assumed a voice that she didn't recognize at all: "I know . . ." *This is the third time! Always, "You are aware."*

He was oddly upset. Never before had he found Nuran to be as beautiful. She was neither the Nuran that he'd seen during the months of fatigue during which they'd arranged for their divorce, nor was she the fiancée who appeared like a white dream behind the mists of years. She was a different woman altogether, one he didn't know, a complete stranger, a woman he didn't recognize despite having lived with her for a decade. *I was so surprised that . . . I wasn't able to speak properly with Fatma . . . I acted as if she were someone else's child.* But was this the real reason he'd behaved so coldly toward his daughter, or was it because of Emma and his fear of aggravating her? *I'm so weak that I'm susceptible to any base folly . . .*

He raised his head and was met by Emma's eyes, which seemingly read from memory everything he'd been thinking. She said: "I understand, Fâhir, if you want to make up with them. I'd never want to come between you and your daughter." And in order to emphasize the resoluteness of this decision, Emma, as if announcing a general strike in the midst of the day shift, rested her fork at the edge of her plate. Her entire face bespoke forfeit and reverence for human emotion. With a habit that came from a lifetime of only pitying herself, her expression changed and contorted.

Emma never asked. She just took. Her experiences as a fallen woman had absolutely forbidden her from asking for anything outright. *Take it, grab it, lay siege, don't let it catch its breath! But above all don't ask!* This was her motto. *Begin with friendship! Always be understanding and patient! A man should sense that you understand him. Then spread your wings, don't give him a chance to catch his breath . . . but ask? Never.* The rich Swede was gradually sensing in his flesh Emma's understanding, her wise compassion, and her generous companionship.

Fâhir gazed at Emma. "What does this have to do with anything, now?"

She understood that she'd made a faux pas. She shouldn't have mentioned anything about the matter! She bowed her head and continued to devour her lobster. Tonight, she had to speak in frank terms with the Swede.

For a week Fâhir had been contemplating what Emma had just suggested on her own. But he couldn't manage to decide, being too insecure, too bound to habit, and because the life into which Emma had initiated him was too exceptional. Not to mention that he had no idea how Nuran would react to such a proposal. Nuran had earlier given him repeated and numerous chances to make up and put the past behind them. *What's really hard is leaving Emma.* Not because he loved her, but because he'd always been a slave to his baser desires. He'd never been a man of determination, nor had he been wise enough to leave her at the right time . . . Not to mention that Emma could display this very determination in his stead. Maybe she'd truly grown tired of him. *Who knows, maybe . . .* He thought about what he could recollect vaguely through the drunken haze of the previous night. The South American captain's chin, hard as a straight razor, and his penetrating glances, appeared. For a time, he and Emma had vanished together. He couldn't manage to extricate himself from the bridge game. *Who knows, and maybe . . .* and like a fresh knife wound, he suddenly recalled memories that constituted the paradise of his life; Emma's full gallop to ecstasy and the frenzied clench of wrestling holds. He raised his head in anguish. He watched, as if witnessing a genuine wonder, Emma's thirty-two teeth grinding up the lobster before her, slowly, quietly, almost as if she were reciting a poem by rote, her eyes exceptionally innocent and languid. The best course of action would be to abandon these meaningless thoughts. He raised his glass. As if to remind her unfaithful lover of the wonderful times they'd once shared, Emma awkwardly repeated the first phrase she'd learned in Turkish: *Şerefinize efendim,* "Here's to your honor, sir."

Her eyes filled with tears of separation that she'd prepared to shed on command. And deep inside she honestly thought: *Over the entirety of my life, I've always been kicked around by people who didn't recognize my worth, haven't I? In Bessarabia, hadn't that landowner done this?* Granted, Emma had made another faux pas then. What call was there to sleep with a stableman, not to mention in broad daylight in the room above the stables? Her entire life had been a chain of misfortunes caused by petty mistakes and lack of foresight. But what could she be expected to do? Men were this way. The landowner, instead of firing his servant, chased her out. The stablehand had pursued her nonetheless. Her fiancé had also left her on account of a similar fiasco. Even if it hadn't transpired exactly the same way, it was close. But that time she wasn't to blame. Her prospective brother-in-law was so much younger than Mihael, they had three sisters between them.

"If it's all right with you, Emma, let's not go anywhere tonight, okay?"

"As you wish, Fâhir . . . You are aware, I'm also quite exhausted, last night . . ." But there was no need to discuss the previous night.

As soon as the words had left her mouth, she blushed. Would they really be staying in tonight? She returned to her lobster in the wretchedness of having to spend the whole evening alone with Fâhir.

Fâhir stared at his mistress with astonishment. He'd never heard Emma complain of fatigue. *And what if I don't actually leave her, that is, what if she doesn't leave and go away!*

"You are aware, Fâhir, you've changed considerably . . ."

But Fâhir wasn't listening. He'd become fixated on the popped button of the waiter's frock. A popped button could at times be a lifesaver. The space of the missing button gave his thoughts unexpected liberty. *Seeing that I'm actually annoyed by these creatures known as the fairer sex, for whatever reason do I bother myself with them?*

Sabih's aunt was a portly lady whose face emanated decency and joie de vivre. For thirty-five years she'd suffered the tribulations of an asthmatic and ornery husband whose temperament altered hour to hour; one by one she'd paid off his debts, the whys and hows of which she was ignorant, and raised four children whose dispositions and morals, her husband in mind, she couldn't trust; nevertheless, she'd married the children off one after another, helped them buy homes and settle down, and now her sole occupation was entertaining visitors in her parlor. In her youth, due to her husband's temperament, she'd nearly pined away for friendships with other young women. For the past seven years, she'd invited countless guests to her house, serving them all the delicacies of a cuisine, the secrets to which very few ladies were privy.

She greeted Adile and Sabih, whom she quite admired, before the garden gate.

"Where on earth have you been, dearest? I've long been expecting you." She felt for one of her triple-tiered pendant earrings. On such days, Sabriye never failed to wear these earrings, which were a gift from her beloved mother-in-law. Since one of the earring's middle pendants had snapped off, she'd tied it back together with a piece of thread. And since she feared losing the large diamond and small ruby that it held fast, she checked it every second. As Sabih kissed his aunt on the cheeks, he looked at the roof of the old gardener's shed; it was still in the same state of collapse as three years ago. Sabriye had no concept of repair or upkeep. In any case, what snapped off and got lost was of a different order than what caved in.

"I've prepared such delicacies for you." Turning to Sabih: "And your dietetic meal is also waiting."

Adile regarded her husband's abruptly puckered face without concealing her delight. "Bless your heart, Auntie," she said. "I was terrified he'd eat something that would disagree with him." Rather than trepidation, her voice quavered with joy.

"My dear girl, would I ever forget about his health? He's my one and only Sabih." Adile, contented with this assurance, walked toward the veranda humming the tango she'd learned a few nights earlier. Sabih was simply up in arms. *I'll show you*, he fumed. *I'll show you all!* And he decided to explain to them from A to Z the recent articles he'd read about the question of Poland in light of German economic needs. At length he would be avenged; this was a point definitely settled.

Had they refrained from plaguing him with a dietetic meal, he would have related what he knew about the life cycles of seals. These sea creatures led lives of true fascination. Indeed, as he read what was written about them in *Lu* magazine, he pondered: *It's as if they're fish in the sea and mammals on land*, and he'd decided to talk about them this way. But now he would mention neither seals nor the unconventional beliefs of the Eskimos – of the puppy who assumed the status of a grandfather because it was born at the exact time of an elder's demise. Now, then, in light of this abrupt announcement about diets, he'd been forced into the sphere of German industry and economy. Scorn welling up within him, and no longer worrying about the possibility of the large diamond pendant falling and getting lost, Sabih glanced at his aunt's ear again. All of his detailed information would flow into that funnel projecting at a forty-five-degree angle from the skull! For long years Sabih had used newspaper accounts as something of a means of compliment or commendation. One day, however, while relating a story of this variety to one of Adile's admirers and habitués to the house, his young interlocutor first yawned to declare his impatience and then stood and left, and Sabih quickly realized that everybody's response to world affairs didn't resemble his own. From that moment onward, he'd labored to all but perfect the impact of this "weapon," which his keen memory and plentiful free time helped him develop.

On the veranda, as always, there were seven or eight other guests. All of Sabriye's children had left the house, surrendering their friends to her. They were all there: Yaşar, her oldest son's piquet partner, who was also Nuran's cousin; Nuriye, her oldest daughter's sister-in-law; İffet, who'd introduced her middle son to gambling, causing him to forgo his studies while he himself finished first in engineering school; and her youngest daughter's high school chum Muazzez. Sabriye had long grown accustomed to filling the void left by her own children, who rarely visited, with this group of surrogates.

As soon as Adile stepped onto the veranda, she exclaimed, "Oh my, Yaşar is with us as well. What a pleasant coincidence, my fine gentleman!"

Yaşar combed his prematurely gray hair with his hand and wiped his glasses clean. Next he greeted Adile with full and proper etiquette. He, at the very least, was a man who was familiar with European customs.

"We were just now together with your cousin Nuran. Oh, how dainty she was, you should have seen her." Then she turned to Sabriye. "And Mümtaz was there, too."

Sabriye harbored great affection for Mümtaz because he'd found her grandfather's name and biography listed in the *Sicill-i Osmanî* biographical register of renowned Ottomans. Informing her by telephone that he'd found the entry, which her late husband had promised to locate for exactly thirty years, on the day after she'd brought it up – Sabriye gave particular import to the fact that this musty, bygone account had been conveyed by telephone – struck her as nothing less than miraculous.

"My word, why didn't you bring him along? I haven't seen him for months, it's a shame really. You see, Muazzez is here as well."

Sabih wanted to forestall the matter before his wife had her chance: "We knew that he was going to meet up with his friends and so we didn't insist."

Muazzez rose from the chaise in which she'd been reclining: "Apparently, Suad is ill. He came back to Istanbul for a week, and he's here at the sanatorium. He was going to meet up with them as well. I saw him on my way here."

Surprised that this entire horde had been transported here by the morning ferries, Sabih nevertheless commiserated: "How unfortunate . . . What's he have, I wonder? I mean, is it serious?" *No, tuberculosis isn't such a serious illness; one just needs to eat and drink nutritiously. My own illness, now that is truly serious. I'm forced to diet.* In no time at all, over the torment of eating buttered zucchini and carrots, a frisson of jealousy would pass through Sabih – for practically everyone Suad encountered would advise him to eat heartily, partake of rich foods, pastries, grilled meat . . . Eat well and you'll be as good as new! *Now then, this Muazzez is an anomaly. How does she know all of this? Wherefrom? How did she learn it all?*

Had it been another day, Adile would have been rather upset at hearing of Suad's affliction. Few people were as peppy as he was and understood the feminine soul as well. But at this instant, just when she was about to let the cat out of the bag about Mümtaz and Nuran, to Muazzez and Yaşar nonetheless, the mention of Suad was an obstacle for which she had no patience. Like a well-trained racehorse, Adile hurdled this unexpected barrier: "To tell the truth, it's not that I didn't consider it . . . But he was so consumed with Nuran that we couldn't get a word in edgewise." And she glanced at Yaşar out of the corner of her eye. She knew quite well that he'd long had affections for Nuran and that he was jealous of her attentions. Not to mention that he'd played a very devious role in her separation from Fâhir by both facilitating the relationship between Fâhir and Emma while relaying daily developments of their affair to Nuran. Yaşar's face turned ashen.

He nearly stuttered: "They've known each other for some time, you say?"

Adile answered in a state of virtual ecstasy, "No, *we* introduced them to each other." Then she turned to face Sabriye and added, "Auntie dearest, you should have seen how they twittered and chirped! Honestly, it pleased me no end. You know, it wouldn't be such a bad turn after all! There's a bit of an age difference, but . . ."

Sabih gawked at his wife in astonishment. In Muazzez's company, she shouldn't have ventured such deceit. Dearest Muazzez was so much younger than the rest of them.

"Who is this Mümtaz anyway?"

"He's a faculty assistant in our department at the university." Muazzez shook her hair in the sunlight, squinting. *He's conceited . . .* Her eyes were fixed perpetually on the large Holland stars in the garden. *Bright red, bright red.* Then she unexpectedly changed her thoughts: "We like him very much, you see." She was crestfallen, quite so. She'd come here because she'd learned from Mümtaz himself that he'd be coming to the island. But she'd missed him on the ferry. *So then, this very turn of events . . .* She glared with spite at Adile from behind the lashes of half-lowered eyelids.

"My good fellow, how could you ever forget him? You know your father's friend İhsan, yes? It's his young cousin. You've seen him at our place countless times!"

But Yaşar had completely forgotten about Mümtaz. From inside the house, the clock chimed one thirty. Time for his tablets. For Yaşar, even the possibility of Nuran's marriage to another man couldn't make him forget his pills. He produced a small vial from his pocket. He carefully removed the stopper; tilting the vial slightly, he dispensed two tablets onto the packaging tissue without touching them.

"Have them bring some water." Then he turned to Sabih. "Incredible boost, my friend," he said. "Vitamins. Since I've started taking them I feel much better, more robust."

Sabih missed the glint of ridicule and contempt in Adile's eyes.

III

As if previously arranged, they met at the ferry landing on the following night. Sabih and Adile were nowhere to be seen and Nuran had left Fatma with her aunt. The redolence of spring wafted over the landing. Almost every passenger carried a large blossoming twig. A few held fresh bouquets of roses. Seemingly, the entire crowd was returning from a great plunder of flowers.

When Nuran saw him in the distance she made a vague gesture with her hand. Mümtaz ambled toward her, pleased by this encounter, about which he had absolutely no foreknowledge, and by her interest in him, which seemed even more improbable.

"I didn't think you'd be returning to the city this soon."

"I didn't either, but here I am. How did you spend your time?"

Apparently she was asking for an account of his day. Looking behind her at all the splendor of the Anatolian coast and its pastel colors that appeared to have been smudged with blotting paper, Mümtaz answered, "We conversed . . . It's what is most readily done in this country of ours, conversing." Then, to avoid being unfair to his friends, he added, "But we talked of good things. İhsan was there as well. We solved nearly half the world's problems . . . Later in the evening we listened to a spectacular *ney*-flute performance!"

"By whom?"

"Artist Cemil, Emin Dede's student! He played the melodies of an array of *saz*-lute instrumentals and old Mevlevî dervish ceremonials."

Both of them glanced about furtively, hoping an acquaintance wouldn't appear and disturb them. Finally, the boarding gate at the dock slid open, they stepped onto the ferry as if they were long-lost friends, and again sat in the lower deck.

Mümtaz: "What'd you do with the young lady? Wasn't she upset when you left her? She seemed rather attached."

"No, I mean, she knew that it was necessary. We're worried about the whooping cough that's spreading through our neighborhood. She spent the entire winter sick besides. She listens to reason when it comes to matters of illness and health."

"Four years ago I'd have already known about it, but now in İclâl's absence . . ." Four years ago he saw İclâl every day, learning of news having to do with Nuran.

Nuran didn't hear this remark; she chased her own thoughts.

"Fatma's a queer child," she said. "She seems to live through the interest shown to her by others. If not for the threat of getting sick, she would have raised all hell."

"I'd have thought you'd prefer to stay with her, too."

A rascal of light falling from one side clung to her hair, slid slowly toward her neck, and like a small creature accustomed to human warmth, tussled playfully on her pale, moonlight-hued skin.

"That was my intention, but then I had an unfortunate encounter."

Only then did Mümtaz realize that Nuran was not as carefree as she'd been yesterday – she was distracted, downcast even.

The distress that had seized Mümtaz when he saw Nuran and her ex-husband at the ferry landing overcame him again. He fell silent for a time, then, ever so thoughtfully, said, "I happened to witness that exchange yesterday. I'd been looking for my friends." He blushed, unable to lie. "I saw your confrontation with Fâhir." Nuran stared at him silently. Beneath her gaze, he was uncomfortable having observed an intimate moment in her life: *Had I not made the decision to confess everything to you, of course I wouldn't have mentioned it!* Then he threw all caution to the wind: "The worst part of all is that as you left the landing you wore such a pleasant expression . . ."

Nuran smiled gloomily: "Why don't you just fess up that you'd waited for me to come out . . . I saw you. Don't blush. Such behavior is typical of you menfolk. But, you weren't able to see the worst part of it! Worst of all was that you didn't come to my aid and take the poor girl from me. The two of us were on the verge of collapse." Mümtaz's face was a swirl of confusion, but Nuran paid no heed. "And equally bad, Fatma was a nervous wreck. Her father had begun to recede in her memory. The girl has an odd sense of propriety. Now she's jealous of his affections. She cried and moaned till morning, 'I don't care if my father doesn't love me! I love him.'" Next Nuran completely changed the subject as if to dispense with the matter then and there: "Is İhsan the İhsan we all know?"

"I'm not sure. Which İhsan is that?"

"During the armistice and Allied occupations after the Great War, while my uncle was working for the Defense of Rights resistance, he said that he helped a certain İhsan. Apparently, he was Nadir Pasha's aide. They tried to frame him with Pasha's death. Even though İhsan could have fled, he's alleged to have said, 'With this shadow of incrimination over me, I won't go anywhere.' My uncle was of some help in saving him from the gallows."

"Thanks to a letter that Nadir Pasha had written him. Yes, that's the same İhsan. But why hadn't İclâl ever mentioned this fact? I've seen your uncle a number of times!"

"İclâl is rather like a writer of realist novels. She doesn't make mention of anything but everyday events."

Mümtaz was dumbfounded.

"That means Tevfik is your uncle . . . and Talât is your great-grandfather?"

"Yes, Talât is my mother's grandfather."

"I've even listened to Tevfik perform once. He recited the 'Song in Mahur' to us. Do you like the piece?"

"Quite . . . very much, in fact. But, you know, it's believed to bring bad luck in our family."

Mümtaz stared at her solemnly: "Do you believe in such things?"

"No, I mean, I never gave it much thought. As with everyone, in many respects I feel an unspecified dread lurking inside me. The effect of the 'Song in Mahur' on me was quite extraordinary. The error of my great-grandmother's ways scared me. Many members of our family have – out of sheer ambition and desire – made those closest to them suffer. Since I was a little girl I've been told that I resemble her, and as a result I've thought about her frequently. Maybe for this very reason I've tried to live rationally rather than through my emotions. But what's the use when fate dictates otherwise . . . My daughter's unhappy anyway."

"And you're related to Behçet?"

"No, only by marriage . . . He was miserable too. I have a photograph of his poor wife, Atiye! It's so bizarre. But let's not talk about such things."

"İhsan loves the 'Song in Mahur.' He practiced it with Tevfik. You realize your great-grandfather's composition is something of a masterpiece."

"He'd intended to write a Mevlevî ceremonial piece, but this composition emerged instead." She closed her eyes. Mümtaz gazed at the ashen sea from the window and watched the sky where tullelike clouds of similar hue loomed large. Then he likened Nuran to the delicate rose saplings in his garden that tended to tremble out of their own frailty in such weather. Light emanated toward them from this tulle-shrouded mass like the portent of pleasures foreign to both. The luminance caressed Nuran's face and hands in an effective state of delight.

"It seems like you didn't sleep at all last night."

"I didn't. Fatma complained throughout the night."

"How did you leave her behind like that?"

"My aunt insisted. She told me Fatma would change once I left. So, I agreed. When I'm with her she acts quite spoiled."

"But you're so distraught . . . If it were me . . ."

"If it were you . . . but you're not a woman, are you?"

"True, I suppose, as long as you don't consider that too great a drawback." He genuinely wanted to share in Nuran's fate and he was extremely ashamed and distressed that he couldn't. This particular affect of his made Nuran laugh. They'd established a friendship of sorts. And this friendship resembled a voyage whose course had been predetermined long beforehand. Their lives were so close to each other.

"You're an odd bird. Are you doing it for fun or do you always have such a childlike nature?" *If he isn't actually a fool.* Mümtaz didn't answer, but smiled.

Later he said, "Would you recite the 'Song in Mahur' for me one day?

I know you have the voice." His thoughts were always with the "Song in Mahur," with this ironic and tragic union of love and death. Nuran quickly responded, "All right . . . I'll sing it for you one day." Then she added, "You know, I don't consider you a stranger at all. We have so many acquaintances in common."

"I feel the same. If our friendship continues, its course will seem preordained."

Then they spoke of completely different things. Mümtaz found her laughter wondrous. He wanted to savor it to the utmost. He recounted an array of stories to her. And he realized, as he spoke, that he was poaching from İhsan's repertoire. *So, I'm still living on the surface . . . I haven't been able to find myself . . .* In fact, he was crossing a vast threshold.

This woman of experience, elegance, and beauty had a quality that was thoroughly radiant and enchanting, as if she were the garden of the sun itself; a realm that he hadn't experienced beforehand, one that he'd assumed had been denied him, but had only actually been dormant and was now prepared to be filled and emptied by her presence. Each notion transformed in the awareness of a brisk awakening, and the small and mysterious contractions emanating from the depths of his being sang forgotten songs of life. This music of silence existed in both, rising to their faces from deep within, and Nuran, frantic to suppress it, appeared more crestfallen than she actually was, while in contrast, Mümtaz, yearning to mask the shyness of his character, forced himself to be bolder and more carefree.

Till now Mümtaz's experiences in love hadn't gone beyond a few random escapades and exploits that were attempts at scattering himself to the four winds. Rather than being instances of the advent of a woman's presence in his life, they amounted to small flings and trivial crushes – various dimensions of his own ennui and passing lust. He hadn't even yet sensed the urge for anything more in his imagination, which centered on himself alone. To him, a woman meant Macide's companionship and the compassion of his aunt, things absent from his life and fulfilled by the two of them between the time of his mother's death and his adjustment to İhsan's household.

Now, sitting before Nuran, Mümtaz noted her sublime attributes with a gaze that transcended petty flings, crushes, lusts, and other commonplaces, and he contemplated how spending his life together with a woman of uncommon beauty seemed impossible. His eyes roamed over her face and hands with a forwardness fostered by a kind of indescribable despair. Nuran attempted to evade these bold glances. Each time he allowed her a moment's peace, she withdrew into her shell embarrassed, as if she'd been suddenly caught stark naked, and to hide herself from the man before her, she frequently opened her purse and powdered her cheeks. Each sensed that a particular fate was being concocted for them and they spoke to each other in intimacies.

Open seas in the offing near Üsküdar had become the waterborne manse of southerlies at eventide. In places between Leander's Tower and the open Sea of Marmara, copper sheets covered with the glitter of an array of hammer-wrought gems had been layered into the watery depths. At times these copper sheets floated to the surface as jeweled rafts; at other times they opened up great, bright crimson abysses filled with yearning and the desire to ascend to a truth like the distant vanishing point wherein light merged in representations of divine grace and absolution by painters of the French Primitif school.

Presently, warm colors attempted every possibility of being, from a spectacle for the eyes to an ascension, a Mi'raj of the Soul.

"It's a very beautiful night," said Mümtaz.

Nuran, not wanting to appear surprised, said, "It's the right season!"

"Its being the right season shouldn't diminish our awe." *Your beauty issues from your youth, but I'm awed nonetheless.* But was she truly beautiful? He wanted to view her at a remove from their present exhilaration. No, he wouldn't say anything. He couldn't even see straight anymore. He couldn't see a thing apart from his own bedazzlement. Not to mention that he'd stumbled upon the mirror of awe within himself. Through this talismanic mirror, he observed what lay inside him, the gradual stirring of desire.

Nuran understood that this response was directed at her and that the invitation that had long been secreted in darkness had now emerged into plain sight.

"That's not what I meant," she said. "I meant to say that from now on we'd share evenings as lovely as this one." She grew frustrated with herself because she'd knowingly uttered this double entendre.

Time remained before the second ferry that would take them up the Bosphorus. They stopped in front of Kemal the bookseller's stand. Nuran bought a few newspapers and novels. Mümtaz observed her as she opened her purse and removed cash. These gestures, repeated daily, now seemed exceptional to him. Not to mention that the bridge had transformed as had the bookseller and the act of buying and reading books. He was seemingly living in a fable, a world in which animated lines and bright colors rejuvenated all, giving everything a meaning that approached the most generous state of grace, where every movement shimmied and wriggled to infinity like the play of light in a still expanse of water. The bookseller returned her change.

Carrying in his arms his own gift and whatever else she'd purchased, they walked toward the Bosphorus ferry landing. They walked in tandem. He'd just come ashore in Istanbul with a woman whom he'd only recognized from afar yesterday on the morning ferry, whose acquaintance he'd made by chance; yet they'd be traveling up the Bosphorus together on another ferry. For him, this was unfathomable. Granted, it was of the variety of everyday events that happened repeatedly; granted, hundreds of thousands of people might experience such feelings once or a hundred times in their lives; it made no difference. He, too, realized that it was a commonplace to fall in love, to achieve happiness, to be acquainted before falling in love, and after having loved, to forget one another, or to even become enemies. But sea bathing was this way, too, as was sleeping. Everything was this way for everybody. That the experience was neither new nor the first of its kind didn't diminish the fervor in his soul. Because it happened to be a first occurrence for him, because his body and soul had come to act in unison for the first time, they'd achieved the satisfaction of complete synthesis and symbiosis. Thus, it was exceptional. But did she think the same way? Was she content as well? Did she yearn? Or was she only humoring him? This anxiety, this doubt, made Mümtaz feel wretched. Why was she so silent? Like one whose feet get entangled in string drawn across a dark path, such a battery of questions prevented him from walking straight. *Ah, if only she'd say something!*

Nuran, for her part, was in no state to utter a word. She wasn't waiting free and easy at the intersections of life like Mümtaz. She'd already lived out one life and had separated from her husband. She might rightly assume that hundreds of eyes were boring into her from this throng. *If he'd only leave. If he'd only leave and go . . . His arrival was so sudden. I need to spend time alone. Who does he think I am? One of those chums of his with whom he gads about?*

I'm a woman who's established her life, only to watch it crumble. I have a daughter. Love, for me, is nothing new. I've passed through this experience so much earlier than him . . . At a place where Nuran might have found a thousand pleasures, she only met with affliction.

Am I to once more pass over roads that I've already traveled? Is there torment greater than this? Why are men so selfish? Why is it that they think we women are as free as them? And she absolutely had to get new shoes. These heels were so cumbersome that they made her look like the dotty teachers back at the girls' academy. *These shoes were only good for an address on women's rights at a protest rally. Not the shoes themselves of course . . . It was evident that shoes couldn't speak . . . How could he possibly find me attractive and elegant in these?*

The girl yesterday morning on the ferry, her lips were as red as pomegranate blossoms, and she faced Mümtaz perpetually. Even I, from where I sat, could see the invitation on her lips, and I grew anxious for her sake. He, however, from his vantage point, strained to see me. He had such a peculiar way of stretching his neck. It was so unbecoming . . . She wanted to say to him, "All right then, move along now, let's go our separate ways here . . . What need is there to insist upon this meaningless affair?" But she couldn't manage it. She knew full well that he'd be miserably heartbroken. And she didn't want to make him sad. Rather, she might, if she could console him by taking his head into her hands, if this were possible, she might do so simply to savor this pleasure. Because cruelty also had its pleasures. She sensed this within her now like an urge. Only temporarily, for a fleeting moment only, of course. Because she couldn't endure too much of it; she wouldn't want too much. It was part of her. And this being the case, she needed to feel happiness and torment together. Nuran would introduce all of it to him; because she was aware of this fact, she found herself strong and ever so powerful. Thus, her smile was as thin as a knife blade. Yet the anxiety within her continued to speak: *Others who see us together, who knows what they'll say? It's so obvious that he's inappropriately younger than me . . . They'll assume I've separated from Fâhir to be with him. I wasn't even the one who separated from Fâhir . . . He left.* If only he'd just go away and let her be.

IV

The Bosphorus ferry held crowds of another magnitude. This wasn't a wealthy, luxurious pleasure ground where every feature was ordered and arranged by money, with wide roads of asphalt and ornamental flower beds like the island, which had emerged abruptly during Istanbul's decline, in so short a time it might be termed a season. No, this was a venue that had lived shoulder to shoulder with Istanbul from the start, had seen its fortunes rise with the city's, and had fallen on hard times when the city lost its ways and means, a venue that withdrew into itself when the city changed its predilections, conserving as much as possible the bygone trends in which it had participated; in short, this was a venue that had experienced an entire culture like a single-minded venture.

In Mümtaz's estimation, one did become somewhat anonymous on the island. That was a place for rather conventional people; one longed for what was actually inessential there, at least for what alienated one from oneself and in the process prevented one from standing on terra firma. On the Bosphorus, in contrast, everything summoned one inward, and plummeted one into one's own depths. Here everything belonged to us, those facets that governed the grand synthesis, including the panorama and the architecture, as temporal as it was . . . those facets that we founded and subsequently came into being along with us. This was a realm of squat-minareted and small-mosqued villages whose lime-washed walls defined Istanbul neighborhoods; a realm of sprawling cemeteries that at times dominated a panorama from edge to edge; a realm of fountains with broken ornamental fascia whose long-dry spouts nevertheless provided a cooling tonic; a realm of large Bosphorus residences, of wooden dervish houses in whose courtyards goats now grazed, of quayside coffeehouses, the shouts of whose apprentice waiters mingled into the otherworld of Istanbul ramadans like a salutation from the mortal world, of public squares filled with the memories of bygone wrestling matches with drums and shrill pipes and contenders bedecked in outfits like national holiday costumes, of enormous chinar trees, of overcast evenings, of eerie and emotive echoes and of daybreaks during which nymphs of dawn bore torches aloft, hovering in mother-of-pearl visions reflected in mirrors of the metaphysical.

Besides, everything on the Bosphorus was a reflection. Light was reflection, sound was reflection; sporadically, here, one might become the echo of an array of things unbeknownst to oneself.

Whenever Mümtaz lent an ear to his early childhood memories and listened to the echoes of the ferry horns that reached him after ricocheting from the surrounding hilltops, he might discern from which wellsprings the incurable *hüzün* within him sometimes rose and flowed forth and made him so opulent amid everyday routine.

The ferry gathered civil servants returning from their city jobs, sight-seers, beachgoers, young students, military officers, elderly women, and congregants on deck, the remorse of whose lives, and the day's fatigue, dripping from their faces, intentionally or not, seemed to surrender to this waning evening hour. Like the potter described by Omar Khayyám, the evening took up all those heads and worked them from the inside and outside, transfigured their lines, painted them, varnished and shellacked them, made their eyes dreamier, softened their lips, and filled their stares with renewed glimmers of yearning and hope. They came to the center of this radiance as themselves, but, as if fallen into the midst of sorcery, they changed with the transformations of light. Intermittently, a guffaw verging on the obnoxious rose from the center of a group; in the distance, all the way at the bow, well-to-do children raised along the Bosphorus played harmonicas and sang songs in callow voices; and passengers who'd grown accustomed to commuting together called out to one another. These were passing interruptions, however. Quiescence, rather resembling expectation, expanded again – its arboreal growth and boundless leaves beshrouding all.

The roots of this tree that traced a bright crimson arc amid the gilded design of a finely wrought Herat bookbinding on the horizon lay in the sun, illuminating golden arabesques in increasing prominence, melding them anew each moment and recasting them in accordance with their own phantasies. From there, the tree flourished branch by branch. Through its radiance, Nuran had become a fruit of arboreal silence, with her stony expression, her small, protruding chin ready to reject him, her narrowed eyes, and her hands clenching her purse.

"So much so that you seem like you're drooping from the boughs of the evening . . . As soon as the light has faded fully, I fear you might fall to the ground."

"In that case, the night will gather all of us at once . . . Because you're in the same state." And that's just what happened. Even before reaching Üsküdar, the roses dusk had cast hither and yond faded and the sea grew wine-dark. The large bound tome with Herat gilding was now a deep magenta cloud fragment. On the tips of distant minarets stirred one or two flights of whiteness like belated birds. The wave of illumination that had engulfed the opposite shore sprawled like the last reverberations of a score of Ottoman music.

As night fell, Mümtaz found a nip of winter yet in the air. With an unsettling sense of cold, he recoiled into himself.

"In winter the Bosphorus has a separate beauty," he said. "An eerie loneliness."

"But you can't quite endure it."

"No, I can't. In order to withstand it, one either has to be thoroughly rooted in life or has to live extravagantly. I mean, one has to have had a sufficient degree of experience. As for me–"

He cut himself off; he was about to say, "I'm still like a child." What was there in his life besides a menagerie of dreams? *Tomorrow, won't you, too, become a dream?*

"You know what one of my favorite things is? Since I was a little girl, closed, darkened windows facing the Bosphorus upon whose panes the light plays . . . lights moving with the ferry and changing from window to window sometimes form arcs of fire . . . but don't bother looking now, since you haven't noticed. Look for them from a good vantage, a little farther on."

Mümtaz was surprised that he hadn't noticed a detail so simple. "The nighttime map of the Bosphorus is a bit like these lights for me. Like what you said . . . One lives here as if in a dream, sometimes becoming part of a fable . . ."

The sentimentality into which they'd fallen threatened to embarrass Mümtaz. The grand sultanate of the night began after Üsküdar. Large blocks of houses, their boundaries marked by street lamps burning bright, were separated by black abysses that made them more foreboding, mysterious, and fabulous than they actually were. This harmony was broken by the lights in public squares before ferry landings that alluded to a life of greater comfort. With almost each of its windows illuminated, a vintage Bosphorus residence passed before them like a behemoth that had long been submerged, having relinquished its mass and density.

"There are quite a few people in there," he said.

In fact, each window framed a few heads. They were huddled together, watching the ferry. The sound of a horn.

"The horns haven't yet reached their summertime pitch . . ."

They shared their observations with one another. They were like two small children. Each observed what passed separately, and spoke only occasionally. Nuran pointed to an unshuttered and blackened window: "See," she said, "how it becomes woven like moiré cloth . . . then the arcs . . . there goes another one, like a falling star . . . a little farther on, close to our house, fishermen's lanterns mingle into these reflections. But the most beautiful of all are these arcs: a calculus of light."

Later they straightened themselves as if from a tome over which they both had been poring and stared at each other. Both were smiling.

"I'll walk with you as far as your house," he said.

"On the condition that you turn back at the head of the street . . . unless you want to give my mother a heart attack."

Mümtaz grew inwardly annoyed. *Her mother . . . Allah, how many obstacles must I overcome?* he thought.

As if reading Mümtaz's mind, she said, "There's nothing much to be done about it; we have to accept our lives as they are. One cannot just do as one wishes . . . D'you know that even at my age I have to give an account of my whereabouts? Had Mother known that I was on my way home, she would have been mad with worry by now. She would have conjured seventy-five different catastrophes for this beloved daughter of hers." Then she abruptly changed the subject. "Do you only like traditional music?"

"No, all of it . . . of course as much as I understand . . . My memory for music is limited and I never studied it. You're also fond of it, aren't you?"

"Exceptionally so . . . In our family traditional music is something of an heirloom," she said. "We belong to the Mevlevî tradition on my father's side and to the Bektashi on my mother's side. Early in the nineteenth century, they say Sultan Mahmut II even exiled my mother's grandfather to Manastır in Macedonia for his involvement in the Sufi order. When I was a girl, every night there were musical gatherings and lots of entertainment."

"I'm aware," he said. "I once saw an old photograph of you dressed in Mevlevî robes. It'd been taken without your father's knowledge."

He took care to avoid uttering İclâl's name. An indication of his timidity. Not to mention that he didn't want to constantly mention another woman's name.

"Of course, İclâl was also . . . ," she said. *For the grace of God, there was nothing sacred to that girl. Those who knew her lived in houses of glass.*

Mümtaz: "But she wasn't the one who showed me the photograph. And, moreover, I myself guessed it was you in the picture."

Nuran never imagined that this memory would transport her clear back to those days. She pictured her father holding a *ney* and sitting on the divan in the large upstairs foyer. "Come, sit down," he gestured, as if inviting her to his side.

Her entire girlhood had passed in a birdcage of melodies made by that flute. The world, which manifested for others through a thousand sensations, manifested for her purely through sound and music. Nuran had embarked on life through a realm of pure imagination like the reflections in the orb of pale glass called "New World" that hung beneath the chandelier in that same foyer. "When that photograph was taken, my father was still alive. Only we weren't living along the Bosphorus then. We were staying in Libadiye. I don't know if you're familiar with the Çamlıca district?"

But Mümtaz couldn't take his thoughts off the photograph. "That's a striking picture. You resemble depictions in old miniatures. Granted, the outfit isn't the same, but you somehow recall a youth proffering a goblet of wine to Ali Şîr Nevaî." He added, laughing, "Where'd you learn to sit like that?"

"Like I said, a legacy from my ancestors. It's part of my being. I was born with it."

Shortly thereafter the third significant event of the day occurred. They disembarked together at Kandilli. As if this was how it regularly happened, they strode together across the wooden planks of the landing. Mümtaz handed the official at the exit both of their tickets at once, and the man took them without a hitch. They continued together across the square. They began to walk up the hill. As they walked, they embraced one another's presence. Nuran's shoe caught on a stone; Mümtaz took her by the arm. They turned left into an alleyway. Next they climbed another small incline. At the mouth of a narrow path he and Nuran parted. "This is our garden . . . The house is on the opposite side. It's best if you turn back," she said.

A street lamp above them illuminated a large chinar as though from within. Beneath this fragrant radiance showering them leaf by leaf, and beside the splashing of a fountain and the peeping of frogs, they took leave of one another. Mümtaz regreted not asking her whether they would soon be able to meet. Within him lurked the dread of never again laying eyes on her. Beneath the burden of such misgivings, he returned the way they had come, slightly remorseful, though enriched countless times over by Nuran's allure, his heart yawning open to companionship of an indeterminate order.

V

Days later Nuran watched İclâl enter the house, giddy and amused. She'd run into Mümtaz at the ferry landing, where they'd sat and had demitasses of coffee together. Afterward Mümtaz accompanied her halfway to the house.

While stepping into the house, she was still laughing at the cock-and-bull story Mümtaz had made up.

Mümtaz, figuring that he was certain to run into one of the two of them there, had practically encamped before Kandilli for five days. Of course, had he wanted to, he could have directly requested a favor of İclâl; or by way of İhsan, they could have arranged to visit Tevfik. However, as he didn't want to bare his emotions to a third party, he preferred to slyly lay siege to the Kandilli shore. It wasn't quite sailing season. But taking a caïque out on the Bosphorus didn't depend on any season. That time-honored means of Bosphorus transport was the solution to any problem at any hour and was sport and entertainment for all. Though a New Yorker born without a Ford or other automobile might seem natural, a child of the Bosphorus born without a rowboat of some sort still seemed an anomaly. For this reason no one was surprised to see Mümtaz in his rowboat drifting around the Kandilli landing. As soon as he woke, he'd jump into the boat, by turns hoist a sail or use the motor to travel to the landing, where he'd try to fish, read a book at the coffeehouse, converse with the elderly gardeners and the neighborhood old-timers, and when he grew bored and couldn't find anything to do on the water, he'd head up the hill, and with the understanding that he would keep his distance from Nuran's house, he'd roam among wildflowers and plants, rambling in the austere winds of the Bosphorus spring.

On the fifth day he reaped the rewards of his vigilance. İclâl was on the ferry. In the joy of this happenstance, he restrained himself from jumping into the air only with great difficulty. He caught up with her at the landing. İclâl hadn't imagined she'd ever run into him there. Mümtaz claimed that he'd arranged to meet a friend who hadn't yet arrived.

Nuran hadn't assumed that Mümtaz would attempt such intricate gallantry. When she heard İclâl's story, she laughed as well.

"Why didn't you bring him along?"

"Honestly, I *did* think of it, but I didn't dare without asking you first."

"I've already met him."

"On the ferry to the island . . . Apparently you were with Adile. She sends her regards . . . She said that if it suits us, we should pay her a visit in the afternoon and that she'd entertain us."

When they came down to the landing, they found Mümtaz paddling lazily to and fro. He greeted them with a chuckle. "I'd hoped you'd come," he said.

Nuran found his face thinner than before and suntanned. When the women boarded the boat, he went to the stern.

"What's this, aren't we going to sail?"

İclâl and Nuran preferred sailing, its thrill, and the slight headiness caused by the waves: the rolling undulations of the Bosphorus shoreline, the off-point moves that recalled dancing with a capable lead, gliding through the sunlight and the sea. But Mümtaz insisted it wasn't the right time for sailing. It was still much too early in the season for them to savor this delight. Not to mention that their clothing might be ruined. They hadn't dressed for such an outing.

İclâl, in her navy blue ensemble, was fit for an afternoon tea party. Nuran had lent İclâl a gray overcoat. She wore a red-striped beige outfit, and the lapel of her jacket revealed a yellow sweater lending the exposed portion of her neck a softer and more velvety appearance. Evidently she'd arranged her hair at the last minute with a few randomly placed barrettes.

Her appearance, rather more striking through this hasty primping, revealed the ambivalence that had persisted until the very last. Mümtaz felt his veins ignite with the desire to sink his face into the nocturne of her hair. Throughout his whole being radiated the fatigue of one who hadn't slept in a dog's age.

İclâl admired the caïque. "I'm no expert, but it's nice," she said.

Nuran completed İclâl's comment as if she were more closely familiar with seagoing: "It's a nice boat; it would stand up well in most situations, fishing, touring, or sailing. And it's quite new."

From the end of the rowboat, Mehmet the oarsman answered, holding the boat by one hand on the quay, "I could go all the way to İzmit with this." The presence and demeanor of the young women pleased him. This was the first time he'd seen Mümtaz, whom he called *ağabey*, with friends of such variety and he was happy for him. But when they stepped into the boat, he started as if a load of glassware had been entrusted to him. His woman was of a different ilk. To his taste, he preferred women like the girlfriend of the coffeehouse apprentice at Boyacıköy. One could rely on them at life's every turn. These women here were probably frail; but he had nothing to say against their appearance.

"Do you like to go fishing?"

"Before my father passed away, we'd go out . . . to be honest, before I got married."

At this midafternoon hour, the wind had seemingly retreated to certain strategic vantage points. First they headed down toward the district of Beylerbeyi. Then they returned by the same route. They passed the villages of Anadoluhisarı and Kanlıca. At Akıntıburnu the wind and the waves embraced them as if they'd actually emerged out into the open sea.

Only an arm's length away onshore were parks, a path where children tried to fly kites, fruit boughs in bloom, and fishermen apprenticing in patience with their poles and lines. Beneath them the sea gushed in vast layers of current, spiriting them through the sounds and scents of bewildering invitations.

Mümtaz was conveying the treasure of his life. For this reason he hesitated. "I'm both Caesar as well as his oarsman. So, this is the outer limit of our excursion."

He'd said this while staring into Nuran's eyes. But Nuran was preoccupied only with the surrounding views and somewhat with herself. Over the past five days she'd come to an array of decisions; on one hand, she found her house and life tedious and grew impatient for the young man's invitation; on the other hand, staring at her daughter's bedstead resting beside her own, she believed that no external force could disturb her own repose. But there it was; after an argument with herself that lasted three hours, she'd gone out. Was she being spineless? Or was it the exercise of one's inborn rights? She didn't know. She only knew that she'd plopped like an anchor into the boat with the weight of her entire existence. On the way back they stopped at Emirgân Park. The season of the café had begun. There were habitués of all ages and walks of life. They partook of the approaching evening and spring with the understanding that they'd simply leave early if the temperature dropped suddenly.

Springtime was intense and tremulous, like a tertian fever during convalescence. Over the extent of the outing, they'd sensed this tremor. Everything melded together in the consternation and excitement of fresh, pliant leaves and bright colors, of the discovery of self and shadow in blazing white radiance. From the hilltops where they'd congregated, the heliotrope, the crimson, the burgundy, the pink, and the verdure assaulted one's casing of skin.

Here, however, at this open-air café, spring was only a small contraction, a yearning for life. They huddled together with hot teas in tulip-shaped glasses, among the crowd, and with that bizarre sensation brought about by observing from the vantage of another shore and in completely new light the places they'd just passed.

"Okay, then, please do tell us why you've besieged the shores of Kandilli?"

Mümtaz bowed his head to hide the blush of his cheeks. "I don't know if you could call it a siege. Access by land is completely open. I only took the ferry landing under my command." He laughed, making a gesture that seemed to say, "That's all I could do. What else should I have done?" Yet his expression declared, "I've suffered through this week." A hint in his laugh revealed that his entire face was prepared to accept this torment, which could only be discerned in the rims of his eyes and his lips.

"Why don't you tell us about the matter of the palace in Kandilli, Mümtaz?"

Mümtaz racked his brain for the information he'd imparted to İclâl that morning. "A vision . . . up in smoke. We began looking for the context of a line of verse. To be honest, now, it was all rather fanciful." But he had to say something more. "There was a date given for the restoration of the palace. Of course, neither palace nor its foundation exists today. Not to mention the old gardens. But the line of verse exists:

Yet again Kandilli of yore showers sparks along the shore

"It's a trick that this line has played on me." Next he talked of the Kanlıca inlet and the Bosphorus villages of Kandilli, Çengelköy, and Vaniköy. He had an odd erudition. Rather than knowledge per se, he was interested in bygone lives. "Indivduals are of paramount importance. What's the rest of it to me? In the furnace of time, an individual's life burns away as quickly as a leaf of paper, perhaps. Maybe life is actually a comic game, as some philosophers maintain; in complete desperation a slew of hesitations and trivial, hopeless defensive stances, even phantasies, under the guise of decisions. Be that as it may, the life of an individual who has actually lived is still of great consequence. Because no matter how comic it might be, we cannot completely reject life. Even through our mental anxieties, we still seek out values in life, whether 'good' or 'bad.' We make allowances for love and desire. We distinguish between living creatively and losing ourselves in petty squabbles and wastefulness."

"Okay, what about action?" Nuran made a gesture with her hand. "I mean in the sense of accomplishment. Challenging oneself on paths of greatness."

Mümtaz was overcome with self-doubt: "There's no path great or small. We only have our pace and stride. Sultan Mehmet II conquered Istanbul when he was twenty-one. Descartes presented his philosophy when he was twenty-four. Istanbul was conquered just once. As is customary, a lecture is written only once. But there are millions of twenty-one- and twenty-four-year-olds in the world. Should they perish because they aren't a Mehmet the Conqueror or a Descartes? It's enough that they live their lives to the utmost. I mean, the magnitude of what you call a path of greatness resides within."

Nuran stared intently at the young man. "But action, you're not discussing action."

"I did so discuss it . . . Everyone's obligated to act. Everyone has his fate. I don't know, I like to live this fate by appropriating aspects of it and its inner world. That is to say, I like art. Maybe art presents us with the most benign faces of death, those that we can acknowledge most easily. Certainly one's life can sometimes be as beautiful as a work of art. When I encounter that . . ."

"For example?"

"Take the poet Shaykh Galip in the eighteenth century . . . He died very young, during his most prolific age. He underwent training and etiquette that constituted a cache of wisdom all its own. From the start, this education forestalled a number of mishaps and detrimental influences. He neither developed through a dawn nor an afternoon. Like a serene evening, he'd already been constituted beforehand by movement, by the play of light, by fealty to what we admire; for example, İsmail Dede Efendi around the same time. He composed close to a thousand pieces of music. Look at his life: like any ordinary life. But it was all his own."

"Doesn't the era itself contribute something?"

"Of course. But the exception transcends the era. One might be tempted to assume that they lived lives of privilege. For example, neither of them attempted to reform the world. Meanwhile, your neighbor of fame, the seventeenth-century preacher Vanî Efendi, did just that, and in the process spoiled everybody's peace of mind and contentment. He was defeated by despair . . . My first two examples are artists who discovered the secret of living in a manner faithful to their inner selves. It seems to me that the others are but deluding themselves."

Mümtaz gazed about as if wanting to escape the convoluted diatribe into which he'd fallen. Dusk began a vast suite of traditional Ottoman music. Every instrument of light prepared to play the swan song of the sun. And every single entity was one such luculent instrument. Even Nuran's face, even her hand fiddling with its coffee spoon . . .

"Do you think we should go somewhere from here?"

"What did you have in mind?"

"Büyükdere or İstinye . . ."

The day was coming to a close now. But he didn't want it to end. Maybe there, farther on, the sunlight would continue.

"Why don't you explain what you mean by despair, Mümtaz?"

"Oh, I don't know. Despair is the consciousness of death, or rather the way death affects us . . . the array of snares it sets in our lives . . . the teeth of a vise that constricts our every move. Every act, regardless of type, is a result of despair. Particularly in this period of open fear that won't scab over . . . One by one, our continual rejection of cherished things. The fear of turning into one's father. And, finally, the realization that whatever one does, death is inescapable. At least, they say, let death catch me at an extreme, while hurtling toward one of the poles: either while singing 'the Internationale' en masse or while goose-stepping . . ."

He himself, at this moment, was somewhat in the throes of this dread. A golden light shone in the house windows of the opposite shore and embellished the Bosphorus waves. He felt that this light alone saved them. Without it, they'd suffocate, they'd be interred at the base of this chinar. He was honestly content and wanted to act within this happiness. Though his old dilemma was afflicting him as well.

Nuran no longer asked any questions. She'd become lost in her own thoughts, resigning herself to the will of the twilight. The fresh air had fatigued her. The following question confronted her ad nauseam: *What will the end result of this ordeal be?* The best thing to do was to forget, to not think about anything. She was experiencing the serene pleasure of surrendering herself to the moment. İclâl, however, ruminated. İclâl wasn't affected by the will of the twilight. She hadn't even once brought to mind the etiquette cultivated by death. The petite, innocent youth, dedicated to everything around her, simply lived. Countless days stretched before her, and she dressed them in her hopes like little puppets. She dressed all of them in the fabric and accoutrements of love, longing, a stable household, of work hours, expectations, and even, if necessary, of toil and of friendship. She knew just how they should be appointed. But she couldn't see their faces; their faces were turned toward the wall known as the future. At the appropriate time, these faces turned backward one by one, faced İclâl and curtsied before her, then slowly and without remonstration removed those exquisite glittering garments, and said, pointing into the distance, "Apparently I'm not the one, it's most certainly another in line," before passing beside her and lining up next to all the rest that had gone beforehand. This very spring was also that way. Spring, the spring she'd so anticipated and longed for in the midst of winter . . .

"Should we visit the historic lodge?" İclâl had suggested this seeing as they were so close anyway.

"At this hour of the evening?"

"Why not? And besides, it's not evening yet. We're in a hollow, so it only seems that way to us. It isn't even six o'clock. Not to mention all we've been talking about. It isn't easy, I haven't seen anyone for almost a week. So much detritus has accumulated in me."

Nuran conjured a vision of Mümtaz, this fellow who repudiated action, afloat in his caïque, blockading the ferry landing. An exertion made out of pure despair. But this neophyte knew how to insinuate himself into a woman's life. She nurtured a strange feeling of compassion and admiration for him. Mümtaz knew how to summon his mate. But how lonely he must be to call out with such patience and force. He should have at least been able to clear his mind.

The lodge wasn't as Nuran had anticipated. It had no grandeur. For his favorite beloved, Sultan Murat IV had merely had this small house built. It was barely large enough for her and Mümtaz to live . . . And this thought endeared the lodge to her. She wanted to commit the floor plan to memory, because it might be of use one day. At least while lying in bed tonight as she thought of Mümtaz. Mümtaz informed them that this must be the

Bosphorus overlook of the original structure. "Maybe the woods above had first belonged to this property." Even if that wasn't the case, another, larger manor house certainly once stood here.

Nuran roamed about trying to read the old Ottoman calligraphy on the wall panels and watched her apparition hover in antique mirrors of time past. The peculiar redolence of the historic lingered everywhere. This, our scent within history, was so reminiscent of who we were.

Nuran tasted of this elixir distilled from the alembic of ages. Mümtaz's imagination churned elsewhere. It cast Nuran as a beloved of old, like a favorite odalisque of the age of Sultan Murat IV. Jewelry, shawls, fabric adorned with silver embroidery, Venetian tulle, rose-peach slippers . . . a mound of cushions surrounding her. And he revealed his thoughts to her.

"You mean, like an odalisque, is that so? You know, the kind painted by Matissse?" And she shook her head as she laughed. "No, thanks. I'm Nuran. I live in Kandilli, in the year 1938 and I wear more or less the fashions of my day. I have no desire to change my style or my identity. I'm not in a state of despair, not to mention that these mirrors give me a feeling of the forlorn."

Despite this, she didn't want to leave. As she wandered the lodge, she acquired a taste for its pleasures. Here existed the beauty of simplicity. It wasn't overwrought with excess and opulence like the châteaux at which she gazed in photographs in *L'Illustracion* or English magazines. This was an abode of integrity. It was as overwhleming as the colors of an Indian sari, ornate and shimmering with unrefined gems, or the songs taught to her by her father . . . and she heard the remorse of those songs within herself.

They stepped outside. "What shall we do now?" said İclâl.

"We'll go home. This man overcome with despair will accompany us as far as the hill. As a reward for troubling him so, we'll give him a little sustenance. He might have been dying of hunger over the last five days. Afterward, if he so desires, he can continue his blockade of the landing."

As she spoke, she watched Mümtaz's expression, feeling viscerally the heat of the moment when they had kissed before a tarnished mirror awhile beforehand. Within the waters of the mirror – in whose depths slept reflections of the lives of hundreds of people she'd never known or seen – their heads and hands had unexpectedly united. So abruptly that it had startled them both. And Nuran's jubilation arose somewhat from the desire to conceal this astonishment.

Almost no further conversation passed in the caïque. Mümtaz's feet rested in the hole at the stern as he skippered the motor. The Bosphorus was enveloped in dense silence, a quiet that seemed to embalm them. Instead of being engulfed by the setting sun, these three apparitions were wrapped in golden, honey yellow, and purple ribbons. Nuran disrupted the serenity first, perhaps aware of how brazen she actually was. Or maybe she wanted to further plumb the depths of the man who was attracted to her. "Honestly, you don't have any aspirations to accomplish anything grand?"

"Not grand . . . but you know I have a job. I do that, nothing more."

He was intimidated by greatness. That was something quite sinister. Because more often than not it occurred by stepping beyond the bounds of life. Or else one lost the capacity for freedom of thought, becoming the plaything of historical events.

"In that case, one gets lost in the tangled web of one's own self or of events. In reality, in this concert performance of sorts there's nothing grand or trivial. There's only everything and everyone . . . just like the current surroundings in which we find ourselves. Which of these waves or reflections of light could you dispense with? They glow and die out on their own . . . They come and go, the loom weaves continuously. But why is it that you seek greatness and not just satisfaction?"

Nuran's response surprised him: "People are more comfortable engaging in such pursuits."

"But, then, those around them become more uncomfortable!" said Mümtaz.

They pressed onward, to where the Bosphorus met the Black Sea, taking in the nightfall to its fullest extent. İclâl had sunk into daydreams. A house of her own, work, considerable work, responsibility, accounting, long waits, children's clothes, food and meals . . . From time to time she'd escape them all to contemplate Muazzez. Nuran and Mümtaz were involved. She'd gathered this much. Would she reveal this to Muazzez? Her good friend might actually harbor a fondness for Mümtaz. The only place she herself could permit such affections was in her soul, filled only with the lives of others . . . *No, I can't tell her anything!* But the news was exceptional. *For once in my life I'd have outdone her with this tidbit.*

That night Mümtaz wasn't able to lay eyes on Nuran's house, which he'd so often conjured in his mind's eye. On the walk back, Nuran, taking advantage of İclâl's fiddling with her shoe, had discreetly conveyed to Mümtaz that it wouldn't be fitting for him to come to the house. Her earlier boldness vanished when they entered her neighborhood.

"I'll phone and come pay a visit," she said. But to stay with him a while longer, she suggested he accompany her to the pistachio trees, where they waited together for night to descend fully. There, Mümtaz listened once more to Nuran's rendition of Talât's remorseful "Song in Mahur," along with a piece by İsmail Dede Efendi in the Sultanîyegâh *makam*.

VI

Nuran arrived on the appointed day. Mümtaz recalled that day many times afterward. Its memory was both a dagger twisted into his chest as well as a garden of the purest gold. He hadn't forgotten a single detail. During days of torment, or times he noticed Nuran's indifference toward him, one by one he'd recount these details, reliving them.

Till then he'd only regarded Nuran from a distance as an alluring apparition. But from the moment she'd whispered into his ear on the road, "Don't come now, I'll phone and pay a visit," this alluring apparition, this creature of distances had suddenly transfigured. As if these words, percolated into his ear, were an occult spell, feelings that had a second beforehand functioned solely to embellish, deepen, and enrich each passing moment abruptly assumed the force of fiery humors.

Until that moment, the young man was satisfied simply by the presence of this beautiful woman, and when she departed, melancholy descended over him, yet he couldn't imagine her as a part of his life. His feelings for her had only recently met with the catalyst of his imagination. These feelings amounted to elegant phantasies, trivial infatuations, posturings, and passing lusts. And a relationship could be established, one could love and go his separate way like this. Encounters of this variety included eating a table d'hôte meal, sleeping in rooms of the same hotel, traveling together by car, or laughing and being amused by a play or film.

Mümtaz had had his share of these types of relations. But everything had changed the moment he'd felt Nuran's face and lips pressed to his ear and, in such proximity, sensed her voice inflected by desire. From that moment onward, his imagination blazed. That large and astonishing forge, each second and within his very person, fired and produced an array of semblances of Nuran. These spasms amounted to a process of discovering himself within a state of shock or a new order and harmony.

Nuran's breath surging through his veins ushered in a chain of balmy, redolent springs; desire and lust for life flowed from him toward her, like herds of thirsty animals migrating to cool springs in midafter-noon swelter.

Harboring the mystery of existence, organelles whose very presence was beyond doubt had come alive within the body. Mümtaz, respresenting an iota of being, now felt himself to be as vast and infinite as all Creation. Through Nuran's presence he'd discovered his own existence.

He lived in a universe made up of an array of mirrors, and in each he saw another Nuran who constituted but another facet of himself. The trees, the water, the light, the wind, Bosphorus villages, old make-believe *masal*s, the books he read, the roads he wandered, the friends with whom he spoke, the covey of pigeons that fluttered above him, the buzzing summer insects whose bodies, colors, and life cycles mystified him were all manifestations emanating from Nuran. It all belonged to her. In fact, he languished under the sway of a spell conjured by his being and his imagination. Simply because that bewildering and opulent feminine creature, that profound nature so different from man, had momentarily transferred the heat of her being through his ear.

Bizarre visions plagued him through the night. He was to marry Nuran. Such a love couldn't just be left to chance. Mentally, he prepared his house. He sought out additional means of support. Finally, when on the verge of completing a long European travel itinerary, his eyes closed in Norway to apparitions of them arm in arm, watching the Mi'raj of Light in a fjord. But were they actually in Norway or in another spot in the world? Moreover, it seemed to him that they were passing by Anadoluhisarı on the Bosphorus, and he jerked awake in uncertainty. After that, he slept through a chain of similar fitful spells of lost consciousness. Nuran's face, her smile, or unforgettable aspects of her mannerisms disrupted the nuances of a new dream, at which point Mümtaz would shudder awake, and the phantasies that he'd conjured in his previous interlude of wakefulness persisted. In this fashion, he passed the night living a novel that paralleled his own life.

Unable to keep still, he rose at whiles, roamed about the room, smoked a cigarette, or read a page or two of a book. Then he'd get back into bed and try to sleep. Soon the same apparition appeared before his eyes with the same clarity, breaking the flow of the dream that he couldn't comprehend, and Nuran would emerge abruptly from the downstairs foyer mirror, or the plum tree in the yard would assume her form, or he'd encounter her in one of the rooms of his childhood and when her face assumed its full definitiveness, he'd find himself awake in his bed with the following thought: *Tomorrow she will come* . . .

Before then Mümtaz hadn't fully savored the magic of the word tomorrow. His life had only passed in present days. After the serious illness he'd suffered while a student at Galatasaray, thoughts of the past that had poisoned his childhood had diminished. Now, the word sparkled like a jewel within him: *Tomorrow.* Mümtaz sensed a spiritual opulence within, as if the sun, a golden egg within his own self, would bring creation itself to light from his own being . . .

Tomorrow . . . an astounding, enchanted portal. A gateway that opened onto age twenty-seven, upon whose threshold he slept tonight. No wonder he was so frantic. For behind this door also loomed Nuran. She possessed both mysterious and familiar allures . . . a gentle voice, a warm laugh, and other aspects whose elixir she dispensed at will – one as scarlet as murder, as searing as fire, and, oddly, as soul-stirring as light cascading from multicolored panes along with Koranic chants in ancient mosques. Beyond that was her life, into whose intimacy he desired access, his existence poised to merge with hers. The breezes of how many mountaintops, the waters of how many rivers and springs, how much longing and eternity would thereby achieve a union complete?

He could withstand it no more. As if he didn't want to miss a second of this vast and peerless tomorrow, he sprung from bed. He opened the balcony door; dawn had broken. Fog covered all. Creation was yet working the loom of genesis within the pearl of time. Only the opposite hilltops – removed from actual realities as hermetic forms and giving the sensation, as one gazed, that they might reveal the secret cipher of the origins of all things – floated above this shroud of icy sparkle like a phantom ship. Farther in the distance, a cluster of trees shimmered with more grace and flourish than they actually bore under the first shafts of sunlight that managed to reach them through an atmosphere thick with humidity.

But the Bosphorus remained hidden. It flowed quietly beneath a thick foglike shroud of genesis. Toward the seafront of the village of Beykoz, this shroud accumulated more density.

By the time he sauntered down to the ferry landing, it was at least seven o'clock. The proprietor of the teahouse waited until the sun made its full appearance before setting out tables and chairs. The seawaters were crystal clear. In places within the sea, whorls of light that resembled the memory of color more than color per se constituted a realm of unadulterated, crystalline essence.

Into this twilight world a crimson motorboat, whose flat stern indicated that it had been made in Sürmene on the Black Sea, appeared unexpectedly before him only to vanish within a sense of detachment caused by having issued from the indeterminate. Calmly, the phantom of a more fantastic, narrower-hulled caïque followed in its wake as if it were a manifestation of spirit in a world of ideal forms. Like all phantasms and ideas born of the moment, they appeared ephemerally, then, as if the celluloid of the mind had snapped to be spliced elsewhere, another snippet began to play. Most disconcerting of all was the commencement and cessation of voice and sound.

Mümtaz strolled until he reached Boyacıköy. There he sat at a small seaside fishermen's coffeehouse. The view before him dilated or contracted depending on the direction he walked. In this miraculous play of light, rowboats, motorboats, and fishermen's caïques full of lobster traps, each had surprising qualities based on their distance from him. One or two neighborhood youths and a few fishermen lolled about the coffeehouse. Mümtaz went to one of them, requesting that he inform Mehmet of his arrival. Then they began talking about this and that. Mümtaz's impatience, however, prevented his remaining in one place for too long. Nuran was en route. This idea stupefied him. He could only take his thoughts to this threshold. But as soon as he arrived there, he shuddered as if an abyss yawned at his feet.

He remained in ignorance of what lay beyond. What lay beyond was a radiant chasm where colors seemed to meld, into whose aurora he and Nuran vanished.

At such a moment so personal and particular to him, Mümtaz was surprised to be engaged in everyday conversation with others. Stranger still, no one sensed this state of exception in him. All the characters remained the same. Grinning, the old coffeehouse proprietor was pleased at having overcome the sciatica that had afflicted him last winter while fishing for swordfish. His apprentice must have made up with his lover, Anahit – who'd made a custom of returning to her beloved after lengthy breakups spent recuperating from the fatigues of love – judging by the way he swayed afoot sleeplessly and wearily, like a rudderless boat without sail, lost in the mists of last night's bedroom pleasures, which had yet to dissipate. A pair of fishermen mended a net heaped like a mysterious sea creature, crouching before cork buoys and blackened ropes. All about them, seaweed, shellfish, and the briny tang of the deep sea grew thick. Each member of the group posed questions to Mümtaz and listened to his answers. But none of them knew what he thought. Maybe they were aware of it, but they gave it no import. For him to have a woman, to be loved by a woman, was such a natural occurrence that had begun hundreds of thousands of years before him. Though, like death and affliction, it happened only when it was felt in one's own person . . . and perhaps because of this, it also served to alienate him from the surroundings.

Amid these thoughts, Mümtaz looked at Sadık from Rize, Remzi from Giresun, Arab Nuri, who was the seventh generation from Hisarlı, and Yani from Bebek. All were products of this experience: these wizened faces and calloused hands, these men who appeared to know nothing but the sea, fish, waves, sails, and nets, with him standing beside them – a youth with the countenance of Andrea del Sarto's black-haired, Renaissance Madonnas, a youth whose swimming trunks were wound scarflike around his neck. They'd all either had the experience or were preparing to have it.

Oddly enough, despite the same mechanisms churning within them, they were oblivious to the very aspect of Mümtaz to which they could most relate. No, sitting and talking to them was futile. These men were his friends. Like this coffee-house, these nets, these masts leaning against the wall, the mosque up ahead, and the fountain, they were all his friends, including even the black, curly-coated puppy that waited for him each morning at the landing and followed him here, and might even accompany him all the way back to the house. Yet today, Mümtaz was alone in his joy and this would always be the case. In the future, he'd be alone in his misery, nothing but a riddle, a mystery to his friends and acquaintances. Or else he'd become nothing but a lone cipher flung to life's periphery, and on another day, when he died, he'd die in the same fashion, alone.

He rose slowly. He entered the sea from a rowboat at the dock. The fog persisted, though not as thickly; light shone as if distilled through a pearl-hued alembic. Cold salt water washed away the fatigue of a night poorly slept. In a friend's rowboat, without a thought for whom he'd donned the regalia of fleeting thoughts or rather apprehension, he went as far as the Emirgân ferry landing. And later, with his wet trunks in hand and the black-furred pup behind him, he walked home. The puppy was beside itself, overjoyed by this friendship; it not only traced circles around Mümtaz but made strange barks, small yelps, and growls as it loped along. *At least he knows how to express his joy.* Humanity couldn't be fully content; this was impossible. What with thought, settling accounts, and anxiety. Especially anxiety. Humans are creatures of anxiety and fear. *What great miracle could save us from this fear?* But at the moment Mümtaz was simply full of bliss. Even if it came amid a host of thoughts and experiences that weren't his own, he was blissful. Yet, in the middle of the hill, he was lanced by dread. The scales of the balance suddenly tipped in the opposite direction: *What if she doesn't come . . . or if her visit isn't fulfilled . . .*

Opening the door, he invited the dog inside. The animal didn't enter. He'd only once satisfied himself by being a guest in this house for three days. Then he'd reclaimed his freedom and gone back to the hollow at the base of the large chinar where he'd come into the world. He preferred to wait there for Mümtaz and to accompany him on walks.

And now it was outside, two paws on the threshold, wagging its tail, cocking its ears, asking to be played with a little or spoken to. Mümtaz had no choice but to go inside, leaving the door open. The dog placed its head on the threshold like a bygone lover of a traditional romance and stretched out before the door. Friendly peeps and growls emanated from its throat, and its eyes languished in the anticipated pleasure of reunion.

Nuran arrived amid such commonplaces. By the time she'd come, the dog had long gone. Mümtaz, distraught with impatience, waited for her before the door wearing his blue shirt and wrinkled pants. From the hill, she entered through the door breathlessly.

"Allah! What a steep hill," she said.

She'd debated with herself for three days. She believed that the whole affair was quite unnecessary; distressed, she worried about where this step might land her. She was standing before a shroud of mystery. Should she draw it open, the universe would become a muddle. She acknowledged an attraction to Mümtaz. Something within her, which she liked to think was novel, awakening to the boundlessness of indeterminate hopes, to the warmth of presence in life, persisted in drawing her to him. Despite this, at the same time, she'd been hampered by an array of obstacles.

Over this three-day period, the specter of her great-grandmother never left her. The lady in the faint daguerreotype that she'd discovered in the old hope chest when still a little girl; the lady with her long white cloak and semitransparent veil-cloth, with her pallid, moonlight-hued face, and the eyes of a gazelle startled at the edge of a precipice; the lady who inspired in her such mysterious desires, who'd cultivated the pleasures of time past, and who'd turned traditional music and song into a veritable clime wherein Nuran could thrive, now attempted to deny her the measure of her intimate life. Seemingly, this faded picture incessantly came alive saying, "I was the object of much affection, and that's what led to my ruin. Because I loved and was loved, all those who depended upon me were condemned to misery. With one of your closest relatives as such an object lesson, how do you dare?"

Yet, it wasn't only her great-grandmother's voice or presence that spoke to Nuran. A secondary, deeper and more complex voice emanated from the depths. And this second voice addressed Nuran's heart and soul. It spoke through the cacophony of the treacherous awakenings of her heart and soul. This was the sound of the mixture of bloodlines coursing through her veins. Sacrificing everything at once for the sake of love and desire, the lifeblood of her great-grandmother Nurhayat – charging at full gallop – and the lifeblood of her great-grandfather Talât, prepared to burn in Eros's forge like an object of sacrifice; and later still, her father's lifeblood mixing in with these two, which, after ripening through thousands of manly exploits in Ottoman borderlands, in the Balkans, along the shores of the Black Sea, and stunned at having unexpectedly landed in Istanbul during the Crimean War, exchanging struggles in the name of freedom for a demure and diminished existence, his lifeblood becoming the willing captive of the sybaritic pleasures of ages; all of it constituted an exceptional, rather rarefied admixture. In one strain, purity of adventure; in another, purity of resignation, compliance, and subservience. That second voice articulating itself within Nuran in myriad accents was nothing but the voice of this mixed bloodline. Nuran carried this blood within herself for years like a pernicious legacy, trying to restrain and reject it. But on the second encounter with Mümtaz on the island ferry, she simply surrendered, for fearing something resembled the expectation of its arrival. Perhaps Nuran had enabled the awakening of this legacy within her through her own inner fear. That's why she'd made a throaty recital of the "Song in Mahur" for Mümtaz on the ferry after his initial request, without even eliciting so much as a "please" from him! – shameless! – and she'd furthermore sung that song in the Sultanîyegâh *makam* on the hilltops of Kandilli. This blood was a strange brew. It'd been beaten to froth by the odd whisk of that musical genre known as *a la turca*.

The "Song in Mahur" – a family heirloom with its periodic turpitude and keepsakes of cruelty, with its torments resembling the return to a primordial, primitive state of sorts – created an abyss through twin legacies, an abyss now yawning within her and summoning her. When Nuran pondered her great-grandmother's life, how astonishing it was indeed that the lady who'd provided her with such models of etiquette spoke in a completely different idiom whenever Nuran evoked this song, after which, from the small and faint, austere picture in its chipped, gilded frame, this matron now glared at her life with eyes of rebuke, and passionately overwhelmed like an autumn prepared for burial beneath brittle leaves before the image of her existence, she abruptly cast off her former penitence, resuscitated by the semiferal beauty recounted by the elderly ladies amongst whom Nuran was raised, to begin an eternal fire dance in the furnace of her affections and lust for life. "Join in!" she demanded. "Join in the steeplechase, burn and live! Because love is the perfect form of existence . . ." Even more astounding, her great-grandfather with his downtrodden and subjugated spirit accompanied Nurhayat in this fire dance, an all but primitive rite, and was prepared to again endure all his suffering. Indeed, he didn't speak deliriously and desirously through a bewitching aura like Nurhayat, and he couldn't perform the fire dance with the same agility. He, however, stoked the fires with his own torment like a sappy, greasy log smoldering in a hearth of anguish. "Seeing as you bear my blood, you too shall love and suffer one way or another! Don't try to deliver yourself from fate in vain!" And he went even further, asking: "Haven't you waited your entire life for this?" These were two people who knew nothing of decorum! "I've come here all the way from Hell's half acre to burn in this fire! I've been cast about by countless winds. I've dried off beneath sunlight on nameless shores . . ." And as Nuran listened, she remembered what Mümtaz had told her under the tree in Emirgân, that his fate seemed to have ordained everything beforehand. "Who knows," he'd said. "Maybe because I denied everything from the past during my childhood, I cherish the past now. Or else there might be a different reason. We were peasants three generations ago. We're completing a process of acculturation. My mother used to like music in the old style. My father, on the other hand, understood nothing of it. I could say that İhsan is something of an expert in music. I, on the other hand, have included it in my life. Hasn't it been this way throughout history? Yes, perhaps I'm living the fate of a people. Do you want to know what I really think? Until our music changes organically on its own, our station in life won't change. Because it's impossible for us to forget it . . . Until it transforms, our singular fate will be the fate of love!" When she heard this, Nuran had grown annoyed with him, because, staring into her eyes, he'd spoken of love while in İclâl's company. But, now, she understood him. She saw a figure much like her great-grandfather in Mümtaz. He'd also uprooted himself and come here for the sake of searing experience.

Amid the debate that raged within her, Nuran observed her life and surroundings through new eyes, realizing how this bizarre family legacy regulated her private life and how her great-grandmother's gravity ruled her. Not just her, the entire family. A bygone venture in love, a date torn from the calendar guided them all, preparing individual sorrows for them and their acquaintances in accordance with each of their dispositions. It was her turn. Hers and Mümtaz's! Their shadows would flit and dart inside the golden cage that was the "Song in Mahur."

Nuran knew that she'd pay a visit to Mümtaz from the first day. Not because an available young gentleman had invited her. Mümtaz's voice by itself was inadequate to the task. An entire heredity, which made this love her singular fate, drove her there. Others had hollowed out their lives running away from it. Nuran's mother had been this way. Not once in her life did she laugh openly, acknowledge an innuendo freely, or expose her feelings; she hadn't even once kissed her children passionately. "Above all, a woman should know how to restrain herself, darling!" It was the first piece of advice she'd heard from her mother, who'd involuntarily always been cruel and had verged on oppressing her father – who loved her dearly and had to feel emotion to know he was alive. Her uncle Tevfik's petulance arose on account of her mother. And the inappropriate affections Tevfik's son Yaşar harbored for Nuran – so disquieting under the same roof – again were of the same origin. Nuran, too, had grown up with fear. Out of a coterie of young suitors that she could have loved, she'd married Fâhir, whom she knew she'd be able to love under the assumption that they'd somehow manage through the foundation of a good friendship. And her daughter, Fatma, even now, prepared for a similar fate. Her overzealous dependency on Fâhir and Nuran, the sensitivity and jealousy, were all traces of a legacy, an overwhelming burden that Fatma bore, too. It was anyone's guess how miserable Fatma would become. Nuran, perfectly aware of this, took it all into consideration. Yet she also accepted life as it was. Because life could afflict one if it so desired. After Talât's ordeal, a peculiar fanaticism against divorces seized the entire family. Nothing was considered as disgraceful as divorce. For this reason, most of the bridegrooms who'd married into the family began gallivanting and misbehaving, because they knew upfront that their indiscretions would be forgiven. Some even left wives wanting for a scrap of stale bread. This zealotry took hold not only among the women but among the men as well. Tevfik lived with a woman who openly despised him, her husband of thirty years, because she considered him to be more attractive than her. Despite all of this, you see, Nuran divorced Fâhir. The first instance of divorce in sixty years had been enacted by Nuran. But this legacy, or social etiquette, didn't exist only in their household. There were various martyrs in every branch of this sprawling family: Behçet, Atiye, Dr. Refik, and Salahaddin Reşit, who'd met his demise in Medina, among them.

Nuran politely listened to this harsh tirade within herself for three days. On the evening of the third day, after concluding, *I'm not obligated to give an account of my actions to anyone!* she called Mümtaz. And the next morning, so as not to keep him waiting, she left the house at an early hour. In the end, Eros, like Thanatos, was one of the formative forces of life. On the way there, amid visions of Mümtaz, she began to murmur the "Song in Mahur":

And you left even my soul full of yearning . . .

Recollecting the song's ill fortune, however, she didn't continue on to the second verse. She even forewent singing the middle part and the refrain, which she so loved. At the ferry landing, a petite, muddy-faced street waif approached. She wore a filthy, torn print dress and stretched out her hand like a wooden spoon spattered with drying food. Piping, "May Allah bless your beloved!" the urchin asked for change. As Nuran opened her purse, she thought, *I wonder if everyone can read where I'm going from my face?* She verged on tears. She was in the midst of doing something she hadn't done in her adolescence or youth. *Should I return?* she thought, roaming before the ticket window. But love tempted her through the mystery of the unknown. "I've bought some new Debussy. You have to come . . ." he'd said on the telephone. To admire Debussy and Wagner yet to live the "Song in Mahur" was the fate of being a Turk. As she waited for the ferry, she recalled what İclâl had imparted to her that night after she'd parted from Mümtaz. "If he'd let himself relax, he could be a lot of fun, because he's likable. But he seems to jumble and confuse everything together: love, art, history, and physical pleasure! He could only be enamored of a woman like you." So, then, İclâl had sensed this as well. As Nuran waited, she gauged her impatience. *Is it because I'm bored that I'm doing this? Or is it only a matter of physical desire?* But she couldn't recall being bored at any moment since they'd met. She was comfortable, completely at ease. As she boarded the ferry, she thought, *Come what may, I won't be defeated by myself!* And only by dint of this resolve did she smile at love and the image of Mümtaz.

She gazed out the window at Akıntıburnu. Here and there hovered slight patches of mist. But the Bosphorus slid by like a soaring bird. She watched the elation of waters beneath vernal sunlight. *I'm so reckless! The whole family's foolhardy! Great-grandmother and great-granddaughter, we've fallen for two jesters, two aimless men. One* can *structure life through one's volition . . .*

For Mümtaz, the day delivered delicacies he'd never before tasted. For the first time in his life, a woman revealed the mystique of her intimacy to him. She was neither a goddess nor just any creature with a passion for the tryst. She relinquished all of herself, surrendered the measure of her essence like a garden, to the mate her body had chosen, and laid bare her every secret and potential with a "there you have it, this is who I am . . ." Still, what she was, this self, constituted a realm opulent and exceptional – how many would die without discovering such sublimity. Neither undersea treasures nor the opulence of fables could have been so extensive and astounding. Later Mümtaz would frequently recall when he first caught sight of her stark-naked figure in the twilight of the tightly shuttered room. She delivered starlight and the sparkle of bejeweled affluence. This bacchanal of light, both its eulogy and its worship, was constituted by moments of bedazzlement and blaze in which the fire stirred and leapt into flames a thousand times over from its own ashes. It was a Mi'raj of Harmony made by the corporeal in concert with the soul – such that one sensed the ascension without being cognizant of the heavens to be attained.

162

When Mümtaz gazed upon his inamorata, he'd invariably think of this day, and ponder at length which of the forces of fate had united them.

He wondered where and in which unfathomable depths it had been conjured: all decency, beauty, and simple essence, the soft suppleness of skin, the heavy breathing summoning arcana from the occult of genesis concealed in her body, and her physical presence in its substantiation cascading toward him from the darkness of mysteries; now tenderness, now caress, now stupor like another simulacrum of death, and then facets that were the pleasure and elation of resuscitation and resurrection under the orient of the sun; that is to say, contractions, spasms, and depletions that resembled the self-worship of her being in the Mihrab of the Sun. These profound unions, and upon their release the wellspring of yearning, couldn't be contained by a single existence alone. They could only be the result of forces conjured in a remote and dark epoch before human cognizance or even existence. Nature on its own couldn't achieve this intimacy. Happenstance alone wasn't enough to enable the discovery of another within one with such impact.

Nuran's every aspect drove Mümtaz wild on that day. Her amorous surrender to love in expectation of pleasure, a moored vessel in calm harbor waters; her face veiled like a somnolent Istanbul morning; smiles emerging seemingly from beyond the present moment; each constituted a distinct delicacy and as he partook of them, the infinity manifest in one being awed and surprised him, as did the suddenly changing, incrementally waning rhythm of time: the consecutive descent of eternities. From that day onward, within him, a peculiar feeling of devotion transcending all other feelings began toward the woman whose greatest secret rested in simplicity. He discovered her slowly and gradually, like a landscape, and as he did so his admiration and worship intensified.

Mümtaz never thought he could be so amorous and Nuran, so adored. Sümbül the maid had made all preparations the night before, leaving early the next morning. They took their meal downstairs in the kitchen, after which Nuran prepared demitasses of coffee. Catching sight of her in the old kimono – which Mümtaz didn't realize had been in the house, though it was certainly Macide's – of her skin through parting folds, and of the statuesque form of her figure; watching her as a luculent form in one or another posture . . . these amounted to gradual and sweet inebriations.

Mümtaz had planned an after-dinner tour by rowboat, but the young lady deemed it inappropriate to appear together in public. Not to mention that Mümtaz was besotted by Nuran's nakedness, as were the very mirrors within the silent house that they had all to themselves. The walls, the ceilings, each piece of furniture seemed to have taken benediction from a sacrosanct visit.

Besides Nuran's semblances of beauty, Mümtaz savored the pleasures of observing her appropriate the household.

"From the first day I came, I liked it," she said.

Finally, toward nightfall, they resigned themselves to parting company. Mümtaz accompanied her half the way back. According to Nuran, his presence beside her would be a risk. So-and-so might see them. When her shadow disappeared at the bend in the road, Mümtaz shuddered not knowing what he would do next.

That summer was the apex, the pinnacle, the crowning jewel of Mümtaz's short life. Nuran wasn't only becoming, affectionate, and the object of his attentions, she was a friend and confidant. She displayed uncanny skills of perception and tried new things with grace and discernment. She understood music well and had a voice filled with swaths of sunlight, lucid and nearly bass.

Beyond these qualities, Mümtaz was enraptured by her peculiar shyness and purity of spirit which no sin or sybaritic pleasure could undo. At the end of the season, even when she most assuredly belonged to him, their love remained as novel as during initial days, and the particular embarrassment of couples who'd just become acquainted still entered into their intimacy. Mümtaz spared no effort to prevent the dissipation of her bashfulness and innocence.

Not to say that Nuran recoiled before life or exhibited timidity in the true sense. On just her second visit, she'd learned about his research interests. Mümtaz enjoyed debating every aspect of life with her. This same graceful reticence, along with the sense of measure that constituted one of Nuran's main attributes, was also at play here. Nuran hadn't tried to manage Mümtaz's existence in any respect. She didn't want affection to be a violation of freedom. As Mümtaz made a gift of his life and presence, she, like benevolent Abbasid caliphs of yore, accepted them promptly before returning them in turn. "It belongs to me but shall stay with you . . ." Meanwhile, the possessor of this elegant restraint had relinquished her entire existence to Mümtaz, as she had her days, without even mentioning it or raising the issue. Even so, Mümtaz sensed that accompanying this generosity was an inner fortress that no force, not even love, could breach: a notion of independence, or at least a desire to be true to oneself and to avoid hypocrisy.

From the first days of their acquaintance, adoration transfigured her open and simple countenance, with its hermetic contentment, into something of a riddle for Mümtaz. Without giving it much thought, trepidation of sorts mingled into the awe, the sense of worship he felt toward Nuran, recasting his existence as the tempest of a starry night.

VII

Adile hadn't stepped foot outside of her Taksim apartment that summer. She didn't want to ruin her select and newly assembled inner circle, nor to lose the men and women she'd gathered with such difficulty. Not to mention that Istanbul, even if it was summer, still seemed exceptional. Everybody went away, ventured out and about, yet always returned. And they even came around more frequently, because resorts and outings broke urban habits and forced those who couldn't go anywhere closer together. Even one such as Mümtaz, who hadn't shown himself for months, rang Adile's apartment door around four o'clock one afternoon. As soon as she saw him, she was overjoyed. A smile appeared on her lips that nearly resembled a cry of victory. He'd returned at last. The lambie that had strayed from the flock had wandered and returned. But how transformed and reticent. Beneath his reserve rested a bewildering sparkle, as if ecstasy itself were being suppressed. He all but evoked entertainments of the harem after the premises had been shuttered tight and the windows had been draped with swathes of brocade to prevent the intrusion of unwanted eyes and ears. Not to mention that Adile wasn't able to ascertain anything, that is, until such time as Nuran's arrival. When she entered, the matter changed. Perhaps for the first time, Mümtaz saw the outfit of the lady of his affections appointed with such care. Though they'd belonged to each other for more or less a month, he hadn't assumed that Nuran could transform through dress and attire alone. How everything had changed with her entry! And they'd been together only yesterday; yesterday he'd been in her embrace. While wearing her usual colorful blue summer dress cut from inexpensive cloth, she seemed to say, "I'm at the end of my means; this is all I can afford." Presently, with her carefully collected hair, made-up face, and white linen dress, she assumed a different persona. Mümtaz feared receiving a greeting fit for a distant relative. With the calmness of one who plays her hand openly, the young lady asked him, "I'm not too late, am I?" In this way, she'd all but announced their involvement. Adile seemed to be oblivious to this blow.

Sabih, simply beside himself, hadn't cornered anybody of late with whom to debate political issues. His modus operandi resembled the way predatory animals stalked and hunted. He didn't begin a diatribe immediately; after sizing up his kill, he crouched and withdrew to a corner, giving his prey its liberty in order to increase the effect of surprise. When the unsuspecting victim was most comfortable within an illusion of freedom, Sabih pounced, not allowing his prey to move a muscle. One after another, ad infinitum, he began to explain everything he'd read about world affairs in European papers over the entire week or, perhaps, month. His interests encompassed the whole of the globe like longitudinal and latitudinal lines. Everything from China to America, from British petroleum politics to the schemes of Hungarian landowners, from Hitler to King Zogu of Albania and Reza Shah Pahlavi, from Central Asia to Gandhi's fasts, everything having to do with man's fate interested this keenly perceptive mind. As Mümtaz listened to Sabih talk, he mused ponderously, *What monstrous state would we be in if our digestive systems worked this way?* Only if one turned orange by eating carrots and red from eating beets, only if people who ate rice, drank milk, liked fried mussels, assumed the smell, hue, or characteristics of these blessings of nature in the most obvious places like an incriminating mark, only then might an entity emerge resembling these commentaries that were the very fruit and essence of Sabih's long immersions of research. Tonight Sabih appeared quieter and more comfortable than usual. When Mümtaz arrived, he took the opportunity to gather up the newspapers and put them on the shelves. Such portents could never bode well. Mümtaz knew perfectly well that Sabih would soon fall into a convoluted web of incidents and a tangle of contradictions to which he would have to resign himself without recourse.

"You'll be spending the evening with us, isn't that so, my dear sister?"

Pleased at having lopped eight or ten years off her own age through her use of the word "sister," Adile awaited Nuran's answer. Nuran tried to explain that she'd only planned to stop in for a short visit and that she had to leave but neither Adile nor Sabih was having any of it.

"In any case, you and Mümtaz are friends from over Bosphorus seas. Even if you're going to leave, you'll leave late. Let's have a *rakı*."

"It'd be better for us to leave early. İclâl and friends will be coming by tomorrow . . ."

Only after he'd received assurances that they wouldn't go did Sabih begin to delve into his repertoire about recent developments in Germany: In his good opinion, the German economy was in shambles. War was a forgone conclusion. Yet his austere and perhaps truthful judgments depended upon such long-winded proofs arrived at by such convoluted means!

Excursuses gaped open like large cisterns or grottos; then he'd start again from the very beginning, making analogies and comparisons and sketches of contrasting situations in the air. Opposite Sabih, Mümtaz took the only precaution available to keep the monologue as short as possible: he neither asked questions nor responded, but only made occasional nods of agreement and waited like one beneath eaves during a downpour. These eaves might at times be Nuran's pearls crossing the small indentation at her throat called the Bosphorus, or the cleft in her chin, which he so admired, or at times the puerile gestures and hesitations of her hands. He couldn't fathom how a creature of such beauty had entered his life, and in this regard he had no faith in fortune. He listened to Sabih for hours as he sat in a state of enchantment brought on by the bashful, staccato laughter that transfigured Nuran's face into a rose blossom beneath water.

In Mümtaz's esteem, Sabih was like the flailing tail-end of that baffling and fabled creature the newspapers called public opinion, hydra-headed *vox populi* whose actual number of minds remained a mystery. He understood that one lived through current events. Like a boulder washed by waves, he was content as long as he could feel events passing over him. Sabih had no need for an idea of his own; there was always the newspaper. Genera of papers constituted both his ship and his seas, both his compass and his captain. Excluding an occasional change in temperament, he seemed to issue hot off the press along with the editions and extras he read each day. Yet, as he spoke, associations multiplied, memories deepened, and ultimately he'd mutate into a beast of four or five ideas at once. Tonight was such a night. To begin with, he was a democrat, next he became a very fiery revolutionary. Then he sank into boundless love for humanity and, finally, into the austere need for law and order.

Thank goodness for Adile. A number of items needed to be fetched from the shops. The maid was off and the doorman was ill.

Amid these tirades and the delicious reveries of Nuran that greeted him, Mümtaz surreptitiously wondered how Adile would upset Nuran's pleasure, what details she'd impart, which relic of bygone days she'd uncover; in short, the type of impasses she'd point out to forestall their love. He knew that Adile didn't much care for Nuran in light of her open fraternizing with Mümtaz on the island ferry, her gracious manner with the young lady notwithstanding. A few days after that chance encounter, in the coffee-house they'd entered upon Sabih's insistence, she'd said, "You have no idea, Mümtaz, what a heartless woman she is. Heartless and cruel . . ." Adile knew quite well how worldly Nuran was and with what constant lack of means she'd walled off the will of her heart. Back then Mümtaz had ignored this broadside attack and changed the subject. What Mümtaz wondered now was how this woman, who only concerned herself with her milieu, would try to disturb their peace.

Adile didn't keep Mümtaz waiting long. With a wave of sincerity that gathered momentum with the second glass, she first praised Nuran's beauty then described the automobile of a girlhood friend, her fur coat, and the evening banquets she hosted at her house. Finally, when her heart had drained itself of compassion, she revealed her sincere hopes for Nuran. From that mysterious wellspring called fate, she wished for everything that Mümtaz couldn't possibly provide: ermine furs, jewelry, rubies, and the most luxurious automobiles passed before Nuran's eyes, astonished by the abundance, as Adile concluded: "*Vallahi!* Honestly, my dear Nuran, when I think about all that you suffer to keep an ill child from being distraught! I could never display such patience. You realize these are your best years . . . D'you have any idea what it's like from here on out?"

In this manner, after listing all of life's possibilities to Nuran, she'd reminded her, by mentioning Fatma's illness, that her actual duty was to maternal concerns, before advising her, despite everything, to live her life to the fullest. Only one possible meaning could be deduced from this advice. Had Nuran perchance understood? "Either be the mother of your daughter, or arrange a good future for yourself. You're wasting time with this buffoon." Even if she had, she wouldn't have let on.

Doubtless, Adile wouldn't content herself with such subtle innuendo alone; she'd also make assaults of broader scope. But, two belated guests changed the composition of the night: a friend of Nuran's father who'd given her *tanbur*-lute lessons at one time and a neighborhood friend of Sabih's, a musician who'd be staying the night. With their arrival, the evening became a song-and-drink revelry.

Since Nuran couldn't possibly oppose the insistence of her former mentor, she resigned herself to this new turn.

Though the musicians greatly admired *a la turca* music, they rarely ventured beyond the *makam*s of the Ferahfezâ, the Acemaşiran, the Beyatî, the Sultanîyegâh, the Nühüft, and the Mahur, which were essentially climes of the soul . . . But within these *makam*s, they didn't recite each piece simply as it was. According to Mümtaz, *a la turca* music resembled Ottoman classical poetry. In that case as well, one had to decide between genuine art and simple imitation. More precisely, pieces selected with today's level of discernment, the criteria of Western tastes, could be deemed to be rather beautiful. In addition to these *makam*s, they played Hüseynî: a few works of Tab'î Mustafa Efendi's caliber and some of İsmail Dede Efendi's songs; in the Hicaz *makam*, they played Haji Halil Efendi's famous *semâi;* and they considered Haji Arif's two famous pieces and the Suzidilârâ *makam*, entwined with the fate of the modernizer Sultan Selim III, to represent a pinnacle.

These passions were rounded out by a few ecstatic pieces of rare vintage from the nineteenth-century reigns of Sultan Abdülmecit and Sultan Abdülaziz, *saz semâi* instrumentals, *makam* vocal medleys called *kâr-ı nâtık*, along with the works of present-day masters like Emin Dede, who kept alive the purest of classical tastes in the present like a belated spring or an exotic plant that adapted well to new soil. Mümtaz maintained that these works showed how classical Ottoman music merged with modern sensibilities and tastes. What he discovered in the old masters of schools of painting, considered to be "modern" now for the past fifty or sixty years, who were trained between 1400 and 1500, that is, a genuine innovation in aesthetics and sensibility, he also found in these musical genres, the *beste*, the *semâi* and the *şarkı*, and languid, gilded songs called *kâr* that resembled variegated and intricately carved wood ceilings or, rather, conjured Bosphorus panoramas as might be seen from sixteen-oared caïques, bejeweled and regal. In addition to these pieces, of course, there was the bark, the seed, the branch, and the tree roots; in other words, an entire assemblage of arboreal growth. Notwithstanding, what flourished here was the essential delicacy, the bloom of satisfaction, the absolute idea and the invigorating sap, the vision that was a rare vagary of chance, namely, the true reign, namely, the sultanate of the soul.

In this musical dalliance of Nuran's, her distinction from her beloved Mümtaz was that she loved *gazel* vocal improvisations, perhaps with the corporeal attachment of her muliebrity to the deep masculine voice, to its sorrow and its melancholia approaching primitivism. For her, a *gazel*-song that filled a summer's night was an articulation of beauty, perhaps constituting an art form distinct from music itself. Furthermore, Nuran knew the strains and folk songs that she'd heard and learned from her grandmother, a well-traveled, experienced old Bektashi. A sparkling new horizon opened for Mümtaz through the way this daughter and scion of an established family, raised along the Bosphorus, admired, like an İsmail Dede Efendi or Hafız Post, and recited, with an expression particular to each piece, village dirges, *türkü*s from Rumeli, Kozan, and Afşar, traditional dance music of Kastamonu and Trabzon, old Bektashi lyricals, and Kadiri *naat*-odes to the Prophet. On a number of occasions, while she recited these pieces, Mümtaz felt that Nuran was a daughter of an Eastern tribal clan or a young Kütahya bride going to a maidens' celebration bedecked in pied velvets, atlas silks, sashes, and silver-threaded slippers. Truly baffling was his discovery, in this refined cosmopolitan, of a shared intimacy with the people whose lilts she'd appropriated – as if she were one of them. As days passed, it all constituted a force that transformed and completed Mümtaz's dulcinea before his eyes, giving their love a panorama of the order of the soul.

That night, too, at Sabih's, Nuran successively laid open the bastions of Nühüft and Sultanîyegâh *makam*s; as she sang these songs – her hands, which he so adored and admired, keeping tempo upon the small, crimson, wave-patterned tablecloth amid a debris of forks and knives – a constellation of sisters augmented the Nurans in his life and phantasies by means of the various expressions continually confronting him in her facial guises. In the course of hours, Nuran had herself forgotten all the discretions that she'd so insistently advised him to maintain. Blurting out, "Come then, Mümtaz, take me home, I believe the *rakı* has taken hold of me," she quit the table, which amounted to a declaration of open warfare against Adile. In consult with her other guests, however, the mistress of the house was struggling to dampen some or another nuptial plans with the most strident of caveats, and thereby didn't take full notice.

For Mümtaz, Seyid Nuh's piece in Nühüft represented the most faithful aspect of Turkish song. Very few works conveyed the yearning for the eternal in the soul, the wingèd ascension toward the sun, toward illumination and immolation. The Nühüft, the thrust of its élan vital, was the essence of a civilization's inner world hurtling toward a radiance that obliterated all else. Herein, the singular aim was enthrallment or depletion of a sort. And humanity's infinity, in this instance, casting off rationalism in a single flutter, was in the process of attaining purity of soul. As Mümtaz listened, he was distilled from our material world; and death, at one pole, became the talismanic mirror before a rational life congruent with Creation; death was the downcast sibling living entangled with its grinning doppelgänger.

Truly bewildering was how this miraculous phenomenon suddenly stopped. Listeners were affected in kind as soon as the music started around a simple couplet of inferior quality. In this matter, the *makam* had a vital role to play. The lucid melody was laced with such crepuscular undertones that Eros and Thanatos, the two polarities in which the soul of mankind dwelled, merged involuntarily.

Relative to the Nühüft, İsmail Dede Efendi's Acemaşiran *semâi* in 6/4 allegro was altogether different in its opulence. After a plethora of deaths, it resembled a searing recollection; a hundred thousand souls languishing in the intermediary state of a liminal *ârâf.* Here, too, the occult spoke. Here, too, humanity jettisoned many of its inherent qualities. Yet something was being yearned for. Here, Allah, or the Beloved, remained external. We yearned to ascend toward Him, exclaiming in Farsi:

Wheresoever you reside
Therein our paradise does abide

Mümtaz sat listening to Nuran's voice, watching the changes in countenance caused by her straining, and he, too, like İsmail Dede, uttered, "Therein our paradise does abide."

As Mümtaz listened to this piece and, the *türkü*s and melodies sung by the increasingly impassioned elderly master of music Emin Dede, he contemplated the groundless animus Adile harbored toward their relationship. How *did* life manage to thrive between two polarities? At one extent, an array of vehicles for mankind's exaltation and, at the other, trifling worries, the settling of scores, and random enmities that strove to exclude and banish people from exalted heights.

Or did fate wish to declare, "I will *not* leave you alone with your soul"? At the table he caught two or three glances Adile cast at him and Nuran. The mistress of the house looked at Mümtaz underhandedly as if to say, "I'll show you." But when she came eye to eye with Nuran, she declared, "I'm yours forever. You have no better friend than me." Adile, in this manner, embraced Nuran, whom she thought was weaker and whom she knew had some breaches in her life. The small-minded settling of accounts had persisted in the same way during Seyid Nuh's Mi'raj of the Sun, Dede's expression of love that conflated Allah and Beloved, and the oh-so-profound synthesis of *türkü*s from Rumeli, or "Turkey in Europe," with experiences on another horizon like fate, love, suffering, death, and separation. All the same, Adile admired traditional music and drew enjoyment from it. Yet even fine art couldn't mollify the temperaments of some.

VIII

Nuran invited Mümtaz, whom she'd frequently mentioned, to the house. To Mümtaz, Nuran's residence was like the paradise described in the last couplet of Itrî's Acemaşiran song. On this count, he longed to see it and its inhabitants. Particularly the way the elderly music aficionado had piqued his curiosity that night by referring to Nuran's uncle: "He knows this repertoire as well as we do, but he's a creature of habit. He doesn't show himself often."

He found Nuran's mother to be as he'd expected. Nazife, having come of age around the 1908 constitutional revolution, exhibited a number of endearing characteristics like many who'd grown accustomed to seeing life from beneath a gauzy black veil. She satisfied many a pleasure through a furtive glance. She had a childlike curiosity: "Now I've been exposed to this as well. When I go home, I'll think about it more . . . What's happening on the outside? The world in which you live is so different from ours."

Such thoughts could be understood to be natural impulses among most ladies who'd come of age thirty years ago. Under the influence of those years, she was very progressive in thought but very reserved in action. She'd been loved madly by a husband who was twenty years her senior, and she bore a multitude of personality quirks that accrued from being overly indulged. These traits constituted the persona of Nuran's mother as wife of Rasim, one-time provincial governor and *ney* flutist.

The elderly matron's appropriately timed observations, which she didn't withhold, her almost childlike interest in current events, her distaste for frivolity, her love of politics, and the coterie of luminaries she knew – much later Mümtaz realized that she'd traced the careers of almost every high official in the Committee of Union and Progress and was a repository of forgotten facts retrieved with astounding memory – represented the changes that the 1908 revolution had forged in women of a certain class. That day, Mümtaz learned what a harmonious synthesis these distinct identities made in Nazife. But the manner of the matron's speech really drew his curiosity. Only after hearing her did he understand why Nuran occasionally resorted to antiquated words, even delighted in doing so, and why she lengthened and stressed certain syllables. For instance, Nuran pronounced the word pajamas "pa-*jah*-mas"; in this way, after a very long note, she was able to follow with the slightest of dénouements. Known as the "Istanbul inflection," this equated to one's being raised within the politesse and refinement that the eighteenth-century Ottoman poets Nedim and Nabî had so admired; what in part constituted the charm of established middle-class families and large households, whose progeny were more often than not married off to one another.

Nuran's uncle Tevfik had quite a different disposition from her mother's. As a young lieutenant colonel, he'd marched into Istanbul along with the

Army of Action to put down the 1909 Islamic counterrevolution against the Union and Progress government. During the Union and Progress era, he was able to capitalize on some opportunity or other that had arisen and entered into business; he'd faced bankruptcy numerous times; finally, he managed to extricate himself with enough capital so as not to be beholden to anyone. When he'd lost his wife twelve years ago, he moved into his sister's house, together with his son, who hadn't succeeded in arranging a marriage. In particular, the last dozen years of Tevfik's life under his father's roof were truly bizarre in light of the notorious name he'd made for himself as a gambler, a carouse, and a philanderer during the armistice years after 1918 in the bustling Beyoğlu district. Indeed, he'd dedicated these last dozen years to the memory of his father, whose name he couldn't have recalled previously without stopping to think. He'd collected all his father's calligraphy, imperial insignias, the books he'd had bound, the plates he'd embellished at the Yıldız ceramics factory, and the glassware he'd helped decorate. Tevfik confided various personal details about his father and brother-in-law Rasim to Mümtaz. He showed him ornamental plates, explained the stories behind candelabra and confectionary bowls, and, surprisingly, had managed to collect these objects in just a decade. Tevfik, meanwhile, found it quite natural. "The whole of Istanbul is on sale at the bazaar, my dear boy," he said. Thereafter, passing through the Bedesten or perusing antique shops with İhsan, Mümtaz better understood how he'd often blindly passed before many exquisite pieces, thanks to the objects Tevfik had shown him that day, like calligraphy panels, tapestries, and "menageries of glass" – a phrase Nuran had uttered unexpectedly and that Mümtaz couldn't recall without a chuckle.

As Tevfik sought out his father's objets d'art embellished with the aid of his gilding jar, hair-tipped pen, fine brush, and his search for a palette of colors that resembled a kind of anxiety and escape, he'd become a small-scale collector. Mümtaz was astounded that this final and intricate renaissance of

Turkish sensibility had remained so obscure. Neither the poets nor novelists of the fin de siècle Edebiyat-ı Cedid movement of modern literature, nor the newspaper collections that he'd combed at one time while doing research for İhsan, could convey the era of Sultan Abdülhamit II as much as these "menageries of glass" – where had Nuran found this phrase that was yet another facet of her girlish imagination? Whenever he recalled the phrase, he'd conjure his beloved among subtle and pastel-hued glassware: antique, spiral-patterned "nightingale's nest" vessels of indigo, terra-cotta red, and robin's egg blue; rococo, hull-shaped fruit bowls or plates covered with the ornamental designs of leather-bound tomes; and Nuran would appropriate the refractions and timbre of all these delicate and fragile pieces requiring an infinitude of care. Doubtless, they contained hints of *a la franga* modernity. But they still represented a distinct aesthetic.

The gentleman Tevfik most admired after his father was his sister's husband. He'd kept almost everything belonging to Rasim, conserving in a state of timeless preservation pictures, notes made in his own hand, Ottoman-script penmanship workbooks, and all variety of full-size *ney*-flutes and half-length *nısfiye* flutes. Opposite a calligraphy panel of his father's, hung a photograph of Rasim taken with his uniform of distinguished rank and his decorations. Mümtaz read the calligraphy first:

Through the favor and munificence of the exalted Lord we were delivered.

"In the year of the Hegira 1313, or A.D. 1895, a lengthy secret police file on my father was submitted to Sultan Abdülhamit II. He was detained at the Yıldız Palace for ten nights. When he was freed he made a calligraphy panel of this verse by Nâilî. Look closely, among the ornamental arabesques is an image of the divan upon which he'd slept for ten nights." The depiction of a broad divan appeared repeatedly among the roses and vines that bordered the couplet like a garden wall. The arabesque designs and geometric shapes, the ordered roses and flowers against the gilded and pale red background, had been calculated and arranged with such skill and precision that without being told so, the divan motif wasn't at all obvious.

Mümtaz later dwelled upon this element of realism that amounted to the marring, in a respect, of late Ottoman calligraphic art.

Tevfik had attained a profundity of sorts in this passion to which he'd succumbed. The objects among which he'd lived unawares for fifty years had suddenly come to life and taken on meaning for him. This was no anomaly for Tevfik; he was made to persevere. Despite his seventy-four years, he was possessed of quite a mellifluous baritone; he still took his drink each evening, enjoyed the friendship of young and becoming ladies, and on some autumn nights even went out to catch swordfish with the neighborhood fishermen. "The traditional Zeybek dance that I dance, any old *efe* militiaman couldn't do. Especially your top-hat-and-tails *efe*s, never." He'd made this quip as he recollected the Zeybek dance that two MPs had done together in 1926 at a ball: "I immediately signaled the orchestra and stood up. Everyone was stunned. The Zeybek is an altogether dramatic performance; if it doesn't clear the dance floor, it hasn't been successful."

"I've seen it once. In Antalya, but I was little. Two *efe*s from Demirci had made a wager. Lamb and baklava was prepared. People feasted on the street, then under the light of torches . . ."

Tevfik, gesturing to Nuran, said, "This one has a knack for it."

"You don't say? I had no idea."

Nuran, her expression belying annoyance: "Hadn't I mentioned it to you, Mümtaz? I know most Anatolian folk dances."

But Tevfik wasn't only the faithful warden of things past or the best Zeybek dancer of his circle. One of his greatest qualities or pleasures was preparing an assortment of delicacies to accompany *rakı*.

As Mümtaz regarded Tevfik, his admiration grew.

"Isn't it astounding how my uncle resembles my father in many aspects?"

Toward evening, Tevfik disappeared. But when he reappeared an hour later, the spread on the *rakı* table constituted a spectacle of indulgence.

"Above all, *rakı* must be drunk slowly . . . over a considerable duration of time, only then will the bouquet of its essence emerge."

The everyday comfort and joie de vivre of this old Istanbul effedi were quite rarely seen today. For the sacrament of food alone, he had a special calendar. No one knew better than him which fish was best caught in which season and locale, and what dishes could be prepared with an early seasonal offering or with seafood during such and such a month.

"Ebuzziya, may his soul rest in peace, used to put out a calendar when we were young. You couldn't imagine a more intricate undertaking. It was full of recipes translated from the French and procured from small Beyoğlu restaurants. When I saw two or three copies, I was mad with envy. Later my interest was sparked."

On gastronomic subjects Tevfik was methodological. For him the essence of gastronomy lay in the ingredients. For this reason, *sine qua non* was a calendar for each season and month, even a daily almanac that indicated the Bosphorus southerlies and northerlies, *lodos* and *poyraz*.

"Red mullet is the world's most delectable fish, but it's a different story if it isn't caught in season, and especially if it isn't caught off the Princes Islands, or in the southern mouth of the Bosphorus. South of the Dardanelles, mullet is a tasteless sea creature beyond any categorical description."

Tevfik's epicurean interests had attained the level of a philosophy of history.

"Just consider, if you will, the centuries-long labor of fate enabling us to eat this mullet together tonight. To begin with, as the poet Yahya Kemal explains, the waters of the Danube, the Volga, and the Don had to reach the Black Sea. Our forefathers had to up and travel from Central Asia and eventually settle in Istanbul. Furthermore, Sultan Mahmut II had to exile Nuran's great-grandfather from Istanbul to Manastır for being a Bektashi, where he would in turn marry the daughter of a wealthy major from Merzifon. My grandfather had to buy this manor house with the money earned from a Koran that he'd copied out to console himself after his wife left him and that he'd offered for sale to who knows which pasha . . . My young boy, you understand what I'm saying, don't you? The whole of an exalted Koran for the price of seven hundred fifty gold pieces . . . that is, equivalent to this building and the land out back . . . Then, Nuran's father had to fall ill as a child and his mother had to bequeath him to the good graces of Aziz Mahmut Hüdai Efendi so when he grew up he'd initiate into that patron master's dervish lodge, where he'd befriend my father. Nuran had to be born . . . You, too, would come into this world . . ."

Mümtaz adored this ethnosocial history of red mullet.

Tevfik's son, Yaşar, laughed at his father to the degree sanctioned by him, within the incurable heart disease that he assumed had afflicted him of late. Tevfik represented the nineteenth-century Tanzimat era of reform, which set to work with lofty intentions and finished simply with a weakness for everyday pleasures – he lived in the ease, nonchalance, and pilfered delights of that age. Yaşar was more like the second constitutional period after 1908, and bore all of its instabilities. He displayed a bewildering idealism, fleeting feelings of inferiority, and rebellions that cast both off like a wave taking another's place; in short, he vacillated between ecstatic enthusiasm and immobilizing despair.

At the table, Mümtaz assumed this man of about forty-five would enjoy himself more than anyone. He filled his glass in a state of complete excitement and, raising it toward Mümtaz, said, "Welcome," before downing it in one gulp. Tevfik, as if reining in an unwieldy horse, greeted this eagerness with an extended "whooooaaaaa." Yaşar paid no heed to the warning. The machinery of his body was working well; all day the house had been as hot as a small furnace; furthermore, he'd be going to Ankara in three days time; while *rakı* on the rocks and his father's eggplant salad, along with other appetizers, awaited them, why show restraint? Yaşar would more or less enjoy himself like everybody, but only until he recalled his physiology. At the first signal from his delicate constitution, there began a state of affliction, fatigue, overall disgust, and withdrawal. No lack of jocularity existed between son, who lived more or less through the recent yields of science, and father, who over the span of his entire life knew nothing of medication – apart from the senna plant he had Huriye the maid pound on occasion as a purgative and the galingale root that he himself boiled on the brazier when a winter's cough pestered him. As far as Tevfik knew, aspirin was but a version of the tango.

Tevfik wasn't overly complaining about his son's pharmaceutical obsession. Despite poisoning himself each day by recommended or excessive doses, for better or worse, Yaşar forged through life. Moreover, since he'd succumbed to hypochondria, he'd been liberated of many exigencies related to his career. He no longer grew out the nail of his right pinky "a length of four elifs," and he no longer discussed the young contessa and her very *charmante* mother he'd met in Toledo, the straight, pristine boulevards of Bucharest, or the extraordinary beach at Varna. He neither boasted of his second secretariat in Paris, when he'd been honored to make an evening visit to that exquisite pied-à-terre of French singer-actress Mistinguett accompanied by her maidservant, nor the boardinghouse right behind Wilhelmstrasse where one midafternoon he'd suddenly come nose to nose with Swiss actor Emil Jannings, cigarette in mouth, a large canine behind him, as he stepped from his front door. He'd even forgotten about the large-eyed blonde at this boardinghouse, whose pointed eyelashes dripped blue mascara, about her mad infatuation with Wagner, the way her voice trembled when she recited Heine by heart, the incredible trip they took to the Tyrolean Alps, the folk songs they listened to beneath moonlight, and all the rest, forgotten. Likewise, the weeklong vacation he'd passed in the château of an old countryman of ours located a few hours from Budapest, those high-backed armchairs, horses, thoroughbred hounds, and thresh-ing sites that resembled sets prepared for Marta Eggerth's operetta-like films rather than a real harvest; in short, the thousand and one delights of pleasant music and cheap sentimentality, Viennese cafés, ladies of delicate comportment, and cocktail-party trivia about Mozart had all been elided from memory. Nowadays, Yaşar returned to the house every evening with a tightly wrapped, elegant parcel, undid its packaging as if removing a fruit from its rind, unfolded its thin prospectus, and within a radiance but seen shimmering on the lips and in the eyes of full-fledged devotees of the faith when they beheld the ordered workings of Creation like clockwork, read, stunned and grinning.

Mümtaz knew of Yaşar from his friends in Paris, including İhsan, and somewhat from chance encounters at Adile's apartment. Nature had all but compensated this foreign affairs officer, who held the promise of the brightest future in '25 and '26, with hypochondria since he'd lost a midlevel ambassadorship due to the betrayal of a family friend; that is, since being sent to some Balkan town as head secretary in place of assuming a vacant central post as part of an embassy.

This obsession had occupied his entire life for the past half-dozen years, and it was not to be taken lightly. Yaşar resembled a man who'd been appointed by irade to the captaincy of a dreadnought, and just as such a captain would be preoccupied with the inscrutable workings of the vessel, Yaşar was occupied with his bodily workings, whose secrets, potential, and governing laws escaped him. His primary preoccupation was to synchronize numerous anatomical systems of disconcerting mystery and to coordinate their functions, preventing a matrix of probable disruptions through small and precisely timed interventions. In brief, Yaşar's body remained in dry dock under the scrutiny of his own eyes. His hypochondria had increased, particularly after a careless physician had one day declared that he couldn't actually be suffering from heart disease based on the vital signs of his own body, but added that perhaps his other systems were strained, resulting in some slight discomfort, and his life began to pass in pursuit of an elusive orchestration of bodily function. One could say that the unity known as the body had been lost for Yaşar, to be occupied by a perplexing collusion made up of independently working organs that resembled a governmental cabinet whose seats were occupied by ministers of different parties. From the intestines to the stomach, from the liver to the kidneys, and from the sympathetic nervous system down to the endocrine glands, each part functioned independently and to separate ends. Thus, Yaşar, who strove to lead these distinct apparatuses to a single coordinated goal, was something of a prime minister condemned to struggle against the impossible. In his efforts, he had but one single recourse: pharmaceuticals.

Whoever happens to write the history of this century will most certainly be mindful of the proliferation of pharmaceuticals. Yaşar was one of the biggest casualties of this epidemic. In addition to a few pharmaceutical warehouses in Istanbul, he'd also made direct contact with pharmaceutical factories, or their representatives, who'd gradually begun sending him, as they did with doctors, varieties of their latest product samples.

The medications weren't just the victory of modern-day medical science and chemistry. They also came with individual aesthetics, and even literatures. With their meticulous packaging from the most elegant covers and imitation morocco cases down to boxes resembling the most provocative and expensive perfumes, powders, and toiletries, in every size, shape, and color, some petite, graceful, and friendly, as if exclaiming, "I'm as useful as an idea and what's more, I'm easily carried!" and others with their squat bottles promising all variety of discretion like solemn confidants, they'd instigated a distinct transformation in daily life, or at the least, in urban and street life, with wadding as shiny as velvet and packaging that satisfied one like a new leather bookbinding, its fine linty fuzz shimmering in the sun. These pharmaceuticals wouldn't just remain the products of a few major factories, they represented initial steps toward turning consumers into the ideal of a brave new humanity. With the artificial ease that they brought, they'd secure the gradual death of nature in mankind. To be sure, Yaşar sensed this lofty ideal, embracing it heart and soul. Thanks to six years of patient research, many involuntarily physiological functions occurred as an effect of Yaşar's pills. He slept using pills, he attained the clarity of wakefulness with the few aspirin he took upon waking, he worked up an appetite with pills, he digested with pills, he defecated with pills, he made love with pills, and he desired with pills. Companies like Roche, Bayer, and Merck were the mainstays of his life. He wrote the long reports that he presented each month to the Ministry with the help of the tonics from these factories that multiplied human endurance exponentially. The top of his nightstand held a riot of bottles of every imaginable design, decorated with symbols, some wordy with allusions to minerals, mythology, and cosmology, while others sufficed with intimation and innuendo, like the titles of poetry collections. Thanks to these bottles and packages, the long shelf of his dresser was as dazzling as an American bar, and when Yaşar spoke of these medications, he used the most hyperbolic language. Instead of saying that he'd taken vitamin C, he'd say, "For eighty-five cents, I bought a million oranges!" Describing a bottle of Phanodorme or Eviphane that he'd removed from his waistcoat pocket, he'd declare, "Behold the poet laureate of the ages! Each capsule contains at least twenty visions that would never under other circumstances visit the imaginative faculties of a single author!" The hours of the day were divided according to the drugs he took. "Please don't let me forget, at three o'clock sharp I take my pepsin . . . It seems I've forgotten to take my Eurotropin. May Allah grant that no harm befalls me."

Yaşar loomed as a true neurotic side effect caused by the cooperation between modern science and marketing for the betterment of mankind.

IX

The pleasure of welcome at Nuran's house signified a peak of satisfaction for Mümtaz. Unfortunately, Fatma's tetchiness poisoned this delight.

Since her father had left, Fatma's natural disposition was a state of insecurity with respect to others – the phobia of losing whatever belonged to her. That is to say, she nurtured jealousy of Mümtaz. And other contingencies made her jealousy more distressing.

The girl couldn't manage to find any rapport with Mümtaz. First she wanted to be indifferently cool or simply polite; a while later she'd become malicious and spiteful; and in the end, as if to relinquish her world, she'd abandon their company and withdraw, but since the thought, *What's going on downstairs?* pestered her, five minutes later she'd appear again, moody and spoiled. Since word of marriage frequently passed in the house, Fatma knew Mümtaz's status in Nuran's life. This was the reason her demeanor toward her mother had changed over the past ten days.

None of this could dispel Mümtaz's joy at being present in Nuran's house among the things she'd lived with and enjoyed as a girl and adolescent.

Consequently, for Mümtaz, thoughts of Nuran's home became a separate source of satisfaction. When his beloved went away, leaving him alone, or on days she said she wouldn't be leaving her house, he got in the habit of conjuring her. Now familiar with the most important framework of Nuran's life, thoughts of her never left him. Imagining her at the base of the pomegranate tree in the garden or at the breakfast table, or thinking of her in flower beds that she tended by hand, her hair gathered atop her head with randomly placed hairpins, her white morning gown draped in folds recalling Pompeiian frescoes as they clung to and roamed the curves of her body, amounted to delights that filled his hours of solitude.

Nuran's acts and attitudes as evoked by Mümtaz's imagination were implausibly sublime: how she cast open the shutters of her bedroom; boiled Turkish coffee for aging Tevfik; brought medicines to her mother; read a book in the garden, head in hands; or served tea to guests in the small parlour room, a haunt since childhood, while seated in the armchair once occupied by grand vizier Âli Pasha, who'd come to pay a get-well visit to her grandfather; how she pointed out the framed verse by Nâilî – "Through the favor and munificence of the exalted Lord we were delivered" – that İbrahim Bey had in time made as a memento of his ten-day detainment at Yıldız Palace; and how she showed off the decorative plates and vases in the window whose ornamentation he'd made with his ink pots of gold and other colors, his hair-tipped pens and fine brushes, as well as those "menageries of glass," as Nuran put it – a turn of phrase that augmented her grace through the je ne sais quoi of childhood elation.

For Mümtaz, a personal fable of sorts was gradually woven out of Nuran's time away, and he began to embellish the hours of Nuran's day – just like medieval painters who illuminated the prayer books of such and such duchess or king around a château with depictions of daily life, seasonal and astrological figures, or scenes from the Sacred Book – through a plethora of visions, through sparkling and multihued bacchanals conveying a wealth of potential like unstrummed lutes.

In this variegated realm, this music of silence that appropriated its every curve and arc from her ordinary movements and from the figures she boldly presented to the moment and span of her inhabitation – the actual Nuran, through an image conjured by her name – "twin lights of the sun and moon" – a vision of golden chalices pilfered from the banquet of the sun, or of water lilies blooming white in the gardens of dawn, like a fecund season, she came, went, thought, listened, and spoke while her presence flung a multitude of secrets and splendors upon the landscapes over which she trod.

To imagine her at any moment of the day, anywhere, yielded an always boundless jubilation, whether Mümtaz evoked her waiting for the ferry at the landing, selecting buttons or lace at the seamstress's, describing a dress model, speaking with her friends, whether nodding her head "yes" or shaking it "no."

Two Nurans manifested. One was removed from him, such that her every step transformed her material self a bit more, and through the alchemy of desire and yearning, in effect became a substantiation of the soul, and by bequeathing countless traits of her own to other things, she made all distances and wherever she roamed into a realm of transcendence above the everyday, though she nevertheless lived as always in the center of this realm, constituted by nothing more than kaleidoscopic reflections of her self.

The house in Kandilli was the most striking and wondrous of Nuran's realms, and most transformed into abstract reality by this miraculous phenomenon, down to the open hall's wood siding interspaced with laths. And her transformative alchemy, beginning here, incrementally radiated throughout his life.

Then there was the second, the Nuran of his company, who, by her material presence, diminished his phantasms to nothing but infantilism, who, from afar, in one stroke erased whatever he'd conjured. As soon as she made her entrance, the instant she appeared at a prearranged rendezvous, a ferry landing or street corner, Mümtaz's imagination sputtered and ceased.

Mümtaz tried repeatedly to ponder the emotions raised by her approach. Her approach, he decided, constituted a sort of mesmerism of the intellect. Everything seemed to vanish the instant she appeared at the top of the street. Anxieties evaporated, apprehension abated, and even exhilaration lost its former radiance. The proximate Nuran focused the bewitching aura emanating from her presence onto one single entity, one individual, Mümtaz, whom she took into her palms and formed into luculent clay.

Even Mümtaz ceded his fundamental conception of the real whenever confronted by Nuran; Mümtaz, who in previous relationships belittled the fairer sex with near derision, who found his own exuberance laughable, and even amid the most poignant pleasures, in flagrante delicto, carefully tracked his bestial stimulation with a cerebral facet of his yet-lucid mind as if observing the workings of an automaton he'd cranked up himself, and who, beyond visual stimulation, received no purity of pleasure from the female *figura*.

True, this wasn't just a figment of the imagination. He didn't think this way because a lunatic had taken over the asylum of the intellect, either. Even had he not lost his mind, her mystery would survive in his delirium. Thus, whether near or far from Nuran, no wisdom or established truth could provide succor. Neither the Old Testament, which never left his side at one time, nor the philosophers or mentors he admired offered anything that might counter his agitation. These thinkers wrote of the dangers of women, carnal desire, and lust. In Mümtaz's esteem, his escapade with Nuran was of another magnitude entirely. Nuran was the fountainhead of life, the maternal source of all realities. Consequently, even when fully satiated by her, he still hungered for his beloved, his mind didn't turn away from her for an instant – as he sunk into her, he achieved wholeness of being.

On occasion Mümtaz attempted to explain his affection for Nuran through an absolute cellular affinity, and through the sensual chemistry they shared, he learned about the vast enigma nature had instilled within them. Perhaps what Plato had said was true, and in the circle of being, fate, by means of their love, had again reunited the halves of a singular presence rent asunder. Mümtaz, in other words, believed he was living through a Mi'raj of Being and an Exaltation of *Eşya*.

So fully did he feel the forces of Creation in his flesh, during certain nocturnal hours he wondered why he wasn't indeed conversing with rocks, birds, and blades of grass in the garden. The secret of this enigma again rested with Nuran. She was no ladylove of sterile contentments, hidden and jealous. Complete abandon issued from her person. Nuran depended on a minimum level of selfhood. She lived through her milieu. Despite attempts by both to avoid burdening each other with the tribulations of their lives, Mümtaz understood how at times she pitied him on account of people she'd never met.

Twice per week they met for morning trysts. Nuran quite liked his house in Emirgân. "I no longer feel the incline, that's how I've gotten used to it. It isn't exhausting because I'm approaching you." Hearing this surprised Mümtaz; Nuran, who discussed everything thoroughly, who revealed all of herself, hadn't imparted a single word about their relationship. She'd even found the question "Are you happy?" superfluous. For her, love wasn't the expenditure of emotions through words, but the complete surrender of herself to the tempest in Mümtaz's soul. Perhaps, captive in his arms, she assumed he could read her every thought from her face. This proved to be somewhat true. In the changing expressions of her countenance, he could read everything except the ciphers of feminine nature, the elements of the esoteric present even in Nuran.

Not a single spot existed on her small face with which he wasn't familiar. For Mümtaz, her face became his panorama of the soul: the way it blossomed to love like a flower, closed definitively upon a despairing smile – the metallic radiance burning in her eyes asquint – and not least of all the way her face changed by degrees like a daybreak over the Bosphorus. Nuran spoke, listened, and agreed or disagreed through smiles and gazes, rather than through words.

She resorted to glances that vacillated from the most radiant jewels to the keenest scimitar glints. Before these various implements, Mümtaz at times found himself in a state of vulnerability more precarious than death. At other times her eyes coronated him with the most opulent of crowns known to the world, spreading at his feet pelts of reverence that destiny deemed unfit for the soles of others. With a look, she dressed him up and stripped him down, at one moment turning him into a pitiful, forsaken malcontent with no recourse but Allah, and at the next into the very master of his fate.

Day in, day out, Mümtaz harbored Nuran's glances and the sounds of her laughter, which resembled sobs of embrace and ecstasy. Her gaze and gaiety confronted him at every turn. His soul – tirelessly diving into the sea of her eyes – at each moment discovered new sources of strength and anguish in this ocean of riches. Her smile left a series of gardens blooming on his skin, in his blood, and throughout his being. Endless *gülistan*s drove him mad with pleasure such that they almost provoked him, more than once, to breathe in the bed upon which he lay, the objects he touched, and the lifeblood coursing through his veins. Inanimate objects accepted a godly visitation, coming to life through the memory of encounter, and in transitory but wistful moments of enlightenment, became cognizant of the past, the present, the future, and the immediate environment.

On any given morning of Nuran's impending arrival, he woke early, heading straight for the sea and returning after bathing. Fully aware that he wouldn't be able to accomplish a single task, he made the attempt nevertheless, but in the end just waited impatiently before the door as had happened on their first day alone.

> *O Nâilî, whensoever the moonlike beloved nears step by step,*
> *Does that not equal world upon world of separations suffered?*

Mümtaz's most faithful companion at such times was this couplet by the seventeenth-century poet Nâilî. Then, in time, a mysterious force would erupt within him as if announcing the approach of the anticipated presence. When he saw Nuran at the top of the street, his entire being emptied toward her strides.

"Couldn't I find you preoccupied with your work just once, Mümtaz? If I could only catch you distracted and unawares."

"Only if you were sleeping in the next room or preparing artichoke hearts."

"You mean to say that after we're married I'll be left to rot in the kitchen?"

Overwhelmed with apprehension and a guilty conscience as if he'd in fact forgotten her amid quotidian tasks or a consuming idea, filled with the agony of oversights beyond redress, he'd pause to kiss her then and there.

Nothing matched the surrender of Nuran's initial kiss. Then she'd say, "Let's see what you've done?"

Reclining in the armchair between the table and the window, she smoked a cigarette and drank her demitasse.

The moment of Nuran's departure, like the hours that passed in her absence, belonged to Neşâtî, another seventeenth-century poet. Nuran repeated the couplet with Mümtaz:

> *And you even left my soul full of yearning*
> *Nor could I bear the company of friends without you*

Nuran's amorousness represented a faith of sorts for Mümtaz. He was its sole devotee, a high priest waiting before the most sacred spot in the temple and keeping the hearth forever lit, the one chosen from among mortals by the goddess so that her mysteries might find substantiation. This comparison contained a measure of truth. The sun rose each day and the entirety of the past replayed its epochs as if for their sake alone.

Some mornings they trysted in Kanlıca at the Bosphorus residence of Nuran's relative. Watching Nuran on the quay in her white bathing suit – though only as a friend, due to others in the vicinity – represented an initiation into new tastes and torments. When he couldn't quite approach her, or if she didn't remind him at whiles of their intimacy, in his thoughts she'd become an unattainable promised land, a cruel goddess of unfathomable mysteries whose choice of him as mortal prophet hung in the balance; Nuran, a presence harboring the riddle of all potentialities and that of death and birth in her womb, became mistress of seasons, of every creature who plodded in her wake like a compliant slave or a captive beast of burden.

Anxiety fueled the deepest mechanisms in Mümtaz's soul. He would later realize that succumbing in excess to his imagination played a primary role among factors poisoning his contentment.

Over the duration of the summer, however, Mümtaz believed the human soul to be freer than it was – convinced that one could take control of oneself in a trice; that is to say, he was one of life's motley fools.

X

On days Nuran didn't come to Emirgân, the couple met either at the ferry landing or at Kanlıca, wandered the Bosphorus by caïque, went to beaches, and at times forayed as far as the heights of Çamlıca. Mümtaz always returned from these ventures sated. Continuing the custom begun on their first night, they came up with various monikers for places they admired. The coffeehouse in Çamlıca's interior was *derûn-i dil*, their "Heart of Hearts," because in that setting Mümtaz had listened to Nuran sing, in the Beyatî *makam*, Tab'î Mustafa Efendi's offbeat Aksak Semâi: the song that began, "Your endearments, my companion, will not abandon the heart of hearts," and contained reminiscences that transcended death. In that summer midafternoon among the buzz of insects, the occasional flutter of wings, and the shouts of bored, idle urchins, the panorama, having withdrawn into its beauty as if unsure of what else to do – with its small, sloping hillocks, its gardens on either side rolling down to the sea, its orchards, old manors, and copses whose dusty jade had been brushed on by cypresses amid deep naphtha green, the infinite empyrean overarching all – shrugged off its slumber, ceded itself to the laments of Tab'î Mustafa Efendi resonating through Nuran's voice, and fused to the skin of lover and beloved. Mümtaz listened often to the piece afterward, never abstracting it from these hours spent with Nuran at the coffeehouse located above the cistern and fountain, remnants of Sultan Mehmet IV's seventeenth-century hunting lodge.

Another night, returning to Kandilli from Çengelköy, they'd named the otherworldly shadow cast onto the Bosphorus surface currents by the trees before the Kuleli Military Academy the "Nühüft song." This was such a realm of inner radiance that its faithful representation could be found only in the dark emerald mirror of the Nühüft, reflecting spectacularly sparkling stirrings of a reclusive countenance.

By and by, they gave names to locales of their choosing along the Bosphorus, as the Istanbul landscape of their imagination merged with traditional Ottoman music, and a cartography of voice and vision steadily proliferated.

As Mümtaz slowly gathered around Nuran the things he admired and longed for, he found himself more in command of their powers. Like great novelists of the age, he began to feel that he was truly living only when he relied upon his woman. Before, he'd read widely and had weighed and considered matters; but now he understood that these things had become part of his life with more vitality; through his love for Nuran, they'd now entered into a living and breathing realm. She effectively became a cluster of light between that which rested in his thoughts and that which existed in his surroundings, illuminating everything such that the most disparate elements became part of a synthetic whole.

Ottoman music was one of these elements. After he'd met Nuran, this art form had in effect thrust open its doors. In music, he found one of the purest and most rejuvenating wellsprings of the human soul.

One day they roamed together through Üsküdar on Istanbul's Asian shore. First, to avoid waiting for the ferry at the landing, they visited Sinan's mid-sixteenth-century mosque of Mihrimah Sultana, daughter of Sultan Süleyman the Magnificent and the storied Roxelana. Then they went into the early eighteenth-century Valide-i Cedid Mosque of Emetullah Gülnüş Sultana, the queen mother of Ahmet III.

Nuran quite admired the *türbe* mausoleum and the mosque, whose decor resembled the inside of a petite fruit. They'd long missed the ferry. So by taxi they went to Sinan's sixteenth-century Valide-i Atik Mosque, built in honor of Nurbanu Sultana, queen mother of Murad III, and from there to the seventeenth-century Çinili Mosque of Kösem Sultana, queen mother of Murad IV.

By coincidence, these four great mosques of Üsküdar had been dedicated to love and beauty, or at the very least to a maternal sensibility.

"Mümtaz, in Üsküdar a genuine Sultanate of Women reigns . . ."

On the following day, again in Üsküdar, they visited the fifteenth-century Rumi Mehmet Pasha Mosque and the eighteenth-century Ayazma Mosque, and wandered the Şemsipaşa district on foot. Only days later they walked aimlessly beneath scorching sunlight around the area of the Selimiye Barracks, first built in 1800 to house the reformed Nizam-i Cedid army of Sultan Selim III. A confounding nostalgia for the past seized him as he saw the first geometric boulevards made in Istanbul and the handsome streets with window-on-the-past names that conjured a genuine feast of an Istanbul evening.

"Istanbul, Islambol," he repeated. "If we don't truly know Istanbul, we can never hope to find ourselves." In his soul, he'd now become brethren to destitute masses and houses verging on collapse. He wandered feverishly through the Sültantepe neighborhood. But the place he most loved was the Küçük Valide Mosque, located in the market square, though he wasn't partial to the tomb.

"If I had my druthers, I wouldn't be buried here. It's too out in the open," she said.

"After death, what does it matter?"

"I don't know, even after dying, this much in the midst of everything. Anyway, death can't be felt . . ."

"But when the mosque was opened, the markets had been closed down so no one would see the arrival of the Valide Sultana and her entourage."

Nuran especially admired the mosque and its interior half-light at eventide. She loved the eaves embellished with kilim motifs amid marble and gilt ornamentation.

As they returned from these excursions, she pressured him about his unfinished novel on Shaykh Galip. This historical novel, set during the turn of the eighteenth-century era of Selim III, contained elements of Mümtaz's own life. With Nuran in mind, Mümtaz had sketched the characters of Selim III's half-sister, Hatice Sultana, and his younger sister, Beyhan Sultana. Now, as the young lady read the descriptions in the drafts, she became rather meticulous, as if selecting a pattern at the seamstress's or organza at a fabric shop.

"In one you're with Antoine Ignace Melling; in the other you're with Shaykh Galip . . ."

This was Mümtaz's unfinished song: have as many dalliances as your heart desires.

"You mean I represent all the dead women? A thoughtful gesture, honestly . . ."

Üsküdar, which knew no end, was a treasure. A little distance beyond the Valide-i Cedid Mosque was the sixteenth-century Aziz Mahmut Hüdai Efendi Mosque. This spiritual sultanate from the era of Sultan Ahmet I had entered into Nuran's family lore. A little farther ahead was the mosque of Selâmi Ali Efendi, who held the reins for a few years during the rule of Sultan Mehmet IV. In the Karacaahmet district rested Karaca Ahmet – tradition tracing him back to the time of Orhan Ghazi, who ruled the House of Osman in the mid-fourteenth century and was the contemporary of

Geyikli Baba of Bursa, one of the mystical "Khorasan dervishes," and maybe a fellow ghazi of his – and in Sültantepe rested Celvetî Bâkî Efendi at his eponymous mosque.

Nuran was quite curious about the dervish orders, but since neither she nor Mümtaz bore a mystical side, they didn't dwell upon it. One day she'd said in that girlish tone she assumed when the urge struck, "If I'd lived back then, I would've certainly become a Celvetî."

But did they actually believe in all of this?

"This is the Orient, and herein resides its beauty. A lethargic world loath to change, all but embalmed within its traditions; but the East did discover one secret of significance. Though perhaps because the mystery was discovered prematurely, it proved to be harmful . . ."

"And what is that?"

"The secret of being able to see oneself and all existence as constituting a single entity. Maybe because the East sensed future agonies, it came up with this panacea. But let's not forget that the world might only be saved by this mind-set."

"Do you suppose the East was able to create an ethics out of its discovery?"

"I don't think so, but because the East took solace in the discovery, it restricted possibilities of action for better or worse. Within a semipoetic dream, the Orient lived on the peripheries of reality. Needless to say, I don't find this worldview appealing; it strikes me as plodding and tiresome, like a journey by camel caravan . . ." In Mümtaz's mind, the camel trains of his youth that had once lined up before the hotel in Antalya came to life. And he worried he might not be able to return from that time of agonizing *türkü*s. "How exceptional: the image of a camel-train on the empty horizon during twilight . . ."

"Allah, what a bizarre people we are," she said. With an intimation that suddenly rose within her, she asked Mümtaz, "Why is it that we're so bound to the past?"

"Whether we like it or not, we belong to it. We admire our traditional music and for better or worse it speaks to us. For better or worse we hold this key that unlocks the past for us . . . The past relinquishes its epochs to us one after another and dresses us in its clothing. Because we harbor a treasury within ourselves and perceive our surroundings through a Ferahfezâ or a Sultanîyegâh *makam*, even Lebîb Efendi is a source of art to us."

In Mümtaz's esteem, everything from an Istanbul *paysage* to the entire Turkish culture, its filth, its decay, and its splendor was contained in traditional music. The Occident roamed dumbly in our midst like a stranger due to its inability to fathom our music. And many a vista appeared before our eyes accompanied by a melody.

"Not to mention that when a work of art, something of intrinsic value, is underscored by music it is transformed. Strange, isn't it? In the end human life doesn't embrace anything but sound. We exist as if passing over material things, as if barely touching them. Yet through poetry and music . . ."

Mümtaz's obsession with things past gave Nuran the inkling that he wanted nothing more than to be shut up in catacombs. The world certainly offered myriad pleasures and other modes of thought. She liked Üsküdar, but it was dilapidated and its inhabitants impoverished. Among the throngs of unfortunates, Mümtaz forged ahead, blithely spouting "Acemaşiran" and "Sultanîyegâh." But what about society? Where was the overture to life? Actually doing something, treating the afflicted hordes, finding work for the unemployed, bringing smiles to crestfallen faces, delivering these people from being nothing but relics of the past . . . Or had the episodes that he'd confided about his childhood affected him more profoundly than she'd assumed? *Am I living in a country vanquished by Death?*

Taking Nuran by the arm, he pulled her away from the front of the ablution fountain. "I know," he said. "A new life is necessary. Maybe I've mentioned this to you before. In order to leap forward or to reach new horizons, one still has to stand on some solid ground. A sense of identity is necessary . . . Every nation appropriates this identity from its golden age."

Mümtaz nonetheless suspected that he, too, bore traces of ambivalence. Not because he admired time past but because he couldn't deliver himself from the annoying assault of the consciousness of death.

Their frenzied infatuation arose somewhat from this realization. The fact that he, and maybe he alone, knew this better than anyone was troubling. Often Mümtaz suffered under the assumption that the disquieting notion of death separated him from others. Didn't this absolute comprise the clockwork that had regulated his dreams since childhood? In his love for Nuran, didn't he consider her courage to live and her beauty something like life's victories? Whenever he took her into his arms, wasn't he declaring to the afreet of death looming just beyond her head, "I'm on the verge of vanquishing you. I've defeated you, here, regard my weapon and my shield"?

Nuran's likely discernment of this truth made Mümtaz anxious.

"We need to separate two things. On one hand there's a need for social progress. This can be achieved by analyzing social realities and by continually working to develop them. Naturally, Istanbul won't remain just a place that produces lettuce. Istanbul, and each part of the homeland, requires a reform program. But our attachments to the past are also part of these social realities, because those attachments constitute one of the manifest forms our life has taken, and this persists into the present as well as the future.

"On the other hand there's our realm of pleasure. Or, in short, the realm we inhabit. I'm no aesthete of decline. Maybe I'm searching for what's still alive and viable in this decline. I'm making use of that."

Nuran concurred through laughter, "I understand that, Mümtaz. However, at times one risks remaining on the sidelines of life, living through just one single idea. In which case, completely different images come to my mind."

"For instance?"

"You won't be upset with me?"

"On the contrary, why should I be?"

"Something like an ancient corpse interred with all its adored objects, including jewelry, gold ornaments, and images of beloved friends and family. Once entombed, he comes alive and his former life begins. Stars shimmer, lutes play, colors speak, and seasons produce their progeny. But forever on the other side of death. Always conceptually, like a dream that belongs to another . . ."

"First, like an Isis, a fertility goddess bearing the golden disk of the sun, your image engraved upon a wall comes to life ever so slowly, sloughing off the constrictions of the ancient design, and you lean over my decayed body . . . but honestly, genuine art *is* created in this way. The dead are living in our heads at this very moment. To just live one's own life through another's thoughts, or to force time to accept an aspect of your being. Take, for example, the 'Hunched İmam' . . . the Hunched İmam, what a comical name! But what do we think about when listening to Tab'î Mustafa Efendi through his Aksak Semâi today? To us, he's a genuine warden of life and death. And just conjure, if you will, his existence for a moment. An unfortunate soul living off alms from a mosque charity in Üsküdar on one of these hilltops, residing in a suffocating wooden house squeezed between the manors of pashas. A casualty of life condemned, after removing his shoes at the threshold, to sit on his knees in a constricted corner at the gatherings of grand viziers from Fazıl Ahmet Pasha to Baltacı Mehmet Pasha. Maybe he wasn't even able to find his way into such gatherings. He might have spent his days among the lower echelons. Maybe he survived on handouts and small donations. Whenever we recite his songs, however, he makes an astonishing resurrection. He overtakes the roads of Çamlıca through which

Sultan Mehmet IV rode his charger bedecked in gold and gems, or rather, he infuses the entire panorama. And suddenly the man waiting for a more cunning compatriot to give him the opportunity to earn an extra five or ten *kuruş* with a 'Master, come join us in the *mevlûd* birth song of the Prophet tomorrow!' is transformed into one possessed of ample means of admiration and recognition . . . and maybe we've learned to appreciate each other by these very means."

"Isn't love the same in every part of the world always?"

"Yes and no . . . That is, not at all in terms of the physiological! Just think of the differences between insects and mammals. Think of the wretched reproductive habits of fish and crustaceans or the variations between humans and other mammals, not to mention the disparities between tribes, clans, societies, and civilizations." With a chuckle he quipped, "For instance, had you been a praying mantis, on the first day you'd come to Emirgân you would have devoured me."

"And as a matter of course I would have died from indigestion."

"Thank you, my dear . . ."

Mümtaz gave open regard to her unrestrained elation. Standing, they conversed on the grounds of the former manor whose grandeur and frequent guests Sezai Bey had detailed in his memoirs. The entirety of the distant Istanbul horizon, including tulle shadows of *hüzün* and a seascape gradually appropriating the twilight, became an enchanted backdrop for Nuran's visage! "Among elevated classes, an entire realm of culture, discernments, and web of associations serves to transform that fleeting moment of ecstasy, that physiological act, into divine pleasure. In contrast, conditions of life or ignorance in our *vatan* leave some of our own people bereft of the simple pleasure of a kiss." Then he added, "Everything from trendy boutiques or the demands of modernity, from sexual etiquette or feelings of shame, from the fear of engaging in sin to literature and the arts is a factor in this act of intimacy."

"What's the upshot?"

"Who knows, maybe it is just what it is. For in life, everything's a facsimile of all else in a certain respect. The female kangaroo carries its young in a stomach pouch. Anatolian women wrap their newborns to their backs as they work. And you carry Fatma in your head."

"I might be preoccupied with my daughter, but you're meddling with corpses seven centuries old."

Mümtaz was startled by the harshness of her retort. He'd only wanted to say something amusing to make her laugh.

"Are you upset?"

"No, but was there any need to mention Fatma?"

"I was reminded of how she never much cared for me and–"

"Then try to make yourself likable." Her tone was cross.

Mümtaz shook his head in despair. "Do you think that's possible?" Nuran didn't reply. She, too, knew how difficult it would be.

"As for the corpses in my head, they're certainly just as manifest in you. You know what's really depressing? We're their sole guardians. If we don't give them a modicum of our existence, they'll lose their only right to life. Poor forefathers, maestros of music, poets, and everyone else whose name and influence has reached our day, they wait with such longing to enrich our lives . . . and accost us in the most unexpected places."

They lumbered along, boarding the Kısıklı trolley. Nuran had forgotten about their squabble. She dwelled only on two comments: *First the praying mantis, that is, the female that eats its mate, and then Fatma? I wonder, is this how he perceives me?*

Even Mümtaz was surprised by these two comparisons that had come to mind. *Why on earth did I recall this insect? Or am I suspicious that she's a woman who considers only her own pleasures? Maybe she finds me to be overly sentimental and a know-it-all. She's justified in doing so; I hold forth on so many topics . . . but what am I to do? Since she represents everything to me, I'll submit to her with all my being!* At the trolley stop, a young couple – they were eighteen or twenty years old – was having a fiery argument. The woman's face in the twilight was a picture of despair, and the man, as was evident from his bearing, pressured her, displaying a formidable posture. Mümtaz and Nuran fell silent upon seeing them. *Love-stricken on the streets* . . . Or was his caravan of poetry, his thoughts, all of it, in fact, nothing more than what these juveniles were doing? For the first time he felt the anxiety that he was wasting his days for Nuran's sake.

Nuran had been gradually growing tired of his life and thoughts. The anxiety that he was confined to an absolute idea, to an orbit of sterility that took him outside of existence gnawed at him like a worm. It represented a vein of decay that would only grow with time.

Even if not in this way, uncertainty overwhelmed Mümtaz. The anxiety of losing her settled within him. For no reason, fate and the bewildering isolation with which he'd been acquainted since childhood resurfaced.

Their summer nonetheless persisted as the paradise of their worldy sojourn. The day after this outing, Nuran asked to be alone with him in Emirgân till evening. She wanted to sketch out the garden.

Half-recumbent on the sofa, she sketched repeated designs on a sheaf of paper held atop a sizable book on her knees. Her amateur, even childlike, line indicated each detail. She listed the names of flowers and palettes of colors in the margins. "Colors not to mix!" she wrote. A cluster of flowers, for example, was purely ruby or heliotrope. Each season, would boast a few swaths of color. The idea had come to her from seeing poppies sprouting in a fallow artichoke field. Only the roses would be distinct, burning like multi-armed, solemn torches, like lanterns and lamps left aflame.

Nuran, an avid enthusiast of roses, was mad for the velvety variety known as Dutch Stars, which were a sultanate all to themselves. *Let my clothes be démodé so long as exquisite roses bloom in my garden.* Next came chysanthe-mums. She found tulips to be too rigid; instead, she adored violets. When

Mümtaz mentioned that there had once been a violet garden at Keçecizade Fuat Pasha's Bosphorus-side *yalı* in Büyükdere, she became enthralled by this Tanzimat-era vizier. Besides roses, her favorite flowers were the blossoms of fruit and nut trees. Thus, the garden required plenty of almonds, plums, peaches, and apples. Though they bloomed briefly, lasting for only five days, they conjured visions lasting the entire year. Along with her love of flowers and trees, she also had an interest in keeping chickens. How might both be managed together? In the end, they agreed to have a largish coop made at the far end of the garden, a chicken house along with a small open space enclosed by wire.

Since coming to know Mümtaz, Nuran had dreamed that she'd live out the rest of her days in Emirgân. As Mümtaz became aware of her desires, he sought a means to purchase the house. But one way or another he hadn't been able to corner the landlady to negotiate. She didn't come to Emirgân. The pain of having lost four children in succession prevented her from visiting the neighborhood, not to mention the house she'd first occupied as a bride, and where she'd lived within splendor unimaginable to either Mümtaz or Nuran amid maidservants and adopted handmaids, *saz*-lutes and genteel conversation. He left his rent with the coffeehouse proprietor from whom an old servant from Rumelihisarı took it and sent it onward to the island of her residence.

Toward evening they continued to Büyükdere, eating dinner at a small restaurant there. Being the thirteenth of the month, they'd be able to make a *mehtap* outing beneath August moonlight. As soon as the moon rose, Mehmet arrived. Mümtaz found the youth's face pale and wan. He revealed strains of annoyance. Mümtaz had known for some time that Mehmet was in love; maybe his beloved lived here in Büyükdere. Chance had cast their lives in the dual plot of a Molière farce. Considering the affair of the Boyacıköy coffeehouse apprentice and Anahit, the story line was actually tripled. Do what he may, or wander in whichever sublime or unattainable climes that he might, Mümtaz was relegated to living by the laws of humanity and existence. Likewise, there was Mehmet, a man who could love without having known Tab'î Mustafa Efendi or Dede Efendi, without having been awed by Baudelaire or Yahya Kemal.

The difference between them was that Mümtaz perceived his beloved through a matrix of abstractions. Some Nurans traipsed along the Bosphorus seafront at the Kanlıca residence in shorts or a bathing suit; others struggled against sail and gale in a caïque, or slept beneath the sun with eyelashes fanned downward, their firmly ripened faces fruits, deep within whose flesh swirled rejuvenating and redolent essences; still other Nurans floated face up in the sea, clambered aboard a rowboat, spoke, laughed, and plucked caterpillars off tree branches; yes, a plethora of Nurans congregating as a multitude of figures with experiences spanning the centuries entered into Mümtaz's imagination.

Some of these figures, like poses and fleeting facial expressions, emerged from her deportment at any particular moment. Others, meanwhile, belonged to the consecutively manifesting identities in Nuran's living presence, through the awakening of a surplus of legacies inherited from her forebears. Had he never seen the photograph of Nuran wearing a Mevlevî outfit that İclâl had once shown him, Mümtaz would have still compared the seated Nuran, legs folded beneath her as she listened to a gramophone record, to miniatures of an Orient even farther east than Istanbul.

During any ordinary moment, in her comportment, her clothes, her changing expressions during acts of love, his beloved had a variety of personas conjuring figures that had passed before her into the immortal Mirror of *Ars*; personas evoking, with augmented intensity and perhaps in an agonizing way, Mümtaz's near obsession and the pleasures of her possession. Renoir's portrait of a reading woman was one such figure. Beneath a radiance falling from above, illuminating her hair like a golden spray, the flaxen dream burgeoning like a posy of roses between the dark naphtha green background and her outfit of ferrous black cloth, with pink tulle concealing her neck, served as one of the most faithful aesthetic mirrors to certain passing hours of his ladylove through a handful of similarities including the pleasant calm of her face, the dark line of her lowered eyelids, the abrupt gathering of the chin into a small protrusion, and the sweet, almost nourishing smile upon her lips. Mümtaz's imagination, within its obsession for Nuran, at times took her resemblance to the Renoir even further, and uncovered in her figure a likeness to the exuberance of flesh depicted by venerated Venetian masters of the Renaissance.

Tonight, however, against the backdrop of the gilded night issuing from the open window, within the wide décolleté of her gown, the woman with bare, sunburned arms and her hair parted down the middle ever so hastily after leaving the *hamam* of the sea was not the lady of intimate hours – evening light dripping like honey into a room with drawn curtains – pursued by so many poets and painters from the 1890s onward and captured by Renoir after repeated attempts. Presently, through the harsh cognizance and intense vivacity of her half-shaded face and head, and a keenness in her eyes that threatened to devour her entire face, Nuran more closely recalled the Florentine woman in Ghirlandaio's *Presentation of the Virgin at the Temple*, recalling the semiancient earthly glory that flowed through her entire being and into the piazza receding to a distant vanishing point, her left hand perched upon her hip and her head cocked gracefully, highlighting the slight protrusion of her temple and the dimple on her chin which all but touched her shoulder.

Semblances of Nuran, transforming from moment to moment, became the young man's agony and ecstasy. These medallions, or labryses, warranted individually by a momentary thought, a feeling of pleasure, a sudden sensation, or a gesture didn't leave him in hours of solitude but emerged through a recollected sentence, a page in a book, or an idea. The most poignant pleasure, however, and naturally the sharpest anguish, came with

Nurans that came to life within a piece of music heard out of the blue. These semblances manifested abruptly within the arabesque of the melody or the golden rain of the musical ensemble, they appeared and disappeared there, and they glared and jeered at Mümtaz from a measure of time transcending everyday experience, and consequently, the mode of the memory altered and became an echo of prior existences stirring awake.

The venture of living augmented exponentially through the enchantments of seeking Nuran in his surroundings and his past, discovering traces of her seasoning in all experiences, and seeing her before him in the legends, faiths, and arts of centuries – essentially through different personas yet always as herself.

Nuran, in his perspective, represented the golden key to time past as well as the seed of the private fable that Mümtaz considered the first condition for all forms of art and philosophy.

Mehmet's beloved, whom he never saw, neither passed through the ring of these personas nor did he digress in his private fable, which was omnipresent in all things.

Mehmet adored and thought of his girlfriend without seeking in her the traces of any literary heroine, without savoring her bouquet in any chance chalice of music, and he approached her with the virility of a primal man who satisfied everything, every pleasure, through his body. The pleasures Mümtaz sought across centuries were for Mehmet satisfied solely by the flesh.

Likewise the Boyacıköy coffeehouse apprentice didn't regard Anahit as a presence whose semblance might be found in the heavens. He neither sensed his own fate in the depths of her eyes, nor thought the rites and rituals of a forgotten faith had revived as he burrowed in her flesh. He didn't fear that she'd leave him, and when she was away, he rested by laying out his tired body on the dusty stones of the quay or the fishing nets heaped before the coffeehouse, or he teased the neighborhood housekeeping girls; and later, when he understood within his being that he needed her, stretching slowly, he cast off the torpor that had overwhelmed him and called for her, placing beneath the customary stone the key to his single-room inside the old fortress walls so that she might easily enter; and knowing that she'd rouse him when she arrived, he slept heartily without giving it another thought.

Tonight Mehmet was downright irritable and doleful. Mümtaz had grown accustomed to reading like a book the face of this youngblood who'd worked for him for three years now. He must have certainly argued with his girlfriend. Or else he'd caught sight of her hereabouts in a garden or restaurant with another. Maybe this was the cause of their quarrel. In any case, Mehmet's manner of enduring anguish varied completely from his own.

Mehmet represented a facet of undaunted humanity. He found resolve in his own self. Alone now before the restaurant, he puffed out his chest like a fighting cock. This conveyed respect and adoration for his physicality. Essentially it amounted to a primitive narcissism of sorts such that he only accepted a woman's body as a mirror, and when his reflection became slightly blurred therein, he cast it aside contemptuously and took up with another. Women were capable of the same. Nuran might one day act similarly toward him.

This thought, descending upon Mümtaz, assumed such cruel proportions that Nuran took notice: "What's happened? Is something wrong?"

"Nothing," he said. "A bad inclination of mine. The tendency to mull over an idea until it assumes its cruelest possible form."

"Tell me more."

Mümtaz explained, somewhat mocking his own state of mind. Why should he conceal something from Nuran relating to her? She listened, at first with ridicule, and later through a changed expression.

"Why don't you live in the present, Mümtaz? Why do you either dwell in the past or in the future? The present hour also exists."

Mümtaz had no intention of denying the present hour.

He experienced it distinctly through Nuran's face and imagination, and through the nocturnal Bosphorus that had become her earthly peer. Presently, her sweet state of intoxication merged with the benighted Bosphorus. Nuran's face gradually assumed intensity by internal surges and radiated inner light just like this blue nocturne.

"It's not that I'm not living in the moment. But, you came to me at such an unexpected time, when my experience of women and life was so slight; I'm at a loss as to what to do. Intellect, aesthetics, and lust for life all intersected in you. All of it merged through your person. I'm afflicted by the disease of being unable to think beyond you."

Nuran indicated the rising moon with a smile.

The ridge of one of the opposite hilltops reddened. A fine shimmer of radiance appeared, resembling half of a fabled fruit, and at once the deep cerulean clarity of the nocturne transformed.

"Whereas you'd once maintained that one had to separate existence from other notions. You said it was the inaccessible section of the house. Neither love nor other realms of life could intrude upon it."

Mümtaz abandoned the fabled fruit sliver: "That's what I'd once said. But with you it changed. I no longer think through my head but through your body. Your body is the abode of my intellect now."

Then Mümtaz explained the game he'd once made up as a boy: "One of my greatest pleasures is the refraction of light, and its variations. When I was at Galatasaray, I'd peer through my curled hand like a telescope and watch the light refracting from the ceiling fixture. It happens on its own, of course, all over the place, all the time. But making it happen pleased me to no end. Rare are the jewelers who could make ornaments of this kind. Certainly many hierograms and religious symbols have their origins in light and its refraction. To me, it was a poetics of illumination, like gemstones or even certain glances. You know the way a light source changes from brilliance to the glimmer of polished steel, to violet, pink, and pale purple flashes, and to sparks that needle and mesmerize us through the faculty of sight? An essential secret of art rests here: it's a dream conjured in the simplest way, almost mechanically. Now, for me, all Creation refracts prismatically through your body, which I madly crave." He thought momentarily, adding: "Nevertheless it doesn't constitute art per se, it constitutes something approximating art; that is, they're analogous."

By the time they'd stepped back outside, the moon, encircled by a faint halo of mist opening out in spectral shades, had risen considerably.

The equivalent of this night could only be found in Ottoman music; a nocturne attained through musical arrangement and orchestration. Here, everything was a repetition of all else in measures of the infinite. Yet these successive refrains, when one paid careful attention, mingled with each other to such a degree that separating or culling them was impossible. Mümtaz and Nuran floated in the rowboat. The entire panoply was in a state of perpetual becoming with golden seaweed, lucid undulations of waves, aggregate shadows in the peripheries like truths of unfathomable mystery, streams of radiance, and abysses deepened by darkness. In effect, creation, as Shelley wrote, had become a flowing power. Or rather at the threshold of reason, like a very bold idea, and hence not yet come to final fruition, Creation loomed in a state of ambiguity, that made its every feature more alluring.

A *peşrev* overture of the moon. A prelude breathed through innumerable lips into metaphysical *ney* flutes. Fragile chalices of light shattered, elixirs of bejeweled essences were quaffed in doses, quick and bedazzling, and archetypal gems were hurled to sea as if the rites of sacrifice were being performed.

As if chasing the moon, a group of dolphins passed, sewing their paths into the sea. Farther ahead, a ferryboat searchlight illuminated to yet another degree of lucidity locales where lights had already gathered. As if elucidating an ancient and exquisite manuscript, all ambiguous glimmers attained vivid clarity. Wherever the currents pooled, swans by the hundreds experienced a lifetime of momentary dread. This fragile translucent world of glass fell into its own music, into the strange state of expectant listening wherein principal instruments played perhaps in a nethermost region of unlikeness.

As Mümtaz placed his jacket over Nuran's shoulders, he said, "Behold the Ferahfezâ Peşrev of the Moon."

Truly, as with Dede's Ferahfezâ Peşrev, they'd entered a world that issued leaf by leaf from invisible *ney*s. Like the melody of a *ney*, their surroundings constituted a mirror reflection of gentle, profound, and unattainable mysteries. They rambled as if through the consecutive ripples of a numinous idea or of a love that had vanquished every defect, and they passed through a proliferation of unadulterated springs.

"We're on the verge of entering the universe of Neşâtî's couplet:

> *O Neşâtî, we've been burnished to such extent*
> *That we're secreted in mirrors purely radiant*

Nuran laughed, "Fine, but the material world of *eşya* exists, and we, too. Our bodies are material, aren't they? I mean, as is true for everybody."

"Praise be to God a thousand times over . . . but in my opinion, yours isn't like the rest."

"Blasphemy."

"Call it blasphemy or the shortest route to Allah. Don't forget that tonight we're in the divine body of the godhead: *Vahdet-i Vücut.*"

A fish leaped from the sea beside them, tracing an arch of brilliants in the air. Later, a little farther onward, within the steamy blue illumination of the sea, a whiteness of sorts frayed open.

Their satisfactions were beyond doubt. Despite their minds working furtively in contrary directions, they were happy to abandon themselves to the present. Mümtaz seriously doubted whether their love constituted the shortest possible route to Allah, or to any other destination for that matter.

Despite acknowledging the lofty and central place love held in life, he also recognized it as a single emotion that didn't minister to one completely. Also, he no longer worried about his naïveté being a source of annoyance to her. Besides, Nuran had accepted his manner of expression and thought. She'd forgotten her spite from the prior evening at Çamlıca. She'd only become irate with him because he'd shattered life's serenity. She'd confessed this to Mümtaz that morning: "Any woman is a little lazy when it comes to such matters. But I prefer being with you to my own comfort. I'm happy to accept you as you are."

With Mümtaz by her side, she found herself to be a submissive, naïve woman who went wherever her man took her. She trusted him. Despite his youth, he had stature, strength, and a distinct character, one that challenged others. In the face of life, he exercised the fortitude of one forged by a singular idea. She told herself, *Let him give my life some direction, and that should suffice . . .* The rest was her business. She could follow her man to the end. A warm surge of twofold trust emanated from her entire person, because sharing the thoughts of the man she loved and accompanying him was another variation of love itself. And, like the other variety, it involved being reborn from a state of depletion without potential, being pregnant to a world in womb and body. In her affection for Mümtaz there existed a maternal feeling, love, adoration, and a modicum of gratitude. *He's discovered aspects of me . . .* she mused.

They fell silent. Mehmet turned the bow of the rowboat away from Sarıyer. House lamps and streetlights, within shadows inaccessible to the moonlight, appeared tragically more crimson. The lights burned independently like selfish and envious souls that weren't part of the talismanic totality of Creation.

"You know what would happen to me at times when I was a girl? Maybe it's something that everyone experiences. In certain absentminded moments, summers at Libadiye or while sitting lazily along the Bosphorus, I'd have the sensation that I'd suddenly left my body. It approximated floating in emptiness. Strangest of all, it happened one night while I was dreaming. Again, I'd left my body. And I knew very well that I'd left it. I was extremely cold. For some reason, however, I didn't want to rejoin it. I awoke in that agonizing state, my teeth chattering wildly. You know that when I die, you'll no longer be attracted to my body."

"Who knows? I find death to be a matter of unthinkable ugliness. But you'll live on in my thoughts, . . . of course, if I don't go mad first."

"You'll fall in love with another. Your thoughts will settle in other abodes. The way we frequently moved houses in our childhood . . . it was so strange. At first we'd find it alienating. We'd always think of the former house. We weren't able to fit either our evenings or our mornings into those new rooms and halls. Later we'd grow accustomed to it."

As if embarrassed by this sentimentality, she began to describe her girl-hood. The house in Süleymaniye, the inner courtyard with a fountain and pool in Aleppo, the splashing of water, the ice cream at the Aleppo bazaar, the commedia dell'arte performances of a boisterous royal comic named Behçet in the tumbledown theater next to the hotel, the way her rather devout grandmother once stormed out in the middle of the show; then later, the frenzied exile, jam-packed trains, terror, crowds, the wounded abandoned en route, the anguish of leaving everything behind and heading away, of painful recollections like an amputated limb after surgery; then later, the house in Bursa, the Çekirge road . . . the beauty of the Bursa plain, and the manor house in Libadiye. Elementary school, the year spent in Sültantepe . . . Every detail revived before Mümtaz's eyes in ablur as if all of it constituted inseparable parts of their lives. A multitude of memories and sources merged through their relationship . . .

As Mümtaz listened, he thought about his historical novel on Shaykh Galip. The outline or the sections he'd written hadn't satisfied him. It needed further revision. He wanted to proceed through a resolute idea, not through trivial, amusing passages. As the moonlight spilled into the sea in the Kanlıca inlet like a golden channel, he explained to Nuran: "There are too many digressions. I don't want it to be that way. Listening to you talk now, I sensed the need for a kind of organization beyond the synthesis of an ordinary plot structure. Does a novel have to start at one point and end at another? Do the characters have to move rigidly like locomotives on fixed rails? Maybe it's sufficient if the story line takes life itself as a framework, gathering it around a few characters. It's enough if Shaykh Galip appears in this framework amid these people through the effects of his outlook and a few biographical scenes." Then, looking at the opposite shore, he added, "Under one condition . . ."

"Under what condition, Mümtaz?"

"The narrative should describe us and our contexts."

The Kanlıca inlet reveled in bygone moonlit nocturnes. Almost no other boats remained. The night had progressed significantly. Lingering sounds of radio programs coming from open windows gradually fell silent. Only the moon reigned: her realm of golden dreams along with the music of silence and themselves. The melody slowly increased its intensity, overwhelming him like an obsession.

Nuran repeatedly let her hand dip into the water, tugging and straining one corner of the sapphire silk cloth that the moon had pulled tightly around itself – only then did Nuran understand the oneiric and phantasmic nature of the night.

"Only this way can I avoid getting stuck on the page. Like the flesh of fruit that clings to the pit, the essential idea . . ."

Nuran said, "I've got it! The entire Bosphorus, the Sea of Marmara, Istanbul, the seen and the unseen, and all of us are like the fruit around the pit of the moon. We've always clung to it. Just look at these hilltops."

One by one, everything in their surroundings received the moonlight. The setting declared with almost feminine instinct, "Come, transform me, work me, transfigure me into something else, polish my leaves, turn my shadow into a harder and darker element." And the moon proceeded to draw it all inward from the casing, the sheath, or the face, appropriating it into her own being. Nuran's face sparkled like a fully splendent crystal bowl. The oars of the rowboat passing beside them dipped into and out of the sea within the glimmer of objects made of brilliants. Creation was a halved fruit around whose lunar kernel everything coalesced.

"Your so-called essential idea, what is that?"

Mümtaz fell silent; truthfully, what constituted the essential idea?

"The hidden face of life that smiles within us," he said. "Eros."

The night grew increasingly colder. From time to time slight winds blew, forming a spring of pure essences over the surface of the sea out of the floral scents wafting from hither and yond, forming a garden of visions. Waves fluttered and peaked in spots along the dilapidated quayside and where the currents met.

"The garments of the moon are being washed," said Nuran.

They existed in a world of pure sapphire: a misty, translucent blue along with a gilded deluge dispersing mote by mote, leaf by leaf, and flowing in wide runnels; *ney* melodies sounded by hundreds of unseen mouths, sheathed by an accompaniment of proliferating silence that transformed and progressed with the music.

Through the nocturne, street lamps, indeed all sources of light except the moon, assumed a bizarre torpor. In silence, being nothing more than what they were, lights extended columns, arches, and portals of golden fringes over and into the Bosphorus. At times these lights grew attenuated, nevertheless merging into one another like patches of golden seaweed.

The moon in the midst of all, the kernel of a fruit beginning to shrivel, drew about itself this exquisiteness at the height of its ripeness. A stunning sultanate reigned. All things exposed themselves to its rule, accepting its authorial order, and in kind, the order transformed each entity intrinsically, recasting it as the reverie of a vast and mysterious substantiation.

"The arc of genesis has descended over us. We're part of a single unified realm."

Before them, the village of Bebek obscured a large swath of the Sea of Shadows. The coastal lights, however, even those shining all the way from the opposite shore, jutted into this nexus of shadows, working prodigiously toward a future of inscrutable intent . . .

XI

Wandering through Üsküdar had given Nuran the desire to know Istanbul more intimately. An oppressive heat notwithstanding, they descended into the old city a few days in a row. Beginning with Topkapı Palace, district by district, they visited mosques and *medreses*. Toward evening they rested in Beyoğlu cafés or parted company to run separate errands before meeting at the ferry landing again.

Awaiting Nuran at the landing or focusing on the face of the clock when she failed to appear gave Mümtaz deep pleasure. It surprised him that men complained of the tendency women had of making others wait, a favorite fallback for comedians. Waiting for his beloved was delectable. Anything promising her presence was delicious.

As Nuran further came to know Istanbul, she felt Mümtaz was justified in his perspective. One day she'd asked, "Lambie, at your age how did you ever come to admire all these historical things?" Mümtaz didn't hesitate to describe İhsan. He explained that during İhsan's youth in Paris, he'd set out on the path of socialist Jean Jaurès for a time; and later how he'd abruptly changed his tune upon returning to Istanbul during the Balkan Wars; how İhsan had wandered through the foundations of our Turkish presence here, and how he never tired of reliving it as part of his subjective experience.

"İhsan's influence on me is immense. He's my true mentor. Thanks to him, I was spared such unnecessary intellectual exhaustion. İhsan's greatest virtue is that he points out shortcuts."

Nuran's desire to meet İhsan grew in proportion to Mümtaz's stories.

"In that case, let's go pay them a visit, or invite them to Emirgân. I want you to meet them anyhow. Truth be told, we're a little late as is. I refer to him as my older brother, but I consider him a surrogate father."

Nuran thought it over, then came to a decision, "Forget about it. It's annoying to be introduced as a fiancée at my age. In any case, we'll meet each other sometime and I'm sure I'll like him and Macide as well."

They returned to the topic of the sites they'd visited that day. They'd wandered through the Cerrahpaşa neighborhood. Nuran was stunned by abandoned *medrese*s, those dens of the destitute, weeds flourishing in their courtyards, roofs collapsed, by the ruins of the Tabhane district, and the gemstone design of the Hekimoğlu Ali Pasha Mosque.

On this August day, these areas of Istanbul were worn down by filth, dust, and heat. The piquancy of ruins, the fatigue augmented by heat, an array of sick and exhausted faces and the physiological collapse overwhelmed them. The city's inhabitants bore an uncanny resemblance to the city itself. Tired glances or bodies complemented houses squeezed into an area of four or five square yards, their boards bruised purple, their terra-cotta shingles broken, and their corpuses listing alee; had Mümtaz and Nuran not recognized this as the city of their birth, they might have taken it for a motion-picture set.

Like the private automobiles and luxury cars brushing and bumping the throngs on the street, occasionally an old white-and-sesame-hued manse appeared like an astonishing remnant of bygone wealth or of the luxury of life's bloom beside dilapidated, semicollapsed houses gnawed by neglect down to the window-box geraniums. Most houses were unpainted. From open, bare windows poked heads of desolation incongruent with these relics of the past.

Adjacent to them were twenty-year-old brick houses of indistinct architectural style, exceedingly tall or squat, that could never be part of any archetypal pattern, neither one matching the next, backs turned insolently to the aesthetic character of the neighborhood, their walls painted with blue-hued lime-wash.

Among the disarray of this poverty and filth, among the crippled and tired men and women who clogged the street, clothes in tatters, unkempt or having darted out without the luxury of a moment to comb their hair, in an unexpected place, its gilded stones cracked, sparkled a fountain of time past like a vamp who overcame her disheveled dress with her gaze, her figure, or through the intensity of her persona, a seductress who gave others no option but to focus on her face; farther ahead, a tomb with a collapsed dome maintained its integrity through an orderly and dignified façade; later still, a *medrese* appeared, a melee of children's voices emanating from within, its white marble columns toppled over, a fig or cypress tree sprouting from its roof; and naturally, an as-yet standing mosque with a broad courtyard welcomed passersby to go beyond the bounties of this world.

By the time they'd arrived in Koca Mustafa Pasha, they were exhausted. First they sat at the coffeehouse before the mosque, drinking tea. Next they paid a visit to the nearby sixteenth-century saint's mausoleum. Nuran quite adored the protective railing that had been placed around the dead chinar, the story of the tree, whose circumference was etched in Yesarî script, as well as the history of the site.

To Nuran, Sümbül Sinan still sat under the shade of this chinar. The care shown in the maintenance of the desiccated tree gave this garden of death the profundity of a masterpiece.

Along with this, the mausoleum, devoid of architectural style, housed a body that had influenced life from where it lay for four centuries. Supplicants placed hands onto walls and railings and offered their prayers. The saint cured the sick, opened doors of hope for the disconsolate, pointed out sources of light transcending death to unfortunates whose world had collapsed, and taught patience, renunciation, and perseverance.

"What kind of man was he?"

"All of these saints believed in spiritual causes, went through a degree of spiritual training, and learned to supress worldly desires. Therefore, they were exalted after their deaths. Sümbül Sinan is a little different from the rest. To begin with, he was a noteworthy scholar. Not to mention that he had a sense of humor and a sharp tongue."

Mümtaz paused for a moment and added with a chuckle, "Each of them has a few distinguishing characteristics. D'you have any idea how the man resting here got the nickname 'Sümbül'? He used to place blossoming geraniums in his turban. He was so in tune with our own sensibilities that he adored the Istanbul seasons."

"What about his contemporary Merkez Efendi? What was he like?"

"He was of a completely different nature. He wouldn't harm even the vilest of creatures. Despite having a great affection for cats, he wouldn't keep them in his house because they pestered our friends the mice. Could you imagine that a sultanate of the soul could be so easily established?"

Nuran thought and said, "I wonder if such men exist today?"

"They must exist, considering that neither the notion of salvation nor the door to sainthood has come to an end . . . The paths to Allah are always open."

Nuran stared at her companion as if she'd glimpsed one of his hidden faces. She'd expected to hear a modicum of derision, even disparagement or denigration. Meanwhile, Mümtaz had expressed himself in rather unanticipated terms.

Mümtaz felt the urge to explain himself: "I wouldn't say that I'm exactly religious. At this moment I'm certainly quite bound to the world. But neither would I intervene between Allah and his subjects, nor would I question the greatness and potential of the human soul. Not to mention that both constitute the roots of a national life. Just consider how many days we've spent in Istanbul and Üsküdar. You were born in Süleymaniye and I in a small neighborhood between Aksaray and Şehzade. We're both familiar with the inhabitants there and the conditions under which they live. They're all orphans of a civilizational collapse. Before preparing the formula for a New Life for these unfortunates, what good does it do to destroy previous forms that have provided them with the strength to persevere? Great revolutions have long experimented with this, and they've served no purpose besides leaving the masses naked and exposed. Not to mention that everywhere, even in societies of extreme wealth and comfort, existence contains myriad relics and is full of interruptions and half-formed lives. Sümbül Sinan and others like him are mainstays for these fragmented people. Just take a look at this elderly lady."

Nearly doubled over, she approached from one end of the road, leaning upon something between a crutch and cane, and neared the mausoleum with timid, feeble steps. She prayed, her toothless mouth mumbling; with her hands she clung to the railing and remained motionless. From the mosque front, Mümtaz and Nuran watched her every move. How meager her dress . . . everything she wore was in tatters.

"Who knows what afflicts her? As we speak, Sümbül Sinan is whispering in her soul and promising her immeasurable consolation. And if he can't provide anything else, at least he can embellish visions of the afterlife. All else aside, don't you think this human suffering, this search for refuge and despair, is enough to sanctify this place?"

As she turned around, stepping to the front of the mosque, something approaching hope shimmered in the woman's squinty eyes and distraught expression. She stopped there as well to pray.

Nuran, as if having stumbled into a labyrinth with no exit, shook her head. "A good dispensary, a few hospitals, a little organization . . ."

"Even if you established all of that, there's still the abruptness of death itself."

"People accept that, however . . .We're raised through its socializing force."

"We accept it in others! Not in ourselves. We don't easily accept the deaths of our relatives and loved ones. Through our own deaths all matters find resolution, but when our loved ones take final leave we're shaken to our foundations. What then? Are you prepared to just dismiss the downtrodden? I'm not saying *you* in particular, but there are fools who think this way and consider themselves powerful as a result. Take the Nazis, for example. Meanwhile, from the day we're born, humans are helpless and in need of kindness.

"Not to mention that your good dispensaries and hospitals aren't so easily procured. They demand high levels of productivity to support them, a social life of comfort and welfare, and an ethics fostered and created by work. This is what I mean by the transformation of social conditions."

As he spoke, he thought of his all night discussions with İhsan. Most of these were his ideas. When Mümtaz was yet an eighteen-year-old lyceum student preparing to submit his diploma exam, he'd been tossed into this forge of ideas. Now, as he conveyed them to Nuran in the courtyard of this small mosque, he recalled, as if distantly, İhsan's inspirational expression, his fiery rhetoric, his epiphanies, the measured gestures of his hands, his repartee flashing abruptly amid the heat of the oration, and his biting sarcasm. As they spoke, Macide would listen to them from a corner, her wool knitting in her hands, a honeyed smile on her lips, laughing at their banter and startled by their ire.

It'd been a week now since he'd seen İhsan. He wondered about him. What was he doing? What state were they in?

As chance would have it, they encountered İhsan and Macide walking arm in arm on the Galata Bridge that same evening. In his other hand, İhsan carried a weighty piece of luggage. Mümtaz introduced them to Nuran. Then he inquired, "Where are you coming from like this, *Ağabey*?"

"Over the past week we've been lazing in Suadiye."

"Don't listen to him, Mümtaz, for a full week he rowed us around until nightfall or swam as I fried beneath the sun."

Both of their faces were ruddy. Mümtaz could indeed imagine what Macide had suffered. İhsan couldn't stand being apart from her. Each moment of his life he needed his wife beside him. At times, in class at Galatasaray, after İhsan had signaled the respectfully standing students to sit down with an ambiguous hand gesture – was it a greeting or a blessing? – Mümtaz was all but convinced that he might produce Macide's head from his leather bag. Lost in nostalgia, he stared at the face of his "Pearly Sis." But Macide was preoccupied, all of her attention fixed upon Nuran, whom she candidly scrutinized as they conversed. When Nuran began speaking a little, Macide's face relaxed as if a taut spring had loosened. Macide laughed at her interlocutor. The human voice had a peculiar, almost metaphysical effect upon Macide. Neither clothes, nor age, nor occupation, nor even beauty affected her so.

She existed within the human voice, residing there in her most collected posture. When meeting somebody for the first time, she mustered all of her attention, listening to the voice and passing judgments based on its cadence; in accordance, she either approved of her interlocutor, simply remained impassive, or announced her animosity by declaring, "His voice slithers through one like a snake."

This vocal gauge of hers didn't consist of the "high," "low," "cracking," or "soft" descriptive words that others might use. One might describe a voice as being "pretty" or "ugly." For Macide, voice was distinguished by different criteria. Even its mode of perception was a factor. Like specialized devices used to pinpoint certain foreign objects or to measure the functional potential of sensory organs, her ear was effectively removed from her body. A keenness had developed within her like the olfactory sense of canines, or that of desert or woodland animals unaccustomed to human society; and as these creatures discovered certain special qualities in things only through smell, similarly Macide, through listening, uncovered moral characteristics in others and judged them accordingly. "So-and-so is a good person," she'd say. "And a very good person . . . but I think something's troubling him; his voice virtually bleeds," or, "He's very selfish, he's conceited . . . his voice eclipses his vision." These were the phrases Macide used to describe various states of affliction. Each individual speaking before her would either disrobe through his or her voice, exposing innermost secrets, or be sentenced by the verdict of a solitary judge.

One entered Macide's life aurally. She was attracted to İhsan through his voice and had accepted Mümtaz in like manner. Presently, she opened her soul like a giant clam to Nuran's voice where snippets of conversation would transfigure into a string of pearls.

Eyes closed, Macide listened to the people she admired. Perhaps as they spoke, she sensed the pleasure of bathing in cold, restorative waters rich with the untapped attributes of roots or minerals or even stars. When she abandoned herself to the current of a voice, traits of hers broke away and floated like objects drifting toward the unknown; and as people got to know Macide, they came to recognize the phenomenon. Her entire being conveyed the inertia of a flower-laden boat.

One might say that her strained nervous system transcended value judgments such as "good" and "evil," existing through an aural aesthetic of sorts. Macide had once described her condition to Mümtaz: "It happened before I fell ill, too. But less so. Now it's intensified. When I hear certain people speak, my body becomes rigid. It's as if I'm wearing a suit of armor."

İhsan attributed this peculiarity of his wife's not just to voices alone, but to the presence of the other person. Mümtaz inherently believed what Macide said. Since the experience was specific to her, why not believe her? This pointed to an effective variance of method between İhsan and Mümtaz.

İhsan went on to describe what they'd done over the week and with whom they'd met.

Mümtaz asked why they hadn't traveled up the Bosphorus to visit. İhsan answered, taking great satisfaction in the blush of Nuran's cheeks, "So as not to disturb your honeymoon." Later he promised that they'd pay a three-day visit. "The children will be going to the farm with their grandmother. We'll be free. Expect us in the coming weeks." İhsan spoke to them as if they were actually married, pleasing them both.

Once on the ferry, Nuran said, "Macide is quite beautiful. But she does have a way of giving you the once-over, doesn't she now?"

Mümtaz explained the phenomenon of voices, wanting to close the matter half jokingly and half seriously, "The lot of us is a little eccentric."

But Nuran's inquiry persisted. "You'd mentioned that Macide was ill; she seemed quite well."

"She'd been ill, but İhsan returned her to health."

"How d'you mean?"

"Through the birth of their child . . . İhsan has conviction in life, you see. He believes life consists of miraculous transformations. And the secret to life resides in existence itself. During Macide's episode, the eugenics employed by the Nazis were a widespread topic of debate. It enraged İhsan. Not even entertaining the possibility that a child born of a mother such as Macide might be unstable, İhsan believed that her maternity and new sense of responsibility would return her to health. He also considered the deprivation of the rights of motherhood a crime against her person and nature. Some doctors considered Macide a lost cause and advised them to separate their beds.

"In the end İhsan stood by his decision. Of course it was a calculated risk. How should I put it, a contrary outcome would have led to catastrophe. İhsan might have caused the death of the woman he loved. The birth might have further strained Macide. But İhsan trusted life. Sabiha was born without a hitch. And what a beautiful girl. Macide's previous state of melancholia diminished; only slight traces remained. At times she still loses herself in daydreams, but she doesn't tell stories to the ragdoll in her arms the way she used to."

"Could you have ventured such a thing?"

"I said we were an eccentric family, didn't I? If it'd happened to me, I would have done so too. But when İhsan asked for my opinion, I debated with him at length."

Nuran drew completely different conclusions: "As with every such gamble . . . the observer is skeptical about the act in question. Later he applauds the venture. Should the venture fail, however . . ."

"No, not at all, had İhsan failed, I wouldn't have blamed him. When I debated this matter with him, I gave it considerable thought.

"What he did was somewhat courageous. It was an act of commiseration; he was attempting to resolve a problem holistically. Had he failed, all of us would have been devastated. Maybe it would have spelled his demise or downfall. But I wouldn't have blamed him. Because İhsan, in this case, wasn't tinkering with the lives of others, he was playing with his own contentment. I knew he couldn't stand to live without Macide."

"Is he that enamored of her?"

"Excessively so . . . his whole existence passes in her company. Without her he wouldn't be able to work. He's even more articulate in her presence."

"Is the girl healthy?" Nuran thought constantly in terms of her own life.

"Yes, she's normal. She's only four years old, so it's too early to tell completely, but did you notice the beatific expression on her mother's face? You see, Sabiha has that same demeanor. And she has a vivid imagination.

Perhaps later she'll suffer some. But she'll persevere through life, the experience of which is quite sublime."

Living was sublime, quite lovely. The most exalted prayer couldn't approach it. Nuran learned this after coming to know Mümtaz, this naïve man-child who only displayed confidence when engaged in intellectual discourse. Living was lovely from daybreak to nightfall, to the hours filled with a thousand pleasantries including sleeping and waking, from dreams to fantasies to losing herself in the embrace of this affectionate buffoon, and later, to regaining her wits in those same arms again.

And what she observed today was lovely, even the one-legged man limping before them, and the solitary and suffering urchin whose face was ravaged by fire or disease that left one eye protruding. Seeing such things, agonizing and exquisite, before sitting beside Mümtaz on this ferry bench in the midst of an evening, even the remorse stirring within her felt exquisite as she thought about how she'd find her family waiting expectantly at home. Because it all wound the apparatus of consciousness by which we appropriated existence and objects. The ferry had made its stop in Çengelköy and continued onward.

They entered a profound night and the heart of the Bosphorus. In a short while they'd be at Vaniköy. She remembered the day they'd talked, sitting on the landing's hawser mooring post. Existence was a cornucopia, yet summer waned; summer, the pearl, the singular season of their lives. If only she had faith in life like Mümtaz and İhsan. But she did not. She was feeble before life. Due to this frailty, she might one day lose Mümtaz, one so vital to and dependent on her. For she knew herself well. She was incapable of relinquishing herself completely to a thought, or an idea, or a love. As soon as she entered the house, her mother's cross expression and Fatma's annoyed behavior would make her forget everything else. Her life lay in so many fragments.

She resided in separate homes. She resided in abodes of love and obligation. Passing from one to the next, she more or less underwent a transfiguration.

She knew all of this hadn't escaped Mümtaz's notice. One day he'd said, "Our bodies are what we can most easily give each other; the real challenge is sharing our lives. For a love to be genuine, two people must enter into a mirror and emerge as one soul!" Only searing insights that ravaged and exposed Nuran could make him utter such a statement. Mümtaz shuddered as if her silence oppressed him. "What's wrong?" he asked.

"*Hiç*. Nothing. You've gone and muddled my thoughts. Sümbül Sinan, Merkez Efendi, Macide, and everybody's intrinsic right to life. I'm exhausted and want nothing more than to be myself."

XII

Toward the end of September, the bluefish runs offered another excuse to savor the Bosphorus. Bluefish outings were among the most alluring amusements on the straits.

An illuminated diversion stretching out along both shores beginning from Beylerbeyi and Kabataş in the south, extending north to Telli Tabya and the Kavaklar near the Black Sea, and gathering around the confluence of currents, the bluefish catches gave rise, here and there, to waterborne fetes, especially on darkened nights of the new moon. In contrast to other excursions that developed as part of a venture demanding long outings, this carnival dance developed then and there, with everyone.

Since childhood, Nuran had adored the seas over which caïque lanterns shimmered like brilliants swathed in black and purple velvets, the translucent darkness beginning where such radiance ceased, shattering a little farther onward due to another cluster of anglers, the wake of a ferryboat or small swells; she adored the rising of this luminous silhouette within a thousand prismatic refractions, the way it spread through the setting as if it might abduct her; in brief, she loved these nocturnal excursions for bluefish that conveyed a sense of occurring in a realm where reflection, glint, and shocks of light alone appointed a highly polished, radiant palace accompanied by crescendos progressing from small melodies and musical measures to vast and idiosyncratic variations.

Before she'd married, and even when younger, her father, who considered his daughter and Tevfik his only like-minded cohorts in the house, would take them fishing for bluefish. When she reminisced about these nights with Mümtaz, he didn't miss the opportunity to take summer, which had already been so wondrous, to a plane of higher pleasure. Tevfik was more than ready. He'd grown tired of Kandilli, his sister, and even Fatma. "I'll be spending the month of September in Kanlıca . . ." Since Nuran and her uncle would be there together, she'd be more comfortable.

When Tevfik went down to Kanlıca from the manse in part to present this plan to Nuran, with the excuse that the hill in Kandilli was difficult to climb after midnight, he'd abruptly turned into the Tevfik of twenty years prior. He stared into the windows of the old Bosphorus residences he passed as if to ask, "Have the damsels I'd courted grown younger as I have?" Twenty years ago, Tevfik himself was a popular diversion, just like the Bosphorus reveries of the Bebek inlet and the pleasure grounds of Göksu, the "Sweetwaters of Asia." Whenever he crooned from his rowboat of an evening or in the middle of the night, windows opened furtively, colorful and timid shadows extended out into the aether, heartfelt "ah"s, the frissons of reunion, might be heard, and flowers fell to the water's surface from trembling fingers or locks or dresses being straightened. As had been rumored, each of these songs and serenades was an explicit cipher or love letter of single intent between Tevfik and the ladies who'd opened their windows, let down their hair at the exact moment his rowboat glided past and, swooning from the music, had been brazen enough to drop a flower they held or wore into his rowboat below. Come what may, on the following day one of them would be certain to make a "stop at the tailor's," to visit an old acquaintance, a wet nurse, or long-standing maidservant, or perhaps, in a predetermined fashion, one of the garden gates of her Bosphorus residence would be left unlocked on such a night with a devoted servant or handmaid waiting knowingly behind it.

Mümtaz adored this old-world philanderer, who, around the time of Mümtaz's birth, declared his love for the neighborhood ladies five times a day as if it were an inseparable part of the call to salvation sounded to the entire neighborhood from the minaret of the quaint mosque. Tevfik was possessed of a gentlemanly Epicureanism that found open expression only in the subdued air of satisfaction that collected in his eyes when he wiped his grayed mustache with the back of his hand.

A gentleman of rare experience, he facilitated Nuran and Mümtaz's appreciation of Bosphorus bluefish outings and their understanding of the role of ardor in human experience. From the very first day, he'd taken Mümtaz under his wing, diminishing the atmosphere of animosity in the household created by Fatma's jealousy – which had found a most fertile ground under Yaşar's wardship. Mümtaz was quite cognizant of the part Tevfik's friendship played in his amicable reception by Nuran's mother in the Kandilli household. Even when most resistant toward Mümtaz's visitations, she couldn't withstand her brother's enthusiasm and was oftentimes swayed by him.

That this salty philanderer regarded their love so earnestly astounded Mümtaz. Tevfik's profligate life contained little that might indicate his admiration for such passion. At first Mümtaz assumed that Tevfik's mask of approval concealed expressions of mockery toward his inexperience, or that he took Mümtaz seriously only out of respect for the feelings of his dearest beloved niece. Later, as Tevfik gradually entered Mümtaz's life, he realized that his rakish, extravagant, and at times brutal existence obscured bewildering pangs of nostalgia. One day Nuran's uncle casually confided to him that most ladies' men – objects of envy during a reckoning of one's life, or whilst one wallowed in depression after a missed opportunity for gratification due to a bankrupt phantasy – hadn't had the chance to love a woman fully or had lost this chance and attempted to make up for it by chasing after contingencies, an ideal, or an array of tired repetitions of the same experience . . . In short, men like Mümtaz who lived through a single beloved were the objects of genuine envy.

In Tevfik's estimation, it was impossible to be in love before a couple knew each other's physical natures. Most novelists made the mistake of concluding stories where they ought to actually begin. Genuine love was predicated on the experience of the body and persisted through it. People who'd been betrayed by fortune in their first experiences of the flesh would fumble through frustrating ventures till the end of their days should the inaugural experience remain untempered by others.

It pleased Mümtaz to find variant strains of his own ideas in Tevfik's notions of romance, although he didn't confuse this business with metaphysical colorings the way Mümtaz did; he saw only the realities.

This was like a human soul reincarnated in the body of a turtle that nonetheless continues to bear and recollect his former condition without ever revealing so in form, habit, or need. As with men in political and social life who goaded genuine ideals despite a base and carnal existence, there were those who goaded feelings of the eternal in matters of romance while nevertheless knocking on every available door.

It was likely Tevfik was one such profligate, though still bound to aesthetic beauty, the eternal, the pure, and the decent.

He more or less admitted this himself: "Don't end up like me, I'm stranded between forking paths."

As he spoke, sorrowful life experiences could be intimated in the shadows of his face. He was a man who'd paused at least once before every wellspring, overcome by the phantasy of cooling himself only there, but as soon as his lips touched refreshing waters, without even slaking his thirst, he trotted off, saying, "She wasn't the one, it must certainly be another." Like a wayward soul condemned to chase his own body in the indeterminacy of an *ârâf* windswept by chill breezes, he possessed body after body without remaining beside any for long, and now after the collapse of ventures, he'd come to warm his bones at the *aşk* burning between Mümtaz and Nuran.

For a decade, as he'd formerly done, Tevfik hadn't ventured out onto the Bosphorus properly, hadn't crooned aloud, hadn't attended reveries of debauchery, and hadn't sent letters of invitation here and there to the inhabitants of Bosphorus residences. Such dedicated renunciation in a man with such a weakness for social diversions surprised one and all. Some attributed it to the misery he suffered upon his wife's death; some claimed, "He's suffering from a guilty conscience," and others, within the justified incredulity arising from his decade of reclusion, were prepared to completely whitewash the past of which he boasted furtively and recollected with relish, concluding, "Maybe they've mistakenly accused the poor man and wrongfully slandered him. Could a man so bound to his wife commit such indiscretions?" According to the former group, Tevfik hadn't refrained from a single act of cruelty against his wife. The latter group, however, believed he was nothing but a victim of gossip and slander. Actually, Tevfik hadn't ever really loved the long-jealous, overly sensitive, and haughty wife who'd gifted him with Yaşar's psychological impairments – it was *his* son after all – and who'd been self-sacrificing and steadfast in her attempts to exact compensation a thousand times over for every act of decency. And he'd only mourned her passing as much as any stranger despite their long, shared life. He performed the traditional rituals of benefaction in homage to her soul within the spiritual security created by knowing that she resided in a distant place of no return. Had she been willing to live apart from him as he'd so desired, he'd have spared no expense to ensure her comfort and contentment, and thus in like manner, he made outlays for her lamented memory. When his wife was alive, Tevfik would have entertained any price for a separation, and he recognized such deliverance as a blessing – even if it had only effectively come toward the end of his days – repaying it as fully as he possibly could. But where the dear lady presently resided, she didn't need one red cent. And each year the few diligently arranged recitations of the Koran or recitals of the Prophet's birth epic were negligible expenses compared to the money he'd once set aside.

Tevfik's decade-long seclusion, his withdrawal from the world of dalliance and diversion, arose for different reasons. Due to old age, he didn't want to be relegated to the secondary, tertiary, or lesser tier of a lifestyle in which he'd once reigned supreme. Tevfik, who'd always lived in moderation despite his wanton social life, gave himself an age limit when he noticed his waning prowess, and of his own volition chose to recuse himself. Like a Roman consul who'd emerged victorious from battles to later step down from his post and busy himself with vineyard and orchard in a secluded village, Tevfik lived in the Kandilli household through his reminiscences. Now, in the new atmosphere fostered by Nuran and Mümtaz, a completely different Tevfik once again went out on bluefish outings, wandered along the seaside, and at least observed from the sidelines the diversions that he'd once so loved.

The day Mümtaz realized this he also understood that the sparkle of satisfaction shining in Tevfik's eyes as he frequently groomed his whitened mustache with the back of his hand contained a complete life philosophy. This gesture, a glyph of silence, amounted to erasure of the self and simple withdrawal when nothing remained to be accomplished. Whenever he straightened his mustache in this way, he said for better or worse that he'd lived his life and could now distance himself. Because this Don Juan didn't disappear amid lightning and gale in a climax befitting his past grandeur as in the tragic legend, he'd simply interred himself in nothing but this curt and curious gesture.

The husband-and-wife residents of the Kanlıca house – "relatives, one on Nuran's father's side and the other on Tevfik's wife's side" – couldn't seem to fathom these newfound traits of Tevfik's; they still regarded him as a distressed and downcast widower, and they spared no effort in putting him at ease by avoiding any reminders of his anguish. For this reason they'd even considered preventing him from staying in the quarters their son-in-law had first shared with their daughter when he'd moved into the house as a bridegroom. Clearly it'd be agony for Tevfik to stay in a room that harbored such sweet memories. But they were stunned when Tevfik boomed at the top of his voice, "Enough of this foolishness, I know that room, and it's the best one in the house."

In counterpoint to the bluefish season's opera of light, a sly comedy played in the Bosphorus residence. Mümtaz and Nuran met this farce with laughter, whereas Tevfik regarded it at times rather gravely, but more often than not in feigned bouts of ire.

Since good old Tevfik imposed himself at will upon others – his sister excepted – the established customs of the household were immediately broken.

Till then, they cultivated a life of tranquility and ever so timid gestures meant to avoid anyone's disturbance. Mukbile and Şükrü had no desire in life but horticulture. The lion's share of their days passed in the back garden and hothouse.

They filled the remainder of their time by culling seeds at the table, writing and responding to famous flower and bulb companies as far away as Holland, Italy, England, and even America, and instructing and advising neighbors and acquaintances who'd adopted their hobby. Since their tenants, a family of three living in another part of the house, had taken up the same hobby over the eight or nine years they'd lived there, the flowers made up a communal garden.

By the start of summer, the household routine had changed anyway through frequent visits by Nuran and Mümtaz. No longer did anybody make polite apologies for an unintended disturbance in the night or because someone had drawn open the shutters of his room before others; instead of initiating every conversation with, "Excuse me, I believe I might have bothered you just then!" all was relinquished to a "How are you?" With the arrival of Tevfik, the issue spun completely out of control. Evenings, the old man's *rakı* and hors d'oeuvre table was laid out on the waterfront terrace by the Bosphorus. Neighborhood fishermen could no longer pass by without stopping to chat, and the radio played without permission being granted individually by each resident. In this way, the owners of the residence and their tenants had embarked upon a brave new life.

Nuran and Mümtaz dined at Kanlıca or at the tavern in İstinye; or rather, they brought their food out onto rowboats. Under Tevfik's insistence, one night on the rowboat, in keeping with bygone revelries by moonlight, they'd quaffed their fair share of spirits.

When Nuran grew tired of fishing, she joined in the melody being hummed by her uncle, and upon notice of his niece's accompaniment, Tevfik raised his voice and the bluefish run became a reverie of musical delights.

Old Tevfik was friends with all the boatmen, the oldest of whom had known Nuran since childhood. And she'd become friends with them all. Boatmen aware of her imminent marriage to Mümtaz had even begun looking for vacant residences nearby. Mümtaz, pleased by such undertakings, because he believed they'd hasten the marriage protocol, noted down addresses so he could scout them out once the tenants had vacated in the fall; Nuran, on the contrary, took the opposite view so that the dreams she'd nourished regarding the Emirgân house, its garden and decor wouldn't just evaporate: "Hold off for now!" she said. "I can't spend day after day thinking about all that again."

The caïquier in his sixties who'd said, "Nuran won't be able forgo the proximity of the sea . . . Her father had a great affinity for it as well," added, "When you find a *yalı* and settle down there . . . just wait and see how I'll tend to you with a cornucopia of fish." If it'd been within his power, the obliging man would have presented the entire Bosphorus to Tevfik's niece as a wedding gift.

The couple admired the sensitivity of this old salt. Some nights he stepped aboard their rowboat and described old reveries with a spirited rhetoric that came from first-hand experience.

In his turbulent life he'd met with great success and gained vast experience; he'd both lived it up and fallen on hard times. Since the sea constituted the measure of what he loved, he could never consider himself down and out as long as he kept its company: "My grave, should I die with my wits about me, will be nothing less than the sea." Following the illness that he'd suffered at winter's end, after doctors informed him that he'd no longer be able to venture out to sea, he descended to the shoreline early one morning without attracting anyone's notice, set off in his caïque, and vanished after surrendering to the currents, a stone lashed to his ankles. Mümtaz, later informed of the death, mourned as if he'd lost a close relative, though he was heartened that the old man hadn't perished through some mishap far from his one and only love. In this abiding passion, the caïquier had discovered a trait befitting his character and fortune. With the quip, "I've gotten used to poverty, but not to old age . . . ," he displayed an ease of life held over from an era when wages amounted to less than a silver coin but tips could be worth upwards of twenty – or perhaps even a golden lira. While he described fetes held at the Egyptian khedive's *yalı*, boat revelries by moonlight on the bay, and Bebek reveries, the attentive couple felt that they themselves were reliving them.

To be certain, he saw in Nuran's beauty a reflection or memento of time past: "I've seen many things in this world, but never a lady as beautiful as this bride-to-be." Such adoration coming from beyond Mümtaz's milieu gave him childish pleasure. As the caïquier admired his beloved, Mümtaz believed that in this one respect he'd been reunited with a once-familiar world, his usual distance from which filled him with misery.

But the true marvel rested with Nuran herself. The way she waited silently, fishing line in hand, gave Mümtaz a taste of the precocious maturity of children.

To Mümtaz, Nuran's interest in her surroundings seemed astounding given her casual demeanor, her focus solely on the line she held. The rowboat lantern illuminated her face and brisk movements, which, within the waves, bobbed to and fro, at times straight toward him out of the watery depths as if from enigmatic realms and back, to affect him like alchemy that resolved problems beyond cerebral solutions. Mümtaz would thus leave the ambience cast by her petite, puerile, and coy vision to face the exigencies of his psyche.

At the first tug of the line Nuran's face hardened into clarity, and later, when the fish emerged, she began worrying about its quality. She made a childlike, headlong lunge toward everything that drew her admiration. Her excitement, or rather impatience, filled Mümtaz with delight.

Mümtaz, fully aware that this opulence emerged from his own imagination, knew nonetheless that some trait in Nuran sent his nervous system into a frenzy.

Time would come when his adulation would reach such a pinnacle that Mümtaz found his mortal jouissance excessive, and he began to worry about the consequences. Mümtaz's imagination might readily believe, for example, that in a chariot drawn by enormous sea serpents, a sea-foam-splashing Poseidon would take Nuran by the hand and abscond with her to an undersea castle like the ones found in Andersen's fairy tales, around which gathered radiant sparkles and curled scaly shadows of every velvety hue and shade, as if a multicolored taffy were being spun from pliant, mingled seaweed.

Doubtless, this amounted to a figment of the imagination. But during such nights, a mood in Nuran that drew his curiosty gave these phantasies prominence. At certain times, while standing before him, Nuran might seem completely withdrawn from his life. And this phenomenon raised the possibility, in accordance with Mümtaz's own mental states, that he was viewing her through a death shroud or across the space of oblivion.

His fantasies and anxieties bore a hint of truth; Mümtaz in essence lived in a dreamscape.

By means of their friendship, Nuran discovered a season of exception where possibilities flourished. Her every desire, every action, every thought, her passing annoyances, flirtations and overindulgences, and even crassness amounted to diversions as wondrous as art, drawing mysteries and aesthetic beauties to her, and transforming life's order through happy-go-lucky discoveries. Beneath Mümtaz's enamored gaze, it seemed that Nuran perpetually created herself and the objects in her midst anew: the response of the beloved, who senses ardor, to the lover's affections. Those outside the alchemy could never hope to understand this esoteric exchange. Nuran later discovered these separately experienced moments still present within her, involuntarily recollecting each in order to reexperience them.

She wove the weft of their days with vivid beauty and creativity.

On their return, after Tevfik had parted from them at Kanlıca, they enjoyed gliding before *yalıs* whose waters assumed the colors of naphtha-hued atlas silk, *yalıs* interred in the dark density of a laurel forest, a few of whose leaves were varnished by light; that is, they plied silhouette, arcana, and silence. This voyage to a semiemotional realm progressing by lunges from light to light cast from a balcony, kitchen door, or the windows of a house whose residents hadn't yet retired, was disrupted by the moon and its luminance in a suddenly yawning cove; and within the eerie serenity that the Bosphorus assumed after midnight, a ferryboat searchlight occasionally caught them atop a swell, focusing insistently on them as if rehearsing the tableau of a *mi'raj* quite different from accounts of the known variety – yearning to spirit them to lofty heights of the esoteric.

Through a matrix of phenomena that went unnoticed when Mümtaz wasn't present, Nuran grew alarmed under the illuminating fishnet of radiance approaching them, and she cuddled up to him: "If I'm frightened by a dream when we're together in bed, I'll cuddle up like this."

At times their surroundings became nothing but quiet sparkle, as if they existed within vast turquoise. The dark seawater filled with large gem clusters extended by the stars, and the silhouettes on one shore sauntered by as if chasing after rowboats on the other side.

During daylight hours, the oneiric mood in which inlets, hilltops, and copses manifested in perspicuity, as if each edge and curve had been individually embellished under luminous sunlight, became a mirage or phantasy of which the two of them became a part; for Mümtaz, this wasn't just ephemeral exuberance; it might simultaneously be an epiphany of aesthetic secrets approximating alchemy. Whenever he remarked, "This resembles a passage through your soul," he, too, realized how three distinct modes of beauty – that is, the aesthetic order, the cherished order of the natural world, and the feminine order of undiminished allure – mingled together in his soul, and how he existed in a peculiar dimension of sorcery and dreamwork.

He occasionally wondered, "Do we love each other or the Bosphorus?" At other times, he attributed their state of satisfaction and lunacy to the exuberance induced by Ottoman music. "These alchemists of old have us wrapped around their little fingers . . ." he'd said, trying to conceptualize a distinct Nuran or to locate her hermetically within her own aesthetic. But the fusion wasn't as superficial as he'd thought, and Nuran, by unexpectedly entering his life, illuminated things that had been present within him for a considerable time and constituted the lion's share of his spirit, and she'd established her sultanate in contexts that were more or less prepared to accept him; as a consequence, there was no possibility of extricating Istanbul, the Bosphorus, Ottoman music, or his beloved from one another. The Bosphorus contained a prearranged existential framework through its history, the hours of the day it regulated, at least in certain seasons, and through its diverse beauty that bespoke vivid memories. As for Ottoman music, its Dionysian effusion, writhing through rigid arrangements and unleashing a tempestuous deluge of roses, inspired one to be the prey and sacrifice of an absolute thought or desire, to burn in its forge, only to resurrect and again burn to ash; likewise, the satisfaction music provided the couple in seeking each other among age-old and virtually forgotten splendors, while inducing them to inhabit a prearranged existential framework opulent enough to confront any and all eventualities, demonstrated how this might be accomplished, and finally primed them emotionally to make themselves at home there.

But Ottoman music wasn't an art form that dispensed with humanity or depleted it by imparting a sense of devotional awe. All of those saintly souled and humble virtuosi, no matter how lofty the pinnacle of their art might be, were pleased to remain within society and to live communally with others.

Due to these two enabling forces that clung tightly to Mümtaz's identity, Nuran became an enigmatic being returning to live as the mortal substantiation of the historical, the sublime, and the vital; she became a spectacular presence vanquishing time through urge and beauty; and through her, he deciphered the logic of his aesthetic and emotional realms. Being next to Nuran, embracing her, and loving her assumed the quality of a force transcending the limits of her person.

Mümtaz was exhilarated by the semblances of fable and faith adopted by her in his imagination over these nocturnal returns.

When Mümtaz said that he'd experienced a *mi'raj* through Nuran's love, or declared that he'd seen visions of her distinct personas, like variations of the divine incarnate, in the ever-changing ornament and progression of the arabesque of Itrî's Nevâkâr song, in the Rast *semâi*s and melodies of Hafız Post, and in the great gale of Dede Efendi, whose cantus firmus would forever accompany Mümtaz, he genuinely, as it were, approached the true architects of this territory and culture, and Nuran's mortal presence actually became the miracle of a reincarnation. Within the figure of the beloved, Mümtaz craved the concentration of the cosmos and the gathering of a mode of compassionate love specifically Turkish, descendant from forebears whose moral code even reappeared as a carnal and bloody dream, at least in the most visceral folk songs. Synthesized within this mode were *evliya* folk saints as well as *türkü*s of Istanbul, Konya, Bursa, and Kırşehir that recounted romances of *efe* militants and youngbloods and also, resonating through forgotten years whenever he cocked an ear toward his childhood, adventures of murder and vengeance in sonorous strains, Bingöl and Urfa dialects and Trabzon and Rumeli *türkü*s filled with yearning, desire, and the urge for self-depletion.

Under the effect of such a bloody and violent phase of Creation, Mümtaz wasn't stifled by having limited himself to a single love or to the corporeal splendor of, in a phrase borrowed from the French, "a petite mademoiselle," but rather witnessed the construction of his own inner world stone by stone through their romance.

They'd finally get out of the rowboat either near the Vaniköy factory or at one of the empty waterfront quays on the outskirts of Kandilli. The last of Mümtaz's pleasures was to walk the remainder of the way back, sharing the weight of Nuran's fatigue in his body.

She often remained oblivious to Mümtaz's thoughts over these walks, made even more solemn and unendurable due to the advanced hour and the silence, his nerves frazzled by pleasure.

Soon, confronted by the high wall surrounding Nuran's house, he'd part from her company before the door that led to what seemed like the flip-side of fate.

Mümtaz detested his solitary returns despite the vivid and splendid memories of the previous twenty-four hours.

Dread filled Mümtaz every time he accompanied Nuran home, thinking it might be the last. He believed the human soul tolerated contentment the least of all emotions, most likely because nothing lay beyond it; one was obligated to endure contentment ignorant of its duration. One could forge through anguish, striving to escape it as if picking through brambles, hobbling down a rocky path, or trying to break free of a swamp. But one carried contentment like a burden until it was involuntarily laid down at the edge of a road or elsewhere.

Take prisons for example, or comb court proceedings or newspaper collections where daily misadventures are recorded in columns of minuscule type; there's no shortage of malefactors who've cast off burdens of joy simply because they've tired of shouldering them.

Aware of this, Mümtaz also knew that they were content; therefore he feared the impending loss of delight. The postponement of their marriage despite Nuran's open desire to live together filled him with misery. The actual meaning of separate homes was separate obligations, pleasures, and strifes. Nuran lived two lives at once, between which she maintained a precarious balance. The balance could suddenly tip against him through any randomly placed counterweight.

Even so, he believed that she regarded their summer as something exceptional. He discerned in her an outlook that quite simply anticipated the best from the march of time: "The summer's all ours, Mümtaz; we can engage in all manner of madness." Under the anxiety of losing her, this declaration assumed a thousand and one shapes in Mümtaz's head.

Each of these cruel and fleeting thoughts came with their opposites, and Mümtaz quickly cast them off. After Nuran had fully entered his life, she'd changed character a number of times in his mind. To be exact, beside the Nurans that inspired fear and awe respectively, a third Nuran emerged through sacrifices she'd made solely for him and the way she'd divided her life into hemispheres without any complaint. This Nuran, both loftier and deeper than desire, love, and adoration, as well as removed from any individual anxiety, was the Nuran of compassion that rose like endless inner tidewaters. Even when apart, Mümtaz wished for her happiness and holistic harmony of soul. His discovery of this emotion marked a genuine salvation, a maturation of sorts. He thus stopped regarding his contentment as solely limited to his own self, and his soul opened to human fate in new ways.

Toward the ides of October, their joy ever so gradually began to wane. Each felt inwardly and indeterminately that their contentment now suffered from mummification due to its dormancy. They discussed this at Kanlıca's İsmail Ağa coffeehouse on one of their most beautiful days together. They'd trysted at the *yalı* and toward noon crossed the Bosphorus to Emirgân. By evening they'd gone down to the ferry landing. Emirgân Square and its coffeehouse were cool and tranquil.

When they left the European shores of Emirgân, the sun had descended significantly, casting the Asian shore under the direct sunbeams of evening. It was a nostalgic, warm radiance that seized one, stuck in one's throat, and weighed on one's chest like an age-old *türkü*. Moving toward this radiance over a sea agleam from horizon to horizon, unlike the regular workaday trips they made, was like hurtling toward a land of promise.

Neither Mümtaz nor Nuran quite recalled ever before seeing the cerulean cast of the frequently cresting waves. A final wave that mixed deep mosaic gold and gemstone dust into a phthalo blue reminiscent of a Fra Angelico canvas – the wave infused by like like a downpour of divine absolution – virtually tossed them onto the Kanlıca ferry landing. One gunwale edge of the rowboat remained all but hooked onto the quay.

Mümtaz had never in his life seen such a carnivalesque setting. This was

241

no projection of the felicity of his inner self. Maybe all Creation, including people, houses, trees, the phalanx of Bosphorus shearwaters that soared past sipping the sea, pigeons and cats, the watermelons and casabas piled off to the side, had been roused from a deep hibernation. In the twilight, the sea bream dangled on the fishing line held by a policeman as if experiencing a peak moment and flopped along with the to and fro of the line, appearing quite satisfied to be a pendulum ticking out the remainder of its fleeting life. The officer, perhaps astounded by the jubilation of colors or pleased by the joy in Nuran's expression, with a solemnity that didn't in the least match his unbuttoned collar or unbelted overcoat, made a salutation by waving his pole above them, along with the scaly, titanium white symbol of forbearance and tolerance and said, "A hearty welcome to you both; your arrival has brought good luck."

Laughing at this semiformal and, with the sea bream gasping for life on the line, well-nigh tragic greeting, they took seats before İsmail Ağa's coffeehouse. Opposite them, two ladies waited for the ferry; behind them, a few aged gentlemen savored the evening in silence.

Something smiled through the surrounding objects quite separate from their radiance, their edges, their volume, and their attributes: a force superseding all of that. It was in effect the memory of previously lived time. The fullness of its warmth rose from the depths like nostalgia. Mümtaz paraphrased Yahya Kemal's then popular couplet: "Behind us, the old men of Kanlıca are preparing for autumn . . ."

Nuran slowly recited the couplet verbatim:

The days foreshortened, agèd men in Kanlıca
One by one conjure memories of past autumns

And she added, "I'm in awe over the way one poet could vanquish a city through verse this way. Every time I hear this couplet, Rodin's *The Burghers of Calais* comes to mind . . ."

Mümtaz rounded out her thought: "The couplet captures something grand, an essence that will never change." This autumnal hour could only be described in such a manner. All indications were that summer had ended. This thought alone filled them with a feeling of foreboding within which they took in their surroundings.

Summer's end saddened them. A few days beforehand, Nuran had pointed out an early flock of swallows passing south overhead. And this morning, he'd arrived at the *yalı* with three crisp oak leaves collected en route. Worms of death had gnawed the leaves along their edges and had slowly traced a path toward their centers within the cerise of an evening. The once pliant leaves had assumed a hardened, calcified form, as if plucked from nighttime itself.

The song of a solitary bird sounded two or three times in stark yearning, the way a flute solo might bestir among violins and violas in an orchestra. They contemplated the likely tragedy that had caused this affect, yearning doubtless linked in some unspecified measure to the accident that fed it and gave it poignancy. At present in sprawling woods, trees sensed their sap gradually recede and longed to link their branches and huddle together for warmth while their desiccated leaves fell from the slightest tremor. The panorama was as variegated as springtime. The mastic trees of autumn had turned red like the Judas trees of spring, though more sorrowfully.

"Early one morning let's go to the Emirgân woods. It's exquisite the way the trees virtually shiver as they wake."

A cloud set into motion by a small wind kicking up out of nowhere first became a rose garden then, breaking into thin wisps, progressed until it was overhead, spreading out like a carpet before the forelegs of a fiery-maned black stallion.

Rising, they sauntered away. The shadowy road between the hills and *yalı* walls, under the twilight, resembled the tunnel of an ancient temple. Within this tunnel, from among the canopy of branches, they observed the nocturne that ambled together with them.

At this hour, when everything struggled under its own weight, they walked until Anadoluhisarı, holding hands and harboring intense intimations of fate. There they entered the small coffeehouse to the right of the pier. Night had completed its thorough descent. The dock was crowded with rowboats returning from bluefish runs. They watched their customary evening's entertainment as if it were a rather exotic ritual. And if at that moment someone had asked whether they trusted life, both would have responded, "Nah, but we're happy this is the way of the world!"

"Nah, but what difference does it make? We're happy now."

On the way back they mostly talked about the small apartment they'd just rented in Talimhane, near Taksim. Nuran's mother had declared that she'd be unable to remain in Kandilli this coming year. And Tevfik's rheumatism had flared up. Maybe the bluefish outings hadn't done the old man any good. For this reason, they were to move to Istanbul proper. Mümtaz said, "Not for the world would I ever live here alone!" Even if they'd stayed in Kandilli, the wintry silence and serenity permitted no possibility of their comfortably rendezvousing as in summertime.

The apartment satisfied them. Thanks to Nuran's frugality, it didn't end up costing much. When furnishing the place, Mümtaz gauged the degree to which foreign furniture had entered Istanbul at one time. Every sofa shop displayed furniture of every sort and style. As Mümtaz roamed with Nuran, he thought about Istanbul's changing standards of taste and lifestyle.

"There's no doubt that our minds are this way also."

Later they discussed Fatma's condition. All of Nuran's sorrows focused on this one point.

For days now Mümtaz had been anticipating an evening dinner invitation at Nuran's house in Tevfik's good company. Before she moved out of Kandilli, Mümtaz assumed she wanted to expose him once again to her everyday life in the house she'd occupied before they'd met, if for no other reason than Mümtaz, a man of daydreams, knew how to live in various dimensions at once and liked doing so. Thus, while they took supper in the garden, amid a conversation with Tevfik, or responding to Nuran's mother, he might readily contemplate Nuran's childhood dreams or the visions in little Nuran's sleep inspired by the rattling windows and rustling leaves over lengthy autumn nights. But Fatma's petulance made these phantasies irrelevant.

From the moment he arrived, the girl began her defiance, although she did nothing specific in opposition to Mümtaz. But she disappeared often, sending everyone into a frenzy of worry. She was unruly and always found an excuse to interrupt Nuran's conversations with Mümtaz. She nevertheless addressed Mümtaz in a hospitable manner, describing her new school and her friends there.

"I'm a big girl now. I'm tired of dolls. I want a pet like a cat or a dog to play with."

When Mümtaz said that he'd make a present of a puppy if she so desired, she abruptly furrowed her brow. How could she possibly play with a puppy he'd given her? It'd be like allowing the friend of one's enemy into the house. "No, I don't want that . . . ," she said. When others within earshot insisted, "Is that any way to talk, dear? Why don't you say thank you?" she was taken aback. Being reprimanded before Mümtaz was more than she could bear. Lips trembling, she said, "Thank you . . . ," and disappeared again.

Had Mümtaz been permitted to leave at this juncture, perhaps his life would have taken a different shape. But fate dictated that he stay. Besides, he wasn't a man who'd been born with an instinct for self-preservation. Any misadventure in life might find him like a deer startled in the middle of the road. That's just what happened. He couldn't bring himself to part from either Nuran or Tevfik. He'd been invited to dinner and he would stay.

Toward eight o'clock, they sat at a table of hors d'oeuvres accompanied by *rakı*. Old Tevfik had spared none of his skill in the orchestration. Even Yaşar, when he set eyes on the table, dispensed with all his health concerns and decided to indulge in a *rakı* or two. The evening began pleasantly enough. Despite the persistent rains, it was warm outside. Something about this evening of delights affected Mümtaz as he sat in the garden under a pomegranate tree and a solitary lantern, letting the gloam of the autumn night descend around him. Everyone was jubilant. Even Nuran seemed to have escaped the troubles that had plagued her as of late.

Fatma's arrival at the table, however, changed the atmosphere: "Let me sit with you, please, don't make me eat by myself . . ." Within a short time, she couldn't tolerate the way Mümtaz and Nuran sat facing one another. These were reactions they'd long been accustomed to; the coffeehouse storyteller's yarn that Tevfik spun persisted through her moody interruptions. On the third round of drinks, Fatma left to get something she'd misplaced but didn't return. She'd gone and invented a game for herself at the mouth of the well: a combination of dancing and running. Raising her hands ever higher toward the newly risen moon, as if to catch a ball she herself had tossed, her face revealed bizarre elation as she grinned, exposing her teeth. They watched her from where they sat. Her laughter increased and her movements quickened. At each turn, she slapped her hands back down to her sides before raising them again, stretching her entire body toward the golden ball of the moon.

Mümtaz, astounded by the rhythm in this child's maneuvers, said, "Just let me take you under my wing, and I'll be sure you get the proper instruction!"

He cherished her with odd insistence as Nuran's daughter and because he somewhat sympathized with her suffering. Besides simply liking children, Mümtaz recognized traits in Fatma reminiscent of his own childhood. Her sorrows and jealousies evoked the solitude of his own youth, despite its different manifestations. If he were to one day grow jealous of Nuran, he knew with certainty that he might resemble Fatma – moody, sullen, and overly melodramatic. Anyway, it was impossible to watch her in the short blue dress, her spindly legs turning at the rate of her own glee, as if preparing for a voyage to un-attainable spheres, without adoration and fondness. Despite this, a troubling unease had begun. Her laughter and jerky movements rather resembled a bout of hysteria, and as they intensified, the balanced maneuvers appeared to be forestalled moments of collapse. Her grandmother, Nuran, and the rest certainly noticed, for they began to shout, "Enough, Fatma, you'll fall . . ." But as they shouted, the girl increased her velocity. Mümtaz, to prevent the disaster that he foresaw, darted from his seat. But he was too late. Fatma lay stretched out fully at the base of the well. As Mümtaz raised her up, Yaşar came to his side. No indication of injury on the girl's body was apparent, though her knees were scraped slightly. The hysteric laughter had condensed into an tight knot of sobs, her body stiff as a board.

Yet the incident of the evening that truly affected Mümtaz came afterward. Yaşar, instead of attending to the girl, turned to him and ever so slowly, in a snakelike hiss, said, "Unhand the child. You've done quite enough already . . . Do you intend on killing her?"

Mümtaz thought that he would sense the frigid presence of Yaşar's glare on his back until the end of his days. He'd never witnessed the urge to lethal violence expose itself in a single glance. In comparison, a knife blade, a draught of poison, and even the voice that had hissed into his ear were innocent playthings. Mümtaz carried the girl downstairs to the room used during winter. After Yaşar had unburdened himself, he'd remained but an observer. Mümtaz laid the girl on the sofa and entrusted her to Nuran, following close behind him, and then he noticed a change in Yaşar as he stood by the doorframe. His face had become like white parchment and he was covered in perspiration. As if a vital coil had snapped, he was trembling, on the verge of collapsing to the ground. Involuntarily Mümtaz asked, "What's happened? What's wrong with you?" Without responding, Yaşar climbed the stairs.

Mümtaz returned to the garden to discover Tevfik sitting right where he'd been. The elderly gentleman was tranquil, as if nothing had happened at all. Shortly thereafter, Nuran reemerged. But the trio couldn't find the wherewithal to continue the evening.

XIII

Nuran arrived in Emirgân early the next morning, her first unannounced visit to Mümtaz's house. She'd spent a sleepless night. Fatma's intemperance had convinced her, if temporarily, that they must put their future hopes and plans on hold. Mümtaz still sensed Yaşar's vengeful glance like something daemonic that had been sicced on him as he lifted Fatma from the ground.

Yaşar, pitiful fool. Yet Nuran's mother would heed him. They might soon enough sway Nuran against the marriage. A number of impediments existed. Sooner or later, Nuran would be forced to forgo Mümtaz or she'd do something misguided and their lives would be poisoned.

Mümtaz hadn't slept either. He didn't even bother getting into bed, wandering and pacing until the wee hours of the morning before sitting in the downstairs hall till dawn perusing books to which he couldn't fully give himself over.

When Nuran appeared before him, everything changed. He loved her. One way or another they'd find a way out of the impasse. They chatted in the garden, one sitting on a small, recently painted flowerpot, the other standing and holding on to a tree branch. Mümtaz's solution was straightforward. They should simply elope immediately. As soon as the legal waiting period ended – one month remained – they'd apply for a marriage certificate and resolve this predicament in one fell swoop. Faced with a fait accompli, neither Fatma nor Nuran's mother could lodge objections. A child could cry for three days at most. Nuran knew that her uncle thought this way as well.

"Don't waste time . . . for the sake of a child's dream don't risk your own happiness."

But Nuran feared her mother's sorrow: "You mean unannounced? Not in this world, that day would be her last on earth," she said. "She wouldn't allow a chair to be moved from its place without being consulted first. Eloping would strike horror into her heart."

"She'll be fine."

"Not to mention Fatma. What if she were to do something rash? Our entire lives would be poisoned. I know about Fatma. I know about the characters in my household."

Nuran was a picture of pessimism.

"You'll see, Mümtaz, sooner or later they'll ruin us."

Mümtaz didn't want to cause her any more distress. At least they had some time. Anyway, he'd done nothing more than to survey a landscape with which they were already familiar.

"Let's wait," he said. "As long as you don't forsake me, we can find a solution to every problem."

Nuran staggered backward as if yet another abyss had opened up. "Mümtaz, don't touch me," she said. "My misfortune arises from others pressuring me. Accept that you'll have to be by yourself if necessary. I'm in this very state due to people who can't bear to be by themselves."

She knew her advice was futile. Mümtaz was one of those people. This was her fate: everybody became a burden on her miserable shoulders. She'd only yesterday received a letter from Fâhir: "Living without you has proven to be difficult. What would you say to letting bygones be bygones? Let's start a new life for ourselves centered on our daughter!" This was most certainly Adile's handiwork. Who knew the degree to which she'd incited his jealousy.

Nuran's assumption was on the mark. But there was an additional factor. Emma had apparently separated from Fâhir and fled to Paris with the Swedish magnate. Emma, always bemoaning the intrusion of an unfortunate mishap into her vision of a stable life, hadn't succumbed to the South American yacht captain this time, and had kept this alluring threat away from her new love.

So Fâhir wanted to return to his ex-wife. He needed a woman whom he could shelter and whose companionship focused solely on him. Despite their carnal incompatibility, he'd acknowledged and cherished Nuran's friendship. Now, in its absence, this warm intimacy came to life through a thousand phantoms. Not to mention that in just two or three chance encounters with Fâhir, Adile had conveyed how much Nuran loved Mümtaz, detailing her contentment: "Honestly, Fâhir, you don't have to be upset on Nuran's account. The girl is happy. And you're happy, too. Anyway, you two couldn't see eye to eye. But I worry about poor Fatma. She'll be torn apart between the two of you.

"They're in love with each other. The entire Bosphorus is their oyster! If you could see her now, she's not the old Nuran at all . . . I'm just wondering about everything you did for her, it's a pity, really, a pity."

Possessed of exceptional skills and methods in reawakening dormant desires or instigating a nervous breakdown, Adile, with two or three choice comments, by simply exposing Nuran in the setting of her new love affair, had succeeded in conjuring a fresh and completely unfamiliar figment of Fâhir's once tiresome spouse whose bed he'd abandoned of his own free will. As Fâhir listened, he realized that he'd never truly acknowledged Nuran, and since Adile never broached the possibility of reconciliation, Nuran's love became an eternal paradise lost. Furthermore, like the most sentimental of novelists, she dwelled on Fatma's existence and fate, perpetually describing the girl's misfortunes.

But that wasn't all. Nuran's former classmate from her university years, Suad, had also corresponded with her. Writing that he'd come "from Konya sick and desperate," and that he was recuperating in a sanatorium from where he'd recalled their onetime relationship, he declared, "You're the only one who can return me to a state of health!"

Nuran, aware that Suad had once harbored affections for her, assumed that by choosing Fâhir over him she'd effectively dispelled the affection between them. To add insult to injury, Suad was Mümtaz's distant relative.

"Come see me once in a while. For a decade I've lived for your sake. I'm at your mercy!" he wrote. There was nothing between Nuran and Suad; nonetheless, he was at her mercy . . . Who would come to her aid? Who would provide her with yearned-for peace of mind? Half the city was putting upon her; meanwhile, nobody came to her side.

"I'm not a nurse."

Mümtaz noticed that she was on the verge of tears and embraced her.

"Trust me, you'll see everything will straighten itself out."

"Nothing will straighten out, Mümtaz. Our lives will persist like this. You save yourself, I'm the one who's condemned."

Mümtaz hadn't ever seen her in such a state of lament. This couldn't just be due to Fatma's misbegotten behavior. They'd been experiencing that for some months now.

"What's going on with you? Is there something else?"

"What d'you expect? I'm being imposed upon by everybody. Here, read."

She handed him the two letters. Fâhir's letter was brief and filled with a slew of meaningless whining. He conveyed a tone ready to overlook all indiscretions through a single longed-for amnesty. But Suad's letter was bizarre. This married man, fully aware that Mümtaz and Nuran were involved and soon to be wed, expressed his feelings of love and extended an invitation, writing, "Come visit!" Along with his deteriorating liver, it was as if this decade-old or older love had erupted like a volcano, and in place of *Koch bacilli* spewed a magma of fiery words, gripes, and entreaties. He revealed the intimate details of his married life, explained the banality of his life outside of Istanbul, and repeatedly stated that he couldn't be content with anyone but Nuran. Neither his wife nor his children were of any concern.

"I'm at your mercy . . . Without you I'll be destroyed . . . I've made a number of ventures in life, but because you weren't by my side, today, you see, I'm nothing but a zero, a cipher, *sıfır*."

To Mümtaz, this letter was more threatening than the former because he knew Suad well. He'd periodically accosted Mümtaz since childhood. The entire household knew how Suad couldn't stand Mümtaz, who nonetheless displayed some affection toward him; *He's jealous of me on account of İhsan . . .* Clearly Suad displayed certain virtues. He was well-read and a bold thinker. Mümtaz also knew that Suad wasn't quite content in his marriage. Despite his continuous mockery of, and his delight in shocking, Mümtaz, at times displaying open enmity through his quizzical temperament, and despite his attempts to devastate him psychologically, Mümtaz still liked him. He admired and feared Suad. But he never expected such audacity. When Nuran and Fâhir became involved, Suad immediately married and moved far away. Mümtaz realized that the renewal of this love also bore a desire to contaminate others that had been brought on by the disease itself. The letter, full of impatience, pessimism, and protest seen only in that variety of affliction, filled him with greater dread. Yet another factor alarmed Mümtaz: Nuran's vulnerability to those in her circle. No other conclusion could to be drawn from her excessive reaction to these letters. Mümtaz was certain that one locus of Nuran's thoughts rested with Fâhir while the other dwelled beside Suad's sickbed. Within this oppressive anxiety, Mümtaz couldn't even look at his beloved's face out of the fear of reading her every thought.

And perhaps as a result, for the sake of doing something, anything, he slowly shredded the letters.

From where she sat, Nuran watched, as if from a vast distance, the destruction of pages pleading for her intercession.

"What I do know is that Suad was sick at the start of summer; he must have regained his health by now."

She looked at the painted flowerpot upon which she sat, at the plants wet from the night's rain, and at the chestnut's wizened leaves. A viscous sunshine of well-blended tincture, rich with mystery, filled the garden. The season had changed. Aspects of their existence constituted solely by love and diversion or simply by daydream and joy had been depleted. The remainder would be shouldered like a burden. Yet so many loads were being extended that she didn't know which to bear. The best option was to surrender herself to the nearest, most endearing beloved. With Mümtaz's arm about her shoulders, Nuran walked through the garden where she'd once been so satisfied, over whose every hand span of earth she'd cultivated a separate vision, and entered the house.

For Mümtaz, that day was more unbearable than the previous one. They weren't going to give Nuran any peace. He knew this. She had a side that was vulnerable to others. They ought to marry at all costs. However . . .

Will I be able to find the strength to compel her? He absolutely had no conviction. He couldn't venture a single move for his own sake. He'd become conscious of the extent of his own feebleness.

The day was miserable. They spoke as if amid great crowds, over distances, or through a shroud. It seemed to Mümtaz that Nuran's voice was reaching him from afar, as though large amplifiers positioned between them perpetually broadcasted the mind-sets of Fatma, Yaşar, Fâhir, and Suad.

He found himself in an odd, disconcerted state. Till yesterday he'd lived only among those he loved; whereas today, like mushrooms sprouting overnight, a horde of enemies surrounded him. Fâhir, whose accounts he'd thought had been settled and canceled, had reappeared. Suad, father of two in Konya, from a hospital corner, amid coughs, phlegm, and dried blood, had begun penning epic letters to poison his life. Fatma, whom he'd wanted to adopt, to whom he'd been so attached, had orchestrated a full-fledged drama to antagonize him, to publicly announce that she didn't care for him, and to cast him as scapegoat and orphan. Not to mention she'd collapsed at the mouth of the well after making three trial runs. And then that gray-haired buffon Yaşar, that demented fool, had declared his hostility for no apparent reason whatsoever. Who else and what else would emerge? Worse was the slow and gradual birth of opposition in Mümtaz toward these expressions of enmity. Before then he hadn't even felt anger toward the Greek *palikaria* who'd murdered his father. Now vengeance took root within him, as well.

A rising fury told him so. Mümtaz, too, would become the sworn enemy of select individuals all due to the fact that he loved and was loved in return.

All this was due to an emotion as lofty and noble as love, which ought to be one's sole savior, from which one might expect all types of salvation in this fallen world. These afreets were born of love. Maybe tomorrow his own heart would turn into a crucible of lethal poisons like that of Fatma, Yaşar, and Fâhir, and he'd wander in their midsts hissing like a snake. Reading Suad's letter, he could imagine his fingers, yellowed by fever, crawling over the pages. It was daemonic, an act of evil. From a hospital corner, a man struggling against tuberculosis was attempting to afflict others on the outside. This letter wouldn't be the only attempt, of course. What other acts would arise from a desire to contaminate? Was this the way the disease targeted health, joy, and decency, or simply an act of hostility?

Fate had directed Suad's afflicted mind to believe that Nuran represented everything he pined for while recuperating in the sanatorium; consequently Mümtaz, now spiteful of an ailing and needy man, wanted nothing more than to pummel his face and protruding bones. This was one nexus of mankind's fate.

Fate is what confronts us, he thought. *What we wrestle against without being able to overcome it.*

Oh, how mankind, enemy of the sublime, unknowingly desired the destruction of its own happiness as well as that of others; humankind, enemy of peace and decency, enemy of its own self.

And perhaps Suad, during his days of illness, in a letter received from

Istanbul, had learned of Nuran's separation from her husband and recognized the opportunity for one last conquest. The desire to settle an old account. *Seeing that I'll be going to Istanbul, I'll take care of this business as well. A lonely woman, an old friend, and so many memories between us.*

A day of rain followed; Mümtaz descended to the old city. He had to attend to a number of small errands. Afterward he stopped at İhsans' house in Şehzadebaşı to inquire about Suad. Despite having spent a distressing night thanks to him, he also wondered about his present state of health. One by one, the topics they'd discussed together at the start of summer at the island restaurant came to mind, along with Suad's gestures, his derisive and mordant laughter, and his bizarre glances that made one forgive his every affront.

It was as he'd feared. Stopping by the house, he noticed Ahmet and Sabiha at play with two girls, then he caught sight of Macide's relative Afife in the parlor, eyes swollen, face distraught, in the midst of confiding trouble and woe. A becoming, well-dressed, and polite lady, her demeanor, more than anguish per se, bespoke the pain of wounded pride. As Mümtaz listened to her, he remembered the letter Nuran had received. Hearing but a single sentence from those eight pages, directed toward her, would have revived this devastated woman, remaking her into a new person. But Suad wasn't interested in his wife. He thought only of Nuran. Out of some perverse logic, his afflicted head had turned to face and fixate upon Nuran. Suad likely thought of Nuran while committing the trivial indiscretions that Afife presently enumerated or even while trying to seduce his secretaries. He'd again thought of her while vomiting blood into the basin held by these woebegone hands and while signing the consent form.

As soon as he'd been admitted to the hospice, he'd told himself, *I must write to her this very evening,* and with eyes trained on the ceiling, his face tense with fever, his chest wheezing as it rose and fell, he'd pondered over and again the sentences that would make up the letter.

Mümtaz lent an ear to Afife's testimonial as he thought to himself,

Disgusting ... Disgusting ... Everything was reprehensible. Nothing simple and comfortable could exist between people. Mankind, the enemy of contentment, struck wherever happiness appeared or made its presence felt. He quit the house in a strange state of revulsion. He walked briskly down the street. Yet Afife's voice persisted, cursing her fate: "He's destroyed himself. I ache for him, Macide. If you only knew how my heart aches for him. It's just my fate."

Revolting. Her pity and consciousness of fate revolted him. Her attachment and complaint revolted him. All of it revolted him: the way Suad fell into his life like a stone crashing through a window, the way he wrote to Nuran, the way Mümtaz perpetually thought about this ailing man as if he were now an inseparable aspect of his existence.

Afife's voice: *Macide, you can't imagine what I've suffered. Just think about it ... for nine years ...* Suad's voice: *My entire life has passed at a remove from you so that I could establish some stability. But I haven't succeeded. You'll come see me, won't you? I'm in such need of refuge ...* Afife's voice: *A month will go by and he hasn't once looked at the children's faces. Let him just get well, I wish for nothing else!*

This was disturbing. He could observe Suad's life from two opposing perspectives, one represented by Nuran and the other by Afife. This doubled perspective should have removed Suad from the equation entirely and dispelled him. Yet Suad continued to be. Feverishly, he ogled the bodies of the nurses sashaying in and out of his room, and when he improved a little, he smiled at the youthful ones to spark their friendship, tried to caress their arms and cheeks, addressed them in a haughty tone meant to reveal his masculine pride, asked about their work, teased them with meaningful innuendos, and listened to their responses with a cocked eyebrow. When his health improved somewhat, he'd receive an earful from these nurses, and maybe in a quiet moment a slap. But this was on the sly, for when he met with doctors, he'd most certainly request that they address him as "sir," and he'd hold forth in a sonorous voice on politics, human rights, and public affairs.

For nine years... With a desire honed by nine years of disease, Suad had struck here and there contemplating young and voluptuous bodies; he'd sought mature women or he'd weighed and considered the possibilities of trysts like an engineer making complicated assessments about a tunnel or railway system, concluding, "There's nothing to be had with this one, but the other one there is just right!" or, "This one demands patience; as for that one, friendship is an absolute precondition"; he'd come up with schemes to dance with them or get them alone in a room or apartment.

Suad did exist. Yes, he existed in his hospital room, in Mümtaz's thoughts, in his wife's swollen eyes, in his children's thin necks, in the women's lives he entered like a hand under cover of darkness, feculent filth dripping from grimy, tacky fingers, padding through and besmearing a closet of pristine laundry; women, each of whom he stained with a fondle, yes, in all things he existed. And to add insult to injury, this Suad was a man of Mümtaz's acquaintance.

Beneath hard rain, he strode aimlessly. Once in a while clouds separated and everything on the street shone brightly down to the terra-cotta shingles; the fleeting presence of shimmering droplets on the electrical wires and the leaves of the municipality's freshly planted saplings, tops cropped *à la garçon*, conjured a vision of pearls; everything and everyone was bathed in childlike jubilation. Then the downpour began anew, children with jackets pulled over their heads scattered, older pedestrians took shelter in this or that nook, and the street, the houses, everything vanished. A blackish, murky shroud resembling ashen muck encompassed everything; the material world became the prisoner of rain. It pelted everything with a great clangor, emitting loud sounds from the tops of streetcars, the wood boards of police booths, rooftops, and shingles as if they were grand organs or harpsichords; at whiles lightning flashed, and this thick, pasty muck abruptly, but in a disconcerting way, lit up temporarily before the redoubled descent of webs of fine thread.

Mümtaz walked, head exposed. He'd never before felt such anguish. Everything revolted him. All of it was absurd. Everywhere he saw Suad's filthy hand and Yaşar's gray hair, framing his fresh "guard of the harem" expression. *This is how it's going to be then.* One could transform in twenty-four hours' time to become the sworn enemy of two people, two wretches. Two souls, say a despised tenant and an unwanted guest, could just move into one's life from where they might spew poison through their presences alone, by simply respiring under the sun, by looming and using words approximating one's own while describing their feelings and thoughts.

A taxi stopped short. With the affection of a kiln-fired roughneck, the driver said, "Let's ferry you along, young man . . ." Mümtaz looked around. Unawares, he'd come all the way to the mosque of Sultan Selim . . . a little beyond it. For a moment he wanted to disappear into the cool serenity of this old cathedral mosque. Beneath the downpour, however, everything was so miserable and sorrows of such intensity writhed within him that no matter where he went he'd be endlessly distraught.

Before the car door, which the driver had pushed opened, Mümtaz asked under his breath, "Fine, but where to?"

With the same cadence, the driver said, "Wherever you'd like to go, sir . . ."

"In that case, to the Galata Bridge." His head spun; he felt nauseous. He hadn't eaten anything. He wanted to go home immediately. But in this rain, what would he do at home? Nuran was gone today; had she come even, she'd have left by now. He imagined his writing table, lamp, and his books. He gave his seventy-eights some consideration. All of it bored and taxed him. Often, life could be endured by clinging to something. At this moment Mümtaz couldn't locate such a miraculous locus of attachment anywhere.

His thoughts resembled a disk whose diameter gradually decreased each instant, heading toward zero, toward nothingness. In this dizzying vertigo, everything shriveled and shrank, changing color and character until it became a strange accretion like the disgusting stuff of Suad's miserable and contaminating presence; the muck absorbed everything of note along his route, spinning and turning it in a tacky mass, and taking it all to nil.

It was a disgusting jumble . . . and he didn't want to enter his house with it. As a matter of course, this meaningless distress would end in a short while. Or else it would deplete everything like the emptying of a mill sluice.

He loitered on the bridge. No, it was futile. He wasn't able to return home. He felt intolerable agony imagining his garden, the melancholy of flowers and branches beneath rains that beat, briskly whipped, then bore down with great gusts upon the large chestnut in back and the clusters of trees in the distance.

"I'm afraid of loneliness," he said. "I'm afraid of loneliness." Actually, it wasn't just loneliness, he was afraid of entering into the circle of Suad's existence and instabilities. He turned and sought out the taxi. The cabbie hadn't yet gone.

"Take me to Beyoğlu," he said.

As they passed Şişhane, clouds parted momentarily. Above the Süleymaniye Mosque, sunshine gushed as if from a sluice through a massive, single-hued, nearly translucent cumulus cloud, the likes of which appeared in old miniature paintings. The entire city had become the opulent and ornate decor for a fairy tale of sorts, or a Scheherazade fable. He exited the taxi at Galatasaray. Under the pure, make-believe golden light, he at first wanted to walk up toward Taksim Square. But in the dread of running into an acquaintance, he turned back. He walked toward Tepebaşı. There he entered a small bistro. The rain had quickened again. Through the dirty window, he stared at the rain pelting the façades of the apartments opposite, pondering the immense radiance he'd just witnessed.

In the empty establishment, the garçon, bored from lack of business, repeatedly cued the gramophone with dance tunes. Mümtaz ordered beer and some food. The cold drink brought his wits about him; he looked around the sleepy setting. Despite appearing ordered from the outside, the tables and chairs whose paint and patina had flaked, and the multihued bottles of alcohol crowding the old shelves slumbered head-to-shoulder. Such a strange somnolence reigned, disturbing the ongoing downpour of rain and tango; it overtook them like waves of indifference rising in the wake of longing for the faraway and the unattainable. Nonetheless, he wasn't the only soul in the place. Upstairs, in a pantry-like alcove, a couple conversed, backs to the door. Amid the patter of rain and music rose a female voice from an indeterminate station of life, confirming its place at a fringe; a voice whose person was face-to-face with fate, perhaps satisfied, perhaps desperate; intermittently, the growl of a deep masculine voice responded in turn. They were any of hundreds of couples one encountered. But Mümtaz's distraught nerves reacted at once to these sob-like chortles. His emotions anticipated something significant. The vertigo that had turned his surroundings into disgusting muck on the verge of overtaking all Creation had slowed along with everything spinning dizzyingly toward zero about the axis of Suad's face or name.

The voices intensified:

"It isn't possible, dontcha know? I can't, I'm afraid, I can't bring myself to . . ."

"Don't be insane, we'll be ruined, Hacer, my sweet, we'll be ruined."

"I can't do it . . . I can't take my own child. Won't you divorce her?"

The snarling gramophone soon came alive. A downpour pelted the windows of the apartments opposite with a longing for the Andes and the Panama Canal, through the yearning of Singapore shipmen and Shanghai fishermen, the longing for things and people removed and estranged from the here-and-now, for whomever and however many things lay beyond thresholds of death, far away and alienated. Yet Mümtaz, now indifferent to the longing, couldn't be drawn back by any invitation.

The man's voice strained like the wail of a violin whose strings verged on breaking: "Just think for a second, I'd have no other option but suicide . . . If you want to see my demise, that's different."

She paused a while; then her already relenting volition made one final feeble and half-hearted stand: "Supposing something should happen to me, or I should die?"

"You know as well as I do that nothing of the sort will happen."

"What if word gets out . . . and it becomes legal?"

"Did anyone hear of the time in Konya? We know the doctor . . . go tomorrow, it should be handled tomorrow, you understand. I'm fed-up enough already."

A screeching chair . . . and perhaps the perverse affection of the sound of a kiss falling to the ground, then a hysterical sob. With visions of Havana, nothing remained but the ship of hard rain uprooting everything in its path as it churned toward shores of mystery . . .

"*Haydi!* C'mon, let's go. I'll miss the island ferry."

Mümtaz withdrew farther into a corner; and from there observed Afife's husband, the man who'd concealed his love for Nuran for a decade like a beacon of salvation, his back hunched, the skin of his face drawn over its bones as he descended the stairs followed by a thin woman – poorly combed brunette hair jutting out from a mauve hat – trembling visibly under a thin calico dress as she contemplated the misbegotten plans of her life. As the man settled the bill, he thrust his hand into a pocket. He removed and lit a cigarette. "I thought you'd quit," she said.

He answered as he wiped his forehead with the backside of the pack, "You never know . . ." With him leading, they exited and vanished into the downpour.

Mümtaz stared from where he sat, the cheapest variety of eau de toilette cloying his nostrils. The windows opposite had begun a new dance beneath hard rain; they spun, centripetal force drawing everything toward them as they jeered at the scene through reflections of death.

The estimations that he'd been making were correct: it was Suad, Suad who'd been in love with Nuran since before the beginning of time!

Out of fear of making eye contact, Mümtaz only fleetingly looked into Suad's face. Fate cast this instant as a revelation. The moment Mümtaz glanced, Suad cackled slyly, wringing his hands as if to say, "We've dispensed with that noise, haven't we now?" His laughter preoccupied Mümtaz for days. To fathom it fully, he'd have to search beyond human will and even conscientious life. This laughter was the suppressed chortle of a beast. No matter how much Suad praised and admired himself, boasting of grace-under-pressure by declaring, "An intelligent man knows how to get out of a tight spot!" his cackle and its bestial gratification belied an instinct less cunning than the fabled fox who purported to be wily though its pelt was to hang in the furrier shop, and this instinct seemed superior and success-ful because it only addressed what appealed to it directly, as a ready-made solution. No, this instinct was neither a dark temptation around which supernatural mysteries congregated nor a rarefied and rapacious appetite that caught its prey, regardless of the level of the heavens, to tear feather from feather and bone from bone. In Suad, there existed not a single fable or a single wingèd ascension toward decency, the sublime, or loftiness. The way she had resigned herself to defeat demonstrated that she was a bird of the same feather. They'd grappled and she'd lost. Tomorrow they'd separate, each on a distinct path, she in pursuit of dreams of marriage, Suad longing to forget through other conquests the vagrancy he imagined in his soul; in short, they'd entertain various encounters and possibilities before one day meeting again, and amid bygone dreams and dread, they'd reunite, frolic one atop the other, perhaps pay a visit to the doctor again, and by and by another embryo in the nighttime of formation, eyes yet sealed, would be tossed to the city's sewers without having seen the rays of the sun ... and so on and so forth, till the end, till the woebegotten fruits of the tree of death rotted fully and fell away, they'd live out their fate.

He stood, paid his bill, and stepped out into the street. He walked slowly. His previous vertigo and nausea had ceased; now, another strain of agony rose within him. He thought about the fetus. Tomorrow the fetus would be plucked from its mother's womb with a fine set of forceps. It, too, had been appended to Mümtaz's life through its brief misadventure. Tomorrow it would perish. Tomorrow evening a quivering, bloody clot of being, an anomaly resembling a skinned frog, would float in a cesspool of the city.

Tomorrow the central operator on Heybeliada would hear a bell. A voice from Istanbul would exclaim, "Sanatorium!" and the operator would plug the cable into the appropriate slot. A conversation would transpire; Suad would be roused from his bed: "Hello, hello, is it you, sir?" He'd ask, "Is everything in order?" and until he received an answer, his brows would furrow, and briefly with his entire being he'd swing between two extremities, before the lines on his face softened, and the perspiration on his forehead dried. "Thank you, good brother, thank you so much. Send her my best regards, I'll go and see her myself later."

It was the last venture of an unborn fetus as would be experienced by other people tomorrow. Later a taxi would be summoned, and a sallow-faced, afflicted woman would return to the home of a relative or a friend as elsewhere the doctor's attendants sterilized the instruments and washed the basins under copious amounts of water.

He wiped his brow. He walked from Galatasaray up to Taksim Square along İstiklâl Boulevard neither gazing at the shops nor the throngs inundating him from either side.

A tiny fetus, an unborn child. This, too, had been appended to Mümtaz's life. Over a period of forty-eight hours, his life had grown and expanded.

What else and who else would yet enter into it, all due to the fact that he loved a woman who loved him in return? A day in the life. Living meant being besieged by others and slowly suffocating. To exist . . .

But the tiny fetus, the children conceived by Suad and that woeful subservient woman wouldn't live. Tomorrow evening it would perish.

An urchin begged for alms, his feet, face, eyes, and hands covered in mud to such an extent that his voice seemed to come from a swamp.

"For the sake of Allah . . ."

Mümtaz verged on asking: "But how quickly you've emerged from the cesspool into which you'd been tossed? How have you managed to grow like this?"

"For the sake of Allah . . ."

His hand went to a pocket. When the mass of dirt and mud before him saw this, it became a bit more animated; its twitching hand closed over the money, and without saying thanks, it went on to approach the man behind Mümtaz.

"*Allah rızası için*," he pleaded again.

He would die. For the sake of Allah. He would die, tomorrow evening. The perplexing vertigo had begun again. Everything was spinning around him. It spun like a hoop spinning at the speed of light, and as it spun, everything blurred and lost color and shape.

"*Allah rızası için* . . ."

A child was to die. Tomorrow she'd have to call him. She'd have to say, "It's all taken care of, it's over!" This was living. All of it was part and parcel of life. All of it constituted existence: the sea bass marinating in mayonnaise displayed in the window of this restaurant, its membranelike skin before him, the saltfish whose rather frigid eyes lit up like a varnished yellow tin canister – whose extinguished eyes glared with the sheen of unpolished zinc – and the white-frocked waiter stepping on Mümtaz's toes.

They surrounded him as if they'd long awaited the moment of Suad's entrance into his life, and they gradually constricted him in that bizarre vertigo, closer and more firmly, without giving him the chance to move a muscle.

"What should I do? Allah, how to escape?" A small beam of sunlight shone suddenly. Like the soft angel hair of children, a treetop was illuminated by an iridescent light. Mümtaz stood stark still. He'd undergone an abrupt and astounding transformation. Neither the prior revulsion nor the constricting pressure remained. He looked around as if he'd awoken from a deep, extended sleep. With a feeling of satisfaction foreign to him and in a state of profound longing, he remembered Nuran. His eyes fixated on the radiance atop the tree, as if the wet light led to Nuran, emanating from lands where she resided; staring, he pined for her. Nuran was also part of his life, and as a result, the remainder, the confounding faces that filled the dark side of the medallion of life, had simply vanished.

But he wasn't at peace. The torment that had incapacitated him for two days hadn't dissipated but had only transformed. A profound yearning for Nuran and the dread of having lost her forever rose within him. He felt her absence viscerally as if he hadn't seen her in ages and he believed that he'd insulted her in unknown ways. He was convinced she despised him. Though he wanted to pursue her, the distances between them were impossibly vast, and it drove him crazy.

By the time he'd reached Beşiktaş, evening had fallen. The sky had cleared behind him; only the eastern sky was enshrouded in deep purple clouds. Within their shadows, the hilltops, buildings, and gardens receiving the last of the sunshine assumed unrecognizable, grotesque forms that stuck in one's imagination, as if they'd sprung from a spell or séance.

A dark and dank ferry landing: within a bizarre shiver, a fever of sorts, he awaited the Bosphorus ferry. Like a prisoner of fate, his face pressed to the iron bars of the pier fence, as if maintaining contact with his world through bars and interstices, he stared at the Asian shore, toward haunts of Nuran's habitation. In that state, Mümtaz might have recalled each prison *türkü* that had embellished his childhood with sorrowful *hüzün*.

Perhaps through this remembrance and through his own enduring efforts, he'd descended into a phantasy that would prepare the way for an episode of psychosis, or hysteria of sorts. Beset by delusion, he stepped back from the fence and sat on one of the wooden benches in the waiting room.

The waters before Üsküdar embraced an opaque night. This was no longer a summer's or September's night exposed like a daisy, whose charms laughed with open abandon. A few days of rain had drawn an impermeable shroud separating the *yalı*s and seas before which the ferry passed and the summer diversions and iridescent, languid hours that howled in a mother-of-pearl seashell, hours that had lasted till a day beforehand. Nuran, behind this shroud, gazed at him in remorse brought on by fathoms of separation, as if through a maddening lack of possibilities. Everything remained behind the shroud. His whole life, what he admired and believed, fables, songs, hours of intimacy, riotous laughter, unions of intellect, and even his own self, languished there, beshrouded.

Tonight a faded and feverish shadow consisting only of desperate memories and vague intimations remained exiled along with Mümtaz; instead of paving stones, the sidewalks were covered with memories reviving at first contact and assuming the form of reminiscences of days-past; tonight resembled a passageway from whose walls seeped melodies of nostalgic songs instead of water, Mümtaz could do nothing but roam, seeking out and searching for his former self by striving to sidle up to familiar sources of light one by one so as to warm his bones – yet whatever light he approached simply sputtered out.

From the lowered shades of *yalı*s filtered fuller and more woeful lights different from the radiance that had caught them so unawares on nights of the bluefish; street lamps sparkled through denser haze, and gardens and copses – like massive flowers with withered petals and faded colors – persisted as shadows that coiled around a name or a memory.

Things withdrew farther into the nether reaches, to an inner realm from where they sparkled like the scattered traces of ancient lives or legacies removed from anything personal, isolated and atomized. Just like the fiery glimmer of jewels in the old Topkapı Palace that he'd visited in Nuran's company, with their own particular astral shine in protective glass encasements, displayed without any recollection of the luminaries who'd once borne and worn them – numerous white hands and slender, straight fingers – without any recollection of chests and necks that were the matron and mirror of all desire. The ferry passed before each, as if wanting to acknowledge them one by one; and Mümtaz, from the corner into which he cringed, watched the deserted streets twisting and winding down beneath street lamps until reaching the Bosphorus and the ferry dock, whose boards yet glistened, and the small public squares and humble coffeehouses recalling the solitude congregating under oil lanterns in Anatolian train stations, coffeehouses living sequestered lives behind misty panes of glass in a state of introspection; each its own presence, they were satisfied to conjure this autumnal night at a complete remove from all other things. Mümtaz frequently murmured to himself, "As if they're part of another world," astounded that the life he'd lived up until yesterday had exiled him overnight; and he wanted to be beside Nuran so he could simply ask, "This isn't really true, is it? I'm mistaken, aren't I? Do tell me I'm mistaken. Tell me that everything is just as it was, that everything is actually the way it's supposed to be . . ."

Part III

Suad

I

Stepping through the garden door, İhsan exclaimed, "I saw the pair of them, they're on their way!" Then, in genuine elation, he quickly approached Tevfik, who was resting in one of the wicker armchairs beneath the large chestnut tree, his legs extended, feet resting on another chair: "The pleasure of your company, my dear sir . . ." His jacket and hat were in hand, his breathing labored.

The old salt said, "You're getting old, İhsan!" Tossing away the small throw that he'd placed over his knees, Tevfik gathered his legs and invited Macide, "my fair lady," to his side. Macide, tossing her sandy hair so it shone in the sun, kissed the elderly man's hand. He smiled silently at Mümtaz and Nuran as if to say, "You're a fine couple!" İhsan seated himself before Tevfik.

Mümtaz observed İhsan. He had worn the signs of age for some time. His hair had grayed and a slight paunch drew his torso to the fore. Large circles marked his eyes. But his arms were still sprightly and his body athletic. An expression of inner strength radiated from his face.

"Exquisite weather. *Allah sizden razı olsun!* May Allah be pleased with you lovebirds." He closed his eyes tightly against the penetrating autumnal light, turning his face squarely toward the sunshine.

"What's Sümbül prepared for us, Mümtaz?"

Mümtaz, smiling: "Today Sümbül is but the sous chef. Today's offerings have been prepared by Nuran herself."

"Under my supervision," Tevfik quipped in his sonorous voice. The childlike defiance of a gentleman of refined habit flowed from his face. He was pleased to see İhsan. In fact this invitation of Nuran's had consumed him. When Nuran announced that she and Mümtaz would be inviting İhsan, he said, "In that case, I'll prepare the food!" He'd made the list of offerings and selected the ingredients himself.

İhsan uttered effusively, "Oh . . . !" He hadn't partaken of Tevfik's fare for some time. "But is it only your fare? How long has it been since I've had the pleasure of your song?"

Tevfik raised his eyes to the firmament before gazing at the garden, the crimson-leaved trees, the tree trunks and branches turning purple in the distance, and the last of the grasses. His eyes traced the path of a bee to the garden gate. A peculiar and chilling warmth passed through his aging body. "D'you suppose anything remains of that voice, İhsan?"

His thoughts turned to bygone seasons, to a time when he'd been given the nickname "Honey-Toned Tevfik."

"Certainly. It's no secret that you bear a treasury." The honor of the moniker had been made by Tevfik's first mentor, Hüseyin Dede.

Through this recollection, the elderly man grew mournful and said slowly, "May Allah rest his soul. And besides, today you'll be hearing quite a lot! Mümtaz also invited Emin along with Artist Cemil," and in a soft voice he added, "I haven't yet had the honor of meeting this Cemil."

İhsan, overjoyed: "This Mümtaz is a true anomaly! He's expanding his entourage to be sure. But how did you get the idea for this?"

"In three days' time I'll be moving to Istanbul. Before Nuran goes, she thought we should all gather again."

"Where did you come across Emin?"

"I ran into him on the street. And he's promised to play the Ferahfezâ suite."

Tevfik leaned toward İhsan. "How many years have we turned back the clock, d'you suppose?"

"We exist in a region of timelessness, that is to say, forever in the same place."

"Yes, always in the same place." He felt like an aged, massive chinar that reigned over its surroundings. It'd be of no consequence should death catch him in this state. Hopefully he'd pass quickly through that portal, surrounded by everything he loved. He coughed slowly, and made as if to test the cadence of his voice: "I wonder if I can still keep pace with Emin Dede's *ney*." *Dying and succumbing to death are two separate things*... He'd witnessed the demise of acquaintances from a few generations one after another. The forests around him had thinned so this old chinar might stand out fully. The experience was so unsettling that for a time he'd thought, *Maybe I won't die at all! Maybe death has forgotten me*, and such a thought was becoming of his self-confidence, his bodily strength, and the sybaritic selfishness nourished by them; but for a year now... Thus, he wanted to go up against Emin's *ney*. Fifteen years ago such a contest wouldn't have entered his thoughts. With an "Ah!" emanating from the depths of his being, he'd have made the parlor chandeliers where he was being feted chime, or with a single resounding high C, he'd have shattered the glass before him.

Communing with Emin Dede might demonstrate that everything hadn't yet come to an end. The old man had even brought his *kudüm* drums along.

For a year now Tevfik had been curiously preparing for death. And he did so with the noble composure he'd displayed throughout life. He knew how to assume responsibility for his actions. And now he was attempting to confront fate. Not that he wasn't afraid. He harbored a great affection for life. As he approached frailty and senescence, he'd come to appreciate the tastes and indulgences of this fluke phantasy, a chance composed of the material. He'd ceded all his visions and his existence became what it was; that is, a body riddled by all manner of disease. And this body wanted to reaffirm its existence.

İhsan: "Suad shall grace us with his presence as well." Mümtaz's face fell.

Macide, who'd witnessed this, exclaimed innocently, "Don't do that, he's the only person who's flattered me in my life."

İhsan, wearing his always saintly grin, said thoughtfully, "I knew it wouldn't please you. But he does have an unusual appeal and strain of intelligence, though he's the type who doesn't know where or how to apply it . . . And maybe that's why he's disturbed. It seems to me that he's always banging his head against some wall or other. Apparently he caught sight of you the other day in Beyoğlu, but you pretended not to see him!"

Mümtaz fumed with spite: "I did so see him, but he was in such extenuating circumstances that I felt I'd be imposing if I greeted him!" Then inwardly, *Let's see what else I'll be accused of and how I'll be belittled . . .* He described the encounter in the small tavern, the woman with the mauve hat, the impending abortion, all of it. *It's as if I've fallen into the depths of a deplorable well!*

"As he descended the stairs he gave such a caustic laugh . . . and the way he wrung his hands behind the woman's back, as if to say, 'Thank God we've dispensed with that.'" Mümtaz wrung his hands awkwardly. He knew this was despicable. An expression of disgust on his face, he fell silent.

While recounting the story, he hadn't even once looked at Nuran. He spoke with his eyes trained on the ground; lifting his head from time to time, he addressed only İhsan.

"So that's how it's going to be then, eh? Whereas, he'd made mention of your weakness for alcohol. He commented that you probably drank in excess of what was salutary."

Mümtaz made a gesture as if to say, "You know me better than anyone!" Strange sorrows flowed through him. He thought he'd driven Nuran to the brink of a rift. *Suad, you're vile . . . accursed! But why am I so agitated! How is it that love has abruptly donned its mask of cruelties yet again? He's con-*

fused me with himself, one more step and . . ., he looked at Nuran, practically with spite, as if to say, "Let's see what else I'll have to endure on your account."

Nuran's expression was a picture of indifference. But when she came eye to eye with Mümtaz, she smiled. "What's it to us, Mümtaz? He's a perfect stranger."

İhsan tried to change the subject. "Three years ago this hill was nothing, but now I still haven't been able to overcome my fatigue."

"You're still young, *Ağabey.*"

"No, I'm not young, and furthermore, I've never been young. Neither have you. My father used to say that in our family we're born head to hallowed ground." He sighed, "I'm not young, but I'm full of vigor . . ." He raised his arms above his head as if doing calisthenics, then he embraced his own chest in a sort of expression of strength, as if squeezing something beside his body. Mümtaz carefully observed the grace of his athletic form. His movements seemed to challenge the flow of time. "For humans this is genuine satisfaction, understand, Mümtaz? Knowing full well what's ultimately in store yet nevertheless embracing oneself . . . it's a simple maneuver, isn't it? I'm wrapping my arms over my chest. I'm feeling my musculature. Quite simple. And despite the workings of death's inexorable cogs, I've rejuvenated myself. I'm declaring that I exist, but I might not tomorrow, or I might become another person, a fool, a dotard. But at this moment, I exist. We exist, understand, Mümtaz? Can you appreciate your existence? Do you worship your physicality? Hail eyes! Hail neck! Hail arms! Hail seats of darkness and light! I sanctify you in the palace of the momentary, because we exist in symbiosis within the miracle of this instant, because I can move from one moment to the next together with you, because I can connect moments to create a continuous expanse of time!"

Macide heaved a sigh. "Doesn't existence belong exclusively to Allah, İhsan?"

Mümtaz longed to listen to her voice, eyes closed as he used to do as a boy. He mumbled, "Adagio . . . adagio . . ."

"Of course, Macide, but we exist nevertheless, we also exist, and maybe because we do, He exists with such omnipotence. Mümtaz, what d'you think of this Macide?"

"Eloquent; eloquent and beautiful . . . She's become increasingly more youthful."

Macide chuckled. "I think I've grown old, İhsan, I'm easily flattered now. On the previous evening Suad–" Without finishing her words, she turned to Mümtaz. "Mümtaz, you've lost a pair of wings today, are you aware of that? But don't worry about it. If today was only the first time, it's of no importance. The first three losses are of no consequence, but on the fourth time . . ."

İhsan looked at his wife. "Did you make this up?"

"Not at all. Grandmother used to say so. It's apparently written in the Sacred Book."

Nuran, reappearing from inside the house, wanted to know what they were discussing. "What's written in the book?"

"Macide's asking Mümtaz whether he knows he's lost a set of wings today."

"But they grow back three times . . . don't dare be upset on my account, Nuran. My feet haven't yet touched ground."

"To tell the truth, I've never seen Mümtaz without a pair of wings behind him . . . ever since he was a boy. Even those days I'd go pick him up from Galatasaray on weekends, I'd catch sight of his wings before anything else."

Nuran, laughing: "Oh, Mümtaz, *now* I see how you've been indulged!"

Then Nuran grew annoyed, astounded that she was playing the game of guest-and-host in this residence, whose mistress she was not, wherein she maintained she wouldn't be able to make herself heard.

"We're experiencing the best of Istanbul days. The fall has been unequaled." said İhsan, turning to Nuran. "Don't mind Mümtaz. In fall, with thoughts of winter rains, he'll grow heavyhearted. Do you know why?" He looked at Mümtaz with affection and laughed. "His covering up too much, wearing too many clothes. When he was a boy, I always advised him not to overdress. People who do end up with overly active imaginations. Mümtaz, on a single God-given day, how many times do you live out the measure of your life in daydreams?"

"Honestly, I don't know for sure, sometimes five or ten times . . . but no more."

"Hah, is that so? That means you've learned to live in the present. In that case, Nuran has triumphed where I've failed. May Allah be pleased with you, dear Nuran."

Autumn hung before their eyes fully ripe, like a large, golden fruit. They partook of it and all its particularities, wanting to make it part of everlasting time or, in other words, of memory.

"If you lowered this wall, would the Bosphorus be visible?"

They all turned toward the garden wall. The reddish ivy that overwhelmed it evoked a small, insular evening. To conserve this exquisite twilight and the warmth of the memories it roused, Nuran quickly answered, "No, it wouldn't. The house isn't located on the ridge. In front of us is a small plateau upon which rest the neighboring houses; after that, the downward slope begins."

"Nuran made a worthy design for the garden." Mümtaz's eyes filled with affection as the couple recalled the semichildish composition of the designs that had lain on the table. "It upsets her that she's two years older than me, whereas I at times love her like a child!"

Tevfik grumbled, "If you want to see the view, you can go outside. If you want to gaze at the Bosphorus, go down to the shore! The garden's better this way, İhsan."

İhsan: "Yet, your seasonal flowers are few. You've been snared by roses."

Nuran, who'd dreamed all summer about planning the garden, looked about. For some time now she'd meditated over the first day she'd come to this garden, the apiarian buzz, the passing downpour they'd watched from the picture window, and above all the night entwined with bizarre emotions evoked by knowing Mümtaz; the night, a springtime hurricane. Ladies' voices distilled from Debussy's music scattered in her memory like the white petals of wild roses.

"Our climate produces wonderful seasonal flowers, all variety of Rose of Sharon, evening primrose, morning glory, Caracalla bean blossoms, and begonias." He raised his sights toward the sky. "This light shouldn't shine without blossoms." Then he asked, "What was the name of Cem Sultan's mother?"

"Wasn't it Çiçek Hatun, Lady of Flowers? Anyway, how did the journey to Bursa go?"

"Yes, Lady of Flowers, a nice nickname. Nice, in fact, quite beautiful!"

Nuran blushed and with a childish lilt said, "We were meant to go, too. I'd very much like to!"

"Let's go then . . . the season hasn't yet come to a close."

Instead of answering, Nuran made a doleful gesture with her chin as if to say, "Under these circumstances it's not possible. We've locked lips within mirrors of the past . . . None of our desires will manifest with any facility or felicity." İhsan paid no attention to them as he chased his thoughts.

"In the fifteenth century, had Cem Sultan succeeded to the Ottoman throne or had Mehmet the Conqueror lived twenty years longer, what do you think would have happened? His untimely death amounted to the greatest of tragedies. History dictates that lengthy reigns are always beneficial. For example, consider the rule of Queen Elizabeth or Victoria. Of course, if the conditions are right! Had Sultan Mehmet reigned for twenty more years, perhaps today we'd be a nation that had lived the Renaissance in its time. A bizarre wish, isn't it? Time doesn't flow backward. Even so, one succumbs to visions moving from the known to the desired."

"Even stranger is how we're unable to transform our lives despite all this accumulated experience."

"Had Mehmet lived . . . but he did not, and Cem Sultan was unable to triumph in his struggle for the throne. All the frenzied commotion, even betrayal, the desire, hope, and agony reduced to nothing but a small mausoleum. He rests beneath an ordinary dome together with his mother amid an array of tiles. But their remains, along with hundreds and thousands of others, made Bursa what it is. I visited during its most sublime season. Granted there was still considerable heat. But in the evenings the air cooled. I was mad for the flowers. Everywhere, they made the music of silence or a musical idyll."

Macide temporarily quit her blue voyage: "İhsan, do you remember the solitude of the evening lightning, you know, when we looked out from the Green Mosque . . . and later, the morning star?"

"Macide adores the firmament," İhsan said.

"As long as the skies aren't cloudy . . . I can't tolerate cloudy skies. At such times I always turn inward." She'd uttered this softly, as if for her own sake. Her disposition revealed the distinct bow of cut flowers wilting toward vase water. But the autumn light in this garden, transfiguring it into a lute and filling it with music, wouldn't allow Macide to indulge in melancholy. Resisting this required an emotion quite different than melancholy or misery, one of those despotic desires that occluded and erased everything. She turned her face back again toward the skies, to the sole and elegant, metaphysical and grand leaf of the firmament, losing herself in a venture of the infinite.

Such escapes constituted moments of great bliss in her life. One day in the hospital, a day she'd wept frequently, passing through numerous pincers of death, she'd discovered a window open to this azure invitation, from where her thoughts had taken wing toward the infinite. From that day onward, a part of her always passed from one deep blue stratum to another. Like a tired desert traveler, at times she'd come to rest at the base of a cluster of light. No one knew as did Macide how the light and its lucidity surpassed the confines of any reality. Presently more than half her being existed in this illuminated sky. She and İhsan sat at the base of a tree of radiance, conversing.

Tevfik made a hand gesture. "Hold on, now, I'm going to test my voice!" He smiled at İhsan as if to say, "Turn back the clock." And he began the Farsi melismata of the Nevâkâr song:

> *Whilst the rose sapling of the gathering does flourish,*
> *where is the rosy-cheeked cupbearer?*

This was Itrî, an alchemist of genius. Nuran kept tempo with her hand on her knee, her gaze intent upon the peculiar sparkle in her uncle's eyes.

İhsan harmonized in a low voice, as he'd done during the armistice years after World War I in the penitentiary where Tevfik had visited him.

Tevfik fell silent after reciting the first lines that set the crystal of the Nevâ alight then, upon completing the variations of the *makam* progression, said: "That's it . . . it's been years since I've sung that. I practically followed the memory of my voice. I've completely forgotten the rest."

Mümtaz and Nuran stood stunned as if they'd returned from great distances.

Tevfik's voice assumed a force through the Nevâkâr that they'd rarely witnessed, as if somewhere a Simurgh had erected a grand palace from a river or a flood of luminance. But more phenomenal was the way material objects in their surroundings suddenly transfigured through Itrî's alchemy!

"What's done is done. Might you honor us with a recital of the 'Song in Mahur' as well?"

Tevfik grumbled, "The Mahur song?" He looked at Mümtaz with ridicule! "Very well then, but in a slow voice." And he actually searched for the *makam* in slow meter before his voice took wing:

And you left even my soul full of yearning . . .

No, this was something else; none of the glory of Itrî existed here; just now they'd all had the same thought. Each had been incarcerated separately in a stone cell carved from igneous rock. İhsan said, "Itrî is quite communal! But this is nice as well." He fell silent for a while; he felt that they'd each again been imprisoned in the same manner. "It's difficult to escape the mood of certain things," he said.

Mümtaz: "Yes, it's difficult . . . so difficult that at times I ask myself, 'What are we?'"

"We are this . . . this very Nevâkâr. This very 'Song in Mahur' and countless other expressions that resemble them! We are their semblances as they manifest within us; we are the ways of being they evoke within us."

"Yahya Kemal used to say, 'Our novel is our song,' and he had a point there."

"Vagary . . . each day I turn to music a number of times. And each time I return empty-handed."

İhsan: "Patience."

Mümtaz, thoughtfully nodding his head: "Yes, patience . . . *patience dans l'azur!*"

"That's exactly it, Valéry's *'patience dans l'azur'*! Don't forget that you're only at the beginning. This time in Bursa I made close observation of this phenomenon. There music, poetry, and mysticism are expressed together! The stones pray, the trees intone divine mantras."

Tevfik stared at Mümtaz affectionately. He was pleased by his naïve excitement and enthusiasm. *Will he be able to accomplish anything, I wonder?* He would, of course, should life deign to grace him with the opportunity.

II

A commotion ensued at the door.

Selim, Orhan, Nuri, and Fahri entered in the unchanging pecking order and ceremony that held sway among them. Orhan nudged forward the short Selim, whose company he always kept, and followed behind him as if to say, "What would become of you if it weren't for me?" Nuri wiped his glasses at the threshold to better see the setting. Last of all, Fahri closed the door behind them.

İhsan offered a mild "Welcome!" to the group. Then he continued, "Don't dare misunderstand me!" he said. "I'm not being mystical; rather I'm seizing upon brilliance, upon a concept that is reality itself. I want us to know and appreciate ourselves. Only in this manner, by being ourselves, can we hope to discover what's human."

Orhan asked, "What astonishes me is how on one hand you insist on a context of humanism and spiritual values while on the other hand on social development, demanding the regulation of labor from the get-go. Aren't you being slavish to the material side of things?"

"But it's quite simple" – and his eyes registered Nuran gliding through the back door with a tray of glasses and an ice bucket. She was genuinely beautiful, and she exhibited style and appeal through her stride, her figure, her laugh. If Mümtaz knew his own strengths, life could be quite decent. But, strangely, from the very beginning he'd become mired in a web of tribulations. *And what am I to do? He should just go on and overcome these hurdles!* İhsan couldn't be of any help to his nephew. *If I advise patience, he'll waste time. If I say, "Have conviction, act without giving too much thought to others or your surroundings, act quickly and with abandon even," he'll falter.* In ten days' time the legal waiting period after a divorce ended and Nuran would be free to remarry. Mümtaz went to help her. It pleased İhsan to see them working together.

"Yes, you were saying it's simple."

İhsan waved his glass about. "It's simple because it exists in reality . . . and this need comes paired with the other. In fact, they're not even separate, but two sides of the same coin. On one hand we're experiencing a crisis of civilization and culture; on the other we're in need of economic reform. We must enter into the world of business and trade.

"We're in no position to choose one over the other. We wouldn't be justified in doing so, either. Mankind is universal. It discovers itself through work and productivity; the notion of a work ethic gives birth to modern society."

Mümtaz, contemplating: "In that case, work both fosters its own civilization and culture as well as gives rise to society. It falls to us to simply organize our material lives."

"Do you suppose it's that easy? First off, for us to do this, economic life must start and flourish, and society must regain its creative impulses. Not to mention that one can't just let life develop on its own. It's too dangerous. The past is always nipping at our heels. A surplus of half-dead worldviews and modes of being lie in wait to interfere in modern life. Furthermore our present engagement with the modern and the West amounts to emptying into a gushing river as an afterthought. We're not simply water, we're human society, and we're not a tributary joining a river; we're a society appropriating a civilization along with its culture, within which we possess a particular identity. Presently, we're doing nothing more than adopting the accoutrements of Europe while neglecting the social contingencies. We're conditioned to regard the modern with suspicion because it's foreign to us, and we look upon tradition as of no consequence because it's outdated. Our existence hasn't even attained the level of meeting our own basic needs . . . It hasn't achieved the prosperity and creativity necessary to present us with intrinsic values and ways of being! This duplicity, this paradox, continues to confound us in our aesthetics, entertainment, morality, etiquette, and conceptions of the future. We're content to simply exist on surfaces. As soon as we delve into the depths, indifference and pessimism overwhelm us. No tribe exists without gods, and we must forge our own gods or rediscover them. We must be more conscientious and willful than any other nation."

Orhan broke from his observation of Nuran: "In that case, you're of the opinion that a crisis is inevitable and unavoidable."

"Not simply inevitable. I believe we're experiencing it now." İhsan took a long sip from his glass. "Wherever I look, my ideas don't encounter anything that can hold out against them. Like an animal trying to make a nest on pliant ground, I can focus my concentration wherever I want to. But this ease is detrimental. It might seem that we can go wherever we want, but we always end up in the same void, amid decayed roots or among a host of possibilities that amount to nothing but impossibility itself. Of course, this stupefies us. Today one could say that a country like Turkey might become anything. Meanwhile, Turkey should become only one thing, and that's Turkey. This is only possible if it develops through its own contingencies. As for us, we possess nothing besides habits and a name, we hold nothing definite in hand. We know what our society is called as well as its population and territorial extent. Of course, I'm not referring to everyone and I'm not talking about vague intimations. I'm referring to culture in the shape of pure knowledge and ethics. But what of context and potential? We were born out of the collapse of an old agrarian empire. And we're still floundering in its economic mode of production. More than half of our population isn't engaged in any form of production. And those who produce don't do so effectively. They just work and expend their energy. But he who toils in vain tires quickly. Take a look, we're all exhausted! Neither factors of human labor nor land reform have been taken into close consideration with respect to our economy or existence. We can't seem to get beyond the isolated efforts of individuals. Today's labor should increase tomorrow's pace of progress. We're living in a dynamic geography full of predicaments; the world is increasingly moving toward unity; crises are erupting one after another. Granted, at present we're in relative calm. We've bound ourselves economically to Central Europe, and through clearing accounts we get by one way or another. But this delicate agreement might be upset, and what'll we do then? Anyway, this isn't the real matter at hand; the real issue rests in not being able to incorporate land and human labor into our lives. We have forty-three thousand villages and a few hundred towns. Venture out beyond İzmit to Anatolia, or beyond Hadımköy to Thrace. Except for a few combines, you'll find the persistence of traditional farming. The terrain sits idle in places. We have to embark upon a rigorous politics of population management and production. And we're faced with similar exigencies in matters of education and training. We have a certain number of schools and we teach various subjects. But we're striving only to fill a deficient civil service administration, nothing more. What will we do the day that administration is complete? We've made it customary to educate children to set ages. Wonderful! One day, however, these schools will only graduate a cadre of unemployed, and a class of quasi-intellectuals will permeate society. Then what? Another crisis. Meanwhile, we could put the education system into the service of economic production, thereby increasing domestic trade. This is the crux of the issue. Developing the domestic market. We could create a semi-agricultural, semi-industrial workforce. We have such exceptional resources in need of manufacturing. Take Istanbul. Only recently it was a city of elite consumers. All the goods of the Near East flowed here. To such a degree that once every thirty years the city burned to the ground, and yet the estates, manor houses, Bosphorus *yalı*s, markets, and bazaars were practically rebuilt from scratch. The farm animals of old Yanya, the tobacco of Yenice, Egyptian cotton, in short, the products of half the Islamic world were consumed in this city. Now eighty percent of the population consists of small-scale traders. At every step there's a small workshop, a tobacco works, or this or that type of factory, and guess how they all get by? Most often by gathering what's produced in the ground. Meanwhile, in Istanbul, a coordinated effort could transform the face of society in twenty years' time. Take Eastern Anatolia. There you'll find a treasury of immense possibilities in agriculture and animal husbandry. Begin from the Tortum waterfall in the north and phase by phase bring electricity southward to the Mediterranean. Not to mention that the Sea of Marmara is slumbering within its own riches."

"Fine, but what's the relationship between this and the concept of humanity or spiritual man that you just mentioned? You're talking about nothing more than transforming life's material means."

"People are also a material part of life. Haven't you read Charles Péguy? What a turn of phrase. Searing. Poverty makes man more decent and noble. But destitution makes him primitive and impoverished of soul. It destroys the human in humanity. Human honor is only possible with a given level of welfare. A level of welfare that enables employment! I'm not referring to the welfare along the Thames or to American enterprise, of course. My point is that a society that has reached the meager welfare we've been able to foster is certain to resort to the very gods that it appears to have cast aside. Social life discovers the values around which it orbits, and a guiding principle anticipates a community that has turned to face contentment. In place of certain haphazard individual efforts, the collective fosters a sense of responsibility."

As he spoke, his expression changed. Mümtaz was pleased that they were conversing like old times.

"One of our poets claims that it would have been great had Sultan Selim III learned a little political history in place of studying geometry. We might add that it would have been great had the men of the Tanzimat known something of political economy. Not to mention that there was quite an interest in learning about it. But by whom? Sultan Abdülhamit learned from Münif Pasha. It's unclear what the latter knew, and the former was an unfortunate man embalmed in his own paranoia, a sultan mad for power who incarcerated himself in a palace for thirty years until 1908. He was Turkey's public enemy number one. You know those unfortunates sentenced to a hundred and one years. He was one of them! What came afterward is well known. Suddenly we pass on to the dictates of historical events. We remained under such influences until the national victory in the early twenties."

Orhan stretched lethargically. The sunshine was quite exquisite and comforting!

"Okay then, won't all of this come about on its own over time? Or rather, aren't these developments that will happen in time?"

"Impossible, because time changes according to context. The time of the growing child is different than that of the ill. We're outside universal time. What I mean to say is that we must change our pace of time. We must catch up to the world. My perspective promotes our participation and progress as part of the procession even if we're at the end of the line, so that from one particular path we might reach the promenade. Time is, doubtless, a factor, but one that's different for the world and different for nations that have joined in the global workforce, and completely different for us in our present-day circumstances. If we just leave it alone, it won't serve our interests but will pull everything down into the depths, as with others in our predicament. Instead of giving us wings, it'll shackle our feet. No, as Shakespeare said, we have to sprint toward time. We have to grapple with it. We must persevere through our willpower. First we must acknowledge our circumstances. Then we must prioritize our tasks. Slowly and surely we must emerge into the global market. We must open our own markets to our own production. We must remake the family, houses, cities, and the village . . . As a consequence, we shall also remake humanity. Till now we haven't been able to focus on the human factor in a constructive way; rather, we've pursued numerous social and cultural reforms. We've been trying to achieve the freedom of establishing political opposition within our society. From this necessity we now need to awaken to greater and more essential challenges. One can't just keep on leveling the field. We need to erect an edifice on that field. What will this edifice be? Who knows the capacity of the new men and women of Turkey? We only know one thing: the necessity of relying on established roots. If we fail to do so, we won't be able to move beyond a state of duplicity. Treaties and agreements are always risky. Tomorrow we might have to pay for the ease that they provide today through the obstacles they cause. We must be very explicit."

Nuri was unable to restrain himself, "What do you mean by 'explicit'? The situation strikes me as being so baffling that–"

"On one hand we're for better or worse attempting to appropriate a certain technique, to become people of a contemporary mind-set. As we adopt that mentality, by dint of circumstance, we have to discard traditional values. We're exchanging models of social relations. On the other hand we don't want to forget the past! What role does this past play within our present-day realities? Apparently, it's only reminiscence or a nostalgia of sorts for us . . . It might ornament our lives! But what other constructive value could it possibly have?"

By 'explicit,' what do I mean? he thought. Then he raised his head. "I don't know," he said. "Besides, if I knew what should be done, I wouldn't be here talking to you, my friend. I'd go down to the heart of the city and gather everyone around me. I'd shout like Yunus Emre, 'I've come bearing your reality for you.' This isn't a matter that can be resolved by the first person who contemplates it. But, here as well, we can find a few things that need immediate attention. First, bring everybody together. So be it if the standard of living among them varies, it's enough that they feel the urge for the same New Life . . . Suffice it that one group isn't the mangled remnant of traditional culture and the other newly settled tenants of the modern world. We need a synthesis of both.

"Second, we need to establish a new relationship to our past. The former is relatively easy, we can achieve it by more or less transforming material conditions. But the latter can only be achieved through cooperation between generations.

"If we neglect the past, it'll jut into us like a foreign object throughout our lives. Like it or not we have to make it part of the grand synthesis. It's the source from which we must emerge. We need this notion of continuity even if it's an illusion. Not to mention that we weren't born just yesterday. The past constitutes our starkest reality. Now then, onto which of these roots do we make our graft? The folk and folk life are at times a treasure trove, at times a mirage. From a distance it appears like a limitless expanse. But on closer scrutiny, you're limited to five or ten motifs and modes; or you'll enter straightaway into fixed life forms. As for Ottoman classical or elite culture, we've broken free of that in many respects . . . and anyway, the civilization to which it was bound has been destroyed."

Mümtaz said, "This is precisely what I see as the impasse; because, as you've said, the past has no legs upon which to stand. Today in Turkey we wouldn't be able to name five books that consecutive generations read together. Except in rare instances, those who take any pleasure in older authors are increasingly fewer in number. We're seemingly the last link. Soon poets like Nedim or Nef'î, or even traditional music, which is ever so appealing to us, will join a category of things from which we've been estranged!"

"There are obstacles. But it's not an impasse. We're currently living through reactionary times. We despise ourselves. Our heads are full of comparisons and contrasts: We don't appreciate Dede because he's no Wagner; Yunus Emre, because we haven't been able to cast him as a Verlaine; or Bâkî, because he can't be a Goethe or a Gide. Despite being the most well-appointed country nestled amid the opulence of immeasurable Asia, we're living naked and exposed. Geography, culture, and all the rest expect a new synthesis from us, and we're not even aware of our historic mission. Instead, we're trying to relive the experiences of other countries.

"You know about the practice of exegesis, right, *tefsir*? Weighing and considering a text to absorb it as part of one's human experience? If only we could initiate that. That's what we haven't been able to do. I just now used the word 'appreciate,' but it's not enough to 'appreciate,' either; we need to go beyond that. We don't know how to experience ideas and emotions like living, breathing things. Meanwhile, this is what our fellow citizens want."

Orhan, incredulous: "Do they really? It seems to me that our citizens have been indifferent from the get-go. Throughout history they've remained at such a remove from us that . . . they're practically helpless in this regard; or at the very least harbor suspicions."

"Yes, our people do want this. If we stopped looking at history through the lens of today's grievances, you'd think this country was like any other. The distinguishing factor is the lack of a middle-class here. Developments were always pregnant with the possibility of its formation, but it didn't occur. The point of divergence begins with this fact. The indifference or suspicion of the people is nothing but a fable that we've concocted. Nothing but a rhetorical tactic we've seized upon to pin our opponents in ideological skirmishes. You know what I mean; those fleeting Pyrrhic victories that glimmer for an instant only in a reader's mind or that simply remain confined to the editorial pages of a skimmed newspaper? Victories of that sort! In fact, our city dwellers and villagers do confide in intellectuals and do heed them. What other recourse is there? Two centuries of political upheaval has forced us to live in a sort of battle formation. Threats of absolute certainty gave rise to such protocol. Our citizens have always confided in intellectuals and have walked the paths they've blazed."

"And they've always been misled, haven't they?"

"No, or more precisely, when we've been misled, so have they. I mean, as is the case in every nation. Do you really think there's something like rational progress in history? That's beyond the realm of possibility. But the cumulative strength of the society transcends the missteps of a single generation. It gives us the illusion that everything's progressing apace. Rest assured that we've been misled and have made as many mistakes as any other nation."

"Do you even like the ordinary folk of this country?"

"Everybody who admires life has affection for the folk . . ."

"For life or the folk? It seems to me that you admire life or the concept of it more, isn't that so?"

"The folk themselves constitute life. They're both its human landscape and its singular source. I both admire and savor the people. Sometimes they're as beautiful as an idea, sometimes as crude as nature. With them, all things are writ large. More often than not, they'll fall as silent as vast seas. But when they find the tongue with which to speak . . ."

"But to approach them – you aren't able to approach them! Their miseries, agonies, anxieties, and even pleasures remain closed to you. I mean to say closed to us all. When I worked in Adana, I felt this quite tangibly. I always remained at the door."

"Who knows? Certain doors appear closed because we aren't before them but behind them. All comprehensive things are this way. When you try to confine it to a formula, it recedes. You descend into trivial miseries. One moment you'll be stuck in reason, logic, cynicism, and denial, and in the next you'll be overcome by impossibility, incapability, and revolt . . . Meanwhile, if you seek it within yourself, you'll discover it. This is a matter of discipline, or even of method."

"Okay, but how will we find it? It's so confounding . . . At times I feel confined to a glass container like Goethe's Homunculus."

İhsan, musing: "Don't suppose I'll answer by advising, 'Break out of your shell!' In that case, you'll just dissipate! Whatever you do, don't break your shell! Expand it and make it part of yourself, refine and rejuvenate it with lifeblood. Make your shell part of your skin." He suspected he might be playing rhetorical games to avoid being cornered by his former students, but no, these were his genuine thoughts. The individual ought to preserve itself. Nobody had the right to dissolve into Creation. Individuals should remain as individuals, but they ought to fill themselves with experience. He added: "The error of the Homunculus was that he didn't turn his protective vessel into a living organism, he didn't unite with all of Creation from that surface; in other words, his mistake was being unable to coexist fully. The problem wasn't the shell per se."

"But you've misunderstood me, sir. You haven't been able to achieve that state of mind either! Had you, you wouldn't be seeking or trying to foster it within yourself. You'd be regarding it as reality imposing itself upon you and the setting, like a collection of values and truths. You wouldn't be attempting to discover it like a truth belonging to you alone. I don't buy it. In a sense you're the one who's fabricating, whereas I'm talking about approaching what already exists."

İhsan looked at Orhan's face compassionately before saying, "I'm not sure what good such talk does. But I'd like to be more explicit. I understand your doubts. You want me to forgo myself, to deny myself. You see affection as a voluntary matter. In this respect, it's dissatisfying. Your advice is to:

Toss your heart to the vortex and venture out as the soul of vastness

"Or else you're confronting me with the people and folklife as a single reality or obligation. You think the same way about yourself, and it pains you because you can't actualize it. But you're overlooking one point, namely, that before all else you constitute an autonomous self. Above all I aspire to be faithful to myself. This comprises my spiritual integrity. Only after I've attained that might I be of any use to others. Being faithful to myself, that is, adopting certain ethics, is what has separated me from my surroundings from the beginning. Necessarily I'd slip away from ordinary people. After finding myself at this extreme, I'd return to them again. That's why I'd admire them and, as you say, nurture them in my being. To enter into a mystical trance state or to lose myself in the 'oceanic' would serve no purpose for me or my surroundings.

"This means that I perceive life through the frameworks that I want to preserve. These frameworks are my self and my historical persona. I'm a cultural nationalist. I'm a person whose reality reflects a guiding principle. But this doesn't mean that I'm estranged from the folk; on the contrary, I'm at their command."

"But you can't see their suffering, can you?"

"I can. But that's not my locus of intervention. I know that as long as I see them as being wronged, I'll only lay the groundwork for their eventual cruelty. Why do we endure such suffering, I mean, the world at large? Because every struggle for the sake of liberty gives rise to new orders of injustice. I want to end tit-for-tat retaliations with the same weaponry. I want to begin the struggle from the very vessel within which we've been kneaded and formed. I'm about Turkey. Turkey is my lens, my measure, and my reality. I want to perceive Creation, Humanity, and everything else from there, from that vantage point."

"That's not enough!"

"It's enough to avoid the pitfall of utopia. And it's even enough for those who want to do something positive."

"Okay then, go ahead and define the 'Turkey' about which you speak."

İhsan sighed. "That's the crux of the matter. Locating that . . ."

"At times I verge on answering this very question. I tell myself that we're a nation of displacement and exile. A nation that's been formed and socialized by distances. By the love, suffering, and liberty of distances. Our history and art, at least among the folk, is this way." Mümtaz paused to think. "And even our classical *musiki*."

> *Were there a sacred campaign that I might join*
> *Were I to sink into sands on a pilgrimage to the Kaabe*

Nuran had been listening to İhsan's ideas for the first time, surprised to learn that he was this bound to real circumstances: "The cerebral way that you regard society, as if preparing a synthetic concoction . . ."

And she repeated to herself phrases that she recollected from Yaşar's vitamin prospectuses: "*Vitamin B cannot be readily extracted from foods in which it naturally occurs. As a result of great scientific endeavors, our laboratory has consequently . . .*"

"Generations that are obligated to take a formative role can't look upon life any other way. We're forced to work, to prepare the foundations for labor, and even to make others do so."

"But some thinkers claim the contrary, that work dehumanizes people and dims their horizons."

"Those same thinkers espouse a number of things before coming round to that point. They're chasing a kind of mysticism within established Europe. They want the opportunity to meditate on the soul . . . First I desire the formation of my soul and organization of my material being. What they desire constitutes the essence of any mystical sect. But the social life of a nation is not that of a sect . . . and that comes from someone like me with collective leanings. Were I in France, I'd also focus on the individual, contemplating how it might thrive despite society. Or this, or that other thing . . . I'd be dissatisfied with the status quo and try to address the deficiencies I'd discovered, and I'd struggle for that newfound cause. In Turkey, now, I'm contemplating what's in the interest of Turkey."

"A minute ago you said you wouldn't abandon your personality or your individuality, whereas now . . ."

"Why should I abandon my individuality? And moreover, why shouldn't I possess personality? The individual is a fact of existence." In the indeterminacy of reluctance İhsan added, "Just the way trees are the foundation of a forest."

III

There came another knock at the door. Mümtaz said, "That's Emin for certain," and darted from his chair. Most of the others rushed behind him. As Nuran passed before her uncle, who rose from his armchair, she smiled. She knew that he hadn't seen Emin Dede for years. A few days ago he was ecstatic, exclaiming, "If we winter in Istanbul, I'll go visit him frequently . . ."

Artist Cemil held two *neys* wrapped in cloth cases in one hand, and helped Emin Dede out of the automobile with the other.

Emin, extending his hand to İhsan, inquired, "Has Tevfik come as well?" He'd been longtime friends with both. He'd first met Tevfik at the Yenikapı Mevlevî dervish lodge during his early youth. Cemil, who played a long-necked *tanbur*-lute, had introduced İhsan to Emin during the Great War. İhsan hadn't much cared for the *ney* before meeting Emin, rather preferring the *tanbur* as the archetypal instrument of Turkish song, in admiration of the ecstatic feeling it could evoke. But his inclinations changed one night in the Kadıköy house of Tanburi Cemil's sister, where he'd heard the integrity of its essential force. It happened after the concert Emin and Tanburi Cemil had given in the Şehzadebaşı Ferah theater for the benefit of the Hilal-i Ahmer Red Crescent Society. Once the concert had concluded, Tanburi Cemil wouldn't let the *neyzen* flute-master leave his side, and they'd up and forced İhsan to accompany them as well. Holed up for two days and two nights, they'd settled before a *rakı* table provisioned with meager victuals yet alcohol aplenty. Over these two days İhsan had come to understand the degree to which both men were artists of exception: "I realized through firsthand experience all that's been lost to us since it isn't customary to *talk* about lives yet in the midst of being lived." At the mention of this night, gastronome-cum-teetotaler Emin Dede, who was quite taken with

Tanburi Cemil, recalled, "Written on all the *rakı* bottles were an array of honorary dedications: 'To my master, my esteemed master, the venerated Cemil . . .'"

Since that day, İhsan hadn't forgotten Emin, and until recent years he'd visited his house on the crest of Tophane's Kadiri Hill as much as his free time allowed. He'd even referred to this old Mevlevî Sufi, once a student of Albert Sorel's, as comprising his "mystical side!" – for some of Emin's friends were convinced of his sainthood.

Emin greeted İhsan using the customary epithet: "My holiness, you've up and vanished again!" Turning to Tevfik he added, "We've lost trace of you for years now, but it's my fault, I knew the route to your house all along!"

Gesturing to the *kudüm* twin drums that waited in a bag on the floor beside him, Tevfik said, "I haven't touched them for years. I took them out of the closet today."

Culture itself had tapped Emin Dede as the apparatus of its sophistication. His appearance alone could be said to be more delicate than his *ney*. He slowly entered the garden like any other creature plucked from everyday contexts, even bearing his quotidian troubles, small discomforts, and anxieties. He shook the hands of the women, addressing them as "Sultana!" and he flattered Mümtaz's friends. Then he sat comfortably and calmly in the armchair beside İhsan. From behind him, Artist Cemil appeared with the accustomed smile on his composed, angelic face. Regarding the man he exalted in his esteem, whose every gesture he extolled despite variances in lifestyle and milieu, something in Cemil's very bearing said, "See, he's the one, this weedy man, the last sentinel of the treasuries of our entire past, this man whose head is the golden buzzing hive of six centuries, whose breath alone preserves a civilization!"

İhsan, smiling: "So they deign to wear you out with a trip here, do they?"

"Pay no heed, my holiness. We've come here because we so desired.

We've partaken of fresh air and we've commiserated with friends. Is it always others who are to visit us? Allow us to exhaust ourselves a little as well."

He was a swarthy man, with gray-blue eyes and of middling height, whose shoulders sagged, giving his body a scarecrow-like appearance. A large, hooked, drooping nose practically divided his gaunt face into two halves, such that the sharp, straight lines of the lips, and the closely cropped, mostly graying mustache that followed managed to round out the face only once the nose ended. In this disposition, rather than one of the greatest music savants of the age, Emin resembled an unseen yet hardworking civil servant of a bureaucracy like customs or the postal service, virtually aloof from the city's public life. However, should one happen to raise his head and closely regard the eyes resting beneath the thick and curly eyebrows, this diminutive, ordinary-looking man might commune from a realm far exceeding his material being. On their first meeting, mindful of not being a pest, Mümtaz tried to befriend Emin, disciple of Aziz Dede, close companion of Tanburi Cemil – considering the difference in temperament between them, Emin was a patient and tolerant companion – and the last of the Mevlevîs privy to the "secret of the reed." Mümtaz recollected how his eyes had seized and censured him, nevertheless gently, as if saying, "Why be so preoccupied with my material being? Neither I nor the thing you call 'art' are as important as you might suppose. If you can, aspire to the secret of universal love articulated within each of us!" Centuries of Mevlevî cultivation had eliminated everything relating to the ego in him and had seemingly dissolved the genteel, inspired, and patient man within selflessness of sorts; by means of praising his master, Emin often related that one day he'd practiced eight or ten hours straight to reproduce a seven- or eight-note phrase that he'd heard Aziz Dede play and to attain exactly the same modulation. Emin had no individual aspect beside his wee material self half-melted in the intense heat of who knows what inner sun. And this material self hid and vanished each moment behind myriad formalities, decorum, and the acculturation of considering himself one with others and of denying everything individual in a state of humility that we'd consider bizarre today. As Mümtaz looked at him, Neşâtî's couplet came to mind:

O Neşâtî, we've been burnished to such extent
That we're secreted in mirrors purely radiant

And this couplet conveyed a truth. Emin Dede was a man concealed in his material being and culture. It was futile to seek, in such a venerated artist, any pretentious flourish or affect fostered by withdrawing to a corner and wallowing in inner fugues. Rather, he resembled a small sea stone licked, swallowed, and ground down over centuries by repeated waves that pounded eternal shores; a stone whose particularities had been erased; one of those smooth, dense stones, thousands of which one sees while walking along the coast! Nor did he give any indication that he'd preserved the final rays of a worldly realm that had withdrawn from our midst to become its affluent treasurer of sorts. In humility, friendship, and equality before one and all, he knew nothing of transformations in social existence or the repeated renunciations that made his person and his art a glorious vestige, a ruin, or even the final setting of a blazing sun.

Mümtaz observed him, seated like anybody in the garden, under autumnal sunlight in his black garb, and he thought unwittingly of much-venerated virtuosi now resident in other worlds and masters who'd formed Emin's seasons of the soul, about which the master himself scarcely knew a thing.

A Beethoven, a Wagner, a Debussy, a Liszt, or a Borodin was at such variance from this luminary of the literature sitting before him. They were possessed of maddening ire and vengeance, of desires that treated life in its entirety as a banquet spread before them, of a hubris taut with improbable Atlas-like exertions of the single-handed shouldering of such temperaments – of numerous theories and eccentricities that cast their personalities in various lights, and of natures, whose mildness alone cut like the swipe of a leonine claw. Meanwhile, the life of this little-known dervish consisted of repeated self-renunciations. Such denials, the resolve to twice disappear in absolutely reciprocal love and in the general commotion of being, weren't things that solely concerned one such as Nuri. By perpetually pressing his persona – eclipsed by his own will, or by the cultivation of his culture – into the past, it was possible to uncover Ottoman musicians like an Aziz Dede, a Zekâi Dede, an İsmail Dede, a Hafız Post, an Itrî, a Sadullah Ağa, a Basmacizâde, a Kömürcü Hafız, a Murat Ağa, or even an Abdülkadir-î Merâgî; in sum, to reclaim one of our traits, and perhaps a genealogy of our most opulent sensibilities. These men preferred to live reclusively as single stalks within a bushel of wheat. They hadn't driven themselves to the point of obsession, but through a pure ideal they were content to unleash numerous springtides out of the burgeoning and bleary incipience of their inner worlds; they recognized their art not as a means of avowing selfhood above all else, but as the sole path to vanishing in sempiternal oneness. Interestingly enough, their contemporaries also saw the matter this same way. The most individualistic of the lot, who by-the-by contaminated us with numerous maladies of the divine, the younger brother of Abdülhak Molla, in his diary, deigned to refer to Dede Efendi in such simplistic terms, as if ignorant of the import of his artistry, almost in a state of blithe igno-rance. When İhsan one day lamented the vacuous material relating to the virtuoso Dede Efendi in Hafız Hızır İlyas Ağa's *Reminiscences from the Inner Palace*, his interlocutor Emin Dede replied, laughing, "My holiness, you're barking up the wrong tree . . . Others make art. We simply abide in a state of pure devotion. You know, in some religious orders having one's name inscribed upon a tomb was considered bad form, let alone creating works of art." This, you see, was the way of the East. According to Mümtaz, the East that was both our incurable affliction and our infinite strength! In this extraordinary renunciation, Emin Dede was the people's last heir, one who might snuff out the lightning flash of his own existence were it within his power.

Emin spent a large portion of his pure and pristine life beneath the harsh wardship of his older brother. He didn't indulge in alcohol or cigarettes and had no excesses. Very soon, they'd all witness him speaking as the voice of a civilization through humble observations. He told countless amusing anecdotes relating to masters like Aziz Dede, his actual mentor *Neyzen* Hüseyni Efendi, Cemil Bey, Zekâi Dede, and their forebears. Apparently Aziz Dede was a harsh, meticulous, portly, and unlettered master who was exceedingly chaste. One day, as the story went, he noticed that the pen he'd dipped into his inkwell bore no trace of ink, and interpreting the meaning of this portent, he resolved to embrace Allah through heart and devotion alone. By resting his *ney* onto his considerable paunch, which made him resemble certain mullahs, he simply played it wherever the urge struck him.

One night he'd entered a tavern around the Beylerbeyi ferry landing, thinking it was a coffeehouse, and after losing himself in the Bosphorus seascape, he was moved to improvise on his *ney*. Because he played with eyes closed, eyes that normally burned like two hearths beneath black, bushy eyebrows, he hadn't noticed that the establishment had gradually filled and that a stream of spirit-soaking habitués had congregated at the table of spiritual inspiration, where they absorbed without a peep, and the waiters came and went on tiptoe to avoid disrupting him. When the *taksim* improvisation had concluded and Aziz Dede saw the crowd and the *rakı* glasses around him, he darted from his spot. Whenever he related this story, he ended with the following sentence: "My holiness, I felt such humiliation that I didn't leave the house for three full days, and I was afraid to see any of the brethren for another month."

Despite this, Aziz Dede's disciple didn't object to alcohol being drunk at the table. He only cautioned, "Don't overdo it. Elation fills me today . . .

One doesn't see good Tevfik that often anymore! And be wary about plying Cemil with drink lest he slip up when he plays." As he said this, the depths of his eyes smiled. He actually admired Cemil greatly. They'd come here on his insistence and after considerable rehearsal. Cemil made no secret of Mümtaz's partiality to the Ferahfezâ and the Sultanîyegâh.

Emin Dede savored the blessings of the table. His older brother Vasfi, a master calligrapher, was renowned for his culinary prowess; his roast turkey in parchment was ballyhooed throughout Istanbul. They'd nicknamed the dish "turkey with death shroud" in the sybaritic sensibility of ancient Rome.

Yet he said nothing about the meal except for sparse words in praise of the sumptuous fare. Only when the pullets prepared according to his own brother's recipe arrived at the table did he exclaim, "Doubtless your uncle Tevfik taught you how to prepare this delicacy!"

Tevfik, grinning: "If talents don't pass from hand to hand, they wither..." He'd been upset the entire afternoon. Activities with which he'd once easily occupied himself now strained him. He'd forgone all pursuits with a resentment brought about by senescence and limited physical activity. Now he recalled a creature that had reached a sclerotic phase in anticipation of death. As if out of his existence and surroundings he was preparing a sarcophagus of diversions. Traditional music was its most vivacious aspect; with each melody he remembered another day, but rather like something that wasn't his, like this seasonal hour absorbing the bright sunlight of the luculent diamond over his head, enticing him by reminding him of mortality, a memento mori of faded leaves of garnet and agate, of distant pomegranate and Trabzon persimmon trees that he compared to a vanishing evening, and of the buzzing apiarian drone, not as something he experienced viscerally in flesh and blood, but only as a blessed cornucopia to which he was but an invited guest.

Emin went on to describe his avid interest in gastronomic delights and the sumptuous feasts he'd once hosted. With the same distinguished and essential human joviality, he recounted, mirabile dictu, the characters of old Mevlevî lodges, the chef-cum-dervishes that he'd personally known, and the lamb pilaf banquets they'd held. As Mümtaz listened to him he thought, *So the* a la turca *style that so repulses us is really something else altogether . . .* Then the topic passed to Nuran's father. Emin knew full well about the ornamental plate designs and calligraphy that he'd made for the Yıldız ceramics factory. He himself was a calligrapher besides. Some claimed that if not for the iron rule of his older brother, he would have honed this talent. Mümtaz, listening to Emin's discussion of arts and music, noticed that he always maintained an earnestness close to folk sensibilities without any notable aesthetic discernment. His tolerance toward styles late to enter Turkish tastes and traditions, rather degenerating them, also arose from this humility. This Mevlevî possessed of politesse had come of age amid changing sensibilities, feeling in his being the reverberation of every new stirring. Thereby he had no desire to seek out and feel pure forms of the past, which had entered our tastes through the poet Yahya Kemal. Just as the previous generation displayed a regard, which approached the esteem of proponents of classical verse, for a *gazel* written in the ornate language of the fin de siècle Servet-i Fünun school, Emin simply resigned himself to various transformations in writing, painting, and music. He wasn't one to make comments by interpreting particular themes on the subjects he broached. He rarely indulged in such rhetoric. Despite this, he instinctively knew how to be discerning. However he'd managed to protect himself from the transformations in tradition with respect to calligraphy or music, he similarly guarded himself in his oratory. He spoke of his art with the care of a meticulous artisan, without any jargon, and, though unwittingly, he became the center of gravity of the table and the gathering. For his sake, Macide had forgone the visit to her lamented daughter beneath a canopy of white clouds and had been liberated from her anxieties regarding Mümtaz's final fate; meanwhile, Nuran had surrendered herself to this experienced master, to an affection for patriarchs and elderly men that dominated her life, and to an accompanying sense of deference. By admiring and listening to Emin Dede, she felt the absolution of countless sins and transgressions.

Claiming it would upset his stomach, Emin Dede declined the offer of ice cream. He concluded his meal with nothing but a demitasse of traditional coffee without sugar, as dictated by custom.

IV

The houseguests truly came to savor Emin Dede's exception when he began his *ney* performance in the second-floor hall, where they'd retired after the meal. Few musicians could thus transform to assume postures dictated by virtuosity.

First he inquired of Tevfik, "My lordship, are you up for performing the Ferahfezâ?" Tevfik hadn't recited this piece in years. But he was up to the challenge; this amounted to revisiting his youth in a completely unexpected season. During Emin Dede's introductory *taksim* improvisation, Tevfik rummaged through his memory for the ceremonial piece that he'd added to his repertoire while yet in the civil service. Thereafter, *kudüm* drums in hand, he waited half recumbent on the sofa, in that peculiar position necessitated by *a la turca* instruments when seated cross-legged, one foot adangle.

Emin Dede briefly made the rounds of the various melodic progressions and then embarked upon Dede Efendi's *peşrev* instrumental prelude in the rhythmic cadence of *devr-i kebir*. Mümtaz had heard this piece played a few times by Cemil. But now it issued before him as a completely different fugue.

Beginning with the first notes, a strange yearning, nay, pining overwhelmed them in its resemblance to lust for the sun amid thousands of deaths; then, without any dissipation of the effect – Mümtaz regarded the particular substantiation of Nuran before him through this sensation – they were scattered about leaf by leaf in an autumn eerie and eternal.

A serene pool in whose waters floated reflections of gilded firmaments, large bronzed leaves, and extraordinary water lilies, expanded in an unknown dimension, perhaps – yes, without a doubt – in a dimension of their own selves.

Emin Dede's *ney*, with no wane in timbre of breath or wind, in a metallic or, more precisely, idiosyncratic and variegated crescendo, emitted a tone in which cohered the sparkle of gemstones and the pliancy of foliage. Yet how resonant, voluminous, and broad. The music filled the large hall, gushed out windows, and through its effect the garden, overcome by the remorse of final flowers and yellowed leaves, was effectively transfigured. At times everything melted as if reverting to its own essence and from there to a more profound quintessence; beneath the cascade of sound resembling a deluge of roses, the small chandelier hanging from the ceiling blazed in stunning rainbow spectra, and then, with a brazen hairpin bend – or, with that implausible and entwined climb seen only in ivies, wisteria, and fine fibrous plants that conformed to shape without relinquishing any color – it was born of its very self as the ostinato of a short while before. As Mümtaz sought out Cemil's *ney* amid his master's voice, the first section, or *hane*, came to an end. The second *hane* pranced out of the melancholic nostalgia conjured by this denouement in a more solemn tone. Yet again they were spirited away by repeated gusts, passed through squalls of the soul, and regarded their solitude in the mirror of drastic yearning – lo, the anxiety that all was lost in perpetuity. And the Ferahfezâ *peşrev*, or the soul attempting to forge impassable deserts of seclusion, plunged for a fourth time into nostalgic *hüzün*, that crepuscular realm that blazed beneath water.

Each listener was seemingly scattered by the gale of a life span. Only Emin Dede remained standing in his meticulous and straightforward outfit, his expression hardened, like a symbol, a personification of the sentinel of mystery and melody. The entire secret of being that was centered in himself rested in the physical firmness of his inner countenance; beside him a bit to the rear, Artist Cemil, with his fair Saxony bone-china countenance and its sweet smile, though slightly narrower than before, seemed to gaze over the terrain they'd just now passed. Opposite them, Tevfik waited, *kudüm* on lap, in that disconcerting discomfort that *a la turca* instruments added to his reclining form.

Unable to restrain himself, İhsan said in a very soft voice, "My dervish, you possess an exquisite palette of colors . . ."

Emin Dede, with an eye on Tevfik, who was prepared to play his *kudüm* drums, answered with the glance of a true *neyzen* and in the same soft voice: "My Holiness, forget not the succor of the master . . . furthermore, what you refer to as 'color' in our lamented Dede Efendi, I'd actually call 'love.'" Emin didn't just refer to old virtuosi and patrons as if they were still in our midst, he erased both the remoteness of their deaths *and* his self through deferential terms like "our master," "our elder," or "our lord," thereby unifying himself, his life, the master to whom he alluded, and the abstract time of death.

But the true marvel began with the Mevlevî musical rite itself.

Dede Efendi's Ferahfezâ ceremonial was not simply devotion or the striving of a faithful soul seeking Allah. It was arguably one of the most rambunctious pieces of music that never abandoned the secret, the élan vital, the very traits of mystical inspiration, and the express, compelling impetus of immense and unyielding desire. Emin Dede had so managed its progression, which consisted of roaming the *makam*s of *a la turca* music with small flourishes, transformations, and resolutions, that the ceremonial inherently transformed into a symbol all its own.

After revealing the entirety of the Ferahfezâ *makam*'s attributes in the first two couplets of Rumi's *Mesnevi*, which began the ceremonial like two bejeweled façades of a single palace –"Hear the lament of the *ney* whisper stories of separation/Since I've been pulled from the reed bed men and women weep at my wailing"– within varied phrasal arcs resembling a prolonged excursion, he ran the *makam* a number of times, in an arrangement that resembled distinct variations achieved through consistent structural motifs, before slowly abandoning the melodic progressions to associated ones. Thereby the entire ceremonial sequence, in the first lines – or couplets – became a universal journey of sorts within the lust of the lucid and majestic Ferahfezâ that struck the ear; the ear, which never forgot such delicacies, or rather the soul, which never forgot the yearning for transcendence bedazzling it such that acoustic sense and soul grew ecstatic in the conviction of the measure-by-measure approach of desire and delight. However, as soon as this satisfaction was revealed, the eternal longing, the journey, began anew in the softer or simply variant tenor of the Nevâ, the Rast, or the Acem. Apparently, Dede Efendi wanted to manifest the complete predestined course of mystical experience through this bewildering piece. Ephemerally, absolute spiritual truth, or the spirit that was absolute truth, sought itself and its purpose in expansive time and space, disturbed the dormancy of material objects, bowed toward the essence of all things, withdrew into great seclusions, bounded over Milky Ways, and everywhere discovered desires and thirsts akin to its own. It passed from the tenor of the Acem, revealing the Ferahfezâ *makam* to be all but a "rightly guided path" of sorts, to the Dügâh, the Kürdî, the Rast, the Çârgâh, the Gerdaniye, the Sabâ, and the Nevâ; all things were lost, sought, and found within each of them. And the Ferahfezâ, during the entirety of this journey of febrile yearning, extended its bejeweled chalice – that chalice of a singular lyrical line and flourish – at surprising junctures, appearing now like a kaleidoscopic vision, now as a memory or dream of its own self. This quest, this dissolution and self-realization, was at times exceedingly humanist, and Dede's inspiration either exclaimed, "So what if you remain unseen, I bear you within my being!" or fell into desperation as dense as matter.

Yet Rumi was justified: Yearning was the solitary secret of the *ney*. Should someday one make a daring, synesthetic interpretation of Turkish instruments similar to that made by Rimbaud for vowels in the poem "Voyelles," doubtless one would most certainly see in this simplest of *a la turca* instruments the flesh-hued longing of nightfall. The *ney* should be untainted by the sounds of European or *a la franga* flutes, horns, and even the deep emerald green or blood red timbre of the remarkable hunting strains that have for centuries delineated bestial dispositions. In their need to re-create or rediscover nature in new ways, such instruments often forsake the very longing that ought to be one of art's true domiciles. For the *ney* articulates by usurping the place of the nonexistent, by pursuing that very absence.

Why does desire comprise the lion's share of our spiritual lives? Do we pine for the oceanic expanse, one droplet of which constitutes each of us? Are we in the pursuit of the quiescence of matter? Or do we bemoan ephemeral and long-vanished aspects of ourselves because we're children of time, an amalgam prepared in the crucible of time, or because we're victims of time? Do we genuinely seek a state of perfection? Or do we object to the cruel order of time: *zalim zaman nizamı*?

Ottoman music is perhaps the art form that best articulates desire through an arrangement that disrupts what it has created and reduces, with a cursory glance, the dais of time known as the present to nothing but ephemera–the *ney* being its most eloquent implement.

Perhaps İsmail Dede Efendi, feeling such yearning in his soul, began his ceremonial with couplets on longing from the *Mesnevi*. The four-stepped threshold of the *devr-i kebir* talea sufficed to deliver the listener to the realm's doorstep. For here, traditional music, as with the *peşrev*, didn't just satisfy itself with affect; it seized and extracted one from one's place, transforming and shaping one into a kind of vessel whose body and soul would accept deaths of a different magnitude, deaths beyond this world yet full of reminiscences – an echo of sorts. No, this was neither the realm of a moonlit Büyükdere night, of chalices of light shattering across molten emerald and agate, nor of saffron roses scattering petal by petal. The yearning in their presence emerged from beyond a thousand deaths and was directed at all animate things. Therefore, it had no sharpness, no points. Nuran seemed to perpetually awaken anew in an unknown locale, then within the rhythm of the fire dance, suddenly and repeatedly transfigured through inscrutable incarnations before again drawing one of the heavy and excessively gilded clouds over herself at a refrain in the *makam*s, under which she'd descend into an enchanted sleep, before yet again slipping away beneath one edge of this heavy shroud as if she were a coral and yellow artery of light, filtering from the clouds of an evening; involuntarily she gathered again in another place, and again in her exceptional dance became a realm of pure essence, expanded, grew, fragmented, laughed in matter estranged from herself then again as herself, multiplied, pushed the thresholds of improbability, and therein scattered one leaf and one branch at a time like a freshly bronzed autumn. If not for the plodding accompaniment of the *kudüm*, which reached them from subterranean depths as it cast off the ashes of hundreds of thousands of deaths, perhaps she would have flown free completely and vanished, together with the totality of her hylic being. The deep rhythm, however, amid entities transfiguring at each moment, pointed the way for a self no longer hers through the invitation of a time no longer ours, and through wondrous percussion parted certain shrouds in the depths; indeed, Nuran, following in its percussive wake as if she were the counterpart of a twinned soul, sought her self, her other half, perhaps even her totality, in the malleability of this realm of pure essence.

Into the aureate abyss of the *ney*, Tevfik's voice tossed gems of unfamiliar words, ever so slowly displaying the glint of each facet; now the first shout of "beloved" in Farsi, of a "beloved, beloved of mine!" alighted within the vision of a blazing mainmast at sea, and the "mine" syllable, which he depressed fully upon the song, deepened like a silver- and coral-framed mirror of yesteryear, in which Nuran, without clearly discerning her semblance tattered by great gale in wild badlands, at times spied Mümtaz's gaunt face behind eternally closed doors, and at times heard Fatma's voice pleading, "Mother." In this stunning music, all things became a static and profound tragedy in shadows.

The second-floor hall became a galleon tossed about on seas of devotion. Everybody seemed to bid adieu to a sun casting final rays upon familiar shores, the shores of their own lives. Mümtaz gazed at the sun and the surroundings in never-before-felt absentmindedness. He feared the eternal loss of Nuran, who sat two steps away from him; such did the gale of the *ney* verge on scattering them across expanses. This was something of a *rüya*; and as with first dozes that prepared the way for all dreams, it intrinsically affected consciousness, dispersing the self. Nonetheless, this dispersal wasn't total. As the fabric of the music unfolded bolt by bolt, Mümtaz came to realize what it was that defined a genius of ruin. Neither Abdülkadir-î Merâgî's Segâhkâr, nor Itrî's *naat* ode to the Prophet bore the emotional shudder of this ceremonial, nor the Isfahan song – again by Itrî – which Mümtaz had coincidently heard one night at Ahmet's house, sung by the host himself. These pieces sought Allah or the Absolute without ambivalence, conveying their venture of the soul through sturdy architecture and the great wellspring of spirit concentrated within them. Perpendicularly they soared. Yet at present, the struggle was two-fold: The soul couldn't manage to escape the world-worn realm from which it strove to separate. This was neither doubt nor the shortfall of love but a flailing at the confluence of two divergent currents.

Mümtaz seemed to favor one of the two zephyrs in the duel between Tevfik's voice and Emin Dede's *ney*. The Ferahfezâ Tevfik recited in traditional ritual technique was different from the same composer's other Ferahfezâs, which served to instill modes of affection and anguish in Mümtaz. This version found the architecture of the venue somewhat alienating. Perhaps the Farsi lyrics, perhaps tradition itself, had transformed Tevfik's voice, which he knew well, giving Mümtaz a taste of the turquoise hue of tiles in old Seljuk mosques, of the oil lamps within them alight with prayers now illuminating their way, and of the timeworn wood of old folding Koran stands. The timbre and style of the *ney* acknowledged nothing as traditional or modern, but chased after *zaman* without *zaman*, timeless time, that is, after fate and humanity as unrefined essences. And not only that. From time to time, into *ney* and human voice mingled the sound of the *kudüm* that emerged from depths, as if from beneath the ground, an awakening casting off the detritus of a thousand slumbers and laden with forgetting and being forgotten, or rather self-realization amid a multitude of cultures. And these awakenings and self-realizations never succumbed to futility. The sound of the *kudüm* always bore the enchanted call of ancient religions, its percussion contributing an order of earthly substantiation to the celestial journey.

The first ceremonial *selam* ended in a melody without resolution, like a wounded wing in final flutter. Nuran sought Mümtaz's eyes; they stared at each other like strangers. The music had transfigured each into a vision familiar only to the seer – as in a dream. *How disconcerting!* thought Mümtaz.

Emin Dede grinned at İhsan as if in the wake of an initiation the gathered had traveled collectively. Then, with a sweet smile at Tevfik, he placed the *ney* to his lips.

Tevfik, along with the sound of the *ney* – and perhaps to avoid entering into a contest that might ruin the piece – this time all but transformed his voice into a very subtle bas-relief upon a finely cut, precious gemstone, barely discernible to the naked eye. During certain moments of the devotional prayer his voice expanded and intensified. Mümtaz, from his coign of vantage, noticed Nuran waiting her turn at the abyss of music, prayer beads in hand, as if expecting to be sacrificed; she seemed to be saying, "Set me ablaze, oh eternity!" She revealed such an anguished, withdrawn face, yet her shoulders stood strong. Self-assured by all she avowed, she resisted this tempest eternal like the stern of a golden galleon.

Mümtaz pondered the possibility that during a similar ceremonial, Beyhan Sultana, alone bearing five centuries of Ottoman fortitude in her shoulders, resembling Nuran, had gazed at Shaykh Galip from behind lattices in an area designated for royal ladies in the Yenikapı Mevlevî lodge. Whirling Mevlevîs, their ritual robes spinning in the aether, sparkled in a vision of supplication through the refinement of centuries, as one of the dervishes folded his arms before the presence of the one standing behind him.

Mümtaz saw sultan and composer Selim III – to whom he'd never listened, appearing rather like a gardener who, in advanced years, planted an exquisite rose sapling in his garden, with full knowledge that it was meant for some indeterminate future – genuflecting like a gilt and silver icon in the royal loge of a mosque, his face recalling the dervishes of Khorasan, a substantial ring adorning his hand, amid elegant melodies whose potential his royal highness himself had composed.

But what about Dede Efendi? Who was the man who'd arranged this venture of the soul with such fastidiousness, what was he like? On the day that the Ferahfezâ ceremonial was first performed, early in the nineteenth century, Sultan Mahmud II, rising from his sickbed, came to the Yenikapı Mevlevî lodge. All of Istanbul was present, including its most prominent figures, refined foreign guests, palace dignitaries, and opportunists mad with yearning to step onto some or another threshold of fortune. All of them came to hear this new ceremonial composed by Hamamîzâde İsmail Dede Efendi, Royal Chief Müezzen to His Exalted Excellency. Amid this enigmatic tempest, Mümtaz sought Sultan Mahmud II's face, sallowed like worn oilcloth by consumption, beneath a heavily tasseled fez and above the collar of the European-style navy blue uniform with gold epaulets mandated by the sovereign. After moving through the crowd of applauding onlookers lining the streets, members of the sultan's entourage arrived on well-groomed Arabians and listened to these melodies – the ancient protocol of the orient still strong. Within the forge of music, all of them had forgotten the rebellions that had overtaken Anatolia and the entire empire, as well as the foreboding threat of what lay ahead hanging over their heads like the sword of Damocles; they'd become diminutive subjects of Allah, thinking only of the salvation of the soul, and they sank into a reckoning of their lives by turns, exclaiming, "While artworks of such magnitude are yet being created, we won't be destroyed; we're still living through our springtime!"

The third *selam* transported Mümtaz to completely different horizons. Now they entered into the *yürük* song. Here, with increasing momentum, escape from the worldly became a necessity. But this didn't occur. Muslim liturgy bore no symbols; and moreover, prayer and worship existed only through the congregation. This was the case on Sufi paths as well. Spinning steps quickened pace as ritual robes made narrower and more imperceptible undulations. But how bizarre: As the Mevlevî ceremony approached a trance, it abandoned melancholy and solemn aristocratic expression to assume cadences of folk effusiveness. The rhythm became an unfamiliar pastoral, folk celebration. In the lithe dance of the melody, Mümtaz discovered that great wellspring that gave villagers their joy and Anatolia the fortitude to withstand such suffering.

Elsewhere a thin partition cracked. A green sprout came to life like the wonder of a morning. The abode of the soul collapsed beneath burgeoning roses... Purple, stunning rose blossoms... Nuran wanted to soar, to hurtle through the ceiling by her own momentum, to ascend into the skies. She bore her entire world within her self. To soar, verily, to vanish. Why had this music, through its agile expression, recalled the Bairams of her childhood? Why had it erupted in the elation of free and easy times, when the taste of every pleasure came unaccompanied by pangs of conscience? Was it right to resurrect so many of the dead all at once? Through this elation did one arrive at Allah? Or at life itself? She didn't know. Just as during those carefree Bairams, she sensed that as she once faced being bereft of amusement and joy, she now ever so slowly prepared to forgo everything, and felt even the desire to soar abandon her. Oddly enough, she felt isolated. Her inner life was as vast as creation. "I *am a world unto myself*," she thought. Yet she was not in control of this inner world.

And the *ney* persisted. The *ney* had become the secret of constructive and destructive natures. Through its breath, all things, all of Creation, transformed within formless becomings; and from where she was heaped in a state of great devotion, she witnessed this phenomenon unfolding at the center of her self. Here an ocean rose, there a forest burned to ash, the stars kissed, and like honey Mümtaz's hands dripped from his knees.

Mümtaz shuddered. They were now in the fourth *selam*. Shaykh Galip himself verged on joining the ceremony as he grasped the front of his robes. He, too, had to temporarily burn to ash beneath the sun of Shams of Tabriz, to burn in his eternal forge of adoration! During the last of the exclamations, Nuran seemed to grab Mümtaz by the shoulders and implore, "Let us perish together!"

Emin's *ney* played the two *yürük* harmonies that completed the ceremony, then moved through a brief and multihued progression, a *taksim* that wandered the zodiac of melodic progressions as if sketching a map of the firmament, before moving from the distinct Ferahfezâ of twinned *yürüks* to the dominant melody of the prelude, a melody transfiguring everything in its midst into a furnace of desire, before falling silent.

Tevfik let the *kudüm* slip from his hands; he wiped his forehead. The gathering was exhausted, as if it had wrestled with a colossus, the *deev* of time. Emin called out to Tevfik, "You won't be growing old anytime soon! Your future bears nothing of age!" They glanced at each other with affection, the pleasures of which younger generations knew nothing.

"Each of you is a miracle," İhsan said.

V

Suad made an arrival toward the middle of the first *selam*. Though he'd passed through the door with a joyous expression, when he noticed the music and the solemnity of the scene, he sat silently beside İhsan in a manner that bespoke tedium. He sought Nuran and Mümtaz in the gathering, exchanging greetings through glances. From the horizon of intricate return to which the music had transported Mümtaz, he noticed Suad nearly snickering at him amicably, with a hint of derision, before staring at Nuran almost shyly and desperately. Then he severed all exchange with others and focused his attentions on the music. To such a degree that Mümtaz thought, *What a pity he's missed the initial Ferahfezâs.* Toward the middle of the second *selam*, Suad's concentration intensified. Resting an elbow on a knee, he placed his head on his right hand and began to listen, spellbound. But soon – as if unable to locate what he'd been seeking, as if the music offered only empty chalices, as if the climes that the *ney* and Tevfik's voice explored in tandem amounted to only deceptive mirages – he raised his head in sedition. Mümtaz noticed the glimmer of caustic scorn and revolt, even wrath, in Suad's eyes. He also caught Suad's ogles, and not only were his emotions wrenched by a vague sense of jealousy, as had happened when Suad just now greeted Nuran, but he felt intimidated. Later on, while trying to gather his recollections of the evening, he considered how Suad's expression had contorted like a forest under gust and gale. And Mümtaz considered how this restless forest had been illuminated by the lightning of revolt and fear in Suad's gaze. Yes, he was convinced that such feelings lurked beneath the derision in Suad's expression.

Mümtaz, distraught by Suad's presence in their midst, was no longer jealous of him. His mind was nevertheless strangely preoccupied. Suad's affections for Nuran and their friendship made him an agonizing part of

Mümtaz's life, elevating him to another plane; Suad, whom he'd long known, whose sarcasm and insolence unsettled and disturbed him, yet whose off-handedness and quirks he liked, whose intelligence and leaps of intellect he admired, but from whom he kept his distance because they traced different life trajectories. Consequent to the letter Suad had written Nuran, Mümtaz hadn't spent three consecutive hours in which he hadn't thought of him. From that day forward, Mümtaz sensed something resembling the lure felt by all victims toward their victimizers – felt by the sparrow toward the hawk. This wasn't unnatural; as a French poet had put it, between them existed "the hidden allure of the deadly"; they'd confronted each other through Nuran's love. Whatever the status of each in this love, between them arose something like malice. But now in the midst of the music, the revolt Mümtaz had seen overtaking Suad cast him in a different light. He asked himself repeatedly, *I wonder what's happened, what's bothering him?* Then the question became more explicit: *What was he seeking in the music that sent him into such revolt?* He again glanced at Suad. But this time he could discern no meaning or expression in his face. Suad again listened ever so politely in an open and even pitiless state of attentiveness – respectful toward the musical perfor-mance and to the musicians growing weary in its creation – yet revealing the depletion of his faculties of free thought. Suad's indifference bothered Mümtaz as equally as his previous state of revolt and only through willful determination could he follow the finale.

While Mümtaz remained immersed in thought, Emin's *taksim* impro-visation, in the first *selam*, returned the Ferahfezâ with which the com-poser confronted listeners seven times, each through distinct variations, like a time span that now belonged to them – in the first instance simply as something sublime and unexpected, a self-discovery, next as a memory that furthered the conservation of an inner life, and consequently, increased its individuality and intensity. And Mümtaz realized that the suite of Ferah-fezâs, arrived at by the *neyzen* like an inevitable conclusion, like the final station where one's existence discovered its true face, helped constitute their identities – one end of which rested in shadowy presences interred in the measureless blackness of time-past; he realized he'd frequently relive the music along with the others, and, simply due to the sedition he'd observed in Suad, the ceremonial would rule his passions with a mystery illuminated by shooting stars and the glimmering whorl of nebulas.

If one doesn't limit music to technical details or ideas, its effects are subjective. Undergirding each piece recollected in profundity are the peculiarities of the episode in which it was encountered; and in certain respects, the venture of this episode is but the transfusion of the music into one's life.

During the Ferahfezâ ceremonial, Mümtaz, always taking the fugue with him, escaped into an array of phantasies relating to his surroundings, his inner self, and his mental processes. İsmail Dede's melodies independently took refuge in the multihued, fragile, and fragmentary shapes and semblances of images congregating around Nuran's face, which Mümtaz regarded from an arm's length, images dispersing from her to the age of Sultan Selim III, to Shaykh Galip, to the era of Sultan Mahmud II, to Mümtaz's own aestival reminiscences, to Kanlıca twilights, to the Kandilli hill, and to the astounding play of light on Bosphorus daybreaks. Had these visions remained restricted to the music that produced them, like flames in a hearth, they would have burned fleetingly and vanished. Not so. In the passing despair Mümtaz observed on Suad's face, this complex of visions augmented – he realized that the true meaning of revolt, disdain, and ire that he thought he read in Suad's expression was simply despair. And just as the melodies that emerged from the *makam*s of Sabâ, Nevâ, Rast, Çârgâh, and Acem resolved on the Ferahfezâ, just as the manifestation of that woeful, memory-laden suite prepared to bear and usurp the meaning of the totality of their lives, Suad's despair appropriated all these visions, and by means of his own cruel experiences, introjected them into Mümtaz. Instead of the gradual dissipation – as with the other listeners when the *ney* ceased – of the

dreamy twilight conjured around the music and the realm of color grada-
tions evoking life in a spectral rainbow, this gloam settled even deeper into
Mümtaz under the contingencies of augmented intensities and natures.
And throughout the performance, no matter which stations his imagination
attained as it orbited Nuran, this sense of despair, contracted from Suad,
united with notions of Nuran.

Once the performance had concluded and Tevfik and Emin Dede again
played compositions and *semâi*s flirting with the same *makam*, Mümtaz
listened to these long-familiar works through the same despair. And even
when he tried, as always, to distill Nuran's voice, which accompanied her
uncle's, he conjured the phantom of a hindrance between her voice and
himself. He perceived her voice from across great distances and through
mist-shrouded dawns. The tense transfiguration that *a la turca* music caused
in the expressions of its singers seemed not to be exertion but a sign of
separation or distance. As if captive in climes of Sultanîyegâh, Mahur, and
Segâh, Nuran was summoning him to rescue her. But Mümtaz couldn't
reach her.

He knew it was absurd. He realized that the tragic contingencies of his
childhood had instilled the tendency to think and feel this way, to consider
everything he cherished as being far away, in a region of inaccessibility; just
as he'd first been exposed to love in conjunction with death and sin during
impressionable years – as the award and agony of what lay beyond absolution
– so too had this notion of distance taken root within him. Not to mention
that Mümtaz himself had exacerbated these childhood legacies of his own
free will during a maladapted adolescence, cerebral and prematurely inau-
gurated by poetry's influence – legacies that persisted until his introduction
to Nuran. In his opinion, the true destiny of poetry lay beyond objects and
hopes. Poetry resembled the blaze of an entire life bursting aflame like a dry
leaf pile. Weren't all the poets he'd read and admired, Poe and Baudelaire
foremost among them, princes of "nevermore"? Their cradles swung under

celestial signs of negation and their lives passed in the lands of nihilism. How might honeycombs of poetry be filled without transporting one's existence to a horizon of intricate return? Mümtaz hadn't simply denied himself the countless banquets of life and youth, he'd accepted the acrimonies of life as the only clime worthy of experience, despite his elation, his almost algebraic observations, and his diverse appetites for life. As he'd confided to Nuran on the night they'd wandered beneath the August moon, each idea or passion matured within him only once it assumed the form of torture or torment. Short of this, he felt his poetry wouldn't merge with lived reality. That melding and synthesis only occurred at unendurable temperatures, short of which he'd be relegated to the peripheries of a pilfered language.

Perhaps such processes churned in his adoration of Nuran. Mümtaz wouldn't have been so bound to her if not for the enduring legacy of the "Song in Mahur," and the dominance with which she entered his life, brought about by prior love and marriage. The insecurity Nuran showed when confronted by social and emotional life, her surrender to the status quo, and her contentment with what the day offered – in short, her resignation to complacency had fostered a semi-divine persona. Mümtaz had full familiarity with the force behind these tendencies. He sought an inner, emotional order for himself. He was in pursuit of a fiery catalyst that would bring words and images to life. But the rules of the game had changed, and in the trial that he'd willingly entered, he'd failed. A bewildering thought. From time to time Mümtaz awoke from his happy complacency to ask, *I wonder if it's excessive?* The question alone turned the paradise of their love into a mock heaven. Throughout the summer of his content, he'd lived a life that was effectively doubled. And strangest of all was that the suspicion he nurtured against his emotions, his self-scrutiny, neither diminished his affections toward Nuran nor prevented his suffering from the torments of love.

He now spoke to himself in a similar vein: *I'm a fool . . . I insist on incriminating myself.* Each time his gaze fell on Nuran, he felt he wasn't seeing her as usual, but rather through the mediation of memory. This sensation persisted, changing form. He was to love the lady in his midst, who laughed in his embrace, as nothing more than an absence.

Why was *Suad in such despair? What* was *he thinking about? Had he truly listened to Dede with the longing to believe and discover? Or did he begin with a sense of rejection? Why was he so distraught?* As such questions entered his thoughts, he succumbed to bewildering qualms. How did Mümtaz himself interpret this so-called devotional ceremony? One by one he recollected the places his thoughts had taken him during the Ferahfezâ. Not once during the entire performance had he felt any mystical awakening. The associations he'd conjured congregated around either Nuran or the book he was in the process of writing. Was Dede Efendi responsible for this lack? Or was it just a function of Mümtaz's nature? Now he, too, was astounded at his impoverishment of spirit. Or was his stance toward *a la turca* music completely affected? Had he appropriated it as well, like so many other facets of his life, like his love of Nuran, in which he so exalted, as nothing more than a means to an end? Was he only involved cerebrally, forcibly flogging his imagination? Had he furthermore entered into this matter hoping against hope that he'd end up, as a matter of course, in a genuine nadir of his own? How did he feel when listening to other musicians? Did he feel the same while listening to Bach and Beethoven? Aldous Huxley had written, "God exists and is apparent, but only when violins play . . ." The novelist, whom he quite admired, had written this about the Quartet in A minor. Mümtaz had listened to this quartet long before he'd read the book. Alas, he couldn't reign in his feelings.

Suddenly he staggered. In the midst of Dede's "Acemaşiran Yürük Semâi," Nuran's voice wailed in Farsi:

> *Wheresoever you reside*
> *Therein our paradise does abide*

But why did Nuran's voice reach him from across such distances? In this moment of nervous tension, had a presence or an absence intervened between them? Was he seeing her reflected in a mirror of despair? Or was he seeing her like the mortal spark of an Absolute illuminating itself? Mümtaz looked at Suad, as if only he could provide the answers to such questions. But Suad's face was firmly shut.

And perhaps for the sake of doing something, anything, Mümtaz stood from his spot, and went to the spigot in the water closet to wash his face. When he returned, Emin Dede was performing yet another of his celebrated *taksim*s, as always in the Ferahfezâ *makam*. *Music isn't an appropriate vehicle for love* ... For music toiled beyond time. Music, the ordering of time – *zamanın nizamı* – elided the present. Meanwhile, contentment existed in the present. As he wasn't able to attain satisfaction, why should he even bother expressing affection?

But who was content? The plea of the *ney* wasn't in vain. Didn't this voyage through the cosmos reveal the futility of felicity? Had Suad come here to be heartened? Of course not. Were he presently with one of his little damsels, naturally he'd be a thousand times happier. Yet, he *had* come to pester Mümtaz. He'd make both of them suffer; they'd make each other miserable. This was what people did, each day, as if created for this express purpose. Suad listened to the *ney*, his forehead resting on his left hand, elbow on knee. Yet it was evident from his posture that his entire being was cocked and primed. He didn't hear the *ney*; he was simply bored, impatient, expectant. And Mümtaz began to anticipate what would emerge from this hiatus of expectation. He himself began to long for Emin Dede's imminent departure, curious about Suad's first order of action.

Still, the *ney* persisted in its voyage through a realm of spectral illumination.

VI

Emin requested permission to leave upon completing his *taksim*. He entrusted Cemil to them, with the proviso that they not tire him excessively. Mümtaz saw his guest out to the street leading down the hill. He returned to the house reluctantly. Suad's presence had all but made him forget his responsibilities as host. Never before had he felt the desire to flee, to escape in the name of salvation. He wanted to abscond, to hide away. Before the entrance, he counted, *One, two, three . . . one, two, three.* Seeing Suad filled him with dread.

He entered and found the *rakı* table laid out. But no one had begun to indulge. Everybody stood, chatting. He found Suad and İhsan beside the table, where alcohol-filled crystal tumblers cast large luculent clusters beneath the electric light. He approached them: "How did you like the concert, Suad?"

İhsan responded in place of Suad. "We were just now discussing it," he said. "Suad was unimpressed."

Suad raised his head, "It's not that I didn't like it, but I just couldn't find what I was looking for . . ."

İhsan: "You want music to seize Allah, bind Him hand and arm and surrender Him to you. This is an impossibility! You only find what you yourself bring! Allah is neither in Dede Efendi's back pocket nor anyone else's for that matter."

"Perhaps" he snipped. "But I have no complaint to make about that. What bothers me is that incessant gyre, circling around nothingness . . . that flailing in the form of an idée fixe. *That* is what annoys me."

He raised the glass before him. "*Haydi!* Here we go!" he cried out to the crowd. "Maybe there's some consolation in this drink. At the very least the consolation of forgetting!"

İhsan slowly whispered into his ear, "You've come primed for something specific, haven't you?" Then he passed to the other side of the table, joining the company of his wife.

Suad: "To the health and prosperity of our hosts," and finished his drink in one gulp.

"What's the urgency, Suad?" Macide said.

Ruminating, and with a hint of derision directed at no one in particular, Suad answered, "Excuse me, Macide . . . I'm forced to hurry." Then he repeated again, "To hurry!" adding, "Those who don't have time hurry . . . Everybody's born with a sense of one's allotted time. My concern demands urgency."

İhsan, half joking, half serious, protested. "You certainly are speaking in riddles, Suad! You're like the Sphinx."

Suad shrugged. His eyes alighted on the bottle in Mümtaz's hands, and he laughed at the young gentleman, smiling like a boy expecting indulgences: "Please, another glass . . . The train will embark shortly. Would you like to know the worst of it? Not knowing the precise time of departure. To always be thinking it's today, no, it's tomorrow. And thereby frittering away this freely allotted time in the most absurd ways." He stopped, taking back-to-back swallows; he deposited his half-filled glass on the table. Mümtaz, pricking up his ears, continued to listen: "Macide pities me and worries. In a little while she, and perhaps all of you, will attempt to give me wise words of wisdom. I've listened to such advice all my life. But no one considers that I'm a man who's come to the station early and that, naturally, my life will pass at the kiosk counter . . . What else d'you suppose I could do? Like the rest of you, I'm not at home enmeshed in my everyday affairs . . ."

Nuran gazed at Mümtaz; bottle in hand, he filled the glasses including his own but refrained from drinking. *What a perplexing, mutual tie we have, don't we? My former friend and my beloved, his relative . . . but the quantities he consumes . . .* Then she recalled the comparison often made about Suad, back in their college days: *Most horses don't drink this much ... Maybe they never drink.* Raising an eyebrow, she rifled through her mind: *No, it's not that they never drink ... I read in the paper somewhere that certain racehorses drink beer or wine. But of course they don't drink this much.* In trepidation she looked at Suad's glass, which he'd again emptied. When she used to conjure the bit about Suad's resemblance to a horse, she'd laugh. But not this time; so, it's an awkward situation. And because Mümtaz also sensed it, he refrained from drinking. In that case, she wouldn't drink either ... *But I so need to drink ... this music has kneaded me for hours. At times I felt like I'd taken on the form of divine clay ...* She wanted the alchemy of alcohol. But she would not drink.

Next, it was Selim's turn. He'd fled the Caucasus as a boy in the wake of the Mondros Armistice: "Before the Great War, in Russia, students would drink at the kiosks of large train stations. My father used to tell us the story. A chosen leader, bell in hand, would take up the train schedule, reading it at the top of his voice. For instance, he'd announce, 'We've arrived at so-and-so station, our train will remain here for twenty minutes, allowing us three glasses of Bordeaux or one bottle of vodka.' In such a manner, they'd order their rounds. At each station, the alcohol they drank, along with appetizing local delicacies, made for a touristic excursion of sorts. Those who drank themselves under the table before the bell rang again had in effect 'disembarked' at that particular station and the train continued on its route ..."

He glanced about; nobody was listening. He shrugged his shoulders. As a rule, no one listened to the stories Selim learned from his father. On account of these Russian recollections, his friends had dubbed him "Papa's nostalgia." Yet Selim was a fellow who recognized his shortcomings. He took no offense. He sidled up to İhsan. Orhan, seeing Selim in their midst, put an arm around his shoulders with sincere affection. Another of Selim's fates was to serve as something of a leaning post for Orhan, who was twice his size. For some time now, to avoid this embrace, he'd attempted to keep his distance, but under the dismay of his disregarded story, he'd surrendered himself to this clutch of his own volition. *Destiny*, he repeated a number of times internally, and slouching under the weight bearing down upon him, laughing at his own foolishness, he listened to İhsan:

"I'm not sure if it's worth crying over the absence of what amounts to a fiction. If you ask me, our lack of a notion of original sin in Islam, our lack of attention to this matter of the fall from paradise, as in Christianity, affects every field of knowledge from theology to aesthetics. We've given short shrift to spiritual conservation. We should interpret our context intrinsically, as it is." He'd lost track of how he'd begun. He spoke hastily to avoid giving Suad an opening. "There isn't even a foundation for dialogue and debate between these two worldviews. Religion and social constitution diverge. Note that in Western civilization everything is predicated on notions of salvation and liberation. Mankind is delivered in the first instance through Jesus's descent to earth, his crucifixion, and the acceptance of his sacrifice. Later, sociologically, through class struggles, first city dwellers and then peasants find salvation. In contrast, from the beginning we're already considered free by Muslim tradition."

Suad, having finished his third glass, glared at İhsan. "Or forsaken . . ."

"No, first of all free. Free despite even the presence of slaves in the social body. *Fıkh*, Islamic jurisprudence, insists upon human liberty."

Suad persisted: "The East has never been free. It's always been mired in anarchic individualism restricted by despotic groups. We're predisposed to forgo freedom as quickly as possible . . . and by all means."

"I'm essentially speaking of foundations. In the East, particularly in the Muslim East, society is predicated on notions of liberty."

"What difference does that make once it's dismissed out of hand?"

"That's another matter. That's the result of an etiquette of altruism and self-sacrifice. The Muslim East has been in a defensive posture for centuries. Take Turkey. For a period of close to two hundred years, we've been living through phases of vital self-defense and security. In such a society, a fortress mentality naturally arises. If today we've lost the concept of freedom, the reason is that we're living in a state of siege."

Suad extended his glass to Mümtaz: "Mümtaz, please do me the favor of letting me exercise my free will." His voice was as timid as a child's. Or was it hissing? "The very liberty granted to me by Almighty Allah after He's so effectively bound me hand and arm . . ." He took up the glass and stared within. As if he'd seen an ominous portent there, he reared his head and as if to dispel the vision he'd seen once and for all, he clouded the *rakı* with water: "There you have it, the extent of my liberty . . . but not as foolishly exercised as you might suppose. Don't mock it!" Suddenly angry with himself, he set the glass back down. "But why did I acknowledge your censure by saying that? Don't you all do the same?"

Nuran: "No one's annoyed because you're drinking. We've gathered here for a diversion, of course we'll drink." And she raised her glass. Mümtaz turned away to avoid coming eye to eye with her. She felt that they'd all surrounded Suad, in honesty involuntarily, maybe through his own instigation, maybe through their own apprehension, maybe even because they despised him, and had straightaway begun treating him like startled prey in battue or blood sport. This was nothing short of making a bad situation worse.

Not just in this parlor now but perhaps beneath every street lamp in every corner of the world similar scenes were unfolding. Mankind was inept, and for this reason ill-fated. The best laid plans of mice and men *gang aft agley*. An array of meaningless miseries and piddling sorrows . . . Mümtaz sighed. *Suad will make a scene tonight. Simply thinking so is preparing the way for a crisis. Isn't politics this way also? Fear and the defense mechanism, its counterpoint . . . as in music . . . and at the conclusion the golden tempest of a grand finale.* He, too, was surprised at the sudden passage of his thoughts to Western music from the mood that the *a la turca* had conjured within him: *How peculiar . . . I belong to two worlds. Like Nuran, I live between two realms, two beloveds. That means I don't constitute a whole! Aren't we all this way . . . ?*

Suad pretended not to hear Nuran's response: "Everybody chastises and criticizes me. Some allude to my illness, some to my marriage. Neither of them is of any consequence." He grasped his glass tightly. "Everybody brings some malfeasance to my attention. My wife, my friends, my relatives . . . Never once do they consider that I was born without a sense of responsibility. One is either born with or without it. Bereft, I don't have it. My wife realized this during our first week together, but she still complains and nags. Maybe she's waiting for a miracle . . . Won't a miracle happen? Imagine that I experience a sudden transformation and begin to cherish my life! Imagine that at work, I'm pleased with the president, the branch director, the treasurer, and the legal adviser . . . Imagine that I'm happy when my children climb onto my shoulders. Imagine that!"

Macide jeered, "Did you have a little something before coming here?"

"I started last night, Macide. Last night, Yaşar took me along to Sabih's. There we drank till midnight, then we went down to Arnavutköy, where we stayed till three or four. Then . . ."

Nuran inquired about the rest of the night as if after a fabulous adventure: "Then? What happened next, Suad?"

His face was a shambles.

"Next, naturally . . . well, Arnavutköy is *the* mecca. They have all types. Even ethnic types, you might say . . . but since we were being entertained *en famille*, we preferred Gypsies. Greeting the dawn to the beats of a hand drum. You know the infamous entertainment spots over on the Hürriyet-i Ebediye hill? We found ourselves there. From within the night, a Gypsy ever so slowly conjured the rose-faced dawn with his hand drum, as if drawing water from a pump. There was a nymphette there as well, a spring bud, a girl practically. Her name was Bâde, 'wine.' Just use your imagination . . . or Mümtaz should do so, it's his genre. An improvisation on drums, a Gypsy nymph named Bâde, her companions, *rakı*, dancing . . . Then sleeping it off on a divan at a friend's house." His face puckered. He brought his glass to his lips but sufficed with one sip. "It's difficult in the mornings. I haven't managed to get used to the fatigue that comes in the wake of a binge." He deposited his glass on the table. The gathering was in a state of shock.

"Is this enough, Nuran? It's quite shameless, isn't it? But if you want to know the truth, nothing of the sort happened. We didn't go to Sabih's nor did I hit the bottle. I was together with my wife last night, and I came here directly from Paşabahçe." He smiled sweetly: "I'm not drunk, you can be certain that I'm not."

Macide asked: "In that case, why did you lie?"

"To unsettle you. So you'd chastise me. To appear like a man of some import." He was cackling between short, dry coughs: "It bothers me when my marriage comes up."

Nuran: "Nobody brought up your marriage."

"It doesn't matter . . . I mentioned it, didn't I? That's enough, it means I'm under societal pressures!" He wiped his brow and turned to Mümtaz: "Mümtaz, shall I give you material for a story? Think about this, just let me set the scene . . . A man, a man of virtue, a civil servant, a professor, if you like – conjure a saint! Draw him so that he is possessed of every virtue. A man who hasn't once faltered in decency . . . yet he despises commitment. Peculiar, is it not? He's a narcissist: He wants to live only through himself and for himself. His life is full of random but kindly gestures, and these acts become increasingly more generous. He likes to exercise his freedom of thought and he recognizes no sense of obligation. One day he up and gets married, perhaps to a woman he loves, an experience that completely changes him. He becomes grumpy, fussy, and ill-willed. The thought that he's been pigeonholed slowly begins to drive him mad. The burden of being labeled, of living paired off like a draft horse, affects him. He begins to act despicably toward almost everybody; he's cruel to animals and his fellow man, to all things. He becomes petty and he can't endure anyone else's happiness. And in the end . . ."

Hastily bringing down the curtain, Mümtaz said: "A textbook scenario . . . he murders his wife."

"Exactly, but it isn't that simple. He has protracted debates with himself. He ponders his life like a riddle and concludes that his marriage is the only obstacle resting between himself and humanity."

"Why not divorce?"

"To what end? D'you suppose that two people who've lived together can separate, I mean truly separate from one another?" He said this staring squarely at Mümtaz. "And if he left her, what would come of it? Even if he could break off all ties, those intervening years spent together will haunt him. Will he ever be able to escape it all, a vast, terrifying existence of darkness, every excruciating minute of which he's lived through? Not to mention habits of mind. At which point he'll succumb to even greater hesitation. Think about it, this is a man who's consciously committed every affront and indecency against his circle. Leaving his wife would just be adding insult to injury."

"Once he murders, will he then forget?"

"No, he won't forget. Of course he won't forget. But his spite will diminish. The constricting resentment within him will evaporate."

Nuri, unable to restrain himself: "Mümtaz, if you ask me, in place of writing about him, if you happen to come across him in the flesh, kill him outright. It'd be the nobler deed."

Suad shrugged: "What would that solve? We'd only be dodging the issue. Not to mention that Mümtaz wouldn't be able to. To kill him, he'd have to meet and single him out. Why should he kill somebody who resembles everyone else? More or less, everybody resorts to acts of depravity as a reaction to one person or a handful of people. Rest assured . . . behind each downfall you'll find a precipitating one. Each of us digs his own grave. The man in question resembles all of us, he's an Everyman . . . but he refuses to accept this fact. In the end, he seizes upon the only available solution to end this pitiless game. A single act, a bloodletting, a deed that resembles vengeance. And as soon as he takes action, as if having crossed an enchanted threshold, he discovers he's broken through to the other side, to his old world, rich with the treasures of decency he's borne all along. His face shines, his soul assumes all of its generosity, he loves his fellow man, he pities the plight of animals, he empathizes with children . . ."

"How, through murder?" İhsan's mood had soured. Brooding, as if at the edge of an abyss, he recoiled within himself, staring at Mümtaz. Nuran went to Mümtaz and placed a hand on his shoulder: as in an altercation, everybody stood by his most trusted and beloved companion. Only Selim was alone: short of height, his arms crossed, observing the conversation up front with an expression of immense entertainment. Or rather, he resembled an urchin at a neighborhood cockfight.

"There's no *acknowledgment* of murder."

Macide: "Are you crazy, Suad? Why are you discussing such things? Take pity on yourself." And startled by the word "crazy," which hadn't been uttered in her presence for years but had now passed her own lips, she withdrew behind İhsan, her body atremble.

"Not at all, why should I be crazy? I'm explaining the plot of a story. There's no murder in it, but there *is* the matter of salvation. The removal of a single intervening obstacle. There's rejuvenation. Indeed, he rediscovers the world. He's given himself a period of seven days. For seven days he conceals the crime. For seven days, as if resurrected, he lives among others blithely and empathetically in halos of golden radiance. Just like a god, for seven days . . . and on the evening of the seventh day, in a state of peaceful reconciliation with nature and life, in a *mi'raj* of human fate, he hangs himself."

İhsan: "Impossible. How can you account for such a transformation in character? No sense of vengeance, no claim of justice gives an individual the right to kill another. But suppose he assumes this right and murders anyway. How did the transformation come about? The path to self-realization doesn't pass through murder . . . The blood of mankind is taboo. It diminishes and oppresses humanity. Even in the case of social justice, those who mediate through murder are always anathema. The executioner is always a pariah."

"Within the context of our own morality, yes, but by transcending it . . ."

"Morality can *not* be transcended."

"Why not for somebody living beyond good and evil? You're talking about accountability, but my protagonist has no intention to be accountable. He wants liberty. When he attains that he becomes a demigod."

"No one becomes free by spilling blood . . . Blood-stained freedom isn't freedom, it's something besmirched and tainted. Not to mention that a person can't be divine. Man is humane. And this is a station attained through much toil."

"Do me the favor of defining freedom."

Suad stared at İhsan for a minute. İhsan was on the verge of responding, but Macide, genuinely anxious, interrupted: "İhsan, you don't suppose that he plans on killing Afife?" İhsan calmed his wife with a chuckle: "Don't be childish, good heavens!" He added slowly, "No, don't be afraid, he wants to vent . . . He got a little frustrated, that's all." Then he turned back to Suad, awaiting an answer: "I can. It's the grace and prosperity we wish for others."

"But what about yourself, what happens to the wisher?"

"By desiring grace for others, I, too, become free before my urges and appetites –"

"That's nothing but another form of slavery . . . each of us exists independently."

"In one respect, yes, if I don't sincerely desire the well-being of others . . .

but think of it as a joint venture, then it's total freedom. As soon as you say, 'Each of us exists independently,' you've forsaken everything. Existence is whole and we're its constituent parts! If the contrary were true, the world would degenerate. Yes, existence is whole, and we're its transient elements. We might only achieve satisfaction and peace through this mind-set." Then he smiled. "I've made a lot of concessions to you, Suad . . . Understand what I'm trying to say; perhaps we could even agree at some fundamental level. Man, one by one, does not become divine; however, if mankind fashioned an ethics suitable to its circumstance, it might become divine! That is to say, it could assume grand qualities."

Exhausted, Suad withdrew to a corner. He clung tightly to his *rakı*. Mümtaz simply stared at him. *We're having a bizarre night . . .* He wasn't angry with Suad as before. Clearly, Suad was afflicted. But he couldn't fully empathize with him, either. An aspect of Suad's character rejected all feelings of pity. One could rather admire or despise Suad, but he couldn't be pitied. His disquiet closed the human heart to him. Even now, in the parlor under electric lights, he was alienated from each person and from the entire group, ostracized, an anomaly.

"No, this isn't the issue . . . You're conceiving the matter backward. I'm referring to an idiosyncrasy. I'm not referring to a person born into poverty, but to one born into wealth. You're attempting to apply a general system of order to him. He's above that. Don't forget how I started all this. I described him as someone who's already possessed of all virtue."

"What difference does it make?"

"I'll tell you: What others strive to achieve, he already possesses inherently."

"Among these virtues can we name duty and responsibility?"

Nuran closed her eyes. *I wonder what Fatma's doing now?*

"No, not those. He's completely independent with respect to his surroundings, but he's generous."

İhsan asked slowly, "Don't you now realize where you've gone wrong?"

"No, I don't . . . but what difference does it make? Mümtaz should still pen this story."

İhsan continued: "You're absolving people of responsibilities to impose certain preconceived and innate virtues. But being human involves a sense of responsibility. All the rest contributes to the wealth of one's character. In fact, in your account, your protagonist, the demigod that you've conceived, undergoes a transformation enabling him to commit a crime as a result of marriage, a lapse of the imagination, or maybe unprovoked hatred. Nevertheless, a sense of responsibility –"

"The sense of responsibility changes as well. It expands into action. First he'll destroy all vestiges of morality through a transvaluation of values."

"He might destroy them, but then he'll lose his bearings! Because humanity begins from a sense of responsibility."

Suad shook his head. "Where does that lead?"

"I'll tell you: He won't be at peace with others and in society as you suppose. Spilled blood will intervene. To maintain the peace, we each have a reflection of the world and its inhabitants, a fixed and defined persona. Murder, or even the slightest injustice, distorts this reflection. We'd either end up denying the world or the world would banish us!"

"Doesn't suffering distort this persona?"

İhsan answered without hesitation: "On the contrary, it's through suffering that one makes peace with humanity. It's when I'm in anguish that I better understand others. Warm empathy mediates between me and society . . . That's when I grasp my sense of responsibility. Our daily bread is suffering. He who avoids pain strikes humanity in its Achilles heel, the greatest betrayal is to shirk suffering. Can the fate of humanity be changed in a single stroke? Even if you do away with misery, if you provide freedom and liberty for all, you still have death, illness, lack of opportunity, and guilt. Fleeing in the face of suffering amounts to destroying the fortress from within. As for taking refuge in death, that's horrific. That's simply taking shelter in bestial irresponsibility."

İhsan paused. He suffered as much as or more than Suad. Perspiration covered his face. He continued, slowly: "Mankind is the prisoner of fate. When confronted by it, humanity has no recourse but faith and, in particular, suffering."

"You speak of faith, but you're on the path of reason."

"I'm on the path of reason. Naturally I'm going to take the path of reason. Socrates says that the intelligent lover surpasses the impassioned lover. Intellect is the defining attribute of humanity."

"But doesn't the murderer himself die with the victim in the act of murder?"

"To a certain degree that's true ... but, you see, this death doesn't ensure the rebirth that you seek. At least in every instance. Because such transgression removes us from the category in question. You aren't properly situating humanity within the social world. That's the crux of the matter. I'm not one to deny humanity its divine attributes! The soul of mankind is master of the world."

Suad laughed: "Apparently I've come up against İhsan's effusive side. But, Mümtaz, you go ahead and write this story anyway!"

Mümtaz entered the conversation: "That's all fine and well, but why should I write it and not you yourself?"

"Quite simply because you're the writer. You enjoy writing. Our roles are different. I simply live life!"

"Aren't I living?" Mümtaz asked, in a soft voice, as if to say, "Or have I died?"

"No, you aren't, that is, not the way I live. You've withdrawn to a particular vantage where you reside. You have vast and brilliant visions. You have the sense that you'll vanquish time. You strive to seize anything that might be of use. You categorize things: 'This is useful, this is not.' You see what you want and turn away from what you don't." He was all but talking to himself. Often he coughed, and afterward he shook his head as if to say, "Pay no mind, it'll pass." "You sense a world that you want to possess at all costs. Even though it might be an illusion, you stick with it. Do you think I'm like you? I'm a wretched, materialist sot, who shirks his responsibilities. My existence is a shameless waste. I wander aimlessly like water. I'm ill, I drink, I've fathered children whose faces I don't want to see. I disregard my own life to perpetually live in the hides of others. Whether a thief, a murderer, or a cripple who drags a lame leg behind him, each living creature I see becomes yet another invitation. They call to me and I run. Either they open their shells to me, or I open my body to them, and they settle within me furtively and seize my hands, arms, and thoughts. Their fears and anxieties become mine. At night I dream their dreams. I awake with their torments. But that's not all. I feel the anguish of the rejected. I want to feel each and every downfall. Do you know how many times I've stolen from our bank, from the safe entrusted to me?"

Macide cried, "Suad, what are you saying? Don't listen to him, for Allah's sake. Take a look for yourselves, he's covered in sweat."

Mümtaz looked at Macide, her face stark white, her eyes wide. She'd succumbed to a bout of nerves. But Suad didn't heed her anguish: "Don't worry, Macide. It's not what you think. I didn't actually steal. But I've thought of doing so a hundred times. I didn't just think it, I imagined stealing. Maybe a hundred times, I was the last person to leave the bank. I imagined I was being pursued by men who would soon arrest me as I left, receding as I went. I walked over roads I'd never traveled before."

İhsan asked, "Okay, but why?"

Suad only ever responded to Mümtaz: "For the very same reason I lived my life in the most absurd way, for the same reason I gallivanted, caroused, and finally married. To kill time. To live. To avoid rotting away!"

334

He shrugged. "How should I know? I wanted to feel the extent of myself, that's why! To fulfill the need to declare 'I am' to the void at each instant. Now do you understand why I want you to write this story? So that a shudder of alarm might travel up your spine! Your minds house a slew of words like 'love' and 'suffering.' You live through words. Whereas I want to fathom the meanings of those words. That's why I did it. You should write to discover that you don't love someone to the degree that you would kill. But you're not acquainted with death, either, are you?" He laughed and chortled. "I'm quite certain that for you death means waiting eternally in a more pristine and essential state, like objects conserved in a museum after being fired in a kiln. Is that not true? And you're not disgusted by death, but rather you see it as sister to beauty and love. Did you ever consider how disgusting death is? A revolting decay and stench! Maybe some of you believe in Allah. I'm certain you've embalmed this topic in silence and uncertainty. Because you exist only in words! Haven't you just once wanted to talk to Allah? Had I been a believer, I would have liked to speak with Him, to experience Him."

Nuran protested. "Is all this necessary, Suad?" But he wasn't listening. He was spewing as much as he possibly could. What Mümtaz had feared had come to pass. The crisis had begun.

Mümtaz asked in the same childish voice, "Do you believe?"

"No, dearest, I'm not a believer. I'm bereft of this joy. Had I been a man of faith, the issue would have been different. Had I known of the existence of Allah, I'd have no more claim against or quarrel with humanity. I'd then only struggle against Him. At every turn, I'd collar him somewhere and call Him to account. And I'd have assumed that He was obligated to provide a reckoning. I'd say, 'Come. Come, and for a moment enter into the skin of one of your creations. Do what I do every day. Live twenty-four hours of one of our lives! There's no need to select a particularly unfortunate specimen.

You are the Creator; it's impossible for you not to know or understand. Descend into the carcass of any one of them. Live your own lie for a moment along with us. Live as we do. Become a frog of small thirsts in this swamp for twenty-four hours!"

İhsan laughed. "Fine, but only a devotee could say these things. You're a believer all right! And more than any of us!"

"No, I don't believe. But, I am thinking through the thoughts of a genuine follower." He shook his head. "And I'll never believe, either. I'd rather die writhing on the ground from rheumatism."

They laughed awkwardly together. Mümtaz's face was in a state of rigid attention. Suad noticed neither the laughter nor Mümtaz.

"Yes," he said. "I'd prefer to die writhing on the ground from rheumatism! If you like, let me tell the story. Among my relatives was a very naïve but decent man. A devout, earnest, saintly man. We loved him dearly. One couldn't help being awestricken by his perseverance in life. He used to live around Topkapı. He'd come and go into the city by donkey. This donkey became one of the joys of my childhood. One day when we went to their house, we noticed that the donkey wasn't in the yard as usual. 'What happened?' we asked. 'The poor beast has rheumatism,' they told us, and opened the barn door. They'd put the donkey's saddle on upside down, suspending the animal from the ceiling by stirrups. In this way its fetlocks were eased from the humidity in the barn, and it no longer had to stand on all fours. You couldn't imagine how comical the beast looked, its four legs hanging limply, its docile head lolling toward the floor. Pathetic and comic, the animal had effectively become humanized. At first I laughed considerably. But not afterward. Today every metaphysical system of thought reminds me of that animal's pathetic and stupefied gaze from above."

Nuran: "I've never heard of such a thing. Did it get well, at least?"

"Ah, if only . . . It died within a few days, essentially by committing suicide. That is, it managed to get back down to the ground so as to die in contact with the earth. If it hadn't been strung up like that, it would have died from rheumatism."

Mümtaz shrugged. "Nonsense . . ."

But Suad was still laughing. Then he suddenly grew serious. "Perhaps," he said. "But for me, this amounts to reality. Do you understand? For me, Allah is dead. I'm savoring my freedom. I've killed Allah within myself."

İhsan asked, "Do you actually believe that you're free?"

Suad looked at him spitefully. His face was covered in sweat. "I don't know," he said. "I want to be free . . ."

"No, you can't be . . ."

"Why? Who can stop me any longer?"

"The Allah that you've killed still exists within you. You're no longer living your own life. In this state, you're only a tomb, something like a coffin. You house a horrific, cruel death. What freedom could you possibly have? Yes, I, too, know that some people believe that 'without Him, everything is permissible,' and have gone on to plunder the site of His absence for the sake of humanity. I also know about the notion of the demigod, or 'God-man.' What of it? It's only left us face-to-face with our own miseries. The fate of mankind is the same. One is still confronted with the same difficulties. One still suffers the same agonies. Honestly, what you perceive as a new dawn is but a conflagration . . . No, by toying with notions of Allah, you won't be able to escape Him. No wound can heal while it's being ministered to." He paused for a while. "But d'you know, Suad, what a great theologian you would have made? Because what you're expounding is nothing but a theology in reverse."

Suad said, "I don't quite think so. In fact, not at all."

"As you wish, but in my opinion, that's how it is."

Suad glanced at his watch, and lifting his glass toward the gathering, he downed his drink. Only Mümtaz watched him stare intently into the bottom of his empty glass before placing it back on the table.

"I should be going! Farewell to one and all . . ."

Mümtaz and Nuran objected. "Where to? How? The night's still young, there are amusements yet in store." But he didn't listen.

"No, I have the promise of an engagement! Though I'm a tad late, I should go. Good-bye, everyone!" With a gesture of his hand, he abruptly took leave of the gathering. Nuran and Mümtaz accompanied him to the doorway.

Mümtaz, to Nuran: "Why don't you insist that he stay?" As he said this, he felt a sense of dissolution within him. Whether Suad stayed was of no import to him anymore.

Nuran, looking at Suad: "Insisting would be useless, he's determined to go. Godspeed, Suad!" Before shaking his hand, she straightened his collar. "Would you like a scarf?"

"Thanks, but my collar is quite broad. If need be, I'll raise it . . . Mümtaz will accompany me for a distance, won't he?"

The two gentlemen exited together.

VII

Under cover of night, Mümtaz breathed deeply. He felt so tired as to be unable to withstand anything more. In the humid night, they walked past a cluster of shadows, which he'd seen with different eyes a few hours before. The autumn night had engulfed the hilltops of Emirgân in a lonely phantasm of impossibility. The lights of the Asian shore resembled futile distress signals within the desolation. As if unable to see in the darkness, Suad stumbled to the right and left. They proceeded in this way until the middle of the hill where Mümtaz's houseguest said, "You turn back now . . ." But he couldn't complete his words. He was seized by a bout of coughing.

Mümtaz said, "If you'd like, let's turn back. Stay here with us tonight! You won't be able to find any means of transport now. There's an extra bed!" Suad didn't respond until his coughing subsided. He simply held on to Mümtaz's hand firmly. When the coughing died down, he said, "No, I'd best be going. I've disturbed you enough anyway."

"Not at all. But you're not well!"

"True, I'm not, not at all . . . but it'll pass!" And he let go of Mümtaz's hand, which he'd been clasping tightly with two hands. Laughing, he said, "*Haydi!* Go on, have fun . . ." In the darkness he sensed that Suad's eyes sought out his own, and Mümtaz looked away involuntarily. But Suad didn't go; grabbing the collar of Mümtaz's jacket, he accosted him in a low voice, "I've written Nuran a letter. Are you aware of this? A love letter!"

Mümtaz, startled in the face of this lunge, stuttered, "I-I know. She showed it to me. Did you know that we'll soon be getting married?"

"I knew you were involved."

"In that case?"

"There is no *case*. Just another senseless act . . . a half hour before I'd written it, I hadn't thought of Nuran for months."

Mümtaz, in a collected tone, as if there were no matter relating to him in the balance, said, "But with respect to me, with respect to your old friend, I don't know, it wasn't the right thing to do, now, was it?" They came eye to eye. An agonizing grimace overcame Suad's face.

"You wouldn't understand, would you, how impulses, strange and inappropriate, at times overtake one? Perhaps you'll never understand. Because you uphold your measured actions, above all desiring predictable causes and effects. You seek out the logic in all things! But what's done is done! Don't let me detain you for nothing. I only wanted to inform you even if it's an impropriety. Fare thee well." And he began to hastily descend the hill.

Mümtaz cried after him, "Everybody's this same way, so don't be slavish to your damn cause!"

"Good-bye." Suad descended with quick steps.

Mümtaz stood listening to Suad's footsteps sounding a deeper clack in the night and to his gut-wrenching cough. Then he headed slowly back to the house, pleased that his hand was now free of the large, bony, and clammy vise of Suad's palms. Within this eerie night, seeing his own hand in Suad's had alarmed him. This tacky vise had given him the dread of a possession that seemed to penetrate clear through to his soul; maybe this was why he'd avoided Suad's eyes. As he recalled this, he grew angry at himself; he'd been intimidated by a sick man. Nonetheless, his sense of salvation was so profound that he raised his hand aloft in the dark and watched it like a beloved keepsake with which he'd been reunited. Suad's hands, with their sticky warmth, seemed to suck away a potent, rather essential and vital element from the skin of Mümtaz's palm and fingertips. He asked himself repeatedly, *Why is he so tormented? Why is he so cruel?* Mümtaz knew that he'd descended into a mental state that he hadn't experienced since he'd met Nuran. *I'm a hundred steps away from him, and I'm still trembling on this road.* Everyone he considered a part of his social circle was present in the house, but at that moment he thought neither of Nuran, İhsan, nor the houseguests.

On the crest of the hill, he stopped again and looked about. The autumn night, as if resting behind a black and highly polished glass pane, its scattered lights penetrating deeply into him, glimmered in a state beyond any and all potential for change. In the distance, the Bosphorus had become a glowing ashen ribbon. The hazy street lamps beyond, in astral stillness mimicking starlight, illuminated their own silence rather than the existences that surrounded them. Yet, all of it, everything in the environs, the ambient nocturnal sounds, the occasional peeping bird or buzzing insect, as well as the susurrus of branches, was in something of suspended animation.

And what if everything he said was true? Allah, what if all he said was true? Under this trepidation, he raised his head and watched the dome of sky. A debris of stars, luculent pulses that made the darkness of the firmament more aggressive, gleamed like windows of hope, anguish, and dread in houses of the afflicted. Involuntarily he thought, *He's not dead yet* . . . The torment within him was so great that he wanted to escape, to take refuge somewhere. But where could he go? In this black night laden with radiant caravans of infinite time no crack existed into which the human soul might seep. The sated black night wouldn't accommodate one more thing, rejecting every living being and coalescing around him like a bejeweled carapace. Élan vital, the secret laughing and speaking through all matter, had withdrawn behind a thick gem-studded shroud. Somewhere some *thing* rustled, the edge of the horizon stirred. The heavy-laden, fierce night glided overhead like a large turquoise and gilt bird, though its wings maintained their rigidity.

If only it would take me along . . .

Had it been another time, within this night constituted by immaculate gems, by veins of ore not yet roused from pristine hibernation, by granite and black marble, Mümtaz would have found the purest facet of his pleasurable and poetic realms. But now he was rather miserable and closed off to his entire aesthetic world. Great intimations of dread had colonized him.

"It's as if a part of me has collapsed," he said to himself.

Within the house at the top of the street, a lamp burned, transfiguring every receding intimacy on such nights into a sweet reverie; and a window, out of the pure and profound silence into which it had sunk, as if afflicted by the infirmity of existence, approached him together with the glimmering silhouette of the tree before it, like bloody excisions from the vast and opulent silence. Mümtaz remembered that he was neglecting his houseguests. Nuran would worry. He quickened his pace. But this minor snag had only spun him around to face his own dimension of time; it hadn't done away with his inner sense of isolation or the agonizing constriction that afflicted him.

A part of him was still walking through a void. *Why is there such an expanse between my head and my body?*

He stopped and thought. *Is this what I really meant to say?* Maybe what he felt was more exacerbating, more ineffable. He wasn't angry, though he knew what Suad had done was wrong. But he withheld from passing judgment. He'd stopped passing judgment on others. Suad, by exposing his misery, had spoiled their pleasure. The depth of Suad's abjection, or rather, the disarray of his existence, which caused such depravity, astonished Mümtaz. He was obviously in torment. Throughout the evening, as Mümtaz listened to him, he recollected exhausting and semi-nightmarish conversations, phantasms of clenched teeth during fitful nights of sleep. Suad resembled nothing more than a man in the midst of a nightmare.

VIII

The table talk among the houseguests centered on Suad. When Mümtaz entered, Nuran glanced at him as if to say, "Where have you been?" To conceal his misery, he smiled with a furtive pucker, pleased that Nuran wasn't offended by this offhand public display.

"Might I request a glass as well?"

Nuran: "As much as you'd like, Mümtaz dear! We're starting the evening over anyway."

She was pleased to be rid of Suad too. Eager to continue from where he'd been interrupted, İhsan paused in annoyance, waiting for Mümtaz's glass to be filled. That's how he was; he detested being interrupted and he expected the interference to stop immediately.

Looking at Nuran through his glass, Mümtaz said, "In that case, health to one and all . . ."

"Regrettably, the world has already lived through and dispensed with this variety of angst a century ago. Hegel, Nietzsche, and Marx have come and gone. Dostoyevsky suffered this anguish eighty years prior. Do you know what's new in our case? It's neither Éluard's surrealist poetry nor the torments of Nikolai Stavrogin. What's new for us today is the murder, land dispute, or divorce scandal unfolding in the smallest Turkish village in the most desolate corner of Anatolia. I'm not sure if you catch my drift, fully. I'm not accusing Suad. I'm just saying that his concerns can't be taken within the framework of our present circumstances."

Mümtaz emptied his glass. "But you're overlooking one point! Suad is genuinely in torment . . ."

With a flick of his hand, İhsan distanced something unseen from his person. "He might be . . . but what's it to me? I don't have time to chase idiosyncrasies. I'm occupied with social concerns. Let the mother of the sheep who strays from the flock weep in its absence! Did I mention that one day at an auction I discovered a number of old menus, the table d'hôte menus of I'm not sure which restaurant. Probably from the midst of the Hamidian reign. Near the top were written the names of that night's singers. Suad's problems have the same effect on me. Bygone relics . . . Anyone can turn an idea into an exacerbating problem. But to what end? It does nothing but make us dizzy. We're people who have responsibilities and work to accomplish."

"Yet Allah is our eternal question."

"Humanity and its fate are also eternal questions. And they're all tied to each other. Furthermore they're matters whose resolution is impossible. Of course, if one has no faith . . ." İhsan paused to think for a moment. "I know I have no right to speak this way. Of course, our morality and inner lives are tied to a notion of Allah. This game of chess can't be played without Him. Maybe I'm annoyed at Suad for this very reason . . ."

He didn't finish what he had to say. Suad's manner of speaking had disturbed him more than it had Macide. Suad had uprooted all potential for coming to peaceful terms with society. He was a heartbeat away from deeds of madness and excess. İhsan had to discuss this eventuality, particularly with Mümtaz and Nuran. Regardless, Suad's approach didn't please İhsan.

Tevfik, in an infinitely blasé manner, placed an eggplant dolma on his plate. "I'm not sure what Nuran will have to say about it, for Mümtaz hasn't yet begun to meddle in my affairs, but I believe I'm eating the last *aubergine* of the season. And I have my doubts as to whether I'll be able to enjoy them next year. What I mean to say is that the matters with which our boy Suad is grappling, I'll learn about firsthand before the rest of you do . . ." With an extremely cruel and hangdog face he'd made a mockery of himself, Suad, life and the palpable immanence of death. "Do you know what truly astounds me? Our youngsters have lost the ability to enjoy themselves. Was this how it used to be? That so many people, and at this age, gathered together in one place should talk of such things . . ."

Nuran said, "My uncle doesn't much care for Suad . . . He doesn't even want Yaşar to socialize with him. But say what you will, I wasn't at all surprised tonight. Suad has been this way from the beginning. I remember one day, a group of us were out along the Bosphorus, and he'd tossed a puppy into the sea because it was too happy for its station in life. We had quite a time rescuing the poor thing. It was so adorable . . ."

"For what possible reason?"

"Simply because a dog shouldn't be that happy. We're talking about Suad here! In those days he'd say, 'All living things are my adversaries!'"

İhsan made a suggestion: "Friends, if we want to free ourselves from this conversation, let's have Orhan and Nuri recite some folk songs."

Orhan and Nuri were like a folklore duo. Oh, the *türkü*s they knew!

The night, through İhsan's instigation, took a new tack. Orhan and Nuri first recited that beautiful Rumeli *türkü* made popular by Tanburacı Osman Pehlivan. Their voices were stark and majestic:

344

Clouds roll in one by one
Four are white, four are black
You've gone and lanced my heart
Rains, don't fall, O wild winds, don't blow
For my beloved is on the road

Mümtaz listened to the searing, palpable pain of the folk songs as if he'd discovered a panacea. They'd all seemingly stepped out into a bracing, invigorating wind or faced problems which must be overcome; that is, they confronted life itself.

Clouds roll by and the ground does weep
Soaking up wine and growing heady
The scent of my beloved makes me giddy

Mümtaz realized that this deep and maddening desire constituted a world separate from his pain. This wasn't the projection of a bout of nerves, but rather, like warm bread, something full of life, comprising existence.

With the dawn come clouds
With the spring bloom flowers
We'll all be reunited with our beloveds

"You see, this is what we should cherish." İhsan was content. "All truths are contained here, in this vast ocean of meaning. Our satisfaction is relative to our closeness to the folk and our own lives. We're the children of these *türkü*s." Then he unexpectedly recalled Yahya Kemal's line of verse:

Savor it though I have, Slavic melancholy brings me no satisfaction . . .

"Does He exist or not? I exist and that's sufficient. And I desire no freedom for myself that exceeds that of anyone else's."
"But a sharp strain of suffering exists here as well, doesn't it?"

"No, here there's only expression. If the sorrow of this *türkü* and those like it were real, one's heart couldn't endure it for even half an hour. Here we're face-to-face with the collective. The experience doesn't belong to one person but to the totality of the culture."

Orhan and Nuri recited Rumeli and Anatolian *türkü*s one after another, and at times Cemil accompanied them on the *ney*. Toward the end, Tevfik said, "Allow me to sing the Rose Devotional Hymn to you! In Trabzon, more often than not it's women who sing it!"

Mümtaz was cast into a world that recalled Fra Filippo Lippi's fifteenth-century Renaissance *Nativity* of the Christ child amid flowers; the roses scattered by the Ferahfezâ's tempest of desire were gathered up again in this ancient hymn:

> *A bazaar of roses*
> *Roses bartered, roses sold*
> *A hand-held scale of roses*
> *Patrons, roses, merchants, roses, too*

The Hicaz *makam* had suddenly transformed into spring. The final vision Mümtaz recollected of that night was Nuran's face fragmented by scattered thoughts yet reflecting resonances from the deluge of roses, a face that coalesced in an exhausted, mollified, but nonetheless composed smile. Each of his suspicions was no more than phantasm coupled with anguish; he was enamored of her.

IX

During periods of strife between them, when Nuran's social milieu was occupied with her, she trusted in nothing but Mümtaz's composure. Yet,

Mümtaz was far from displaying the presence of mind to respond to her reliance. Instead of regarding the entire matter with calm confidence in his beloved, he was suspicious, accusing her of neglect and carping through a series of letters.

Neither Fatma's on-going afflictions, nor Yaşar's insufferable demeanor, nor the gossip of acquaintances bothered Nuran as much as Mümtaz's unfounded *tristesse*. The interlopers were a hindrance they'd decided to resist together as a couple. But the very attitude of her lover was another matter entirely.

As long as Nuran complained, *Why doesn't he understand me?* and as long as Mümtaz thought, *Why is she turning a simple matter into a can of worms?* each of them insisted on misunderstanding the other.

In Nuran's view, Mümtaz's situation was quite straightforward. Considering that he was the object of her love, he ought to withdraw to a corner and quietly await her final decision. In contrast, Mümtaz believed that if she loved him, she ought to decide as soon as possible for her own contentment as well as his.

The misadventure of moving house, in itself, had given rise to an array of annoyances for Mümtaz. Eventualities like a second rent and furnishing costs prompted him to seek out opportunities beyond his regular means. Granted, they could see each other more easily now because both lived in the vicinity of old Istanbul, where there was no hill to climb in winter and no inconvenience of crossing the Bosphorus, no small ordeal due to the unreliable ferry schedules. Nuran was to visit Mümtaz almost daily. But as chance would have it, a separate slew of hindrances filled her life. By moving to Beyoğlu, Nuran was cast amidst old school chums, a rather extended family circle, Yaşar's endless flood of acquaintances, Fâhir's kith and kin, and not least of all Adile and her cohorts. Nobody understood her dilemma; all of them, knowingly or not, demanded she take up her old lifestyle, and because she didn't have the wherewithal, at least until wed, to say no, she felt obliged to acknowledge these friendships, and the invitations and parties came thickly in turn, to the degree that toward February, when Mümtaz realized that most of the time she'd set aside for him had been usurped by others, he, too, was astounded.

If not for the gossip flying around Fatma's malaise at summer's end, Nuran wouldn't have been so malleable as to reject her own inner life. Meanwhile, all these visits, invites, and friendships gave rise to a web of intricacies. The couple had mutually decided, at least for a time, not to be seen together in public. In a certain regard this was wise. But living separately wasn't easy for Mümtaz. Nearly every day, from near or far, an account of Nuran's appearance at last night's, or the previous night's, invitation, gala, or dance reached his ears. Even worse, under the desire to dispel accusations that she'd neglected her child for Mümtaz's sake, during said soirées Nuran changed and felt obliged to cavort, laugh, and partake of trivial indulgences.

On another front, Yaşar, in his jealousy of Mümtaz, sicced a number of youthful suitors upon Nuran. Yaşar had in effect declared, "Let it be anyone, as long as it isn't Mümtaz." He harbored bewildering enmity toward him. In his consideration, there was neither "good" nor "bad" but simply Mümtaz and the rest.

Within this animus, Yaşar had also forgotten his resentment toward Adile. Practically every day he visited her apartment. They cooperated together without making an explicit pact. Both felt that Nuran would incline toward Adile before long. On their first parlor visit, after having mutually agreed – "Yes, this unfortunate girl must be saved . . . or else she'll be ruined!" – simply by acknowledging each other's opinions, they took all manner of safeguard to distance Nuran from Mümtaz. Whenever Yaşar sent word, "Tomorrow evening we're coming over with a group of friends!" or whenever he said so in person during an impromptu visit, Adile, in response would automatically suggest, "You'll be sure to invite Nuran, won't you? Do insist that she come!" and in this way the date that Nuran and Mümtaz had made a week prior would meet with an unforeseen obstacle.

These measures and ploys slowly began to have their effect. Nuran sensed that her thoughts, at least during these fetes, had shifted away from Mümtaz. The more she feigned composure to escape the prying of her circle and the gossip that tattered her life, the more she acclimated to this new milieu and whatever it tossed her way. Besides, foreclosing consideration of Mümtaz and Fatma amounted to liberation from an array of regrets that had encroached upon her over the last six or seven months. This somewhat resembled the external pressure of a siege felt internally. And toward the end, Nuran realized that she was pleased by the things being imposed on her, that she was satisfied by these swarming hordes, by a life filled with adulation and amusement. Albeit, to silence the plea Mümtaz perpetually made, she frequently told herself, "Wherever I might find myself, I belong only to Mümtaz!" But as she said so, she didn't fail to notice the difference between her surroundings and being with him. "Were I in China even my thoughts would be his!" she insisted. Yet her smiles, conversation, and excitement, that accompanied the thoughts that were always only his, belonged to others; she danced in the arms of other men, she discussed matters that didn't at all resemble what interested Mümtaz, and she didn't think or live as she did when they were alone or when she focused on him. So much so that by the middle of winter she found that she'd truly grown accustomed to this frenetic mental state. At least she wasn't at her family house. At least she didn't witness her mother's surreptitious tsking or Fatma's overt glares of resentment. At least, amid the horde, she didn't listen to herself. And she'd begun to understand how she'd made a mistake by not nipping the whole matter in the bud and marrying him at summer's end.

Trysting with Mümtaz once or twice a week was sufficient for her, as it was for him, but she hadn't at all considered what this measure of satisfaction exacted from him.

Mümtaz's days passed in a stupefying state of anticipation. The apartment in Taksim was small and humble. He'd transferred a portion of his books to this second residence. On the nights that he didn't go down to Istanbul, he stayed there. According to Nuran, Mümtaz was now set up where he could work, in a room of his own. Whenever she went to see him, she did so in the midst of her other business and errands.

By conceiving of the arrangement in this way, Nuran didn't consider the existence to which she'd condemned him. Even had she, there wasn't much she could do about it. Her feminine soul, whose momentum faltered in the face of what she deemed too laborious, had long since instilled in her the notion that she maintained the relationship only to avoid hurting Mümtaz.

Consequently Mümtaz's days passed in solitary anticipation, confined within two rooms and a hallway. More often than not, Nuran didn't arrive on time, and when she did, the visit was limited to the character of a drop-in. To avoid missing her, he'd wait at times the entire day, and at times three or four days on end, excluding those hours when the chance of her arrival was nil.

His torment was genuine. Working or occupying himself with this or that until the promised time was one option. But as the appointed hour approached, the state of waiting commenced, that fragmented and purely agitated existence by the threshold, the doorbell, or the clock. Mümtaz couldn't recollect these hours without experiencing something approaching a headache and sensing in his nerves the remorse caused by living confined to four walls. Over a period of weeks and months, he experienced the passing of the day in his frayed nerves through the intermittent cries of street hawkers. Before now, he'd paid them no mind. Amid everyday thoughts, these cries, familiar to all, had a way of appearing and passing without distinction, like an unnecessary comma or period in a text. Later, when the rational mind entered the realm of anticipation, these sounds gradually became augurs of the phases of the day, and finally, when the appointed hour came and Nuran failed to arrive, they'd be reduced to bitter memories. Toward ten o'clock the call of the yogurt seller simply informed housewives of nothing more than a first-order shortcut, but toward noon the same cry would remind Mümtaz to focus his thoughts on Nuran's arrival, and at two o'clock the same yogurt seller, in the same cadence, would shout, "The hour of Nuran's arrival is at hand," and at three or three thirty he'd declare, "Today will be like last week's cancelation, she won't be coming!" and when he cried out amid the early twilight toward dusk, within the cadence of the call was an admonishment of sorts: "Didn't I tell you so?"

On such days when Mümtaz futilely awaited Nuran, the hours became a creature whose aspect transformed gradually from anticipation to remorse. During the morning hours it grinned with smiling intimations of hope; toward noon it worsened to a mood between doubt and excitement; in the midafternoon its face folded; and toward evening it became a pallid, meaningless miasma, an odd and absurd simulation of Mümtaz's existence.

Meanwhile, within the building, doorbells were rung, conversations transpired before neighbors' doors, in the adjacent apartment preparations began for an evening meal, and the clink of forks and knives mingled with radio broadcasts; afterward the stairs were hastily climbed and descended before finally the entire building sank into silence. Then, willingly or not, all of Mümtaz's attention focused onto the street.

At three thirty the wicker basket of the Greek family on the topmost floor descended by rope to the vegetable peddler, and a conversation began in a pidgin tongue from upstairs to the street and from the street back upstairs; the manicurist in the hairdresser's shop opposite darted out to the street as the hour to make her rounds arrived; as if not wanting to leave the street without absorbing the complete neighborhood news bulletin, she engaged in endless chatter with the laundress – whose Levantine madame, for her part, divulged intimate secrets, while she in turn only expressed her astonishment; and in the next apartment the echoes of a piano lesson would direct the secret ciphers of Cs and Es of every octave toward Mümtaz's solitude. It amounted to an existence through the ears and somewhat through the eyes. More often than not Nuran's arrival put an end to such sorrows. On days she didn't come, however, the night grew terrible under the torment of its passing without having seen her. At such times Mümtaz ran to his beloved's house, and if he couldn't find her at home, he'd exchange pleasantries with Tevfik and her mother in an attempt to await her return. Other times, resentful of everything, he remained captive in his apartment.

X

Monday evening proved to be this way: At six o'clock, on his return from the university to Taksim, he was informed that Adile and her circle, with Suad and Nuran in tow, had spent three days ago in one of Istanbul's popular nightclubs. A pathetic fool who'd practically collared Mümtaz gave him the news in a fashion he wouldn't forget, describing the merrymaking to which he'd been privy from a afar, down to the gowns the ladies wore, Suad's flights of exuberance, his style of toasting, and his boisterous laughter: "I was by myself. Honestly, if you'd been there, I would have gone and joined them . . . I even waited for you for a while. The women there, brother! What women!" He wasn't aware of Mümtaz's involvement with Nuran, just his friendship with Sabih. For this reason, he said whatever came to mind: "And there was one darling, most likely Suad's mistress!"

Then, as if unable to forgive Mümtaz for letting his potential amusements wither: "Brother, where have you gone and disappeared to? Or are you writing something? I guess you're spending time in new places, aren't you? But this is really too much. Why don't you at least tell us where you'll be so we can come find you? Or let's go out together one night, how's that? These friends of yours . . . Anyway, wherever you go, you won't find a group more entertaining than they are!"

Mümtaz stopped listening. He stepped back, virtually pushing away the hand of the pathetic gadfly and freeloader who wouldn't unhand his collar. Had he remained a few minutes longer, he'd have been forced to thrash him then and there. Intense anger toward Nuran overwhelmed him. Mümtaz had spent that very Friday waiting for her. The day before on the telephone, she'd promised with such certainty that she'd be coming . . . Then, exhausted from expectation and suffering, he'd retired to bed without going anywhere. Furthermore, on account of her promise, he'd spent the entire night worried that some random misfortune had befallen her. He awoke frequently, smoked cigarettes, paced in his room, and opened the window, cocking an ear to the silence of the street. And now, he'd received word of how she'd spent the night in question, which had been so torturous for him, of the new dress he'd yet to see, and of her latest coiffure.

After Mümtaz had received such news, returning home was nearly impossible. The isolation, deafening silence, sense of despair, and ire and vengeance that drove into him like poisoned daggers . . . He was so intimate with them . . . Quickening his steps, he walked toward Beyoğlu. He stopped often and repeated the statement he'd just heard: *Most likely Suad's mistress!*

Why shouldn't this be the case? He recalled a trivial detail. Nuran, one day when they were going out, had asked, "Why don't you wear your blue necktie?" before describing a tie he'd seen around Suad's neck three days earlier. This commonplace absentmindedness, or confusion, now incensed him. It happened repeatedly this way. Mümtaz, under the influence of outsiders, would recollect from the very beginning every word they'd exchanged, and in each of her words, in every gesture, he'd seek out hard evidence of betrayal.

The evening of tragic thoughts, which a poet he admired called "the accomplice of villains," gradually relinquished its place to a dark, foggy night. Mümtaz walked down the street, staring into illuminated window fronts that seemed transformed within smells of coal and damp fog. Where should he head? While shouldering such misery all places were equal. Going somewhere meant interacting with others. Meanwhile, Mümtaz wanted to escape the company of others. Their lack of understanding distressed him. They lived easily, unburdened. Or else . . . *Or else, I'm completely hopeless . . . What should I do? Where should I go, Allah?* In a matter of minutes, out of daydream and torment, jealousy had erected its baffling and intricate apparatus inside and outside his person . . . as if a spider were ceaselessly working, spinning webs of steel.

Such was jealousy. Jealousy, the other side of love. Jealousy through which all pleasures and satisfactions, the smiles that heartened us, commitments, and hopes for the future returned inverted, piercing our flesh as sharpened knives and pointed lancets. Mümtaz had known and experienced this for months on end. Long before, the chalice of love had doubled. While quaffing the nectar of delirious desire from one, in the midst of bliss whose each minute resembled devotional worship, the hand of fate pushed another chalice into his palms, and he would fast awaken from the inebriation into a realm of miserable heartaches, petty emotions, and vile suspicions.

In a corner of his mind sat a cruel conjurer who enjoyed inflicting unimaginable tortures. Within a matter of seconds he'd transfigure everything in Mümtaz's surroundings, making the manifest disappear and manifesting what didn't exist, thereby ruining not just the moment but Mümtaz's past and the semblance and meaning of bygone days; the conjurer transformed each of Mümtaz's visions – the pleasures of hours of solitude – into a state of endless torment.

With a fury that he'd never known, he sensed the grating, gnawing voice and subversive stirrings of the conjurer.

Beneath drizzling rain, which had begun again, and in bitter cold, he walked hastily, making frequent stops to talk to himself, frustrated with the inability to control his hand gestures. But neither this quickened pace, as he bumped to the right and left, nor the pedestrians frequently confronting him like creatures of an unrecognizable species, nor the shopwindows, into which he stared without seeing anything, could prevent the further intensification, the moment-by-moment proliferation, of the growing distress, the boisterous rancor and the sense of isolation and self-pity, making them more disruptive, lethal, and unendurable.

He was overcome with the desire to go to Sabih's apartment and catch them all there, gathered together. He wanted to catch them in the middle of a party to which he hadn't been invited. Tonight Nuran was certainly among them, doubtless accompanied by Suad. Seeing them all in the same place had now become his greatest desire. *I must learn everything!* But what would he learn? What was there left for him to learn? *"Most likely Suad's mistress . . ."* The statement wouldn't leave his head. So, then, even a cursory glance from a distance offered such a conclusion.

Slowly he began to walk toward Talimhane. The noises of taxis and car horns had lost their sharpness in the humid weather, and they sounded like mattresses dropped from above. A stranger, grabbing him by the arm, pulled him from before a passing car. Mümtaz, so distracted that he wasn't able to thank the man, only realized what had happened five or ten steps later; turning around, he looked as if to say, "Why d'you go and do that? Why didn't you just let me be? Everything could have ended at that moment." But the stranger had vanished into the night.

Sabih and Adile's apartment: The parlor, the dining room, the small office, in short, the entire side that faced the street, was illuminated. "She's certainly here," he repeated, and walked toward the entrance. But before the door he stopped short. "What if they're actually there and I catch them together?" His resolve, and even his anger, had dissipated. Only now did he contemplate the effect his sudden entrance into this house – which he hadn't visited for weeks, in such a wretched state, and only for the sake of finding her – would have upon Nuran. At such times her expression changed drastically and she gazed with forlorn and reproachful eyes.

He moved away from the front of the building. Not looking at anyone on the street to avoid recognizing belated guests, he walked, in effect, in complete disregard of his surroundings.

From an apartment floor close to street level, a radio sounded. And suddenly Mustafa Çavuş's *türkü* overwhelmed the winter night and the street. "Majestic eyes, majestic . . ." Mümtaz felt a wrenching sensation. It was one of Nuran's favorite songs. He again began to walk hurriedly. But the music became an angel of torment chasing him, accosting him, and pinning him down. "Why? Why does it have to be this way?" He repeatedly brought a hand to his brow, attempting to shoo away dark thoughts.

How long did he walk in this state? Which route did he take? He himself didn't quite know. *If only I had a drink . . .* He found himself at the door of a small tavern in the vicinity of Tünel.

He slunk into a corner amid the smell of burnt olive oil, Greek songs, the shouts of garçons, ready-made smiles careening through the air, wafts of alcohol and cigarette smoke. This wasn't the Mümtaz of old. He'd become a small, puny being. The din around him notwithstanding, the voices in his head persisted. The Eviç *makam* still spoke through his thoughts with the ambience it had gathered from now-lost lands of the Balkans, serving up beautiful facets of Nuran's attributes, of the bitterness of human fate, and of the memories of long-forgotten cities and the old estates of nobles along the banks of the Danube. He mused: *The Eviç* makam *is the Hüseynî of Turkey-in-Europe.*

The tavern was packed to the gills. Everybody sang, laughed, and caroused. A few numbers – learned by ear from a Greek operetta troupe that had recently toured – had fast become famous and sounded from each table separately. Working girls accompanied by friends, prostitutes taken wholesale from their dens for a night's diversion, bachelor civil servants, laborers who erected the days with unknown expertise, and callous-handed coast guard workers, all of them bearing their own human burdens, like little caravans from disparate lands, had stopped here at the headwaters of alcohol, at this strange reclusion shared by one and all, attempting to slake thirsts preordained by their natures and fates – some to forget, others in sorrowful nostalgia, and others still for the sake of taming carnal urges.

Like a sponge, alcohol had wiped away some of their faces while other faces sparkled brightly, like luminous shopwindows. Still, from beneath the alcohol-induced half-sleep, there awoke in each of them, like creatures kept and fed in dampness and dark, a legacy, a repressed emotion, a base representation, or the yearning – of desire, vengeance, the urge to kill, or a sense of self-sacrifice to be forgotten by daybreak, or tragically, lasting a lifetime – to gallop, to satisfy itself whatever the cost; creatures poised, like lizards on boulders crouched and warming in the sun, before, in an astounding metamorphosis, they strove to usurp the place of this human material, this paltry, living prey they'd cornered. Step by step they tried to transport these men and women to their own marked territories, to that assertion present in each individual to be nothing but a singular moment, to the edge of a sharpened knife blade with conflated meanings of Eros and Thanatos.

Whether crude or repulsive, elevated or foolhardy, ascetic or purely sybaritic, everyone hurled toward unity of being. Some, however, simply existed in states of entropy. Like a melting chunk of ice tossed against a wall, they dispersed into unseen particles. Such people hadn't yet seized upon the experience of their lives, or were so benign, they never would, dreamers and desperados who'd in fact, or due to the constraints of fate, remained in a stunning state of dormancy.

A young and naïve whore of swarthy skin and scrawny build, a forlorn

357

waif resembling a corncob marinated in mud, propped an elbow on the knee of her paramour and crooned to him sotto voce. Her voice was like spoiled and fermented dough. She frequently hiccuped, her expression souring under the force of alcohol rising in her throat, though once the hiccuping ceased, she continued her song.

Farther ahead, three men sat together, conversing. The hands of one continuously kept tempo on the tabletop. The one in the center, a lout who was undoubtedly experiencing one of the triumphs of his life – a man in his fifties – in a tone that he tried to make measured and melodious, detailed something as he paused to rest upon each word; frequently, both his hands extended out over the plates of *meze*, without touching them, to mime his plans; after each comment, he stared into the faces of his two friends; what kind of make-believe project or never-to-be castle in the sky was taking root within? A man of ideas. What did it matter if he forgot about it tomorrow? By evening he'd be here again, at this table or another, where he'd be sure to rediscover it with more richness.

Mümtaz glanced at the face of the youth keeping tempo. His posture revealed that he maintained his distance, as much as possible, from this mine of truth. Evidently he envied the man of ideas, and was distressed that his own ideas didn't meet muster. He listened in a state of distraction. More than the third man, who truly looked awed, he missed neither word nor gesture through his feigned lack of attention. He listened in hatred and envy, making separate, internal objections to each articulated word. Tomorrow the exact words would issue from his own mouth and the same gestures would be aped by him; any other outcome was impossible. Mümtaz once again glanced into the young blade's face, overcast with derision. He resembled a closed palm, a category of things that functioned to take and hide. He framed a fierce and greedy emptiness.

A dame beside them, past her prime and wearing too much makeup, rested her head on the shoulder of a tom, listening intently to what he said.

Sporadically, she laughed slowly in a voice that waxed coquettish, then grabbed her glass, took a few swigs, and once again rested her head on his shoulder. In the distance a garçon laughed at them through the experience of many years.

For Mümtaz, the voice of the floozy, alienated from her own experiences so that her crude face resembled a wall whose paint had blistered from humidity, and her sedated and saucy look lost all their tragic proportions through the garçon's silent laughter and were reduced to nothing but a trifle. To be sure, the garçon was an appraiser, an appraiser of human beings . . . And under the terrible effect of this term, which he'd heard since his childhood, he was pushed to the verge. So then, one's life experiences could foster cynical wisdom, which encouraged one to laugh derisively and cruelly before what should be pitied. So then, so-called humanism was the delusion of intellectuals, cockamamy mystics, and dupes who mistook the indistinct glimmers within themselves as the blazing sun of truth. Humanism wasn't intrinsic to life; it was only a mode of thought. This notion transported him back a few months, to that fateful night in Emirgân and heated discussions with İhsan; in keeping with the conversation at the house, Mümtaz conjured a tableau of Plato with a copy of *The Republic* beneath his arm, on the path of exile.

His thoughts snapped. Nuran's face appeared before him in the ambience of the tavern filled with cigarette smoke, the stench of alcohol, and tacky voices, as if she were unwilling to leave his mind in such a state of *hüzün* – not for an instant.

Once again he yearned to be on the street, to ramble aimlessly over roads, to bump up against passersby, to scarcely be saved from a fate beneath automobile tires, and to let his thoughts cavort wildly and aimlessly. The renewed thought of Nuran was so strong that he momentarily felt suffocated. Then he reached for his glass. Alcohol, alcohol should provide some relief. *Humanist experiences devoid of humans indeed . . .* All decent, absolute, blissful, and lofty things like this were devoid of humanity. Profound and reasonable ideas were predicated on a single point: Death! Or else unrestrained chaos, that is, life itself!

Mümtaz stared at the door, wondering which of the two would enter: astounding and illogical Eros or the master of inevitability, Thanatos. The door opened. A young woman and three men entered and sat down at the neighboring table. Mümtaz couldn't recall when this table had emptied out. Then he realized how his attention was skittering over surfaces. Perhaps none of what he thought he'd seen actually existed. His imaginative faculties could have conjured the waif who resembled a muddied corncob, the garçon and his plague-of-torment smile, and the middle-aged, painted lady with bracelets jangling like the bells of an old-world camel. With this thought, he looked about with trepidation. The waiter with the unctuous grin was yet preoccupied with the newcomers. Through hand gestures, which he tried to make polite and agile, he recommended haricots in olive oil, mixed pickles, salt bonito, and shish kebab to the young woman. He never varied his mimes such that these delicacies, whose procurement elsewhere was impossible, emerged from horizontal circles traced by a pair of coupled fingers beneath her nose. The waif continued to croon her song, though now tears welled in her eyes. The middle-aged harlot, from where she rested on her lover's arm, requested a *türkü* from the one-eyed mandolin player.

What's a young man like me doing in a place like this? Alcohol offered no consolation. He wasn't one to attain the paradise of oblivion through drink. *As for this lot . . .* Anyway, should he one day lose Nuran, by dint of circumstance, he'd sup in places like this, he'd adopt habits resembling those of the regulars in this crowd, and he'd desire the companionship of these women. Solely due to this eventuality, half delirious, he darted from his chair.

XI

By the time he'd arrived home, the hour was approaching eleven o'clock. As he patted his pockets for keys in the entryway while contemplating the unseemliness of the night, the door opened by itself. Before him stood Nuran. At first he was alarmed, assuming that he was to receive bad news about Tevfik, her mother, or Fatma. But when he saw Nuran wearing the traditional folk dress that he'd purchased for her a week ago from a Kütahya native, he understood that this was simply an evening delight.

Evidently Nuran had set out on her way Friday to come to Mümtaz's apartment at the appointed hour, but as she'd happened upon Suad just before the door, she couldn't bring herself to make an entrance. For two weeks now she'd been running into Suad on this street. But this time Mümtaz's relative had tightened the blockade and was having his shoes shined by a street urchin before the entrance. Reluctantly she'd turned back, and together they'd headed to Sabih's, from where they'd decided to press on to Arnavutköy. The night described with such embellishment by Mümtaz's friend had amounted to nothing more than this.

"It was completely awkward . . . completely! I was a hair's breadth from having it out with him. And he was being sheepish in an odd way. I dreaded having to openly discuss the situation. But it worked out well." Then Nuran laughed mysteriously. Mümtaz looked at her blankly. "It worked out well because I've made up my mind. I'm fed up with this vagrancy of spirit. My mother has softened her stance besides. As for Tevfik, he's been pressuring me day and night. Today they went to Bursa. They'll be staying for a week. We can finalize this whole business in the meantime. İhsan's acquaintances can make arrangements for us in a snap. Those were Tevfik's own words. He said, 'İhsan could handle the matter in a snap!'"

Nuran had actually succumbed to strange anxieties over recent days.

Being cast in the midst of so many men prevented her from managing her life. For the sake of doing something, anything, for the sake of a direction, she might have entertained another beau. But only for frivolous flirtation . . .

"There's a soirée at Sabih's tonight. She's arranging a party for a dignitary who's helping him in the faience tile business. They insisted on my presence. And this time the invitation came from Sabih himself . . . To avoid going there, I came here."

Mümtaz could only guess at what other ordeals would confront them. Regardless, they had the coming week to share together.

"I arrived at six so we might go out someplace or eat here tête-à-tête . . . You weren't home, so I awaited your return with no other alternative. Then I saw the dresses, realized they were for me, and tried them on. Take a look . . ."

She made a girlish hand gesture.

"Have you eaten?"

"Of course, Sümbül offered me something, but I waited for you. Where were you?"

Mümtaz briefly described his evening but avoided dwelling on his emotional state and thoughts. Nuran listened, nodding. Finally she said, "These are passing worries. But you do make a point."

"What if I'd actually gone into Sabih's house?" Mümtaz said regretfully.

"Seeing as we're getting married, it wouldn't have mattered anyway. Oh, and you should know that I think I've lost the apartment keys . . . I'm afraid Suad might have them. Suad knows the address. He's always wandering in the vicinity."

"'Seeing as we're getting married'?"

"Yes, my uncle insists on it. My mother does as well. D'you know, I'm afraid now, too . . ."

Nuran sparkled like a jewel in the tight-fitting, ginger-colored, waist-length jacket over a purple velvet vest and matching baggy *şalvars*, all embellished with ornate silver thread and embroidery. She herself was quite taken with the costume, frequently looking into the mirror.

"How did you manage to braid your hair and put it up like that?"

"It's not like there aren't combs and mirrors in the house. Sümbül helped as well." Sümbül smiled sweetly, revealing poor teeth. She existed in such a different world than Suad's delirium or Yaşar's afflictions.

"Nuran, you realize that anyone who sets eyes upon you will assume they're living in a fable?"

Nuran longed to sing the *türküs* that she'd learned from her mother and grandmother, from lands she'd seen and traveled.

Mümtaz felt he was living in a newly discovered dimension.

"What name shall we give you now, Nuran?"

"My real name is adequate." Then she added, "It seems that the lives of our grandmothers weren't so bad after all. For one, they dolled up quite nicely! Just have a look at this broadcloth."

Before the looking glass, from which she couldn't pull herself away, Nuran gazed at the vision of herself.

"Purely the early Renaissance of Pisanello! Or one of our own miniatures."

"How much do you suppose a new one would be?"

Mümtaz guessed it would cost no less than a few hundred liras.

"But I doubt whether another like it could be made. The looms and weavers used to make this material . . ." Then he remembered: A school friend from the south had a traditional woolen cloak woven to celebrate the liberation of cities in that region. That alone had cost him fifty gold coins.

"Amazing!" Nuran nevertheless refused to relinquish her phantasy of time past: "Furthermore, their lifestyles were comfortable . . . They lived within a protective cocoon."

Mümtaz stared at Nuran's face remorsefully and said, "It's true. Despite all the liberties we've given to women, we're tinkering with their minds, and not even women, with the minds of young girls . . . Each day we cast a slew of victims out into society!"

Nuran nodded her head. "There's nothing to be done. People aren't interested in lives of ease now; they want to forge ahead on their own . . ."

But tonight wasn't the night to delve into such matters. Sümbül was summoning them to the table. After the evening meal Nuran sang *türkü*s that matched the outfits she wore. Both of them greatly admired songs from Kozanoğlu, though Nuran was saddened at not knowing any *türkü*s from Kütahya.

Early the next morning they went to see İhsan. Wearing his robe de chambre, he was conversing with two friends in his study. Mümtaz drew him aside and explained the situation. "Fine," İhsan said. "It'll be done within a week's time . . . The district official in Fatih will handle it for me. I'll inform him shortly. Give me your papers immediately, or have them delivered to me . . ."

"In the afternoon, then . . ."

İhsan, gazing at both of them, chuckled. "Nothing could have made me happier." Nonetheless, he was preoccupied.

Accompanied by Mümtaz, he returned to the company of his friends. Nuran went to help Macide bathe Sabiha. Sabiha's bath recalled the protocol of an eighteenth-century queen. The little scamp loved the water madly, as well as the soap bubbles and ducklike fluttering in the tub. She had to fully savor each of these cherished things. Everything was done only with her consent. She might say, "Mother, I'm freezing to death," or she might shout and feign annoyance, "Gracious, you've scalded me! You've startled me breathless!" From where he sat upstairs, Mümtaz heard cackling from the ground floor. *Perhaps the last remnant of animal instinct in the species could be traced to the way little girls lived to be adored.*

İhsan continued from where he'd left off a short while before: "Aren't we putting too much stock solely in the idea? Evidently we are. Meanwhile it's forced to transform so drastically . . . Just like elements that lose their properties or transform completely when exposed to air. Just for the sake of an idea, social life won't forgo its own order or lack thereof, or its continual state of becoming. And that's the reason leaders everywhere don't pursue only one idea, even if it's their own. The idea, at times, paves the way for their coming to power. But it cannot reign in and of itself. What actually reigns and endures are episodes in history and, along with them, realities whose resilience doesn't diminish unless the era is disregarded. This is why, whoever they might be, great men of action only represent one passing moment, or else a limited period. Every age has its golden hour. You see, the man of greatness represents that golden hour.

"What should a ruler do with ideas that serve no purpose but to bind him hand and arm in the face of real events? And just let him try to concentrate on a very bold and exclusive issue and to move beyond current events! Just let him give up trying to contain those small, incessant revolts! Then he'll glimpse the fundamental matter. But do you think life, that is, the social context, would allow this to happen? How long do you think he could endure? Had I been a dramaturge, I'd have rewritten Wagner's *Rienzi*, the hero who emerged from the masses only to be burned by them. Or else a character resembling him . . ."

İhsan's old schoolmate, a civil servant in his mid-fifties, staid and experienced, had been a member of parliament for three years now. "The entire catastrophe has to do with one's repeated encounters with others, such that one's ultimately unrecognizable to even his own self . . ."

"Ideas suffer the same fate: after repeated encounters with society, they become unrecognizable. New concepts are bold, but they're susceptible to the disaster of not meeting a countervailing force capable of resisting them. What might serve to restrain an idea? Nothing. But put it into practice and see what form it takes. It'll change from moment to moment, no longer resembling its original shape at all. Here rests the history of great revolutions. There are few epics as grandiose and sublime as the French Revolution. Within a span of twenty or thirty years, mankind had discovered all the principles that might guide it for another two thousand years. However, in the beginning, who would have guessed that the end result would have been bourgeois rule?

"Nothing simply accepts another entity the way it is: Agency resides within us. Outside us there are nothing but tools and means."

"Despite this, for the sake of an idea we witness revolts, revolutions, cruelties, massacres . . ."

İhsan collected the hems of his robe de chambre. He was truly one beloved of oration. He glanced at Mümtaz as if to say, "Do pardon me!" before continuing. "Yes, it happens. But the outcome always changes. The arrow continually veers from its trajectory. As for our current times, it's total horror. All our values and virtues are for sale at the bazaar. The carts have been upturned. On one hand there are engineers of revolution, the most grisly, most destructive legacy of the nineteenth century. Rest assured, as we speak there are 'visionaries' in Spain or Mexico preparing revolutions in random corners of the world based on nothing more than a city map, as if remotely planning any old public works project that intends to bring electricity to its citizens . . . Insurgents are identifying localities prone to provocation or susceptible to gangrene and instigating or inciting them."

The middle-aged parliamentarian interrupted, "İhsan, you appear to be of a rather modern cast. It seems to me that you're not so fond of your generation, are you?"

"I am not. Or rather, let my put it this way: I'm no advocate of revolution. But am I modern, truly? To be modern, I must be a man of the times in which I live. Meanwhile, I yearn for different things! To be modern, I should accept perpetual transformation along with the revolution. Whereas I'm one who admires consistency in certain ideas and contexts."

"But all revolutions aren't this way. Take ours, for example . . ."

"Our revolution is of another variety. In its natural form, revolution occurs when the masses or society transcends the state apparatus. With us, the masses and society, that is, the collective in question, is obligated to catch up to the state. Even including, more often than not, intellectuals and statesmen . . . Walking down a path blazed by an idea! At least since 1839 and the Tanzimat it's been this way . . . That's why our lives are so tiring. Not to mention that there's an enormous legacy of socialization looming over us. Customs and moralities impeding all our efforts and virtually condemning us . . . We're quick to relent: the prevailing characteristic of the Muslim East. The East relents. And not just in the face of hardship, it relents in the face of time, natural time . . . But how did we get onto this topic?" He shook his head. "That unfortunate, lamented gentle man . . ."

Mümtaz quickly recognized the change in İhsan's tone. "What's happened? Who?"

"An old friend. You remember my schoolmate Hüseyin? He passed away last night. The funeral and obsequies are today . . ."

A deep well yawned open before Mümtaz. His own elation, İhsan's ideas, Sabiha's multi-hued, crisp laughter rising from below like fireworks, and a few steps beyond them all: mortal remains being cleansed and shrouded for interment.

XII

Rainfall, having begun the previous night, now turned to snow. Nuran adored the Bosphorus under snow. During the summer she'd spun a phantasy about the winters they would spend in Emirgân, and didn't leave it at that but had Mümtaz buy two ceramic tile woodstoves that she'd happened upon at the Bedesten. On another occasion she'd insisted on a portable gas heater: "This should be available in case of any eventualities!" After having delivered their papers to İhsan and having informed Tevfik by letter of the new developments, she inquired, "Mümtaz, we have a week before us, can't we head off to Emirgân? But we'll freeze from the cold, won't we?"

And Nuran shivered before the stove.

"Why should we freeze? We've got all that wood and those twigs. Or have you already forgotten about the stoves you had me buy?"

"Not at all, we're rich in stoves, but . . . who's going to light them? I mean, that large tiled one? The one we purchased in the Bedesten. I wouldn't be able to figure it out for the life of me." Here in the study, they'd set up a stove salvaged from a former pasha's estate.

Mümtaz, ponderously: "As soon as we've decided to marry, without even waiting to see it through, the first thing we do is change our plans!"

"Don't forget about Sümbül . . ."

"Sümbül will be staying at İhsan's tonight!"

"We'll drop a letter and she'll come tomorrow. She's been pining madly for Emirgân."

"Fine, but what about tonight?"

"I'll light the damn stove . . . C'mon, let's go." He, too, yearned for the Bosphorus. Though it didn't please him in the least that Suad had learned the whereabouts of his apartment.

Nuran, half teasing, insisted, "You'll always rise to the occasion, won't you, Mümtaz? You'll see to the things that I'm unable to, won't you?"

"We're not even married and you're designating chores . . ."

Nuran responded solemnly, "For the sake of our comfort and future peace . . ."

Mümtaz didn't want to let a careless aside slip his lips. He hadn't been able to get used to this apartment building. He'd suffered so much within these walls.

"Let's go! We'll just take what food's available here. Tomorrow, when Sümbül comes, everything will return to normal."

"You light the stove. Food is no problem. I like to improvise in the kitchen. It's a skill that runs in the family."

By the time they descended to the ferry landing, nightfall loomed. Within the span of a few hours, snow had accumulated along the Bosphorus, which was shrouded in mist.

Nuran, gleeful as a child, hadn't been in Emirgân since the evening of Emin Dede's performance. "I wonder what state the garden's in?" The first day that she'd come to the house, Mümtaz had introduced yet-blooming fruit trees to her as "your handmaidens . . ." Thereafter it became an in-joke, and together with Mümtaz she'd given them traditional Ottoman servant names. Presently, recalling each by name, she wondered how they were faring.

It astonished Mümtaz that Nuran hadn't forgotten these sobriquets amid the countless episodes that had so distressed him this winter. Even worse, he didn't conceal his surprise. Nuran said, "How peculiar, you actually think I've been estranged from you! Next you'll thank me for not inquiring after *your* name!" And she continued listing the trees vociferously. "I wonder what state head maidservant Razıdil is in? She'll have a bit of a chill, won't she, now? Poor little dear, Razıdil, she's the solitaire of the garden."

That week constituted the last of Mümtaz's halcyon days. From the gloom of winter, they'd reemerged into sublime days of summer. During this week he tasted of the full zest of that initial seasonal fruit called satisfaction, of all things that filled human existence with poetry and enchantment, forging nothing less than a *pièce de résistance* out of life. Both of them had succumbed to ennui over recent months. For this reason their pleasure resembled a fever of recuperation. As if they'd returned to health and vitality after long illnesses, they clung to each other's presence.

Within the quieting of nerves fostered by his reunion with Nuran,

Mümtaz again began to occupy himself with the Shaykh Galip. He again outlined the entire novel. He discarded everything he'd written beforehand, starting anew.

On the third day of their assignation, he said, "I can clearly see the book now!"

"And I can see the missing button on your blazer."

"Are you doing it on purpose, for goodness sake?"

"Why should I be? I'm preparing for married life. Haven't we divvied up the chores?"

Through the window the evening twilight cast a faint and nostalgic pastel blush over the snow-covered hilltops above the Asian shore. All things out there swam in dreamlike buoyancy beneath a tulle-thin hue. Fog had descended. Snow was in the forecast. Ferryboat horns occasionally sought and found them in the corners of their seclusion, filling them with the mournful *hüzün* of shores abandoned to desolate waves, empty seafront *yalıs*, wind-lashed public squares near ferry landings, and roads as gloomy as a catacomb and abstracted from active life.

The panorama made for a rare Istanbul snowscape. Winter, which had ever so lackadaisically squandered its entire season, duped by the faux summer of southerlies, broke out at the end of February in true Eastern-style haste and, determined to make up for all its shortcomings, paralyzed the city within a few days, using every means at its disposal from storms to fogs and snowfalls to blizzards. The previous day, everything had frozen, up to and including the water in the pipes of the pump. The trees in the garden, large icicles hanging from their branches, resembled, in the emptiness of evening, grave and aged apparitions belonging to a realm of absolute difference.

This *âlem* had overtaken them. For two days Mümtaz couldn't get his fill of the panorama that recalled an unwritten poem, a truth as of yet untainted by the poison of doubt, a totality that hadn't been fragmented by life's shortcomings. He existed in an immaculate dimension of Creation that had overwhelmed his own perceptions and abilities. The couple lived in a world bleached white, as if in the center of a brilliant diamond. Rare silence: Everything, the entire summer, their own lives, their acquaintances, their thoughts, all of it lay beneath a shroud of silence. On pure white pages of silence, each memory could be detailed and each gesture could be described; from whiteness, every description might issue forth without tainting the gesso or disturbing the measured peace of the totality. They passed half their time reminiscing about summer. Mümtaz, half of whose life had been spent in quest of bygone days, was surprised that Nuran resembled him in this diversion, and he asked, "Are you just imitating me?" Oddly enough, since they'd stepped foot in Emirgân, Mümtaz had been preoccupied with Suad rather than their recent past. Mümtaz couldn't forget his words, disposition, laughter, and bizarre point of view from that fateful night. *What had he meant to say?* he asked himself perpetually. About eight or ten times since, he'd been in Suad's company for a few hours. Yet Suad hadn't revisited such dire subjects. *Had he actually recounted what he believed, or . . .* Whenever he brought the matter up to Nuran, she grew livid.

"If you've got nothing better to do, go down and get some breadcrumbs for the sparrows."

Mümtaz plodded toward the door. But thoughts of Suad didn't leave his head. *Why is he in pursuit of Nuran to this extent? I'm certain he doesn't love her. What is it? What's he after?* The entire episode recalled the vagaries of fate. And for this reason he was afraid. At the kitchen table, as he broke apart the soft white insides of bread loaves, he continued to ponder such questions.

The first morning of their arrival, they'd noticed a graceful teeming around the windows, as elegant as lace, inviting, and atwitter. Nuran cried, "Oh my! The sparrows have arrived . . ." From that moment onward she'd assumed responsibility for feeding them. Not the slightest is known about the sense of taste of these birds. Nuran, were it within her power, would have had special meals prepared for the little creatures. That day, toward night-fall, the population of the old house was augmented by one. The snowy, icy weather must have been unbearable and tedious for Emirgân's black bitch, seeing as Mümtaz's previous invitations, toward which she displayed exces-sive demurral, were now met with great delight as she entered. She cleaned herself beside the stove and cast desirous glances toward Nuran's winged companions, preparing – within the comfort of a dream – to taste this twit-tering bounty that all but mocked her from its protective sanctuary.

Mümtaz desposited the bread crumbs on the windowsill and shut the window. Then he turned to Nuran. "Would Tevfik really agree to live with us?" He sincerely desired this. He was nearly as bound to the old man as Nuran was.

"He's hard to fathom . . . But now he probably would. He's even picked out a room." She fell silent and looked out the window: The sparrows jostled on the sill as they pecked at crumbs.

"Mümtaz, d'you really think we'll manage this marriage?"

Mümtaz took his eyes off the Arabic *amentü billâhi vahdehü lâ şerike lehü* calligraphy wall panel – "I believe in Allah alone, who has no peer." He stared at Nuran for a time. "If you want to know the truth, no."

"Why? What are you afraid of?"

"Nothing, or rather, whatever you're afraid of, that's what frightens me as well."

This dread had been with them since the day they'd come to Emirgân. Nuran stood and went to him.

"Let's go back to Istanbul . . . tomorrow! Can't we?"

"Okay, let's head back!"

It was the fifth day. That morning Mümtaz spoke by telephone with İhsan, who said that everything was going to plan and instructed them to be at the Fatih district marriage bureau at four o'clock sharp. "Without stopping back home, go to the marriage bureau! That's how this will get taken care of. Come down from Emirgân and go directly to the license bureau . . ."

Later, Mümtaz would profoundly regret not heeding İhsan's advice.

The next day they returned to Istanbul. Sümbül was to follow behind toward evening, after having straightened up the house. Beneath rain that fell in torrents, the pristine and eternal façade of winter scenery melted away in fragments. Overnight the winds had turned southerly. The ferry forged ahead, virtually tossing and rolling. The surrounding scenery lay behind an ashen shroud. Strangely, through a peculiar play of memory, this shroud further reminded them of the past summer. From time to time the view opened up so that woods, a mosque, or an old *yalı* would descend upon them. A black ship crossed their path as if to declare, "I, too, exist within the framework of your lives . . ." Next everything took on the same washed-out pallor, and the hard rain caused whatever it contacted to meld and merge.

As they churned past Beylerbeyi, Nuran suddenly took hold of Mümtaz's hand. "I'm afraid," she said.

"But why? I don't understand. Not yet an hour ago we spoke to your relatives in Bursa. All of them are fine. Everything's going to plan."

"No, I'm not thinking about them. I'm afraid of something else. Last night I dreamed of Suad."

Mümtaz regarded her with astonishment. Suad had also entered his dreams. Furthermore, it was an agonizing vision. Suad had taken the crystal lamp out of the hand of Mümtaz's father before embarking on a caïque along with the village girl from his childhood. As Mümtaz flailed his arms frantically from the quayside – although he knew not where precisely – worried whether they had or would capsize, he awoke. Few dreams could be so terrifyingly vivid. Even now, on this ferry bench, he could clearly see the same pitch-black bargelike caïque, Suad's long, bony face, the girl's expression, and amid rough seas, the lantern dimming to the verge of going out.

"Pay no mind, for five days we've talked of nothing but him!" Then he changed the subject: "Will you have a coffee?" He lit the young lady's cigarette and began to make plans for coming days.

But Nuran wasn't listening. Finally she couldn't restrain herself. "For God's sake, let's not build castles in the air! Once it's all done and finalized, then, afterward . . ."

They stepped out of the taxi before the apartment. Holding their bags in one hand, Mümtaz allowed Nuran to walk ahead through the door. The solitude of the building and the street had settled her nerves. The wife of the doorman mopped the tile floor in the foyer. Nuran briefly exchanged a few pleasantries with her. Before they'd left for Emirgân, Mümtaz had helped procure a treatment of diphtheria serum for her child. She learned that the boy had improved. Mümtaz, bags in hand, waited for Nuran on the bottommost step of the stairs. The surroundings had faded in the sepia light that fell in the wake of snowy weather. The foyer's blue tiles appeared black beneath such illumination. A cat pressed its head to the casement window opening onto the air shaft and letting light into the stairwell, gazing at them with eyes so near the color of dried straw that they all but crackled. In the backyard the doorman's eldest son sang his usual song in a feverish voice:

Floodwaters have overtaken Erzincan
A stranger has taken up with my girl

Mümtaz had earlier resolved to give Nuran a kiss as they passed through the door. *Before we enter . . . on the threshold.* And he smiled internally at this gesture of satisfaction. But when he climbed to the top of the stairs, he saw severe light fall onto the landing through the door's small diamond-shaped window. Nuran, with the ball of one foot on the final step, stopped in her tracks.

Nuran: "It looks like someone's home."

Mümtaz, to calm her: "Sümbül most likely forgot to switch off the light in her haste . . ." By the time they'd pushed open the door, he'd forgotten that he'd even hazarded such a guess. The image that they encountered would stay with them for the rest of their lives. In the hallway, beneath sharp electric light, a human form slowly swung toward the door. At a glance Mümtaz and Nuran both recognized Suad. His bony face was contorted into an expression of strange and daemonic ridicule. On his limp hands were patches of dried blood. As Mümtaz took a closer look, he noticed blood on the ceramic floor tiles. The couple stared dumbly for a moment. Then, in a state of coolheadedness that he'd never be able to muster again, Mümtaz shuffled Nuran, who verged on fainting, from the apartment. Unaware of what they were doing exactly, they descended flights of stairs. It had all occurred with such speed that their taxi was still idling before the entrance. Mümtaz, as in a dream, all but ignorant of the import of his actions, helped Nuran into the vehicle. He sat beside her. İhsan was home. As usual he'd gathered whoever else was there into his study. Neither he nor Macide had the opportunity to be startled by this impromptu visit.

———

Through İhsan's machinations, the incident was handled without either Nuran or Mümtaz appearing in the press. Suad's note explained everything. Afife officially identified her husband's handwriting. During a brief investigation, Mümtaz learned that Afife and Suad were on the brink of divorce. Nuran quickly departed for Bursa. In a letter to Mümtaz, she stated, "What remains for us to do, Mümtaz? Fate has ntervened! There's a corpse between us. Don't expect my return! The dream is over."

As soon as Mümtaz received the letter, he rushed to Bursa. There, he was confronted by Fâhir, who'd arrived sometime beforehand. He and Nuran still spoke at length. She now regarded love as nothing more than frivolous and farcical. "With regard to us, I shall always be your devoted friend. But don't mention words like 'love,' 'happiness,' or 'marriage' to me! What I've witnessed has revolted me."

"But what fault is it of mine?"

Nuran: "You don't understand! I'm not blaming you. I'm only saying that our happiness is no longer possible."

In this fashion, they separated.

One month later, upon Nuran's return to Istanbul, Mümtaz's hopes were somewhat rekindled. He met her a few times here and there. These encounters, however, didn't produce any new developments. Nuran was disgusted by love. The horrific smirk on Suad's face haunted her. In one instance she'd said, "I don't think I even have the wherewithal to read a book that touches on love."

A devastating life began for Mümtaz. He existed as if trailing in Nuran's footsteps, but he could never quite reach her. Their lives moved in parallel and nonintersecting courses. During infrequent chance encounters, he couldn't match Nuran's breeziness; he was nothing but an annoyance to her in his absentminded and irritable mental state, at times madly jealous, at times excessively subservient.

One quickly loses sight of the impetus for one's responses. Not to mention that one's social circle interprets each event as isolated. And one's imagination fabricates other causes for each incident. This was the case for Mümtaz. Despite their having shared the same misadventure together, he somehow couldn't accept Nuran's distance from him. Soon he sought out other reasons for her separation. He began to scrutinize her life with renewed suspicion. He attributed surreptitious causes to her devastation by Suad's suicide; in short, he was jealous of a corpse.

He hadn't forgotten about Suad, however. His wretched demise or confrontation – for Suad's death elsewhere, under other circumstances, wouldn't have had the same impact – appended his death to Mümtaz's life. He'd obtained a copy of Suad's letter from the police. Occasionally he read it, trying to comprehend Suad's underlying motivation.

During nights, amid confounding dreams, Mümtaz almost always struggled against him. He was neither able to fathom Suad's enmity, which rather verged on the obsessive, nor his denials or his torments. On occasion he discussed the matter with İhsan. For İhsan, the enigma of Suad was simple: "He was born with a rebellious streak. For such people, contentment is an impossibility, as is forgetting about themselves . . ."

"What about his suicide?"

"That amounts to nothing more than the great act of provocation that he'd longed for his entire life . . . but don't try to put your finger on Suad through motivations of singular intent. He was a man of contradictions. He exhibited astounding hubris. He was sensual, rebellious, and in the final analysis . . . he was disturbed."

XIII

An April's day: Mümtaz came down to Istanbul from Emirgân to visit İhsan and escape the memories besieging him from all sides as if to asphyxiate him. They conversed in İhsan's study. As a twist of fate, the offshoot of a cypress tree that had sprouted atop the sheathless dome of the Hazel-Eyed Mehmet Efendi Mosque – a somber witness to his entire upbringing – all but mocked life and death from above this Muslim sanctuary. Meanwhile, spring had initiated an attack. It laughed, hollered "fools!", grew incensed at everything that didn't deplete itself in desire, and perpetually sang *türküs* of love accompanied by the vast orchestra of the empyrean.

İhsan shooed a bee that for some time had been tracing golden arcs about his head. Gazing out the window at the broom shrub that had taken root along the edge of the street, he said, "What have you done about the Shaykh Galip?"

Mümtaz rose. "That's another problem altogether! All of the enchantment is gone . . . I've been grappling with it for three weeks. I haven't even been able to write a single page! Evidently I don't have the ability to finish . . ."

Along with Nuran's absence, his intellectual life had effectively ceased. She had absconded with all of the vibrant and sublime aspects of this vision of time past, leaving in its place an ashen heap much like Mümtaz's own existence. All of the protagonists that he'd drawn with such care, and with whom he'd lived, had been reduced to nothing but silhouettes, attenuated and limp puppets with no chance of returning to life.

İhsan made an ambiguous hand gesture. "Don't dwell on it, it'll pass . . ." Then he abruptly stated what he'd actually wanted to say, "You've been looking at them through the light of your own emotions. You were projecting what you'd envisioned in your own life onto them! You cherished them not for what they were in and of themselves, but for your own sake, as part of your life. Had you sought them out through the particular historical era that you'd chosen, everything would have been different. Whereas you were trying to gather the world around a single individual."

Mümtaz, grasping the edge of the chair, listened carefully.

"But I was attuned to the concerns of the times."

"No, you were simply preoccupied with your beloved, Nuran." Then his face softened. "And this was quite natural. You passed through an experience that's the shared destiny of everyone. Now you'll open up to life! You must become a man of your convictions, not of your emotions! Suad destroyed himself because he'd fixated upon your state of happiness with Nuran. We have no right to create providence for ourselves out of just anything. Existence is so vast and mankind is in the midst of such profound dilemmas . . . To seize life we must be free in our thoughts and our lives." Then, in a lower voice: "Become a man of convictions whose responsibilities you can shoulder! Nurture them like a tree within your own being. Toil around them, patiently and carefully, like a gardener!"

"You realize you're chastising me, don't you?"

"No, I'm not chastising you. Nuran exposed you to a spectrum of inspiration. Others might have arrived there by different means. That's not important. But thoughts of her shouldn't impede you any longer! You can't wallow in the aura of a sole person too long . . . People resemble wells. We're susceptible to sinking into our own depths and drowning. Just pass beside them. Test the free play of your thoughts through the context of an idea . . ."

But İhsan didn't understand one point. Mümtaz didn't see Nuran's love as just an experience. She was part and parcel of his life, and profoundly so. Through her he'd savored an insight shared by few people, a reconciliation that sanctified both love and the self. This constituted his contentment, which he wasn't willing to sacrifice. As they parted company, he thought, *They don't understand . . . They can't seem to fathom . . .*

He wandered along the old Theodosian ramparts till twilight. He ambled, disassociated from his self, hopeless, unaware of even his own fatigue, taking refuge in the torment of his abandonment. At times he could see reality clearly: I'm senselessly blaming Nuran.

This arose out of his sentimentality, an emotion that weakened the entire structure. *We're all overly romantic,* he told himself. *Myself, and İhsan, and Suad as well . . . We couldn't do anything to help him! There's something in us that weakens others!* On account of it, the semblance of miraculous love had gradually withered away.

In a more balanced man this love couldn't have been attained. He stopped short. *Would someone more stable have been able to express love this way? Or could he have even loved at all?*

He was standing before a dilapidated tomb that had taken on exceptional beauty through the aesthetic of a terebinth tree growing out of its center. From the epitaph, Mümtaz learned that here rested Shaykh Sinanî Erdibli.

The fifteenth century, more or less at the end of Sultan Mehmet the Conqueror's reign. He was face-to-face with one of the city's oldest inhabitants. A waif of ten or eleven, her entire being covered in whelks and wounds, sat in the middle of the grave collecting candle butts from the surrounding stones.

When she noticed Mümtaz's attention, she said, "Tie just one votive and your wish will come true."

At this age even, she displayed a posture that was prepared to sell everything for five or ten cents. Mümtaz was saddened, assuming that she'd extend her palms to beg. But, as if reading something on Mümtaz's face, the girl said, "You're upset. You might as well offer a prayer to him, he has experience!"

Mümtaz realized the frivolity of his previous thought, and the superiority of this sick little girl with her faith and conviction. Mümtaz gave alms to the boy playing at her feet with a bone, perhaps one belonging to a corpse. The girl said she lived with seven siblings in a house below the Merkez Efendi Mosque. Their mother was a charwoman, and this was how they survived.

Maybe İhsan does have a point! This society wants ideas and maybe even a struggle out of me. Not romantic posturing! Suddenly a feeling of rebellion rose within him. *But to achieve this end, must I forget about Nuran?* And why should he forget her? Why should he impoverish himself? He walked onward beneath the sun, wiping his sweat and talking to himself. Resentment against İhsan knotted within him. *As if I'm to forgo Nuran for the sake of this urchin and others like her! And will they themselves, in their own lives, reciprocate through similar sacrifices?*

He sensed a base and crude human throng proliferating to unseen and unknown horizons around him, having abandoned itself to its own urges, covetous of what it assumed were its rights, and ready to transgress all cultures and social etiquettes.

But do I even have the right to demand this sacrifice from them? If I give myself over to them, shouldn't I do so without expecting anything in return?

He entered the city through a gate in the ramparts that he didn't recognize.

An Armenian woman crouching beside a small concrete police kiosk stretched out a hand. "My son, help me so I might stand up . . ."

After gazing at her as if to say, "Do you really need to get up?" he lent her a hand. The elderly woman stood with difficulty.

"There's a church nearby. It's a sacred place. It's worn down, though . . . If you have the desire to make an offering, go ahead and do so . . . It'll be granted. I'm heading there myself!"

Mümtaz continued to wander down streets that more resembled abandoned lots and by houses, most of which resembled gramophone cases: *Yes, those who want to benefit social life should devote themselves to it generously.* Yet thoughts of Nuran recast this sentence: *Those who genuinely love do so without expecting anything in return . . .*

He couldn't deliver himself of the notion that he'd been unjust to Nuran, and he couldn't endure living apart from her.

İhsan's always rambling on about conviction . . . But I'm so damn miserable . . . He again felt the same ire and resentment toward İhsan.

Why don't those advocating for society understand people?

Man and life were separate entities. The former created the latter through flesh, bone, sweat, and thought. But they weren't commensurate. It was necessary to be partial to one or the other. Yet Mümtaz knew he'd remain in a perpetual state of ambivalence between them. He'd neither be able to forgo his individual contentment nor forget about the terrible needs of the society that surrounded him, including the hapless ten-year-old girl attending to a saint's tomb and the aged Armenian woman.

I'm feeble, a feeble man simply created out of weakness. Which of us isn't? As he uttered this last part, he realized that he had Suad in mind. In the little coffeehouse that he'd ducked into, he removed Suad's letter from his pocket and began to read it for the umpteenth time.

It was a long, cynical letter that mocked almost everything, full of the quiet torments suffered by the inner self. As Mümtaz read, he sensed that

Suad had seized him at a profound level. He didn't ascribe to any of his ideas. But he did share in his anguish. Mümtaz realized that Suad would no longer let him be himself, that he'd become part of the realities of his everyday life. Then he remembered what they'd discussed the day Mümtaz first saw Nuran, as Mümtaz accompanied Suad to the ferry that would take him to the sanatorium.

As usual, when they were parting, Suad teased him. "Don't look at my face with such remorse as if I'm actually dead," he'd said. "I have absolutely no intention of surrendering this world to you alone."

Suad had indeed kept his word. However his jest had unsettled Mümtaz then, now that it had become a reality, albeit differently and more poignantly, it continued to gnaw at him.

The notion of Suad, like the notion of Nuran, like all the rest, wouldn't let him be, and insomuch as Mümtaz would bear these notions for the duration of his days, he'd be rent asunder by countless maelstroms.

Part IV

Mümtaz

I

It was twenty past five by the time Mümtaz returned to Eminönü after taking leave of İclâl and Muazzez. He watched trolley-borne crowds rejecting each effort made to board. Short of another option, he could hail a taxi. But then he'd arrive at Beyazıt early. He'd run into Orhan that morning and had said, "Expect me at six o'clock at the Küllük coffeehouse!" There was time yet. He didn't want to sit in the coffeehouse by himself before they arrived. He knew so many people . . . For the first time in a fortnight he was to meet up with friends, and he worried that hangers-on would disturb their gathering. *I'm a defenseless man!*

His own thought stunned him; indeed, he was a defenseless man. At will others could impose themselves and their desires on him. And was that all? His thoughts perpetually orbitted Nuran. But he hadn't been as battered and bruised as he'd feared. He trudged absently in the quiet reserve of one accustomed to the betrayals of fate. Beneath the archway of the Yeni Cami, so pleasing to him on a breezy summer day, he once again repeated, *I'm a defenseless man . . . Anyone could just walk away with everything I have.*

He stopped temporarily amid the throngs of Sultanhamam and looked around. This must certainly be the busiest place in the city: a seething array of people, automobiles, and trucks. *A modern painter could represent this jumble framed by caravanserai windows without it being a facile statement! But the cacophony of it all.*

Fine, but why am I not thinking about Nuran? Or rather, why can't I? It was as if İclâl and Muazzez had absolved him of all of his troubles, the torment that rent his heart, and even the opulent love he'd shared with Nuran. *I'm close to saying that I'm relieved this matter is finally over!* He traced this change in himself with curiosity and trepidation. Not that he'd completely forgotten about Nuran; indeed, he was walking alongside a phantasy of her, as though they were separated by great distances, vast currents of water, or unknown obstacles. *This must be an effect of death's etiquette!* The old saw about water under the bridge came to mind. It resembled that.

He slowly climbed the hill. *Death gives rise to the human capacity for accepting the inevitable!* Maybe this was a natural effect of such situations. War was imminent. He'd witnessed with his own eyes how the black market had come to life. But he wasn't too distraught over that, either; at least he didn't harbor any feelings of revolt. *Seeing as it's a forgone conclusion. Seeing as there's no recourse!* Why should he be so agitated? Through the lens of war he again looked around. Would the market be able to sustain this level of commerce in six months? Of course, the abundance in these shops wouldn't last. He skeptically scrutinized the display windows full of fabrics, ladies' apparel, faience earthenware, and everyday bric-a-brac. Automobiles plied the crowds, parting person from person and pushing them out of the way.

A street porter approached in slow motion, bearing a massive load on his back, his neck and torso weighted down under the burden. Walking toward Mümtaz from the crest of the hill, the porter's two arms dangled at either side, and in a rather bold economy of line, his forehead and cheeks appeared to meld as his chin remained tucked away and out of sight. For Mümtaz, this anatomical geometry recalled Pierre Puget's caryatids in Toulon. But he immediately doubted his own description. *Did such an economy of line truly exist?* The porter, more exactly, in order to see his way, trudged forward with his entire face exposed upright. *It's rather that his head isn't situated upon his shoulders but appears to emerge from his torso.* Voilà, this was a head that had been adjoined to the torso. But that wasn't quite accurate either. *We're unable to see! We pay scant attention to detail! We simply speak from rote!* Large beads of sweat poured from the man's forehead; as he passed Mümtaz, he wiped his forehead with his hand so the droplets wouldn't obscure his line of sight. Mümtaz intricately recalled the gesture of the thick, dark hand: It alone constituted a nightmare.

The measure of the porter's entire corpus served to gauge his every step. He saw with his eyes, though he surveyed, weighed, and considered with each step. No, maybe he didn't consider, but only surveyed. Mümtaz stopped again to look back. The porter was only seven or eight strides beyond him. Where the edge of the weighty wooden crate ended began the full, formless, patchwork drape of white muslin pantaloons. *He doesn't resemble Puget's giants at all. They display an expression of taut muscle and might emanating from the entire body. Meanwhile, this poor man has been swallowed whole by the load on his back!* In his mind's eye, Mümtaz once again conjured the man's face in all its vividness. It bore neither any expression of strength nor any trace of thought. The porter signified stride only, stride and one more stride. He lived diminished, fragmented by the steps of his own feet. Only his hands exhibited astounding fortitude.

Mümtaz shook his head, remembering the well-intentioned law that had gone into effect a few years ago prohibiting the transport of cargo on the backs of men. For a few days the heart of Istanbul had been a picture of utter confusion. Newly instituted handcarts and wagons had congested the roads and the business of transport had actually grown more laborious. Then, slowly, the law was forgotten and everything returned to the status quo; this porter and his like had been reunited with their work, and the natural order had returned. *Just like the League of Nations, like peace conferences, like the desire for vast cooperative ventures, antiwar propaganda and protest art.* The individuals of our age and the fate of this porter melded in Mümtaz's thoughts, both were manifestations of lack and impossibility.

Who was he? How did he live and what did he think about? Was he married and did he have children? The wares he'd seen a few hours ago at the flea market, the multitude of those cheap overalls and faded dresses were meant for the likes of him. People whose lives he'd never be able to fully fathom. On occasion in newspapers, amid big, serious debates, photographs of stars mollycoddled like life's rare flowers, and the faits accomplis of world events, a two- or three-line anecdote, report of a murder or an unexpected death might appear – momentarily illuminating the lives of such riffraff, who remained in shadow though living in plain sight – solely because the passing glint of a gun, a dagger, or a Bursa-forged knife shone above them or a collapsing building had crushed them – before they were forgotten yet again. Mümtaz thought of the poor living in houses of mud brick and tin below Taksim Square, on one side of the hill that descended down to Fındıklı, around Unkapanı. Streets in which dirty water and sewage flowed openly, where children of blind chance grew and matured till they transferred their primary haunts to dry fountain basins, sidewalks, or underpasses.

How many wars did it take to put us into these circumstances? Since A.H. 1293, the Russo-Ottoman War of 1878, an array of disasters caused the influx of the downtrodden into Istanbul, and it was unclear whether these refugees were peasants or city folk, as they didn't fit into any evident category besides "destitute" or "needy." *Now it's Europe's turn!* Of course it wouldn't happen through a single war. *But who says the matter will be confined to one war?*

If war breaks out, that porter will be conscripted! I will too! But there's a difference between us. I'm familiar with Hitler's madness and he infuriates me. I'd fight him with pleasure. But this poor man is ignorant of Germany and these ideas. He'll be fighting a cause that he doesn't know about or recognize, and he'll likely die in the process!

He stopped and asked himself solemnly: *Okay then, what's the upshot?*

He couldn't conceive of any upshot. Someone among the street crowd deliberately brushed up against his body, walking briskly away before turning down an alley a short distance ahead. Mümtaz glanced in his direction. "Peculiar," he repeated. The man resembled Suad. *But Suad is dead.* To confirm the resemblance, he glanced in that direction again. Someone who actually did resemble Suad gazed at him from afar, smirking. The man wore a leaden sharkskin suit and held his fedora in his hand. "Impossible," he said. *Or are the dead no longer buried properly?*

This thought bothered him. *It's inappropriate for me to make a mockery of a tragedy. Not to mention that I'm more or less responsible for his suicide. Or rather Nuran and I. If only he hadn't found that key and come to the apartment; if only we hadn't made such an ordeal in plain sight.* But it wasn't just the couple. There was a third person. On his last night, Suad was accompanied by a waif or stray girl that he'd met on the Bosphorus ferry dock. She'd forced him to reassess his life. His letter stated, "It was then that I suddenly saw my life in all clarity, and in short, I was disgusted." A tinge of responsibility for the suicide fell to this unfortunate girl who had no fault besides being young and untrammeled by life. "I immediately sought Allah. Ah, were I a believer, everything would have been so easy and natural . . ." But why had Suad sought Allah by such circuitous means? Why hadn't he sought Him out directly?

As a matter of course, the girl would have read of Suad's death in the papers. How distraught she must have been. How she must have writhed. Why? Because she'd entered a man's life, for only one night, from the peripheries, because she had no place to stay and couldn't afford a room in a hotel. The ways that people exploited one another.

His thoughts lurched. He saw Suad in the entrée of the house in Emirgân, on the night he'd spoken so convolutedly before the *rakı* table. *Emin Dede had only just left!* His surroundings suddenly transformed. A voice, a voice from within him, repeated Rumi's initial couplet from the Ferahfezâ ceremonial suite. As if he were weeping in the wake of a sun he'd no longer see, yearning stirred within him. Never again would he be able to see Nuran. *Or Suad.*

Suad, yet again? He'd been obsessed with Suad for three days now. *And last night in my dreams. Of course, an omen of news to come.*

He realized that he'd been under sway of the *rüya* since morning. But he hadn't been able to pinpoint the dream itself. He only knew that he'd struggled with Suad the entire night. *I was in an enormous house. Yes, an enormous house. An array of corridors, halls, and rooms. I was searching for Nuran, opening each and every room and looking inside. But in each I discovered only Suad. I'd quickly apologize to him for disturbing him unnecessarily. He'd cackle and nod his head . . .*

How bizarre: The man who'd brushed past him had cackled like Suad in his dream. *Yes, exactly so!* But did such a man really exist? It was obvious. Suad was here with him. And perhaps the stray girl and Nuran now recollected Suad the way Mümtaz did. He repeated the first couplet of the Ferahfezâ again. Oddly, amid the melody's roses of lust, rather than a vision of Nuran, he saw Suad: *In my haste to be married, I treated his demise as nothing but a small setback . . .*

He stopped and wiped his forehead with his hand, just like the porter had done in the middle of the road only one stride from him. But his hands didn't resemble the porter's. Mümtaz's hands didn't directly engage in life. They hadn't been cured in life's forge. The porter's hands were black, rough, and thick with distended veins. *Mine are white, refined, soft . . .* And he studied his hands with rapt attention. Suddenly he again recalled the night in Emirgân and the moment he'd parted from Suad at the crest of the hill. He'd extricated his hands from Suad's grasp with difficulty. *And I couldn't look him in the eye. Allah, will this slope never end? Or is this my Via Crucis and is Suad my crucifix?*

Mümtaz looked around, wiping his brow once more. *But what right did he have to intrude into my life, into our lives? Forget about us. What about that wayward girl? "One can't live without trusting others!" She'd said this to Suad. Poor lamb!* He continued to walk. But Suad wouldn't quit his thoughts. What kind of letter was that? Why had he written it? He began to recite inwardly the sentences that remained in his memory:

> *Do you know, Mümtaz, what constitutes the most pathetic aspect of our fate? It's that mankind is preoccupied solely with itself. The entire structure is built upon this foundation, both subjectively and objectively. Whether mindful of it or not, mankind expends its fellow man like material fodder. Our spite, our malice, our desire for greatness, our love, our despair, and our hopes are all bound to others. If you did away with beggars and the poor, no mercy or divine grace would remain and we'd fast become wretched. There are no two ways about it, humans are preoccupied with humanity. People exist by imposing on others. Even artists are this way. Even those you say have "saintly souls." That night, how Dede Efendi impinged upon us. In the violin concerto that I've listened to for one last time, how Beethoven imposed upon me. And the musicians, more so than others. Even you, Mümtaz, the things you say without considering your own position, not to mention in that awkward manner of yours. If you weren't so tedious, or . . .*

He shook his head remorsefully. *He always despised me. But to what end did he die? Why did he burden us this way? Seeing that he knew all this.*

> *Everything İhsan said was true. Only he's quite tiresome, even more so than you. One can at least tease you. İhsan, moreover, has a rational mind.*

He hurried on his way. *I've memorized the entire letter!* If only he'd heeded İhsan's advice and taken a trip. He would have forgotten everything by now. But which of İhsan's ideas had Suad found to be truthful? "Mankind is responsible for all Creation." Yes, it was this one. Suad said, "Truthful, but foolish. I mean, it gives the impression of truth on first glance." And a short while later he began objecting to it; this was his nature. He was certain to attack whatever he'd admired a moment before. "Unfortunate humanity!

Which notion of responsibility? Like Joyce's Leopold Bloom, perched atop our own anxieties, we're spouting philosophy and poetry."

He recalled the expressions contorting Nuran's face when she first read this letter. But he wasn't able to conjure the scene the way it had happened; frequently Nuran's head, along with Suad's head, bowed over the page. Mümtaz made a hand gesture as if to shoo him away. But his subsequent thought was a response to Suad: *I accept responsibility for my ideas. You think how you want to think!* And without a pause, he returned to thoughts of the porter. *I can certainly send him off to war with people he doesn't know. Seeing as I have conviction. There's a litany of things that I believe need protection. If need be, I can expend people like cannon fodder as well!* The porter would perish. Absolutely. And even worse. He'd end up killing somebody. One or a number of others. *For what else but the sake of humanity!*

No, Suad had no admiration for Mümtaz. Because he accepted responsibility for his thoughts. But were the porter's wife and children amenable? His thoughts roamed through the mean and constricting corners of the city, through the mud-brick hovels on streets flowing with filthy water. Why? *So their grandchildren might be content and comfortable . . .* But the porter's wife wasn't willing. Wearing the gaudy wedding gown that he'd seen that morning in a flea market shopwindow, she begged of Mümtaz, *Don't send him off! Don't send him! If he goes, what will become of me and the children? Who'll take care of us?* And she wept at his feet in the gown purchased from a discounter. On the way here he'd seen new conscripts at the Sirkeci train station, inductees who hadn't yet been issued uniforms. Accompanying them were young fiancées and mothers holding the hands of their children, all walking in tears.

I do take responsibility for my ideas. Had Suad heard this sentence, he would have keeled over in laughter, "Which ideas, my dear Mümtaz?" But Suad was of a different stripe. *He never did like me. He never did take me seriously. Yet I can't help but like him.*

Did he truly like Suad? Had he truly liked anybody, ever? The fact was that Nuran had left him; she didn't have a single decent thought for him. İhsan was ill while Mümtaz aimlessly wandered the city streets. *Macide forced me, Suad. She said, "Don't come home before dark! Go out and get some air, otherwise you'll fall ill as well! I can't look after you, too!"* He'd been reduced to defending himself before the judgment of a corpse.

He wiped his brow with a hand. *Why am I so obsessed with him anyway?* He tried not to think about Suad. He wanted to remember a time before all this, a period of trivial and blithe concerns.

"Best not to think about anything!" He hastily passed through the Kazancı market. He walked before Istanbul University's dental school, scattering the covey of pigeons that he'd fed that very morning. Then he crossed the square. He strode apace by café tables beneath the sprawling chestnut to avoid being stopped by an acquaintance and entered the Beyazıt Mosque courtyard. He glanced at the clock out of the corner of his eye: ten to six. *They must have arrived by now!*

Two elderly men took ablution at the mosque fountain. *Which of the prayers will they perform?* A disheveled elderly woman wearing a black chador crouched, cooling herself by awkwardly bringing a palmful of water to her face. Her shriveled hands appeared to be roasted by fire. Stray pigeons dawdled atop the marble slabs of the courtyard as if roaming through a garden of abstraction. *"Like the beloveds in old miniatures . . ."* Annoyed with himself, he struck out this comparison uttered in Suad's voice: *Not even close! If anything, they're thoughts wandering through a mind in solitude . . .* This wasn't accurate either; *they're inklings before the onset of actual thought.* Voilà! Pigeons on the portico traced mysterious shapes through ephemeral flights of lacey design.

By the other courtyard gate, he again observed elderly men performing ablutions and the expanse of the quadrangle. As Yahya Kemal had put it, this space had been an open casement for the soul since the mosque had been founded in 1506. This was what should persist. *I wonder if women in chador would come here in the past?* But this wasn't the only transformation. As he'd passed through the courtyard he'd noticed a lone electric bulb burning as if to augment the dimness of the mosque from beneath the thick, half-raised entryway drape. *Old men performing the ablution at a classical mosque . . .*

Everything that might be termed national is a thing of beauty . . . and must persist eternally.

Then, thinking of the porter, he again retorted: *Don't think I'm making wagers on your head! I'm also speaking on behalf of your convictions.*

This time the porter wasn't alone. He'd been joined by Mehmet, who'd been doing his military service in Ereğli, and the coffeehouse apprentice at Boyacıköy.

Outside the entryway another elderly woman begged for alms in a thick Rumeli accent, though in a gentle voice. She had small hands, as small as a child's. Her eyes resembled mountain springs on her wizened face. As Mümtaz handed the woman money, he wanted to peer into her eyes. But he could discern nothing there – such had they been occluded by pain and longing. Next he stopped in front of the prayer-bead seller peddling the final and paltry mementos of his boyhood *Thousand and One Nights* Ramadan celebrations, having reduced this realm of his genesis to a few prayer beads and two or three *misvak* toothbrush sticks in a small case. Last August, he and Nuran had purchased two strings of prayer beads and chatted with the man. He again bought two strings; but was scarcely able to keep them out of Suad's clutch. *I'm dreaming, I'm seeing things while wide awake . . .*

II

By viscous light of summer twilight the coffeehouse seethed in sound and fury. A gathering of every ilk and class – including expectant ferry-goers, neighborhood locals soon to return home, and day-trippers chatting with friends after the beach – had braved the evening sun filtering through the acacias like the fourteen children of Princess Niobe and were discussing the current state of affairs: *They display a true heroic resilience in this sun! Virtually Homeric.*

Mümtaz walked on as the names of Hitler, Mussolini, Stalin, and Chamberlain flitted through the air. While passing one table, he overheard the vociferous commentary of an acquaintance: "My dear man, today's France can't fight. Its inhabitants have become decadent . . . One and all they're like André Gide . . ."

Alas Gide, alas France! If France can't fight, of course it isn't Gide's fault. There must be other reasons! That this man could today still recollect a France without Gide was truly bizarre. Mümtaz immediately thought of a book comprised of comments and predictions made at each café table. What a testimonial. *To simply convey opinions on the verge of war – if it comes to that!* Read after the fact, it'd be an accurate and fascinating record of the vagaries of human thought. *But documented in the thick of things . . . it ought to be written tonight!* Should these same citizens later try to write down what they'd honestly thought now, intervening events would distort their state of mind and perspective. *Because we change along with events; and as we change, we reconstruct our histories anew.* The human mind functioned like this. Humanity would continually reformulate time. The knife's edge of the present carried the weight of history while also transforming it, word by word.

Prophecies of other voices rose from other tables: "My good man, England isn't as weak as you might suppose" or, "You'll see, the actual victor will be Mussolini! The man could be in Paris in twenty-four hours!"

Mümtaz was transported to the era described by Cabî İsmet Bey in his history of the reign of Sultan Selim III: *"The general known to the world as Bonaparte sent word, 'whoever be my sultan, I shall come to his aid with an army that could fill the Seven Seas . . .'"* Of course, it wasn't quite the same, but reminiscent of what he heard. The commentaries continued: "At the turn of the nineteenth century, we were experiencing a crisis with Europe similar to today's. But back then we weren't familiar with Europe or ourselves"; "How much this country has sacrficed in blood"; "In place of supporting France, if only we hadn't left England's side"; "But, my good man, history is done and over with." At what lengths he'd discussed such matters with İhsan. İhsan, who lay ailing.

His friends sat in the rear of the coffeehouse, their backs against the garden wall. A garçon who'd known Mümtaz for some time said, "They're waiting for you." Should war break out, he, too, would be sent to the front.

The lot of them were gloomy. Selim fiddled with an envelope. When they saw Mümtaz coming they called out, "How's İhsan?"

"I haven't seen him since about three. But he doesn't seem to be in any real danger. Only, I worry about the night. They say that odd numbered dates are always more difficult."

He took a chair. He sank his trembling hands into his pockets.

"You look quite pale. What's bothering you?"

"Nothing," he said. "Troubles." And with a hand in his pocket, he fondled the prayer beads he'd snatched from Suad's clutch. *I'm nothing but a child! I'm driving myself crazy!* "Have them bring me something, would you?"

"What would you like?"

Wiping the table, the garçon recited, "Coffee, tea, *ayran*, lemonade, soda . . ."

Mümtaz gazed at the man's face and perspiring mustache through the lens of his student years. He'd once lambasted him when he'd lost the satchel Mümtaz had entrusted to him. Later they'd become friends.

"A tea!" Then he turned to his friends.

"What's going on with you all?"

"What d'you expect? We're talking about the march to war . . . or not."

Mümtaz glanced at Orhan's athletic shoulders. "Likely so," he said.

He, too, was surprised that he'd pronounced this verdict. "If not today, tomorrow. There's no other way out. Now that matters have reached this impasse . . ."

"Then what about us? What'll happen to us?"

Selim extended the envelope in his hand. "They've called me up to the district military office. I'm going tomorrow."

Maybe they've sent a letter to Emirgân for me. Once İhsan gets better, I'll stop in at the conscription office!

"You haven't answered to my question."

Mümtaz looked at Orhan stretched out bodily over four chairs. His swarthy face, trained on the tree branches drooping from the mosque yard, awaited an answer in its usual state of composure.

"We're tied to agreements: If France and England enter the war, we'll enter."

Nuri was the most distraught of the lot. "I was going to get married this week." In Mümtaz's eyes the wedding gown that he'd seen that morning could change a woman. But no, Nuri was well-off and his bride wouldn't be caught dead in such a tacky dress. She'd wear a prettier, fancier, and more fashionable dress accented with jewelry – perhaps the jewelry he'd seen on display at the Bedesten. But if Nuri were indeed drafted, she wouldn't be that different from the porter's wife. In the midst of a more ordered, more comfortable life, she'd weep for him, yearn for him on quiet nights with stirrings of complete physical longing, and when his absence was reaffirmed, she'd become the enemy of all humanity.

Mümtaz had been friends with petite Leyla since university. He'd given her the nickname "Pocket Lady." She'd once darned his loose jacket seam, lowering her small head to her chest while, in a moment of intimacy, he'd observed the softness of her nape between curly locks and the line of her dress. Leyla truly was delightful. Now she'd lower her head again, but this time to weep.

"You can still get married before you go . . . Or else you'll take leave. Besides, it's not clear what will happen!" Then, as if wanting to deliver himself of these troubles, Mümtaz took refuge in loose speculation: "Maybe war won't break out and some means of reconciliation will be found."

Fâhir: "You just said there was no recourse!"

"Everything hangs on and is held together by a thread. Do you want to know what's truly horrible?" He paused, recalling the phrase of a poet of his esteem: "*Pire . . . Pire destin . . .*" he repeated. "The worst fate."

"Yes, what's truly horrible?"

"This insecurity. Life can't seem to decide on its path. And it won't, either. We know nothing of the era before the last war. We were only children then. But when one reads about it, it's absolutely shocking. The sense of security and stability then! Finance, labor, ideology, social struggle, all of it developed on roads that had been paved beforehand. Now, everything is a shambles. Even borders change from day to day and hour to hour. International crises, and our nervous tension, can skyrocket in an instant. Maybe they'll come to a resolution. But that won't solve the matter. Because this state of insecurity and fear has befuddled the politicians."

Orhan, with the same absentmindedness: "True, if this war happens, it won't happen by accident like the last one!"

"The last war didn't happen accidentally, either. Some believe that it happened because Poincaré wanted it to! Whatever the case, it caught the entire world off guard. Everybody distrusted their neighboring country and more or less armed themselves against each other. But the people on the ground didn't give war much credence. They believed that it wasn't possible in this century of civilization, that consent for this magnitude of death couldn't be given. But today . . . today the world's in the midst of a civil war. Ideas alone are at war. Ideas themselves have begun to run riot."

"But isn't that just a small faction?"

"Not at all! Because these persistent crises have also exhausted more moderate factions and groups that simply want to live their lives. That's why war is a forgone conclusion."

Orhan, after entertaining thoughts of hanging a fist-size lock on the door of the chemist's shop that he'd recently opened, said, "Is it all worth it for the sake of a small harbor?"

"Of course not, but it isn't simply an issue of the harbor. It's uncertain what will follow! Not to mention that there's the crucial problem of Nazi tyranny and aggression! The man's a plague on humanity."

"Mümtaz, do you actually still believe in humanity?"

Mümtaz gazed at Orhan. "What else is there?" He resembled the stray girl whom Suad had mentioned in his letter.

"I don't believe in it. And the spilling of blood for the sake of humanity infuriates me. What's it to me if Europe claims to be in dire straits? When we were in danger, did they give us a second thought? Did Europe even once think of preventing the catastrophe of the Balkan Wars? For centuries your Europe has performed cold-blooded surgery on us. An incision here, an amputation there. They uprooted us like grass from lands in which we'd lived for hundreds of years. Then they transplanted other nationalities in our place as if planting carrots in a field of rice. Didn't Europe do all of this? Hasn't Europe nurtured Hitler and the current state of crisis?"

"But we could come to a mutual understanding that violence unleashed against us and others should end! And it should end once and for all!"

"And you intend to do this through warfare?"

"Seeing that there's the threat of military attack, of course through warfare . . . First I'd repel the threat at the doorstep, then I'd try to prevent its reoccurrence."

"Two wrongs don't make a right!"

"Sometimes another wrong is the only solution. Surgery cures gangrene. Skin cancer can be abraded with a scalpel. Operations are terrible, but at times they're the only available option. Not to mention that establishing a new ethics and morality is laborious and time-consuming. We assume it can happen all at once like a rising sun. But it manifests by means of suffering and trial and error, and through the resulting process of socialization. Ideas are a dime a dozen. Value judgments get absorbed through our skin, that's how common and invasive they are. But they're good for nothing. Because society doesn't simply adopt what the mind conjures up."

"Will it adopt it by force of war? We saw what happened between 1914 and 1918."

"True, the road traveled is no indication of what lies ahead."

Orhan, having finished with the lock, was lost in thought. During such moments, he'd be certain to sing a *türkü*. In fact, in place of answering Mümtaz, he mumbled:

> *Imperiled between a rock and a hard place,*
> *One falls by bullet, the next by knife wound . . .*

Mümtaz recognized the *türkü*. During the last war, while in Konya with his father, Mümtaz remembered that soldiers being transported by evening freight trains and peasants carting vegetables to town toward daybreak always sang this song in the station. It had a searing melody. The entire drama of Anatolia was contained in this *türkü*.

"How strange!" he said. "It's acceptible, even forgivable, for the masses to moan and complain. Just listen to *türkü*s from the last war! What spectacular pieces! The older ones are that way too. Take that Crimean War *türkü*. But these songs aren't liked by intellectuals. So they have no right to whine! That means we're accountable."

Nuri returned to the earlier topic: "And how d'you know that things won't run amok this time? Due to the absence or the surplus of the most insignificant thing, a piece of straw."

Mümtaz completed his thought: "I'm not defending war. What makes you think that I am? For starters, can humanity even be divided into the 'victorious' and the 'vanquished'? This is absurd. This division is sufficient to bankrupt values and ethics and even what we're fighting for. Naturally it's a mistake to expect good or great things to follow in the wake of every crisis. But what's to be done? You see, there are five of us here. Five friends. When we think independently, we find ourselves possessed of an array of strengths. But in the face of any crisis . . ." His friends gazed at him intently as he continued: "Since morning I've been debating this on my own." Abruptly, however, he returned to the previous topic: "On the contrary, worse, much worse things could arise."

"What have you been deliberating since morning?"

"This morning, near the Hekim Ali Pasha Mosque, girls were playing games and singing *türkü*s. These songs have existed maybe since the time of the conquest of Istanbul. And the girls were singing them and playing. You see, I want these *türkü*s to persist."

"That's a defensive struggle . . . That's different."

"Sometimes a defensive struggle can change its character. If there's a war, I'm not saying we'll rush into it at all costs. For nobody knows what the developments leading up to it will be. Sometimes, unexpectedly, a back door opens. You look to find an unforeseen opportunity! In that case, waging or refraining from war becomes a matter that's within your own control."

"When one contemplates it, it's confounding. The difference between those who controlled humanity's fate at the start of the last war and today's statesmen is immeasurable!"

Mümtaz turned to İhsan in his thoughts as if to ask him something.

"Of course there are a lot of differences. Back then humanity seemed to emerge out of a single mold. Values were still regarded in high esteem! Not to mention that centuries-old diplomacy, its gentility and protocol . . . Today it's as if a lunatic has moved into the neighborhood. Europe as we know it has vanished. Half of Europe is in the hands of renegades bent on provoking the masses, on vengeance, and on spinning new fables." The more he spoke, the more he assumed he was leaving his fixed ideas and fabrications behind.

"Do you know when I gave up hope on the current predicament? The day they signed the Nazi-Soviet Nonaggression Pact."

"But the leftists quite applaude it. If you could just hear them rave! They're now all praising the Führer. As if the Reichstag Fire Trial had never happened." Nuri's face was yellow with wrath. "As if so much murder hadn't been committed."

"Of course they praise him. But only until the next news flash. You get my drift, don't you? Mind that one doesn't lose his sense of ethics and value judgments! Despite being opposed to war, I'm not afraid of it, and I'm waiting."

He spoke with unfamiliar certitude. From one of the neighboring coffeehouses a radio or gramophone cast another variety of turmoil into the evening hour. Eyyubî Bekir Ağa's version of the "Song in Mahur" lilted through the twilight, staggering Mümtaz on the spot. As he heard the melody, the version that Nuran's grandfather had composed, that ominous poem of love and death, filled him. *Tomorrow she'll be leaving, and leaving full of resentment ...* Fury, so vast as to be unbearable, rose within him. *Why did it have to happen this way? Why is everybody imposing on me like this?* She'd been talking about her peace of mind. *So then, where's my own peace to be found? Don't I count? What to do in such solitude?* He was all but thinking through Nuran's words: *Peace, inner calm*, huzur ...

"The entire matter hinges on this . . ." Orhan didn't complete his thought.

"Go on!"

"No, I've forgotten what I was going to say. Only you're right on one point. Two wrongs don't make a right. Each injustice condoned gives rise to greater injustice."

"There's another point: avoiding injustice while fighting injustice . . .

This war, if it comes to pass, will be a bloodbath. But the torments suffered will all be in vain if we don't change our methods . . ."

I shouldn't be seeking peace through Nuran, but through myself. And this will only happen through sacrifice. He stood.

"I'm worried about İhsan," he said. "Please excuse me. And purge yourselves of these thoughts. Who knows, maybe there won't be any war! Maybe we won't get involved. We're a country that's lost so much blood, we've learned many lessons. The circumstances might just permit our neutrality." ·

As Mümtaz took leave of his friends, he realized that they hadn't discussed the stages of such a war, were it to happen. Inwardly, this pleased him.

Will it actually come to pass? The voice accompanying him said, "Don't worry about it," then added, "Well-spoken, you've put yourself at ease! That's all you need to do, nothing more!" He ran and hopped onto a streetcar, perhaps to escape Suad's derisive voice.

III

İhsan lay as sick as ever, his gaunt face ruddy from fever. Occasionally he tried to wet his cracked and drawn lips with his tongue. This was no longer the former İhsan; perhaps he verged on becoming a memory. Seeing him in this state meant encountering him halfway on that foreordained path. This was precursor to becoming a remnant, existing only through Mümtaz and other acquaintances. *Should his persona grow a little more exhausted, a little more attenuated, it'll pass into us, persisting only in our memories.*

He gazed at İhsan's hands. His distended veins looked as if they had been roasted. But they were alive. Alive as if they'd been conquered by another dimension of existence and were now living in another climate. A climate of 104 degrees. But that wasn't all. The temperature alone didn't create this environment. An array of small organisms, microbes, known as bacilli, observed through special instruments, isolated in tiny vials and in thin test tubes, introduced into a variety of laboratory animals, and thereby regenerated; for whose preservation and proliferation special methods were implemented, for whom hot and cold extremes were established, concerning whom a variety of tests were undertaken for their extraction from hosts, who were dyed in the most inconceivable ways, and preserved in fluids ranging in color by shades from blood red to dull green; these microbes had certain codes, and these microorganisms, along with the programming they carried, transformed this temperature between 102 and 104 degrees into a clime between life and death quite separate from our own context, transforming it into an unimaginable altitude or a suffocating, noxious quagmire, into the thin air found at a height of thousands of feet or into something like the maw of a volcano active with the admixture of unknown gases.

The afflicted man's chest rose and fell like a poorly working bellows that couldn't manage to find an adequate breath of salvation or preservation; he gulped air hungrily, and exhaled furtively and imperceptively like a tire leaking air; however quickly and noticeably he inhaled, his exhalation was indeterminable to the same degree.

One could hardly recognize this wheezing anatomy as a human torso – reduced to its most basic functions, rising and falling in its own inadequacy. The half-shaded light on the bedstead illuminated this mass of misery in greater clarity. Uncanny was the light of the room of the afflicted: It pointed out everything through idiosyncrasy, delineating certain objects in the fore-ground and others in the background. It was a light that declared, "I am awaiting a state of distinction, a zone between 102 and 104 degrees, a final threshold. That is all that I illuminate, nothing more." But this enunciation, according to Mümtaz, existed to some degree in all the assembled objects:

the bed had swollen along with the patient and had taken on his suffering. The drapes, the wardrobe mirror, the silence of the room, the tick of the clock whose pace gradually increased, and all else demonstrated what a bizarre, mean, rough-going passage the interstice between 102 and 104 constituted – leading from the manifest to arcana, from a numeric quantity to zilch, and from cognizance to absolute inertia.

Here reigned a sultanate. Over a period of nine days, this sultanate had been established in the corpus of the man lying here, whose hands twitched as they'd never before done in the normal atmosphere of 98.6 degrees, who sought oxygen to cool his lungs at the altitude of his ascent only by incessantly working his chest, his drawn lips waiting before countryside fountain spouts through which water hadn't gushed for years, lips chapped like the earth longing for one burst of water and serenity, with eyes that regurgitated light, with a face that receded from within, a man of affliction whose very being declared, "I'm no longer what I once was!" In the course of nine days, he'd been removed from his old self, from resembling others, and had been relegated to the margins of existence, where only if one paid close attention could one discern his astonishing slow and steady metamorphosis.

What remained in this room of the man he used to know? Besides the suffering of his material being, practically nothing. Not even the light in his eyes was a sign of a life recognizably human. Any material object catching any reflection would elicit this much luminance, Mümtaz decided. But no, the eyes of ailing İhsan shone differently. It was as if İhsan could still read Mümtaz's thoughts from the limits of extremity he occupied. *Why do I always succumb to pessimism like this? Why am I this cowardly?* he thought, and leaned toward İhsan to speak. But the man of affliction closed his eyes when Mümtaz took up his hands; he didn't want to speak. Silence of the ephemeral. Silence the likes of which he hadn't experienced before.

One couldn't call this silence, either, because the table clock churned as if all had been relinquished to its command.

With gradually increasing momentum, the clock marked another time, one between *zaman* that could be considered external to humanity and the intrinsic *zaman* of human existence; the time of a being that had traversed half the road, of a terrible metamorphosis that would conclude shortly in a single lunge. The clock represented, if not the exact hour of this abstraction, an impending metamorphosis – a shedding of human skin, the approach of death.

This was a time that had internalized the metamorphosis of a larva into a chrysalis and of a chrysalis into a butterfly, a time that had established such rhythm that it was regulated internally. This was that strain of time. What difference was there between the one who lay here tonight and the creatures that changed character and form this way?

İhsan opened his eyes; he wet his lips as much as his strength allowed. Mümtaz gave him water with a teaspoon, then leaned downward, happy that he'd been delivered from this nightmare, and asked, "How are you, *Ağabey?*"

With his hand İhsan made a gesture that might mean anything. Then, as if reluctant to make any determination about his state, he rolled his tongue in his mouth with difficulty to inquire, "How are you?" He stopped. He attempted to pull himself up but failed. His chest constricted. His hands hastened their tremors. His face reddened as if he were choking.

"Let's call a doctor, Mümtaz. I'm afraid."

Mümtaz knew that tonight was a fateful night. But he hadn't guessed that the crisis would be so severe. He gazed at İhsan's worsening condition in genuine surprise. Frightening possibilities collided in his mind. *What if something should happen while I'm gone?*

Stunned, he imagined how he might act with the physician. That dour-faced neighborhood doctor, whom he disliked, passed before his eyes. All the others, the ones that he knew, were off on vacation. Could they be blamed? Would he himself have been here in the midst of the sweltering season had it not been for this illness? Before his eyes, the diamond-spire road from Vaniköy to Kandilli came to life through the lights of fishing boats, the shimmering of stars, through the sounds of birds and bugs, just like those visions that were pure sparkle and a palette of colors reflected on the panes of grand *yalı* windows with shades drawn at night; Mümtaz – in the event of a turn for the worse – could see himself plodding along this well-lit Bosphorus road with a doctor who would be of no use.

He understood that his imagination, despite such terrible possibilities, still existed in another dimension and that a majority of it was only occupied with Nuran. He stood, ashamed of himself and his selfishness. Macide knew how to administer injections. But how could he entrust her with such a difficult task? He looked at İhsan writhing in a fit of breathlessness. Macide brushed aside Mümtaz's hesitation.

Standing, she said, "I'll give the injection." This was a Macide with whom he wasn't familiar, a ghastly pale woman who dispelled every objection with intense eyes, who'd decided to rescue her husband, and by making this decision, vanquished all doubts in her mind. Mümtaz bared İhsan's arm, and Macide, to avoid losing time, simply swabbed the tip of the needle with alcohol before attaching it to the syringe and holding it to the half-light . . . After, as if she couldn't believe her own eyes, she indicated the ministered arm to Mümtaz.

Mümtaz saw a thin trail of blood on the broad athletic form of İhsan's arm tracing a path over his still suntanned skin. With a stunned expression, İhsan's mother stared in horror at what had occurred. She had no stomach for medical interventions. But İhsan had responded to the shot, and had relaxed.

"Please, Mümtaz, call a doctor."

Had Nuran or his aunt said this? Nuran was far away. She had no inkling of the fear and apprehension that reigned in this house. She'd be heading to İzmir tomorrow. Maybe she was now busy preparing her bags. Or perhaps she was at home conversing with Fâhir, making plans for the future.

He stood within the bizarre and disorienting understanding of one who has slipped out of a dream. The threadlike trail of blood had disconcerted him. But what was blood after all? Something we all carried in our bodies by the pint.

"Do you think it's an absolute necessity?"

Macide concurred with her mother-in-law.

"To be safe," she said. Mümtaz walked toward the door to get the physician.

Calling for a doctor was de rigueur. Whether the patient was improving or not, the doctor must be summoned. Neither life nor its doppelgänger death could take place without a doctor. Death, in particular . . . In today's world it was all but shameful to die without the presence of a doctor. This only happened on battlefields, when people died en masse by the thousands and tens of thousands. For death was quite costly. But at times its price would drop and it'd become available to one and all.

In that case, without the need for a physician, pharmacy, medicines, or compassion, people died huddled together, embracing, entwined, and sharing their greatest intimacies with one another. But dying an idiosyncratic death at home in one's bed had a set protocol: a Koran chanter and recitations, a priest, a doctor, a pharmacist's mortar and pestle, shed tears, blessed water, the peal of bells . . . Only through these acts and signs could death come to fruition. These were accoutrements that the human intellect had appended to the order of nature. This is how things transpired among humans. In fact, nature was ignorant. It knew nothing of the existence of these addenda. Death in nature was entirely different: Sensing the scattering turbine of cosmic time spinning within one's body and soul, losing incrementally first one's memories, then memory itself, then one's sense and sensation, scattering into countless elementary particles that skitter away from each other into the eternal void in proportion to the speed of this whirling blade; this, then, is death in nature.

Through Macide's unblinking courage, this turbine spinning within İhsan had stopped, just like the momentary pause of the ceiling fan above the wardrobe when switched to reverse – a veritable winged creature on the verge of taking flight – it had stopped in an act of no small significance.

Mümtaz again gazed at İhsan's face, and making an ambiguous sign, left the room. He moved slowly, as if wading through water, amid thoughts that he himself didn't quite understand.

Numerous diaphanous membranes separated him from material objects. Or maybe the realm in which he moved, thought, and spoke was not the same realm in which he physically lived . . . as if he engaged his surroundings through a persona that was purely observational. He perceived, registered, and contemplated his environment. But this perception, cognition, and even communication transpired through an identity that had lost its mass and had all but atomized.

He turned on the light in the foyer and, as always, stared into the mirror. Mümtaz never passed up the opportunity to look into any mirror. For him, mirrors were symbols of human fate or the potential of the intellect before the unknown.

He gazed into the mirror; the light settled into the flat, crystalline glass with a slight tremor, taking in the entire foyer. Mirrors were strange; they set to work instantly. Mümtaz had the appearance of somebody who'd just woken up. At the other end of the foyer rested four pair of shoes belonging to İhsan. On the wall hung a thick-handled umbrella. Would he be able to use these items again? Why not? Stopping the momentum of the scattering turbine was sufficient to live. Then one could pass from cosmic time to the plane of people and life. This was a restorative place where all wounds were healed, all flaws smoothed out, where the hours of the clock were friends to mankind.

Four pairs, two of which he'd just purchased at the start of summer. A black and a yellow pair of the variety that could be worn in winter. When Mümtaz teased, "*Ağabey*, you've bought winter shoes in summer!" İhsan replied with the seriousness he displayed at such times, "I'm a prudent man." *A prudent man! Had he been prudent, would he have come down with pneumonia?*

Mümtaz stared at the shoes. *In this world, how little we're able to appropriate the objects around us. These shoes, this umbrella, the things in this house, the house itself, like everything else, belonged to İhsan. There were the things that were his and the things he shared with others. But tomorrow, Allah forbid, if something were to befall him . . .*

All of it would be released from his possession. If only somebody who remembered, or a mnemonic source, would appear. Genuine preservation only occurred with others and through others. The human intellect, the human heart, the human soul, the human memory . . . When the human component withdraws, nothing remains at the center. The center cannot hold. *Granted, certain animals, too, never forget their owners or where they live . . .* But this was a trait that had passed from humans to animals. He switched off the light. The four pairs of shoes, the umbrella, the items purchased that evening and left on the little table, the stove-like brazier, everything disappeared. The glass of the mirror became the realm of certain borderless, even formless, shadows beneath the indeterminate light filtering in through the window. How quickly everything had vanished. With the comportment of a scientist performing an experiment, he switched on the light. Again, on the flat mirror surface that reflected part of the foyer more brightly, as well as in the entryway itself, objects came alive in sharp clarity, through shapes and sizes gathered one atop the other and within silent, relative positioning – vivid, harmonious, cognizant of their substantiation, and over-joyed to exist together, to complete an arbitrary totality. *These things exist with-out me as well! The presence of light is sufficient. Light, that is, any medium of stimu-lus, and under its command, cooperating with it, consciousness or memory . . . In that case, I am indeed necessary! Me or anyone else . . . even the last man, if you like.*

He closed the door with the same care with which he'd descended the stairs. The street, despite the desolate night, gradually filled with some luminance and evening sounds. Certain details were enough to evoke the summer nocturne: the peep of a few frogs, the buzzing of insects, and, in the distance at the head of the street, the gushing spout of an old fountain, which appeared like a scale laid aground, situated between the alley and the larger road onto which it opened.

Onto the spotted and green nocturnal backdrop, which resembled a frog's back, rumblings of empty streetcars and indeterminate sounds leaped like flames before sputtering out. This was the hour when poets claimed that everything slept. A kitten sheltered in a neighbor's doorway suddenly – startled like a wild animal – arched its back at Mümtaz, puffing up as if to pounce. Mümtaz glared at the feline – they usually unsettled him – threatening to teach it a good lesson. It seemed there was a correlation between this kitten's fear and the way everything he'd observed for days in his life, in the *omnium gatherum* of his thoughts, and in his mind's eye, assumed the form of a tormenting idea. *For months now I've been in turmoil . . . Had I remained by myself, everything would have returned to normal. At least we wouldn't have separated on bad terms . . .* Trying to the best of his ability not to think, he quickly turned onto the boulevard of streetcars. He walked, searching up and down both sides of the street for an empty taxicab. The physician's house wasn't far; it was within walking distance. Hopefully he'd be at home, open the door, and return to the house with Mümtaz.

But the doctor wasn't home. The man who'd said, "I'm at your command always, it's my duty!" had vanished by eight P.M. . Not just him, the entire household . . . Mümtaz rang the bell at length and pounded the door. But not a peep could be heard. *Has the entire household entered into the slumber of death?* Finally the door cracked open, and a servant in unkempt clothes stated that the doctor and missus had decided to make an overnight visit at a late hour.

"Who goes on an overnight visit after eight?"

"If one has the means, one goes after eight as well –" The servant, afraid sleep would escape her should she speak for another second, shut the door without finishing.

With no other recourse, he went to Beyazıt and called on the state physician. From the moment he'd left the house, his anxieties had multiplied. With each passing moment he grew more afraid that catastrophe would strike should he be delayed any longer. No one was on the street. Only far in the distance, at a bend where, from his perspective, the street appeared to end, a group of trolley laborers gathered over a node of heliotrope light, which appeared more poignant in the night, repairing streetcar rails within a chiaroscuro play of light and shadow that recalled Rembrandt's canvases.

He walked, watching this illumination within the nocturne, noting the darkness it disrupted, the glistening faces and clothes and the shadows that sank further into the night as he slowly approached the scene of figures. The light embellished each movement one after the next onto the night and, within a reigning shadow, gradually and confidently completed the forms. In this way, an everyday undertaking came to life boldly.

When he reached them, one of the workers requested a cigarette. "We're all out of 'em," he said. Mümtaz left his half-smoked pack with them and continued.

He forged through the summer's night, the sounds of hammers, the susurrus of trees, and the rumbling passage of empty trolleys testing rails in the distance.

Beneath the luminance of two electric lamps, the municipal complex at Beyazıt, within that peculiar and overwhelming starkness specific to this type of official building, slumbered, stealthily poised. And it woke quickly. First a policeman on duty emerged from nowhere, his collar undone, cap in hand; then a janitor appeared in a corridor along with the chair on which he slept. The chair and its partner awoke together: One shape approached Mümtaz, while the other skipped backward.

The doctor wasn't available. A short while beforehand he'd been summoned to a difficult birth. He'd telephoned to say he'd be delayed.

Tonight a child had been born. Mümtaz's mind registered this fact without attaching much importance to it, like a newspaper tidbit. Shocked by his failure to find what he sought, he gazed at the faces of the two men standing before him. The police officer mumbled, "Doctor . . . doctor . . ." Finally he meticulously described the route to the house of a military doctor a short way past Soğanağa: "He's an exceptionally good man; he'd help you even if he were in the most dire situation, but I can't be sure if he's at home."

"What d'you mean?"

"His children have gone to their summerhouse. But he stays here certain nights."

To let a little coolness and an echo of the sea into this stifling night, Mümtaz inquired, "Where do the children go?"

"To Çengelköy, on the Asian shore . . . They have a villa there . . ."

To Çengelköy . . . How Mümtaz would have loved to find himself in Çengelköy or any spot on the Bosphorus removed from the anxieties of recent days. How he would have loved the feel of a rocky road beneath his feet, the treetops of Kuleli above his head, to find himself in the spot where those shadows conjured a realm unto themselves in the dark waters, and farther on; he'd chat with the factory guard, then he'd slowly walk from Vaniköy toward Kandilli, and at the crest of the hill, he'd sit on a boulder and watch the Bosphorus, and take in the scents of the enormous black rose of the night. And he'd think about Nuran and the following day's tryst.

Nuran's name coursed through his body like a feverish shiver. But pleasures of reminiscence weren't as innocent as they'd previously been. Intermingled with them was the anxious guilt of having neglected İhsan. Meanwhile, he'd made it here almost in a run. He realized he was covered in sweat. But he'd continue to run. This was something like one's fate as determined by the stars. Those guilty by birth were fated to run this way throughout their lives, bearing torment. Mumbling, "And me, throughout my life . . . poor İhsan . . ." Mümtaz turned into a narrow alley.

IV

A private, cleanly dressed Istanbul youth opened the door. When Mümtaz inquired after the doctor, the soldier gestured upstairs before vanishing. He came back down immediately, indicating that Mümtaz could go up.

A sizable parlor: Two of its windows faced the Bosphorus. In a corner rested a broad divan with two chairs beside it piled with seventy-eights, and nearby a gramophone played. Without so much as a glance at the doctor's face, Mümtaz recognized the piece being played. The violin concerto approached conclusion. On the bed, the doctor, wearing gaiters, trousers, and an undershirt that clung to his body from perspiration, listened without disturbing his peace. Mümtaz, within the astounding transfiguration of the musical motif, which gave one the sensation of being in a dream, could all but observe himself approaching his own essence. Before his eyes, a seed that had only just been sown grew rapidly, branched out, and foliated.

What unanticipated crescendos, soaring strains, proclamations of self, fits of hesitation, and finally, an arrival like the discovery of truth, repeating its concise development within subtle variations like an autumn cornucopia, before once again vanishing into the marvel of metamorphosis.

Silently Mümtaz sat on the corner of the bed in a spot where the doctor had retracted his foot, and listened.

What was it? Had he been asked such a question, he'd have answered, "Doubtless, one of the things I'm most attached to in this life." But this still would have conveyed nothing. Was it symbolic of human fate? Did it amount to a complaint or a surrender? Was it the dark dance of memory in the light of unconsciousness? Which of the dead did it summon to life? Which span of time did it resurrect?

Or was it simply another realm formed outside life by the single-handed toil of a *deev* in human cloak – a creature unlike man – created for the sole purpose of expending its strengths? Certainly this, too, was a distinct and particular climate like the one he delved into at İhsan's bedside, with its specific extremes, stifling altitudes, harsh and rejuvenating breezes, and devastating siroccos. And as was the case when one's pulse reached 120 and one's body temperature 104, one lived here in a discrete way, facing other challenges of singular intensity.

Suad had listened to this concerto before his suicide. Even earlier, over and over for an entire day, he'd listened to it alone. This was what he'd confided in his letter without indicating why. And the concerto, in its heavy, tormented progression, didn't divulge this secret. The music itself was unaware that Suad had listened to it. It simply scattered and spewed its fiery essence.

Mümtaz gazed at the gramophone as if the entire enigma of Suad was hidden between the small metallic disk of the speaker and the hermetic world of the vinyl record that spun in frozen sparkles. How many times had Mümtaz pictured Suad listening to this piece in his own apartment on that last night? *His face must have been very pale . . . And who knows, maybe, like the protagonist of the story that he'd suggested I write, he laughed at everything with a saintly piety of sorts.* According to his letter, first he'd listened to this concerto together with that girl, and after she'd left the next morning, he'd played it by himself. And at night, while writing his letter, he'd listened to it again. Undoubtedly he raised his head from time to time, and because he knew it was the last time he would hear it, he surrendered all of his attentions to its agonizing progression. And perhaps, like all people facing death, he was absent and indifferent to everything. Perhaps he was afraid. He regretted what he was about to do. He sought a means to avoid it, looking to the door, hoping that someone would enter and deliver him from this predicament.

And Mümtaz wondered whether this concerto had played a part in his demise. For it transported the listener to such realms of impossibility . . . Then, abruptly and vaguely, he recalled that he, too, had listened to the same piece that same night. Indeed, the soreness of memory within him at that moment, the helpless awakening, didn't come from nowhere. *But where? I returned home at night. I conversed with İhsan briefly. He felt well. And I was tired. I went to bed. Then, until Macide woke me up . . .* The first side of the seventy-eight snarled to a halt. The doctor, with nary a glance at Mümtaz, cued the other side. Mümtaz wiped his brow as if he'd been roused awake. *But where? Or else was it in my dream?* Of course, he couldn't have heard the entire piece. *But the vivid pleasure of taste, the pain!*

A hand on each temple, sitting on a corner of a man's bed, a man whose acquaintance he'd only just made, Mümtaz tried to recollect his dream. No, he hadn't listened to the concerto, but he did dream of Suad. And in a very bizarre way. *I was at the Bosphorus, on the quay of a* yalı. *Before me, the evening was being erected just like a theater set. First large boards were carried in – but in an array of colors. Purple, red, navy blue, pink, and green . . . Then these were nailed together. "We're going to hang the sun here," they said. I was shaking my head, saying,*

"The sun doesn't shine in a dream. Neither sun nor moon. Sleep is the sibling of Death." But nobody heeded my words. Finally they raised the sun with ropes and pulleys. Only it wasn't the sun. It was Suad. Yet how stunning and multihued he was. As the ropes cut into his flesh, the smile on his face grew more intense. Then they stretched him out over the evening that they'd built. He must have been the setting sun! Then pulleys and other mechanisms that I knew nothing of were set into motion. The ropes that bound Suad grew increasingly taut. I realized that they were cutting into his muscles, and I was frantic with his suffering from where I watched. But Suad continued laughing, as if he felt no pain; he was surrounded by color and brilliance. The more he suffered, the more he laughed. Next, I'm not sure how it happened. Suad began tossing down part of himself that had been rent asunder. It was as if he'd become a shadow puppet whose binding strings had snapped. In the seawater before me, I could see the colorful body parts that he'd cast away. Suddenly a voice sounded beside me: "See? See what a fate I bear? Suad threw an arm at me!" I turned toward the voice. It was Adile. She was doubled over laughing. Then I woke up. Macide came in and informed me that İhsan's condition had worsened.

Mümtaz wiped his forehead and looked about. *I wonder what the doctor will think of me? Here I sit, listening to music. Who knows what kind of crazy gestures I've made?* Then he returned to the subject of the dream. *Maybe that was the voice of the sea . . .*

When the seventy-eight finished, the doctor let the remainder of the concerto resonate. But when he noticed Mümtaz's woebegotten face, he said, "Tell me then, what troubles you, my young man?"

Mümtaz implored, "Please, let's be on our way, doctor."

"Going is easy, my son. But where are we going, just tell me that . . ."

"Wouldn't it do if I told you on the way, good doctor?" he said.

Smiling, the doctor put on his jacket, which had been hanging on the wall. He grabbed his cap and walked toward the door without fastening any buttons. Inwardly Mümtaz said, *What a strange night, Allah. What an endless, inexhaustible night. It's as if I'm trying to fill a bottomless pit.*

As soon as they entered the street, the portly doctor began breathing heavily. Mümtaz briefly explained İhsan's condition, the attack he'd suffered that night, and the injection. The doctor translated *huile de camphre* as if wanting to satisfy the spirits of ancestors: "Camphor oil . . . camphor oil . . . camphor oil is one of the remedies that has done honor to the field of medicine. But only for the heart. Meanwhile, you didn't need to let the matter go this far. My good man, some colleagues are reticent to take responsibility. With sulfamide, pneumonia can be inhibited from the start. You could have done this as well. Eight Ultraseptil every four hours . . . It'll clear up the affliction. Nonetheless, we've set out on our way. Let's have a look at him. Who's the patient in question?"

"My cousin on my father's side. He's older than I am and like a brother to me. Others expect a great deal of him."

"Does he have any relations besides you?"

"His mother, wife, two children . . . But his wife . . ." Mümtaz hesitated about whether to tell him, as if Macide, wearing her usual expression, had appeared before him and, with a finger over her lips, said, "Don't divulge my secrets!"

"What happened to his wife?"

"Since the day an automobile struck their oldest child . . ." When he stumbled upon the phrase "mental faculties," he was able to finish easily. "She's not quite in control of her mental faculties, or rather, from time to time she'll suffer a lapse."

"Was she pregnant at the time?"

"Yes, in the last days of the pregnancy . . . Then the fever started, and the child was born in that fever."

The doctor turned into a housewife reciting a recipe: "Slight and persistent melancholy, endearing attention to detail and a childlike demeanor, extended silent withdrawals, abrupt bouts of elation . . . My good man, trivial and profound lapses of memory. Oh, the telltale symptoms of that puerperal pyrexia!"

He'd declared this last phrase bombastically, his chest puffed out, as if emulating a Vefik Pasha translation of Molière. Then, without invitation, he hooked arms with Mümtaz.

"Slow down, slow down. The time you'll save by having me rush, I'll cost you by sitting down on the first step of the stairs. I'm not a bad man, but despite my large size, I have modest whims." He fell silent for a time. He removed his hand from Mümtaz's arm, and Mümtaz found life a little more bearable once he'd been relieved of this burden. The doctor searched his pockets before unfolding the layers of a broad colorful handkerchief. He wiped his sweat and took a deep breath. "I don't tire of working. But this weight. Even Varashilov's apple diet didn't do me any good . . . First, mind that a condition doesn't become chronic . . ."

Mümtaz understood that the topic would now turn to politics. *"Mind that a condition doesn't become chronic."* What a horrible judgment. Yet the doctor changed the subject as if he didn't have the courage to pass through a door he himself had opened.

"I see you're a connoisseur of music!"

"Indeed."

"Only European?"

"No, Turkish as well. But not as the same person."

The doctor looked at Mümtaz's face as if to say he appeared to be something of an odd bird. "My child, you've expressed a genuine truth," he said. "So very true. The matter goes far beyond music. East is East and West is West. We wanted to merge the two in Turkey. And we even presume that we've discovered something new in this. Meanwhile, the attempt has always been made and it has always given rise to creatures with two faces."

Mümtaz imagined himself, at this pre-dawn hour, as a Siamese twin, one face looking East and the other West, with two bodies and four legs, scuttling sideways.

"Isn't it terrible, doctor? But," he added, "I don't think with two heads, only with one."

The doctor had also conjured an image like the one that came to Mümtaz. Grinning, he said, "But you think in two ways. And even more astounding, you perceive in two modes. Pitiful, isn't it?

"Just as we will always have our Mediterranean aspect, we will also always have an Eastern aspect, one exposed to the sun, *ex oriente lux*. Forever sensing the sharp prod of piercing mirror shards in one's soul. . . ."

"This is our country's paramount issue, I suppose."

"And it also emerges from geography, that is, from the genius of history. It existed before us and will exist afterward. Does your cousin love his wife?"

"Insanely so. But it isn't possible not to love Macide. After the illness they had another child."

"Their situation has returned to normal then."

The doctor followed the train of his own thoughts: "A life of normalcy within abnormality. You've seen firsthand how many things in the world that we think are impossible do indeed happen. Should there be war, in the midst of this conflagration, it would be something like the continued presence of the sick and needy, of prisoners who are obligated to complete prison terms, of our hunger at regular intervals."

"Do you think it'll happen?"

"As one looking at events from the outside, I don't give much credence to the idea of an immediate war . . . But the world is so fraught and prepared to accept this catastrophe . . ."

He stopped and took a deep breath. "It's a strange state of affairs . . . How should I put it? I don't give much credence to the outbreak of war. It seems unlikely to me because it's so sinister and devastating; I think that almost no one, even the most crazed, the most bloodthirsty, the most robotic, the most inhuman, or the most deluded (phantasies about ourselves are the most insidious), will have the courage, but will refrain from engaging at the last minute; and will suddenly toss the torch away from the stoked hearth of death. Do you know what the last hope is? Often, the last hope rests in expressing the impossibility of the intention!" He stopped again and took a deep breath. Mümtaz noted with sorrow and remorse that they were still only at Vezneciler; yet, he listened to the doctor with rapt attention. "Let me give you an indication of how weak this hope is. For years, all of our hopes were focused on the ones instigating this jingoism, the politicos deliberating as if obsessively over an arithmetic formula. Just think: For years they've prepared for this outcome as if concocting a pharmacological formula, prepping an operating room, or staging a theatrical performance. First they stamped each natural phase of life, every cause and effect as a 'crisis' to find excuses to increase their strength and scope by multiples of three or four . . . Now what are we taking stock in? Nothing short of a miracle: The possibility of a sudden about-face by the same warmongers who have provoked the crisis and made matters so untenable; the abrupt return to peace and quiet after unprecedented instigation; and an organic understanding of things instead of through the lenses of vested interest . . .

"What's truly frightening is that all the players, that is, adversaries, each espouse distinct states of mind and spirit. Some are overcome by the luxury of comfort, inaction, or implausible ideals; some are seduced by the insanity of absolute action. Or, you know, leaders who think that only their own acts of courage can resolve the dilemma. . . Who supports that mind-set?"

This time the doctor wiped his brow with the back of his hand, and, as if afraid of leaving his thoughts incomplete, began to speak rapidly. Mümtaz noticed that the night had clouded like a chalice whose contents had been mixed with another substance.

"This is the tragedy. But there's more. Even the most indecisive are still in the midst of the fracas. Therefore, everybody believes only his own evidence. This belief is goading the most insane actions by Hitler. But that's not all, gradually we've come to believe that war is the only option. And that's not all.

"We assume that there will be war, one of the great wars of history. Meanwhile, the world has united before the faces of politicians, has linked incidents together, and is preparing for a civil war. Civil war, that is, one of the ways in which civilizations slough their skins. We're living through the metamorphosis of such a great organism, so great as to be incomprehensible within its own reality, that it resembles a delirium or nightmare of nature. We're at a point, if the term is appropriate, a physiological point, in which the entire context has prepared for collapse and made it inevitable . . . It's so easy to avoid a political war . . . An abrupt change of course or the temporary return of common sense could resolve the whole problem. But overcoming a crisis of civilization or maintaining one's state of mind in the midst of its stumbling, is like trying to confront it without losing control of the rudder, being swept away by flood, drowning in a typhoon, or being pulverized in a meteor shower . . ."

"You're quite a fatalist, doctor . . ."

"Because I'm a man who believes in processes of nature. For years I managed a physiology lab. I saw tens of thousands of patients. I think I can now tell the difference between what can be avoided and what can't . . . I can tell from a distance the precise spot death has chosen to settle . . ."

"But isn't this a separate matter?"

"Wherever there happens to be the organization of a system, there you will find more or less the rule of biological laws . . . Don't think for a minute that I'm being pessimistic in order to take a comparison to its furthest limit. I believe that interventions will always be possible: I'm a physician; that is, I've been trained in the discipline of interventions. However, the condition has been intentionally exacerbated to spread throughout the organism . . . Look at it from another perspective.

"In an era in which everything's in a muddle, in which disconnected questions are posed independently, parallel to each other, in which each door of hope reveals a dragon's maw, just consider the catastrophe of a human fate held in the hands of a cadre of half-mad fanatics, irresponsible false prophets, determinists of production and overproduction, of utopians who clearly express good faith only through the report of weapons, who find their mettle through death sentences, and who hide behind masks of truth. Take for example Stalin's pact. What a chain of events. An event that could be described as paranoia from Hitler's perspective, is nothing but perfectly premeditated malice for Stalin. Don't forget the way Lenin's mongoloid, prophetic profile turned suddenly Machiavellian beyond all description. How it all became an intrigue worthy of a detective story. How Stalin kept the promise of his own persona and of the stare in his photographs.

"In the name of an ideal that would foster a paradise on earth, how he trained a weapon of death, which bore the possibility of one day being turned upon him, onto the entirety of humanity. He's openly promoting war, preparing the possibility of its outbreak. He's saying, 'Do not fear me, have conviction!' A trivial, but if you want to know the truth, extremely cunning, gesture. The chroniclers of old would have praised him to the skies. But this is nothing but resorting to crime, even if it's for the sake of protecting his own hide. It's like prodding the hand holding the torch toward the hearth. If we enter into his logic, maybe he's justified from his own perspective. But only from his point of view . . . Meanwhile, in today's world, there should be no vantage point reserved only for oneself. It's possible to explain this to you, to myself, to the banker in Antwerp, the railroad engineer in Brussels, I don't know, to everybody. Yet how could one ever explain this to a mystic, to people who assume the world is a vast stage upon which they're only players, to people who start with the assumption that death in cold blood is a viable answer to their desires? One declares, 'Allah determines my role,' while the other claims, 'I've emerged through historical determinism.'"

In the narrow alley onto which they'd turned, the redolence of flowers wafting over the walls of a manse of time-past in the still night settled deeply into Mümtaz with a poignant and lethal sensation – as if through the nostalgia of lost happiness and hope as well as obliterated dreams, like a qualm, like the mercilessly unforgiving consciousness of a criminal affront against the *nefs* of one's desires, afflicting one like an angel of torment for the duration of one's life; yes, just like the dominant melody of the recently played concerto discovering itself more fully at each flare and flourish, yes, ripple by ripple, pulling gradually away from the abundance as its own self, and finally, like a golden serpent, recoiling within one's being.

He felt exceedingly miserable. He suffered as if he'd committed all of these crimes himself, and he understood to a deeper degree, through this torment he bore due to no fault of his own, the extent to which humanity was a totality, and how every transgression against the whole amounted to a primal sin.

He no longer conceived of any of them in isolation: Neither Nuran, nor cousin İhsan, nor aunt, nor Macide, nor the unfinished book, none of them existed. He now saw only the newspaper headlines he'd read yesterday morning, or that he took in rather, without comprehension: BRITISH NAVY MOBILIZED; LAND & AIR RESERVES CALLED UP; GERMANY MAKES 16-ARTICLE ULTIMATUM TO POLAND; FRANCE HONORS ITS OBLIGATIONS. Despite so many intervening ordeals, troubles, and personal crises, he regarded these bulletins inherently as they were, fully aware of their actual meanings.

"D'you know, young man, what the tragedy of the situation is?"

Mümtaz knew the tragedy of the situation. Death's wings had stretched out over the globe. But he listened nonetheless: "Mind that humans aren't deluded into thinking that a sinister possibility is a new horizon. Mind that humanity doesn't catch sight of the abyss. For it won't be able to turn back. It'll adopt that eventuality. Don't ever consider the sale of an item of cherished value – a rare manuscript, a nice gramophone, a Persian carpet – to be something of an opportunity. Don't ever be tempted to divorce your wife, if you're married, or to break up with the lady you love, if you're in a relationship. Should you do so, as a consequence, no matter how much you resist repeating such acts later on, you'll do the same thing as if conditioned, as if others were prodding you from behind. Restraint in human existence doesn't exist. Especially for humans en masse. Especially once the open abyss beckons or the black tongue of death speaks."

Had he or Nuran conceived of the breakup first? In which of them had the destructive desire stirring within humanity to annihilate both itself and all of its endeavors first gained momentum? *I'm a measly narcissist. Look at what's plaguing the world and at what I'm worried about. There's a sick relative at home, and as soon as I stick my head out of my hole, I find that the lives of millions hang in the balance. And all for the sake of a woman.*

He couldn't continue this line of thought, because this woman wasn't as trivial as he supposed, and for the measure of a year she'd erected the most sublime bridge between himself and the everyday world that he had sensed and experienced and been exposed to through Nuran's attributes and body. *My sailboat, my sea, and in the final analysis, a lone man . . .* She was his horizon of truth; he'd deepened his thoughts and had established an inner life through her. *But in which one of us did the abyss first speak? I admit I strained the ropes . . . But she was the one who frayed and tore them apart. No, it wasn't like that. She'd made the decision to separate. She'd reasoned, "Seeing that Fâhir is returning, seeing that he says he's heartsick, dependent on me, and he's Fatma's father, and that I shouldn't reject his overtures, I'm obligated to take him back. I know I won't be happy, but I'm obligated to do so for peace of mind . . ."* As she'd said this, how distraught her expression had been; but this distraught face and the two-month effort that Nuran had exerted to come to this decision was nothing next to the debate that raged within Mümtaz. Over two months he'd become a shadow of his former self, a variation, waiting at a fork in a road, devastated and overwrought. Mümtaz liked to think that the separation had emerged out of Nuran's necessity to "revamp herself," but it didn't. He knew quite well that it didn't. She might be able to love Fâhir somewhat, at the most, because affection and commiseration were forms of ardor. He thought of the last day that they'd spent together. They'd traveled down the Bosphorus to Istanbul together. Until the Galata Bridge, he hadn't mentioned a single word to Nuran about her decision, but once at the bridge he'd again implored. It was vastly different than his former entreaties. It contained the retribution of a spurned lover, wounded self-esteem, and every last thing. "Come back today," he'd said. "You must change your mind!"

"Don't expect me – because I won't be coming. From now on I can offer you nothing but friendship . . ."

Mümtaz wanted nothing of her friendship. "That's impossible," he'd said. "Under these circumstances the last possible thing we could offer to each other is friendship. You know as well as I do that when I sense the withdrawal of your emotions, it spells catastrophe. I turn into the most miserable of creatures. I lose my harmony and focus. I become pitiful and small . . ."

Then came the fateful retort: "Enough already, Mümtaz . . . I'm tired and fed up," she'd said. Mümtaz knew that as Nuran spoke, everything he'd suffered over the past year on her account revived within him. *At that moment I'm certain she carried not one single positive memory of me . . .*

Afterward they said good-bye awkwardly. Nuran went her way, and Mümtaz roamed for hours randomly over darkened and narrow streets, gazing absently at small secondhand salvage shops, street mongers selling food which he couldn't imagine himself or anyone eating, at pitiful houses exuding the misery of rain from every corner, and their deathly black windows whose illumination by inner joy was beyond possibility. He seemed to have left the city of his familiarity and knowledge; as if everything in his midst had appeared along with the incessantly falling, tacky rain – whose gloom didn't diminish even when it stopped. His anguish became his tattered soul's universe. In the course of time, he found himself in Dolmabahçe, by the Bosphorus, intently watching a small crimson sloop unloading wood onto the quay.

All or nothing . . . That was the conviction he'd had at that instant.

All or nothing, that is, death. He came to realize that he was speaking in madness, just like Hitler. You're either with us or against us. Either world empire or the blackest death.

In the order of nature, however, "all" or "nothing" didn't exist. When "all" or "nothing" appeared together, the mind of man, that consummate apparatus of balance, malfunctioned. When this machinery of exception was deluded by its own perfection, this syllogism emerged. Pity to the one who takes it as a premise, who regards this chaotic life from that vantage point! From such a triangulated perspective, humanity might think that all of life rested in its control. From such a vantage only we exist, or, more precisely, merely one facet of us. For even if we should analyze "all or nothing" a little, if the scale should veer just a hair's breadth from its absolute equilibrium, it would lose its orientation, and the realm of torments, delusions, hopes, and regrets would begin. All or nothing. No, not at all, rather, a little bit of everything.

Mümtaz wanted to scramble out of the thoughts into which he'd fallen. But he failed. The doctor shifted his considerable weight and leaned onto his arm with a certain sense of purpose. He stopped. Once again he took a deep breath and exhaled as if confiding to the night.

"Just a few people can change everything, d'you understand? A decent group . . . This being the case . . . Consider this tranquil nighttime hour. Now, just think of tomorrow morning."

Tomorrow morning opened before Mümtaz like a black well. The doctor, however, didn't even look into the well that he'd conjured.

"Regrettable, isn't it? First a nation or a class of people is provoked by means of a series of instigations. Next a madman or a plan concocted behind the scenes ensures the exploitation and appropriation of the masses, who are dragged into the abyss after being bumped from rock to rock as if possessed by a djinn . . . Just take Germany, for instance. Think about it individual by individual . . . Then look at how it can be manipulated en masse once in the hands of a sadist . . . In turn, sadism, worship of power, blind trust in fate, the thought that 'only I can set things straight,' through a retribution taken to excess, passes to others, even those in the opposition . . . A terrifying door is opening up; a barrier is being torn down, beyond which rests only endless catastrophe." Mümtaz stopped short, as if refusing to pass through this doorway.

"I even read the letters that German students had written to their families during the last war. They all sounded like mystics of humanity . . ."

"Mystics you say? The worst of all fates. Above all don't let your feet leave the ground. Then you're susceptible to anything. Anything contracted through the air. Because white noise speaks through your being. Mystics of humanity, mystics of power, mystics of race, the abomination of mystics of torment . . . Because divinity hangs beside us like a theater costume, and it's so easy to simply slip it on . . . Mind that mankind doesn't attempt to deify itself. Mind that it doesn't believe it's an Absolute Idea or that it's the only vehicle through which truth can be found.

"Young man, whatever I have faith in torments me as much as what I doubt. As a result, I bring harm to nobody. Meanwhile, mystics are not that way. They have a mission . . ." He laughed like a boy. Mümtaz, heartened by the innocence of this laugh, waited for him to begin talking again.

"When I was little, a mad Koran chanter, a *hafiz*, would visit us. This man claimed he'd subdued a djinn and had become its master. My father, you see, was bent on discovering treasure. The *hafiz* spent his days and nights in the men's quarters of our house . . . They'd wake up early and go off to who knows where. As I came and went from those quarters, I'd sometimes see him seeking out treasure spots through intercession from beyond. He'd commune with the spirit world. Turning to face the wall, and as if speaking on the telephone, he'd converse with the unseen or with the deficiencies in his own psyche. I could follow the outlines of the conversation from his responses and line of questioning. A kook, apparently, a harmless lunatic. But there's no such thing as a harmless lunatic. Young man, a madman is always dangerous. And the trance states of divine communion are terrifying.

"One day when my father was out, the *hafiz* was again speaking to the walls. Apparently he'd been told that in order for the treasure to be located, a young, adopted Arab girl needed to be sacrificed in the empty adjacent lot. Mayhem broke out in the house. The mad *hafiz* entered the kitchen and began to sharpen all the meat cleavers while reciting bizarre prayers and incantations. The chef first grew leary of the glint in the madman's eye, then of the words he overheard . . . Mind you, he was both sharpening knives and speaking to the unseen . . .

"Thank goodness he was detained in time. What trials and tribulations my father suffered before he'd had the man locked up in Toptaşı. And the *hafiz* didn't keep his peace there, either. Every day he submitted denunciations of my father to the palace."

"Did it at least cure your father of his obsession with treasure?"

"Yes, but this time he fell sway to alchemy, and everything we owned ended up going to a con man from Marrakech . . ." He let out a deep, sorrowful sigh. "Recovering from this variety of illness isn't as easy as it seems. There are so many overlapping symptoms. Take today's Nazi sadism . . . I can almost see the emergence of tomorrow's masochistic literature, a complete underground literature spawned through their worship of power . . . It'll all be submission and tears: Kill me, tear me apart, for as I suffer cruelty and pain, I find myself . . . Later the reactionary rebellions will begin. Oh, take pity on the individual . . . The rights of the individual are being trampled upon, the individual is being oppressed . . . Individuals are nothing but the bloody bricks and tiles of this flesh and blood Tower of Babel . . . Do you remember those who were spouting such blather a decade or so ago?"

The doctor puffed out his broad chest in the night. "Health, Allah, bestow health upon us . . . Not strength, but health . . . The health of humankind . . . Healthiness that accepts life inherently the way it is . . . We don't want an existence resembling that of the gods . . . Let's live a life specific to us . . . Let's live humanely. Let's live without being deluded by anything, without telling lies to ourselves, let's live without worshiping our own lies and apparitions . . ."

Mümtaz thought, *This one's a prophet of another magnitude . . .*

It relieved him to enter their neighborhood. This degree of thought, this contradictory and speculative stream of consciousness, disturbed him. As if wanting to thrust it all off his shoulders at once, he thought of Nuran. When he'd been beside her, life had been so steady. A world in which everything was arranged according to its own value . . . But Nuran was quite a distance away, and in the house they were approaching rested an infirm man whose condition was a riddle. A man whom he dearly loved . . . *Only one hundred paces at most, only one hundred paces.*

The pain of living with countless barriers and limits racked his nervous system.

What's going on with me? Others have also suffered emotional pain . . .

He couldn't complete his thought. Ahead of them on the road a shadow darted through the stinging nettle. The doctor made a start. Mümtaz said, "Don't be startled . . . He's an old Bektashi dervish. He sleeps in an abandoned cistern around here . . . The neighborhood looks after him."

An elderly man stopped and stood before them. "*Hû*, greetings, companions of holiness . . ." He brought his hand to his heart and forehead and recited a couplet by Shaykh Galip:

> *Mind you minister to yourself, chosen of the worldly realm*
> *Mankind, you're the apple of the eye of the living*

In a deep and sonorous voice, as if feeling the surface of a bas-relief, he recited the letters and the syllables, exposing the full force of their intensity. As if he had no other concern besides being understood, being heard and understood, he bore no particular style of expression, no specific poetic flare. The effect was more stunning because he was at a remove from all variety of proselytizing, or even calling. He just left them face-to-face with a truth before vanishing; and this truth was a truth that described their torment. But was it only theirs? No, near and far, it constituted the torment of the world. This couplet was the first instance of a signpost within the night – and all previous nights – within the webbing they traced, the dark and labyrinthine catacomb that they couldn't manage to escape.

The doctor: "Fine, but he's no Bektashi, he's a Mevlevî . . ."

"No, he's a Bektashi. I've spoken to him often. Many nights İhsan, myself, and he have commiserated over *rakı* together . . . He's Bektashi through and through; he recites beautiful strains of verse, and he's particularly fond of this couplet. One day he'd said to me, 'The sole reality is this: One ought to hold humanity in high regard. We ought to sense this regard within us without effort.' In his opinion, this was more important than love . . . In short, he's one who displays respect toward others and humanity . . ."

"He has respect for humanity . . . In that case, he's completely mad." Then he abruptly changed his tone. He gazed at the houses that appeared pale next to the handlike objects illuminated by a feeble light, at the lot overgrown with weeds, and at the face of his companion, whose fatigue could just be discerned. A rooster, fluttering its wings somewhere above them, emptied its radiance into the night like an elixir of molten rubies and agate concealed within its being.

"The East," he said, "my beloved East . . . From without, it appears lazy, foolish, helpless, and impoverished . . . But from within, it has resolved never to be deceived . . . What could be more beautiful? When will we learn to satisfy people from within? When will we understand the meaning of the phrase, 'Mind you minister to yourself'?"

"Does the East even comprehend this?"

"Whether it does or doesn't, it's conveyed the idea, hasn't it, my son?"

V

The small, stray girl spared from sacrifice had seemingly arrived just in the nick of time to turn on the light. As soon as Mümtaz entered behind the doctor, he saw the objects that he'd left an hour ago again in the same position within the illumination of the mirror, with the same blithe invulnerability of an hour before, pleased to simply be themselves, gathered and glimmering. *Oh, the way these objects simply wait, as if for an opportunity to leave us . . .*

The world exists even without me. It exists on its own. It persists. I'm a small trace of this persistence . . . But I exist, and I find the strength to persevere in the consciousness of continuity . . . Through that continuity, I move from my genesis toward eternity . . .

With the demeanor of a man pleading for grace from tyranny, Mümtaz looked about. For he knew that he wouldn't persist eternally, and perhaps this minute, perhaps tomorrow, perhaps a few days hence, one day his presence within this continuity would cease and be usurped by other presences, and he knew he wouldn't be the way he'd been in the past, and he wouldn't sense the same shudders, and furthermore whether or not he would shudder.

Eternity was a nebulous light into which his intellect at times shone. And not even to such a great depth. Only to a part of his being that fleetingly shifted toward the arcane. Meanwhile, reality amounted to this stone foyer that he perceived in a glance through his doubled existence and, as always, through his past; it amounted to the stairs he climbed, and İhsan's room, whose staleness – comprised of the odor of medicines, sweat, and illness – he sensed before even entering; yes, reality was the suffering present there. Other unseen realities also existed that he couldn't sense with his flesh yet that stabbed and twisted into him like a knife: Nuran's disposition of a solitary lily in the white nightgown that they'd selected together; the tree branches that spilled over the garden walls of the house; the stunted fig tree that all but came to life on moonlit nights; the small chinar before the door; the nocturnes through which he passed; and the small table and chairs where he so longed to sit with her and have morning tea – a table whose cloth, left in place instead of gathered up, made the possibility of this pleasure more tangible . . .

But there were other realities. Things he'd never seen, of whose existence he was uncertain, that he sensed had settled into him in light of recent events, infecting him. Telegraph operators conveyed breaking news from one office to another while thinking of their wives, children, and homes; typesetters aligned letters and type with scorched fingers; housewives roamed through their houses aimlessly, feeling as if they'd forgotten something, opening, for maybe the twentieth time, the luggage they'd prepared, yet unable to add anything useful or new that would help confront the unknown; they did nothing but abandon broken smiles, pitiful prayers, and the grasp of their fingers before letting the suitcase close yet again . . . Train whistles, songs of separation . . . These, too, played within him like a knife blade. No, he wasn't in the realm of the eternal but of the worldly. The world resided in everybody. A world that existed at times in a corner of our beings, at times as a single soul in totality, at times a world we forgot about during our

433

workaday lives, though we carried it with us, in our very blood; a world that, like it or not, we sensed in the weight of this evening upon our shoulders. And beneath this burden, beside the patient, the wrestler's physique of the physician seemed slightly diminished.

İhsan was a little better, but he was dazed. On the taut skin of his forehead were drops of perspiration that seemed foreign to it, giving the impression that he couldn't relax. By the looks of his chest, which appeared more puffed out and powerful under the force of his respiration, and his sweaty ruddy face, rather than a sick man, he resembled a swimmer who'd just vanquished the waves that he'd been struggling against for hours, and now waited for his pulse to return to normal where he sat resting on the shore. Had he actually vanquished them, however? His face resided in such an eerie region of remoteness. The worst of all possible prognoses resurfaced in Mümtaz's mind.

"The good lady saved the patient just in the nick of time . . . I'd guessed as much besides. There was no recourse but to increase the sulfamide dosage. Now I'm going to prescribe eight sulfamide capsules. And we'll closely monitor the results. In addition we'll need a bit of syrup and another heart medication. Mümtaz, I'm afraid we're going to have to trouble you again."

From the forest of a life of fragments, İhsan looked at Mümtaz as if to say, "And where did you find this specimen?" Then he extended his hand to hold the physician's and uttered perhaps his first words of the night: "What d'you say, doctor? Will it happen? Will they proceed with this madness?"

The physician immediately answered his patient: "You concentrate on getting well!" Though his eyes said, "I share your concern!"

VI

Once out on the street, Mümtaz found himself more relieved than on his prior excursion. Almost no trace remained of the thoughts that had made his head swell. Strangely, he walked with a sprightly spring that he'd never before felt. He seemed not to be bound by the laws of gravity. *If I had wings, I could fly.* He was astounded by this state: such a stark contrast to the gravity of the circumstances in which he found himself. For he still saw everything just the way it was. Perhaps war would begin this very night. İhsan's condition was still serious. He'd progressed so far down the passageway between life and death that his return would be difficult. Nuran was to leave this morning and her departure meant devastation. With her absence, everything would end. All these realities that had been pressing down on him only an hour ago now felt like distant events unrelated to him or his own world. He regarded them all from beyond the threshold of death.

He felt at ease. *I wonder why? I'm so prone to contemplation, my thoughts form knots inside me and keep me pacing till morning. Why is it that now I can't think of anything?* But even this thought wasn't enough to overwhelm him. *Or am I not in this realm of existence? Have I left the world? Or maybe the world has left me? Why not? Like any old liquid emptying from a container . . .* Despite this, he was aware of the task at hand. He knew the route that he would take, and he hurried to bring İhsan's medicine back as soon as possible; furthermore, his mind recorded everything it encountered with a lucidity that seemed improbable even to him.

The landscape was ensconced in shadows as if the retaining wall holding brightness at bay had cracked in an unspecified locale. Grasses glimmered in the illusion of a greenish patina sprayed over them. The surroundings pulsated.

This was the hour when the dawn tuned its instruments. Soon the empyrean of Creation would be remade. In the foyers of houses, and in rooms, the first morning lights were lit. In the murky weather these lights fostered the artificial glow of the stage. A woman opened a window, her half-naked body stretched against the fading night, and straightened her hair, her arms bare. A dog slowly rose from where it had slept and ran toward Mümtaz, the morning sojourner, but just when it came close, it changed its mind and darted on to the base of a saint's *türbe* where candles burned behind a shut window. A milkman, comfortably seated cross-legged above the copper ewers that he'd hung on either side of his mare, passed beside him at a near gallop. In the distance a car horn sounded.

Mümtaz observed it all as the sky gradually changed hue. But there was a difference in his perception. It didn't resemble the quotidian contact our senses made with their surroundings. It was rather like discovering these external objects and gestures within himself.

A clutch of crows broke away from the trees in the courtyard of the Şehzade Mosque. With sharp caws and metallic fluttering, they passed over-head. The scent of fresh bread from the bakery engulfed the entire street. The laborers who'd been repairing the rails were now before the mosque. The acetylene still burned, extending toward the lavish Rembrandt-like gilded dusk; between the molten radiance and the encompassing darkness, faces, hands, and bodies, each by shades, were transfigured. Mümtaz, a second time, watched in awe the movements of hands and the concentra-tion of faces.

Our neighborhood ... His entire childhood ran toward him from this road and the surrounding streets. *To have a neighborhood, a home, a routine, and friends, to live with them and to die among them* ... One way or another, this future-oriented life structure that he'd prepared for himself did not coalesce around him. Besides, he couldn't see any of his ideas to completion. Material things, all artifacts, existed of their own accord. They gave rise to an inkling, like an echo, before others usurped their places. However oppressive, he longed to lose himself in the passageways of an idea.

As he passed through the Vezneciler district, he sensed that the scenery had grown lighter. When he arrived in Beyazıt, a commotion had begun in the coffeehouses on the causeway. The chairs were still stacked together inside, but the opportunistic garçons had prepared a couple of tables for early morning clientele. When one of them caught sight of Mümtaz, overjoyed he said, "Welcome, Mümtaz, good sir, the tea is presently steeping." But this sudden flashback to university exam mornings didn't arouse any reaction in Mümtaz. With a hand gesture, he indicated something approximating haste. The morning commuters on the side of the road that headed to Aksaray and the calls of newspaper hawkers and sesame *simit* and pastry sellers had begun to erect the city's morning. Mümtaz looked in the direction of the mosque. A covey of pigeons floated toward the ground before ascending again. *I wonder what it was that startled them?* forgetting the question as soon as it had been posed. Yet he could still trace the persistence of his thoughts – at the very least through their absences. *This doesn't constitute lack of possibility but maybe apathy. I wonder if I'm indifferent toward all things in this way? Will I ever again be able to reconstitute the world within myself? Will memories ever again speak through me? Or am I growing delirious while yet in complete control of my senses? Before my own eyes, like this . . .*

The metal shutters of the after-hours pharmacy were still shut. A woman banged on the shutters and frequently stood on tiptoe to glance through the peephole. She held a prescription that she'd evidently crumpled up on her way here. She was exhausted and destitute.

Frequently she said, "Allah," and again peered within on tiptoe, as if wanting to glide inside.

The pharmacist finally arrived. Both of them extended their prescriptions at the same time. Mümtaz received the medicine. He performed all of this with exceeding efficiency, like a man who didn't want to lose a second's time.

The situation actually necessitated this. The part of him that procured the medicine was lucid. It didn't falter. Beyond that, his entire mental faculty labored between two extremes in the vacillation of one on the verge of slipping into narcosis; his mind had become a bewildering apparatus that adapted to its environment instantaneously, and after perceiving its object, immediately let it go. *What's happening to me?* It was certain that a shroud existed between him and the world that he hadn't noticed before. Something translucent, which permitted exceptional focus, separated him from the world.

But could he even be separated from the world? *Life is so sublime . . .* Living at this morning hour was a beautiful thing. Everything was beautiful, fresh, and harmonious. It greeted one with the pliancy of a smile, and Mümtaz had the conviction that at this hour he could tirelessly observe an acacia leaf, the face of a small animal, or a human hand in perpetuity. Because all of it, everything, was sublime. This light of subtlety was a symphony; there, in the mosque courtyard, its first rays danced like a woman disrobed. The fresh smell of *simit*s, the haste of walking men, faces lost in thought were all beautiful. But he wasn't able to focus fully on any one. *At such an hour? Perhaps it's because I find objects to be so beautiful that I'm able to divorce myself from life. Why shouldn't this be the case?* Because this sense of the sublime and within it the accompanying jubilation like an orchestra was no everyday experience. It resembled an epiphany of sorts. It was a variety of epiphany that could come only at the last possible instant, at the moment when the intellect cut off all contact with everything and became its hermetic self, the moment when it functioned in the most idealized way. It was a reality located at the edge of the abyss. The clarity within him could only suggest the lucidity of the previous moment.

"How strange! Nothing is connected to any other thing. I perceive every-thing as atomized," he complained.

The man beside him answered, "Of course it doesn't connect. Because what you're seeing is nothing but unmediated reality."

"But yesterday and the day before, didn't I also see things this way? Wasn't I perceiving reality? Hadn't I always encountered it before?"

He sensed the presence of the man beside him, but he couldn't look him in the face, though this didn't seem unnatural.

"No . . . Because you'd been regarding your surroundings from the per-spective of your identity. You were actually observing your own self. Neither life nor objects constitute a totality. Wholeness is a phantasy of the human mind."

"All right then, don't I have an identity?"

"No. *That*, my friend, is in my palm. If you don't believe me, then take a look for yourself."

He extended his palm toward Mümtaz's face. A small, astounding being, a formation something like an exoskeleton or dermis that he didn't recognize stirred in his palm with small contractions.

So, then, this is my identity! he thought. But he didn't say anything. The man's hand had stunned him.

Mümtaz had never before seen such a beautiful thing. Neither crystal nor diamond could produce this inherent glow – a dull illumination reserved only for him. This light within the palm, this small crablike being, his own identity according to what he'd been told, opened and closed with little contractions like an artery and was silently functioning on its own.

Timidly he asked, "Aren't you going to give it back to me?"

"What?"

Mümtaz indicated with the tip of his chin. "That, my identity. That thing you call my identity."

"If you'd like, take it. Take it if you want to go back into the realm of experience," and the hand again opened at the level of his chin, but this time Mümtaz's eyes focused on the radiance of the hand itself. Mümtaz knew that the man standing beside him, despite the impossibility of such an occurrence, was none other than Suad. *If the dead roam the streets like this, could life offer any pleasure?* With a sidelong glance he slowly looked, as if to say, "Is it actually him?" Indeed, it was Suad. But how he'd been transformed! He was much bigger and more handsome, something like an enhanced Suad. He was even more sublime and exquisite than the Suad he'd dreamed of a few hours before. Even the smirk Mümtaz had observed on Suad's face that day in the hall of the apartment, the grimace that vilified everything, life in its entirety, had now become an opulent smile, emerging from depths and illuminating mysterious planes of being. The wounds on his hands, neck, and face also sparkled. *Cruel and sublime . . .* He was suddenly shocked, and wringing his hands, he began to think: *But what will I do now?* He had to talk to Suad at all costs. But would he even be able to speak to such an exquisite and exalted Suad? *I wonder if all the dead become sublime this way?* He remembered how Suad had said that he was revolted by death and dying. *He's not only beautiful but powerful, too . . .* Yes, he was mighty; some force within him flowed toward Mümtaz continually, attracting him. He would speak to him.

He slowly whispered. "Suad," he said. "Why have you come? Why don't you leave me alone? All day and night you've been harassing me! Enough already! Let me be." As he spoke, his trepidation left him, to be replaced by a bewildering feeling of revolt. "Just leave me alone already!" Then he regretted having addressed a dead man with such irreverence.

"Why shouldn't I come, Mümtaz? I've never left your side anyway!"

Mümtaz nodded his head. "Indeed, you haven't! You've been a veritable plague on me. But more intensely since yesterday. Last night I saw you on that hill. And in my dreams. Do you have any idea how strange it was? I was watching the nightfall. More exactly, evening was falling and frantic preparations were being made. Purple, red, pink, and lilac-colored boards and beams were brought out and assembled on the horizon. Then they raised the sun with ropes and pulleys. Yet, you know, it wasn't the sun at all, but you. Your face was beautiful, as it is now, and because it was more sorrowful, you appeared even more sublime. Then they just crucified you there like some sort of Jesus . . ." He suddenly began to cackle. "If you only knew how bizarre it was, your state of sorrow like that, and your crucifixion like Jesus . . . You, a man who believes in nothing, a man who mocks everything . . ." And he laughed at length again.

Suad, his eyes fixed on Mümtaz, listened.

"As I said . . . I've never forsaken you. I'm always by your side!"

Mümtaz continued walking for a while without saying a thing. He had the sensation that he was walking in the glow of the one beside him rather than the light of daybreak. And this was quite distressing.

"Very well then, what is it that you want from me? What's the reason for this insistence?"

"It's not insistence . . . but obligation. It's my obligation to be with you. I've now become your Guardian Angel."

Mümtaz laughed yet again, though at the same time he recognized that his laughter was rather strained.

"This can't be!" he said. "You're a dead man. That is, you're a person." He felt the need to further clarify his thoughts. "It's so difficult to converse with the deceased . . . I mean to say that you *were* a person. Meanwhile, this business is actually the concern of angels."

"No, they can no longer keep up. In recent years the earth's population has greatly increased. The politics of population growth is on the rise. Now angels are having the dead see to these matters . . ."

At first Mümtaz didn't respond at all. Then he objected. "You're lying!" he said. "You can't be an angel. It's impossible. You're the very devil himself!"

And it rent his heart to speak to a dead man in this manner. Despite this, he continued. "For the sake of deceiving me, you've put on these airs. I'm onto your game."

Suad gazed at his face in a state of sorrow: "Were I the devil, I'd have whispered from within you. You wouldn't be able to see me."

"However," Mümtaz began, "do you know how pleased I am to see you? I'm overjoyed even." Then he again looked at Suad's face fearfully.

"How beautiful you've become! Exceptionally beautiful! This sorrow suits you. Do you want to know what you resemble? The angels of Botticelli . . . you know, the ones that give Jesus three nails during the Passion–"

Suad interrupted him: "Stop making these absurd comparisons . . . Can't you speak without comparing one thing to another? Haven't you yet realized how you've made matters worse due to this vile habit?"

Like a child, Mümtaz begged: "Don't scold . . . I've suffered so much. I haven't done anything all that indecent. I've only found you beautiful. How have you become so sublime?"

"Things that exist in the mind are always sublime."

At first Mümtaz wanted to protest. "Just now you said, 'Were I the devil, I'd have whispered from within you'!" but suddenly another idea entered his mind. *I'm unable to follow the train of my thoughts . . . How dismal!* "But I can now see you with my own eyes. Not to mention that I'm conversing with you . . ."

"Yes, you see me through your own eyes! And you're conversing . . ."

A notion passed through Mümtaz's mind at lightning speed. "And I can touch you, can I not?"

"Of course . . ." Suad had now passed before him and had raised his arms as if to say, "Go ahead and examine me," and laughed at Mümtaz within the sparkle emanating from his presence. Mümtaz turned his bedazzled eyes away.

"If you so desire and if you have no fear!"

"Why should I fear? I'm no longer afraid of anything! But he was reluctant to extend his hands toward Suad. He thrust them back into his pockets as if to say, "In case of any eventualities!"

Suad laughed the way he had that night in Emirgân. "I knew you'd be afraid," he said. "Why don't you inform that porter so he can come and touch me! Or Mehmet, or the coffeehouse apprentice in Boyacıköy! The people that you've condemned to death today."

Mümtaz staggered. "What business could they possibly have with us?"

"They'd touch me in your stead."

"I'm not sending them off to war alone. I'm going as well."

"But without taking your death into account. You've seen their deaths as an absolute certainty and you've duped them into dying."

"No! Not at all . . ."

"Yes, indeed . . ." Suad leaned over him with a cruel jeer, chastising him. "Or the wife of the porter. Let her touch me in your place."

"No, I'm telling you. I intended to go as well. I will go. I don't see them any differently than I see myself."

"But you do, you do. You were bargaining over their deaths. You were trying to dupe them!"

"Lies . . . you're lying."

Mümtaz came to his senses. This argument was futile. İhsan was waiting at the house. He pleaded like a child: "Suad," he said, "İhsan is very ill! Be so kind as to let me pass and be on my way already!"

Suad laughed fitfully. "But how quickly you've grown tired of me!"

"No, I haven't grown tired. But there's a sick man awaiting me at home. I'm exhausted, not to mention that you're no longer one of our kind. I was dishonest with you previously. I *do* fear you. And furthermore, just get out of my damn way. The streets will soon become crowded! You're an anomaly in the world of the living. You're a glaring ghost, why roam in our midst? Isn't what we suffer from our own enough?"

443

"Weren't we in each other's company only yesterday?"

"Yes, but you're no longer the progeny of the sun!"

"Don't worry about that. Since last night, all the dead have been out and about."

Mümtaz gazed down the street, trembling. They were only twenty-five or thirty steps from the house.

"Why is that? What good does that do? This is the realm of the living. Everything here is for the sake of life! At the very least, all of you dead should quit haranguing us!"

"Impossible," he said. "I can't let you be. You're coming with me." He spoke with bitter derision.

"Without Nuran, in the midst of such misery . . . impossible." And Suad spread his arms and tried to embrace him. Mümtaz stepped backward.

"Come . . ." His summons was pierced by a blood-curdling laugh.

Mümtaz implored, "At least don't laugh! Please, stop!"

"How is it possible? You've reduced everything to the limits of your own self to such a degree; everything resembles you . . . You're so bound by your puny existence and its concerns. Not to mention your limited devotion to life, your measured compassion, your trivial torments, your hopes, your states of withdrawal and worship . . ."

Mümtaz let his arms hang down and said, "Don't be vindictive, Suad. I've suffered plenty."

Suad again laughed expansively. "Very well, in that case, come with me and let me be your salvation."

"I can't, I have work that I must see to."

"You won't be able to accomplish anything! Come with me. You'll be delivered of the whole lot. These are burdens that you can't bear . . ."

Mümtaz once again stopped in his tracks and stared at Suad. "No," he said. "I need to take on my responsibilities. And if I can't, I'm prepared to be crushed beneath them. But I can't go with you."

"You will!"

"No, that would be cowardice."

"In that case, remain here in your cesspool . . ."

Suad spread his arms and struck Mümtaz forcefully in the face. He staggered and fell to the ground.

When he stood again, his face was bloody. The medicine bottles were broken in his hands. Despite this, he wore a strange, almost imperceptible smile. From one of the nearby windows, a radio announced the order for attack that Hitler had made that very night. Mümtaz had forgotten about the entire ordeal.

"War's begun . . ." he said. And he opened his palms, which still held shards of broken vials, and gazed at his wounds. Then he slowly plodded toward the house. Passersby at this early hour glared in shock at the odd grin on his bloodied face.

He unlocked the door. The foyer mirror had assumed once again its terrestrial face in the morning light. He stared at his own face for a time. Then he slowly climbed the stairs.

Macide was sitting with the physician in the hall, listening to the radio.

"Good God, Mümtaz, what's happened to you?"

Mümtaz again opened and closed his aching hands before the window.

"You don't want to know," he said. "I had an accident." That strange smile – which seemed to hold within it the mysteries of an entire life – persisted on his lips.

"The medicine bottles broke!" he said. Then he turned to face the doctor. "How is he?"

"So-so," he said. "He's better. He doesn't need anything more. Have you heard the news?"

Mümtaz, no longer listening, had withdrawn to a corner where he stared at his palms, then darted from his spot and walked toward the stairs.

But he couldn't ascend. There, on the first step, he sank back down with his head in his hands. The doctor looked at him as if to say, "Now you're mine, all mine!" Wiping her eyes, Macide approached him. In the stillness of the house, a lone booming voice on the radio spoke for them all.

Chronology

1757–99: Shaykh Galip, Ottoman divan poet and Mevlevî sheikh, establishes himself in the Ottoman court. He is renowned for his mystic romance *Beauty and Love*.

1778–1846: İsmail Dede Efendi, a hafiz, a muezzin, a Mevlevî, and one of the greatest composers of Ottoman classical music, composes more than two hundred works.

1789–1807: Reign of Sultan Selim III, a Mevlevî, a patron of the arts, and a composer. Selim introduces the first military and political modernizing reforms into the empire under the Nizam-ı Cedid ("New Order") and appoints the cosmopolitan painter and architect Antoine Ignace Melling (later landscape painter to Empress Josephine of France) as court architect. Among the regular attendees to his court is the poet Shaykh Galip. (In *A Mind at Peace*, Mümtaz's unfinished historical novel is set during this era.)

1808–39: Reign of Sultan Mahmud II, who continues the legal and military reforms begun by Selim. Mahmud II abolishes the Janissary corps and replaces them with a modern standing army and institutes European-style clothing reform, including the introduction of the fez in place of the turban.

1829: Treaty of Edirne. Autonomy is granted to Serbia, Greece, and principalities under Russian protection. Beginning of secession movements and expulsion of Muslims from the Balkans, Crimea, and the Caucasus between the 1820s and 1920s. (A Refugee Commission, Muhacirin Komisyonu, is eventually established in 1860 to resettle Muslim refugees in Central and Eastern Anatolia.)

1839: On April 3, İsmail Dede Efendi performs the Mevlevî ceremonial suite in the new Ferahfeza *makam* (mode of classical Turkish music). This work was commissioned by Sultan Mahmud II, who listened to it only months before he died of tuberculosis. (The music is described in the "Suad" section of *A Mind at Peace*.)

1839–76: The Tanzimat, or "Reorganization." Begins with the reign of Sultan Abdülmecit I (1839–61). This era of reform attempts to turn "subjects of the sultan" into "modern citizens" by creating a new centralized government and new educational and legal systems. Sultan Abdülaziz (r. 1861–76) continued on this path of reform, and under his successor, Sultan Abdülhamid II (r. 1876–1909), the era culminated in the promulgation of a constitution and parliament in 1876, the first modern constitution in the Muslim world. Though this constitutional sultanate lasted less than two years, it was reinstated in 1908, ushering in a second constitutional era. This era also witnessed the first novels in Ottoman Turkish.

1877–78: Russo–Ottoman War. Concluded by the Treaty of San Stefano signed with Russia. The Ottoman state loses sovereignty over territories in the Balkans and Eastern Anatolia.

1901: Poet, scholar, and novelist Ahmet Hamdi Tanpınar is born in Istanbul. His father was a *kadi* (Islamic judge). Tanpınar graduated with a degree in literature from Istanbul University in 1923, then worked as a high school teacher and university professor, and served as member of parliament from 1942 to 1946.

1907: "Young Turks" in Paris establish contact with the Ottoman Liberty Society in Salonika, uniting to become the Committee of Union and Progress with the goal of restoring the constitution.

1908–20: Second Ottoman constitutional era, which begins after the Young Turk Revolution in 1908.

1912–13: First and Second Balkan Wars. Ottoman Empire loses most of its Balkan territories.

1914: Ottoman Empire enters World War I on the side of the Central powers. After Ottoman defeat, the Allied powers occupy Istanbul between 1918 and 1923 while former Ottoman territories are partitioned into mandates, nation-states, and kingdoms, giving rise to the modern Middle East.

1919–22: With assistance from Allied powers, Greece invades Western Anatolia, and a mass exodus of Anatolian Muslims follows. (In *A Mind at Peace*, Mümtaz's father is killed during the invasion and Mümtaz flees to the southern Mediterranean coast before moving to Istanbul.)

1922–38: The Kemalist cultural revolution (led by Mustafa Kemal Atatürk) introduces a program of secular social engineering, including the abolishment of the Islamic caliphate and dervish orders, the institution of clothing reform, a change in the alphabet from Ottoman script to Latin, and the purging of Perso–Arabic words from the language. (Discussions on revolution and social change by İhsan, Suad, and Mümtaz in *A Mind at Peace* focus on the cultural revolution.)

1923: Establishment of the Republic of Turkey after the Turkish War of Independence against Allied occupations.

1938: Death of Mustafa Kemal Atatürk, the first president of the Republic of Turkey. (In *A Mind at Peace*, Mümtaz meets Nuran around this time.)

1939: Start of World War II. Turkey remains neutral until several months before the end of the war. (*A Mind at Peace* concludes with declarations of war in Europe.)

1942: Tanpınar publishes his famous literary history *The History of 19th Century Turkish Literature*.

1943: Tanpınar publishes his first short-story collection, *The Dreams of Abdullah Efendi*.

1944: Tanpınar's first novel, *Song in Mahur*, appears in serial form.

1946: The beginning of multiparty politics in Turkey after decades of single-party rule by the Republican People's Party. Tanpınar publishes his seminal collection of essays on art and urban culture, *Five Cities: Istanbul, Bursa, Konya, Erzurum, Ankara*.

1948: *A Mind at Peace* appears in serial form in the daily newspaper *Cumhuriyet* and is published in book form a year later.

1950: In the first free elections in more than twenty-five years, voters send the Republican People's Party out of office, putting the Democratic Party in power. Tanpınar's novel on the Allied occupation of Istanbul, *Waiting in the Wings*, appears in serial form.

1954: Tanpınar's parodic novel of the Kemalist cultural revolution, *The Time Regulation Institute*, appears in serial form.

1956: Tanpınar publishes *Summer Rain*, a short-story collection.

1960: A military coup ousts the Democratic Party. The Constitution of 1961 replaces the Constitution of 1924. The "Second Republic" begins.

1961: Tanpınar's collection of thirty-seven poems appears under the title *Poems*. He also publishes a monograph on poet Yahya Kemal Beyatlı (the basis for the character İhsan), his mentor.

1962: *The Time Regulation Institute* is published in book form. Ahmet Hamdi Tanpınar dies of a heart attack. He is buried in Istanbul's Aşiyan Cemetery, next to Yahya Kemal Beyatlı. Tanpınar's tombstone is inscribed with his own famous lines of verse: "Neither am I inside time / Nor altogether without." A novelist of later acclaim, his posthumously published works in book form include *Essays on Literature* (1969); *Waiting in the Wings* (1973, novel); *Song in Mahur* (1975, novel); *Lady in the Moon* (1987, novel, incomplete); *As I've Lived* (1996, collected essays); *Between Two Fires* (1998, screenplay based on *Waiting in the Wings*), *The Secret of Gems* (2002); *Lessons in Literature* (2002); and *The Complete Stories* (2003).

1971: Military coup by memorandum ousts Justice Party. Leftist organizations are targeted for closure and their members imprisioned. Thus begins a period of marginalized voices in Turkish literature, including existentialism and feminism as represented by Oğuz Atay and Adalet Ağaoğlu, respectively.

1970s: Tanpınar is rediscovered among the intelligentsia and his works are reissued or published for the first time.

1980: Military coup ousts government. Leftists are targeted in mass roundups. New Constitution of 1982 replaces that of 1961. Regarded by some as the beginning of the "Third Republic". Ushers in a period of postnational, magical realist, and/or historical Ottoman novels in Turkish literature, as represented by Latife Tekin and Orhan Pamuk.

1997: Necmettin Erbakan of the Welfare Party resigns under pressure from the military in what the press dubs the "Postmodern Coup". The Welfare Party is subsequently banned in the courts for antisecular activities.

2002, 2007: The Justice and Development (AK) Party wins national elections, signifying a fundamental transformation of the secular state. Beginning of a period of transcultural themes in Turkish literature, as represented by Elif Şafak.

2005: Turkey begins official negotiations with the European Union for full membership.

2006: Orhan Pamuk is awarded the Nobel Prize in Literature and acknowledges Tanpınar's oeuvre as a formative influence.